Beloved LIAR

USA *Today* and International Bestselling Author

Lauren Rowe

Books by Lauren Rowe

The Reed Rivers Trilogy (to be read in order)
Bad Liar
Beautiful Liar
Beloved Liar

The Club Trilogy (to be read in order)
The Club: Obsession
The Club: Reclamation
The Club: Redemption
The Club: Culmination (A Full-Length Epilogue Book)

The Josh and Kat Trilogy (to be read in order)
Infatuation
Revelation
Consummation

The Morgan Brothers (a series of related standalones):
Hero
Captain
Ball Peen Hammer
Mister Bodyguard
ROCKSTAR

The Misadventures Series (a series of unrelated standalones):
Misadventures on the Night Shift
Misadventures of a College Girl
Misadventures on the Rebound

Standalone Psychological Thriller/Dark Comedy
Countdown to Killing Kurtis

Playlist for Beloved Liar

"You and Me"—James TW
"Oh, Darling"—The Beatles
"I Don't Want to Get Over You"—The Magnetic Fields
"Bad Liar"—Imagine Dragons
"Love the Way You Lie"—Eminem
"Ready to Let Go"—Cage the Elephant
"Golden"—Harry Styles
"Adore You"—Harry Styles

Chapter 1
Reed

It's a temperate Sunday afternoon in the Hollywood Hills. The perfect day for Hazel Hennessy's first birthday party on her parents' small backyard patio. The birthday girl is sitting in a highchair, wearing a bib that reads, "I'm the Birthday Girl, Bitches!" Her party guests, other than me, are crowded around her, singing "Happy Birthday," while her proud mommy stands over her with a white cupcake topped with Elmo and her smiling daddy records the occasion on his phone.

And where is Uncle Reed in this happy moment? Nowhere good. He's slumped in a chair in a corner of the patio, slugging his third Bloody Mary, while drowning in a dark and stormy sea of soul-searing regret.

Because... *Georgina.*

It's been sixteen hours since she took off in that Uber with her stepsister, without looking back, leaving me to wallow in a brand of pain I didn't even know existed. What I'm feeling in this torturous moment is the kind of pain artists sing about in their most tormented breakup songs. The kind of pain I've heard other people talk or sing about and immediately thought to myself, "Get over it, you fucking pussy. Move on to the next and you'll be fine."

And now, here I am, wallowing in misery, drowning in Bloody Marys, and certain I'll never "get over it" or "move on to the next and be fine" ever again.

1

My phone vibrates in my hand, and I look down, praying I'll see Georgina's name. But, no. It's Owen, telling me something I don't care about. Goddammit! Why won't Georgina respond to any of my texts or voicemails? I mean, yes, I know *why*. Because, last night, in a space of mere minutes, Georgina got hit by a shit storm trifecta that made her question everything. In rapid-fire succession, Georgina figured out I'd funded the grant, she found her stepsister sobbing in an upstairs guest room, thanks to a speech I'd given to her about her demo, and, worst of all, Georgina discovered me coming out of the garage with Isabel, right after I'd kissed her. In that horrible moment that's now running on a permanent loop in my brain, Georgina saw Isabel's smudged lipstick and the guilty expression on my face and decided, *wrongly*, that I'd fucked the living hell out of Isabel in that garage, rather than merely giving her an ill-advised goodbye kiss. And, just like that, Georgina's trust in me was shattered, along with her precious heart. And now, I'm rightfully paying the price for my stupidity.

Out of nowhere, an idea pops into my head. A lifeline. An ingenious idea that will prove to Georgina I did nothing more than kiss Isabel. Granted, this idea wouldn't fully exonerate me in Georgina's eyes, since touching Isabel at all was wrong. A betrayal I wish, more than anything, I could take back. But, still, at least this idea would put an end to Georgina thinking I screwed the crap out of Isabel in that garage. At least, Georgina wouldn't be thinking I cared so little about her, and our magical week together, that I took the first possible opportunity to screw my ex. And, maybe, knowing I'm not *that* big a monster would soften the blow a bit for Georgina and then, hopefully, pave the way for her to eventually forgive me.

My mind begins turning this idea over. Looking at it from every angle. Weighing the pros and cons. And, soon, much to my dismay, I conclude it's a non-starter. Surely, it would create more problems than it solved. Shit.

I take another long swig of my Bloody Mary, and sigh from the depths of my tormented soul. I just wish Georgina would call me, if only to chew me out or interrogate me about the grant. CeeCee is still in Bali, so I'm presently Georgina's only source of enlightenment about the grant. Doesn't she want to hear what I have to say about how that happened? Does she hate me so much she *literally* never wants to hear my voice again? Because, if so, then I've got some bad news for her. She's still assigned to the special issue—including writing an in-depth article about *me*—and I fully intend to hold her to her professional obligations.

The crowd reaches the last note of their song, and I let my eyes drift to Josh's former assistant, T-Rod. Theresa "Tessa" Rodriguez. Nowadays, Morgan. The Woman I've Wanted to Fuck for Ten Years. She's standing next to her asshole husband, Ryan, holding a dark-haired baby on her hip, as Ryan holds their toddler's hand. And, man, she's smoking hot. Hotter than ever. Motherhood definitely suits her. But there's no doubt about it: I don't want T-Rod. Not even in a fantasy. Sitting here now, I know, without a doubt, the only woman I want, the only one my heart and body are *capable* of wanting, is Georgina.

It's a mind-blowing thing to realize, considering how long T-Rod has been my gold standard of hotness. My go-to masturbation fantasy. But it's the undeniable truth. Georgina owns me now. Georgina is my new gold standard. My queen. Before today, I knew Georgina had burrowed herself underneath my skin and slithered her way into my bloodstream. But now, as I sit here trying in vain to "move on" and "get over it" and "be fine," I realize something shocking: *Georgina has embedded herself into the very tissues of my heart.*

T-Rod laughs, along with everyone around her, so, I shift my gaze to the birthday girl to see what's up and discover Hazel has just smashed a large glob of white frosting into her face. She was aiming for her mouth, and missed, apparently.

And the crowd loves it. I don't blame them. It's a cute moment. Objectively humorous. But I don't give a shit. Because... *Georgina.* If only she'd call me to let me explain!

I glance at T-Rod again, and marvel at how much she reminds me of Georgina. In ten years, I bet that's exactly how Georgina will look. T-Rod is a crystal ball showing me Georgina as a mommy. Georgina as a wife.

Out of nowhere, while I'm still staring at T-Rod, her asshole husband gives her a kiss and then glares at me. I quickly look away. Was that a not-so-subtle message to me? Did Ryan notice me staring at his wife and decide he needed to stake his claim? *Fucker.* Calm down, man. I don't even want your fucking wife anymore. I was just imagining she was someone else. Someone who used to trust me.

Aw, fuck. Out of nowhere, I'm having a horrible thought. If I don't win Georgina back, *pronto,* if I don't fix this mess I've created, Georgina is going to "get over it" and "move on to the next" and "be fine." Maybe one day soon. And then, one day, ten years from now, she's going to be standing at a kiddie birthday party alongside her asshole husband, holding his baby on her hip, getting kissed by him when he notices some pathetic loser staring at her. And I won't be Georgina's asshole husband in this scenario. *I'll be the pathetic loser staring at her, wishing she were mine.*

Testosterone whooshes into my bloodstream. White-hot jealousy. Aching regret. And all of it followed by a tidal wave of panic. If I don't fix this right away, Georgina is going to move on to the next. She's going to fuck someone else. Fall in love with someone else. Get married to, and have babies with, someone else.

In a flash, most likely to avoid my head physically exploding, my brain transforms T-Rod across the patio into Georgina. And Ryan into *me.* That's *my* baby on Georgina's hip now. Nobody else's. Georgina fucked *me* to make that baby happen. Nobody else. In fact, in this fantasy, Georgina never fucked anyone else, after me. Ever again. And she certainly never pledged her undying love to some other motherfucker. Hell no. She pledged her undying love to *me*.

Calm washes over me. Obviously, I've got no desire to get married or have a baby, not even with Georgina. But I sure as hell don't want her doing either of those things with someone else.

I finish off my Bloody Mary and check my phone again. But, still, nothing from Georgina. Just more shit I don't care about from Owen.

I shouldn't do it, I know, but I can't help myself. I tap out yet another ill-advised text to Georgina. And then, just because I'm in my texts, I answer Owen, too, including telling him he's fired, just for kicks. But it's no use. Nothing, not even "firing" Owen, is numbing this searing pain. The only thing that could possibly help me now would be seeing Georgina's name lighting up my phone.

"I've brought reinforcements," a voice says, and when I look up from my screen, Henn is standing before me, holding two drinks. In reaction to whatever misery he's seeing on my face, his features contort with concern. "Aw, Reed. If you feel half as miserable as you look, then I'm sincerely worried about you."

Chapter 2
Reed

Henn gives me a choice between his two proffered drinks. When I pick the gin and tonic, he sits across from me with the vodka soda. "You're not planning to join the party today *at all?*"

"It's for the best. I can't imagine anyone wants me walking around, scaring all the little kiddies. Have you made any progress on hacking the football coach yet?"

Henn looks annoyed. "When would I have worked on that for you, since the last time you asked me about it—which was last night, at your party, when I was shitfaced?"

"I think I'm going crazy, Henn. I can't stand the fact that he's out in the world, living his best life, and not suffering at all for what he did to Georgie. She was *seventeen*. He was her *teacher. She trusted him.*" Georgina's words as she screamed at me last night slam into me, yet again: *I trusted you, Reed!* And, once again, my heart twists painfully. I whisper, "I swear, if I could take a hit out on this guy, and know I wouldn't get caught, I'd do it."

Henn rolls his eyes. "Okay, I'm ninety-nine percent sure you're not stupid enough to start searching the dark web for a hired killer. But just in case: don't do it. You *will* get caught. And from what I've heard about prison, you wouldn't like it. No Egyptian cotton bedsheets and the veggies, if you get them at all, come from a can." He sighs sympathetically. "I'll get into his devices, okay? And when I do, the odds are high I'll find something we can use to sink him."

"But, see, I don't want 'high' odds. I want a *guarantee*."

"If that's code for 'I want you to plant evidence,' then fuck off. You know I'd never do that. Will you please just trust me? I'm amazing at what I do. Let me do my thing and stop acting like Tony Soprano."

I lean back in my chair. "I have to do *something* with this manic energy. If I don't focus it on taking down Gates, then I'll have no choice but to focus on what a fucking idiot I am. And I don't want to think about that. I can't believe this is a self-inflicted wound."

Henn looks sympathetic. "What, exactly, did you do? I'm so confused. One minute, you were making breakfast for Georgina and telling me she's breakfast-worthy. And the next thing I know, Hannah is telling me Georgina stormed out of the party, looking distraught over something *you* did."

Midway through Henn's comment, Josh walks up, holding his one-year-old, Jack. "You're talking about Georgina?" He looks at me. "What happened?" He settles himself into a chair. "I don't get it. One minute, you were cannonballing into the pool and kissing her in front of everyone, and the next thing, Kat was telling me you'd done something to make her cry her eyes out."

I groan. "I don't want to talk about it, guys. Suffice it to say I fucked up, royally. And I regret it from the depths of my soul."

Kat appears, out of nowhere. "Exactly *how* did you fuck up? Spill it, Reed. Whatever you did to my beautiful Georgina, I could strangle you for it. I liked this one. I wanted to keep her!"

"I was just explaining to the guys I'm not interested in talking about this."

"Too bad. Tell me everything."

"News flash, Kitty Kat. That's not *my* ring on your finger." I point to the baby on Josh's lap, and then to Kat's baby bump. "And those aren't my kids. Which means I don't have to tell you jack shit."

7

Kat doesn't flinch. She's a girl who's grown up with four brothers, after all. Plus, she's long since learned to take me in stride when I'm in one of my bad moods. "It's in your best interest to tell me everything. Have you forgotten Georgina will be staying at my house when she comes to Seattle to interview Dax and the Goats? Well, when your name comes up, which it surely will—because that's what women do: we shit-talk the idiots we love—don't you want me to know your side of the story, so I can gently try to steer Georgina toward saintly forgiveness?"

Feigning shock, Josh says, "Wait. Women shit-talk the idiots they love?"

"Oh, honey." Kat pats her husband's thigh. "It's our favorite sport."

Damn. I think Kat has a point. She's uniquely positioned to influence Georgina's opinion of me. Plus, Kat's fiery temperament and personality are a lot like Georgina's. Kat's the only person I know who's as gifted at twisting people around her finger as Georgina, not to mention ripping them a new asshole with a smile. Come to think of it, yeah, I should probably use Kat as a sounding board—as a proxy for Georgina—to help me figure out my best strategy for winning Georgina back.

"All right. I'll tell you everything. But this stays between us, guys." I look at Henn. "Although, of course, you can tell Hannah." With that, I proceed to tell Kat and my two best friends the whole story. Everything from the panel discussion to the grant, and how it came about, to my conversation with Alessandra, to my regrettable kiss with Isabel in the garage. "The irony," I say, in wrap-up, "is that kissing Isabel made me realize I only want Georgina."

Kat snorts. "Good luck convincing Georgina of *that*."

"Why? It's true."

"Maybe, but that's the thing cheaters *always* say after they get caught. 'Yes, baby, I cheated on you. But it only made me realize how much I only love *you*.'"

My shoulders slump in defeat.

Kat asks, "Before the party, did you and Georgina exchange 'I love yous'?"

"No. Is that good or bad for me?"

"It's a double-edged sword. On one hand, if you'd already exchanged the magic words with Georgina when you cheated on her, she'd think those words meant nothing to you."

"Can we not say I 'cheated' on Georgina? I feel like that's a bit dramatic for what I actually did. It was nothing but a stupid goodbye kiss."

"It was *cheating*, Reed."

I slump in my chair.

"As I was saying," Kat says, "it's a *good* thing you hadn't already said the 'L' word to Georgina when you cheated on her. That saves you from Georgina thinking the words are meaningless to you. But, on the flipside, if you were to say 'I love you' now, *after* cheating on her, then Georgina will think you're only saying that as a ploy to win her back."

I exhale with exasperation. "This isn't helping me. What's your point? That I can *never* tell Georgina I love her now? That I'm fucked forever?"

Kat's face lights up. "So, you *do,* in fact, love her?"

I pause. I've never said "I love you" to a woman before. I've said, "You drive me crazy" and "I can't get enough" and "I care about you." But, in this moment, there's no doubt the word "love"—and nothing less—is the one that accurately describes my once-in-a-lifetime feelings for Georgina. "Yeah. I love Georgina like I've never loved anyone before."

Kat clutches her heart. "Aw, sweetie." She looks at me sympathetically for a beat, before her features contort sharply with anger. She swats at my shoulder. "What the hell is wrong with you, Reed? Why did you go into that garage with Isabel, in the first place?"

What the hell is wrong with me? Women have been asking me that same question my entire adult life. And I'm no closer to

9

being able to answer it now. "How is this helping me?" I whisper-shout. "You told me to tell you *everything* so you can convince Georgina to *forgive* me. Flogging me for my stupidity isn't useful." I wave at the air. "You know what? Forget it. I'll figure it out myself." I stand. "Someone who isn't drunk, drive me to Georgie right now. She's got to be at her father's condo in the Valley. I'll go there now and tell her I love her and win her back."

Kat stands and points at my chair like she's commanding a misbehaving dog. "Sit your ass down, you clueless, impulsive, drunken fool! Do you want Georgina to swoon or scowl when you tell her the magic words for the first time?"

"I want her to swoon," I admit softly.

"Then sit down."

I flop down, feeling dejected.

"You can't say 'I love you' to Georgina until you're completely out of the doghouse, or she won't believe you. She doesn't trust you, Reed. You need to regain her trust before you're allowed to say those magical words."

"But when will she trust me again?" I boom—but then, I look around the party, realizing I said that far too loudly. I lean forward and whisper-shout, "How can I get myself out of the doghouse with Georgie when she won't even call me back? *Help* me, Kat, for the love of fuck!"

Kat looks at Josh. "Have you ever seen him this pathetic before?"

"Not even close."

She puts her hand on mine. "Okay, Reed. I'm going to help you. But you need to look me in the eye and *swear* you only *kissed* Isabel in that garage, and nothing more."

I look into Kat's blazing blue eyes. "I swear on my life. On my mother's. *On my nephew's.*"

And that's it. Kat clearly believes me now, without question. Because she knows, for all my faults, I'd never swear falsely on my beloved nephew.

10

"Okay," she says decisively. "Let's figure out how to get Georgie back."

"Oh, thank God. Thank you, Kat. Bless you."

Kat taps the little indentation in her chin. "Okay, first off, I think it's important to realize the kiss is your biggest hurdle. I'm sure you were a bit rude with Alessandra, knowing you. But I have to believe Georgie will talk to her stepsister and find out what you *actually* said, versus what she *thinks* you said, and all will eventually be forgiven."

"Good. Yes. That's my thinking, too. Same thing with the grant."

"I agree. I'm sure Georgina felt blindsided about the grant last night—and understandably so—and now she's thinking worst-case scenario about you and CeeCee. But, eventually, she'll talk to CeeCee and find out what *really* happened and forgive you on that score, too. Heck, she might even *thank* you."

My spirit is rising and filling my chest. "CeeCee is still in Bali. But I'll text her now..." I pull out my phone. "And tell her to call Georgina the minute she lands and tell her—"

"No, no, you stupid man!" Kat booms, snatching my phone out of my hand. "You have to let Georgina contact CeeCee, *organically*. And when she does, you need CeeCee to be able to say, honestly, she hasn't spoken to you about any of this. Otherwise, Georgina will think you tampered with the witness. Look, I know you're a control freak who's used to pulling strings every which way. But, this time, you need to release that impulse and have faith the truth will come out, on its own, and set you free."

"But what about the kiss? How do I convince Georgina I'm telling the truth about that? And, then, how do I make her forgive me for it?"

Kat twists her mouth. "Yeah, that's a toughie. Even if you could convince Georgie it was only a kiss, she's going to think you're full of shit if you say it made you realize you only want her."

"But nothing's impossible, right? Come on, Kat. You think like Georgina. You're a hotheaded psycho, just like her. A demon spawn."

"Thank you."

"So, use that brilliant, evil, demonic mind of yours to channel Georgie. Tell me what would work on *you*, in this same situation."

"If *Josh* were the dumbass who'd kissed his ex in a garage?"

"Yes."

She looks at Josh. "If Josh had kissed his ex in a garage, during Josh's party, when our relationship was still brand new, and we were still building trust, and I'd been staying at Josh's house for a week, falling head over heels in love with him, and I'd *just* told him things I'd never told anyone else...? Hmm." She taps her chin again, deep in thought. "That's a tall order, Reed. Not gonna lie."

I groan in pain and crumple over. "It sounds so bad when you say it out loud like that."

Kat shrugs. "I think, if the situation were exactly as I've described, then there's only one solution. Only one thing Josh could possibly do to even have a *shot* at winning me back." She pauses for dramatic effect. "*Grovel*. Reed, trust me on this: you need to grovel, grovel, grovel your arrogant ass off, like you've never groveled before. It's the only way."

I throw up my hands, exasperated. "I've already done that! *Repeatedly*. And it hasn't worked."

"What do you mean you've already done that? That's impossible."

"I groveled my ass off last night! The whole time I was following Georgina from the garage, into my house, upstairs to her room, downstairs to the front door, across my driveway, to my front gate! I groveled like a pathetic fucking idiot."

Kat scoffs. "All of that wasn't *groveling*! It was explaining. Apologizing. Maybe begging and pleading. But real groveling takes time. It takes grand gestures. It takes humbling yourself until the woman knows you're in it to win it, for real. She needs to see you're willing to get down on your hands and knees, over a lengthy period of time, and beg and plead for forgiveness in a way that makes it indisputable you're willing to sacrifice your ego completely, all in the name of winning her back!"

I look at Josh, and he shrugs, making it clear he's deferring to his wife on this one. But I can't sign onto this madness. Yes, I'm willing to do "anything" to get Georgina back. *But only within reason.* I'll apologize profusely. I'll even beg Georgina for forgiveness. *But* I can't give myself a personality transplant! I'm Reed Rivers. A survivor. A fighter. A *hustler.* I'm a man who transformed his name from a badge of shame into a badge of honor—from a cross to bear into a designer label. I'm not a guy who's going to *grovel* in the way Kat's describing. And even if I were, why would I do that, when I'm certain it wouldn't work! Georgina fell in love with me this past week, every bit as much as I fell in love with her. I'm sure of it. Which means, to win her back, I can't turn myself into a guy she doesn't even recognize—some simpering version of myself with no swagger and no game and no pride. The only thing weeks and weeks of groveling would do is make Georgina lose respect for me. Which, in the end, wouldn't help my cause at all.

Once again, that same idea from before, the one that would vindicate me, pops into my head as my best option. But, quickly, my rational brain discards the idea as a non-starter, for all the same reasons as before. No. That's not the answer. But neither is *groveling.* What I need is to get back to basics. And what's the most basic thing I know in life? *Everyone's got a price.* All I've got to do to win Georgina back is figure out her goddamned price in *this* particular situation... which, I admit, is a tall order, like Kat said. But, still, I'll do it. I'll figure out her price, whatever it is. And once I do, I'll give it to her. *I'll bribe her with it.* And that's how Reed Rivers, The Man with the Midas Touch, is gonna play—and *win*—this particular game of chess.

Chapter 3
Georgina

Monday, 7:16 pm

"G eorgie," Dad whispers, rubbing my arm. The edge of my bed lowers with the weight of his body. "There's a delivery guy at the front door. He says he's got a stationary bike for you. Does he have the right address?"

"Oh. Um." I rub my eyes and glance out the window. It's dusk. Nearly dark. When did that happen? When I crawled into bed it was just past noon. "Yeah, uh, the bike is mine. It was a gift."

Dad's eyebrows shoot up—a sure sign he knows that bike wasn't cheap.

"It's from my boss," I add quickly. "CeeCee Rafael gives every new intern a stationary bike. She says it helps with productivity." I hate lying to my father, but I don't have a choice. There's no way I'm going to tell him the bike was a gift from the CEO of River Records.

Dad turns on the lamp beside my bed. "That's quite an employment perk, especially for a summer intern."

"CeeCee is generous."

Dad looks at me for a long beat, his eyes letting me know he thinks I'm full of crap. But, whatever he's thinking, he doesn't say it. Instead, he stands and says, "I'll accept the delivery, then. I thought for sure there had to be some sort of a mix-up."

"Nope. It's mine."

When Dad leaves the room, I grab my phone to check the time. But my phone is still turned off. I turned it off two days ago while sitting in the back of that Uber—right after I'd started receiving frantic voicemails and texts from Reed—and I haven't turned it on since.

When my phone springs to life, a backlog of text- and voicemail-notifications comes up—a bunch of them, not surprisingly, from Reed. My stomach churning, I slide into my texts, and, consciously ignoring Reed's messages, head to one from Alessandra.

Landed safely in Boston. I hope you're feeling better. I love you.

I tap out a reply.

I just woke up. I got back into bed after driving you to the airport this morning. Don't worry. I've decided to stop wallowing now. I love you, too. I'll call you tomorrow.

Next up, I've got a text from Zasu, my co-writer on the special issue.

I've secured a 2:00 meeting with CeeCee on Wednesday, so we can go over all the interviews we've got lined up. It was hard to get onto CeeCee's calendar that day, since it'll be her first day back from vacay, so the meeting will be short. Make sure you're super prepared with your pitches!

I write back to Zasu to say I'll see her on Wednesday, and I'll be ready to slay.

Next up? A text from CeeCee's assistant, Margot.

There are three boxes here for you from the courthouse. I put them into Conference Room D.

I reply to Margot, thanking her for the information and telling her I'll come to the office tomorrow, Tuesday, to go through the boxes.

Next up, there's a text from Kat Faraday, giving me some options on dates for my trip to Seattle. One, as early as the end of this week. I reply to Kat, telling her I adored meeting her on Saturday and can't wait to see her again. I write:

Lauren Rowe

Let's tentatively plan on Friday for my interview in Seattle. I'll confirm after I meet with my boss on Wednesday.

And that's everything in my inbox... *except* for that slew of texts and voicemails from Reed. With a heavy sigh, I steel myself for whatever bullshit I'm about to read and then swipe into his first text. It's time-stamped mere minutes after I'd hopped into that Uber with Alessandra.

But before I've read more than two words, Dad pokes his head into my bedroom. "I had the guy leave the bike in the living room. I was thinking I might want to try it out, if that's okay with you."

"Of course. Enjoy it."

Dad enters the room and stands over me, his bullshit detector visibly flashing "RED ALERT." He crosses his arms over his chest. "That's a *really* nice bike, Georgina Marie."

Uh oh. It's never a good sign when Dad uses my middle name. "Mmm hmm. My boss is *really* generous."

Dad sits on the edge of my bed. "Are you sure that's not an apology of some sort, maybe from whoever made you crawl into bed and cry for the past two days?"

Oh, jeez. Each and every time I cried these past two days, I put a pillow over my face. Damn the paper-thin walls of this condo.

Dad strokes my hair. "I could tell you were trying to muffle your crying, but I couldn't help hearing. You want to talk about it?"

I exhale. "I'm sorry, Dad. I lied to you about the bike. It was actually from a guy I really liked." *No, a guy I loved,* I think. But, of course, I'd never say that out loud. I continue, "I thought this boy liked me the same way I liked him. But it turned out, he didn't. He rejected me at a party on Saturday night. That's why I came home and cried my eyes out."

"Aw, honey." Dad grabs my hand. "You can't let a boy rejecting you send you to bed crying for two days. It's the

16

same thing you did when that stupid basketball player broke your heart. You came home for a weekend and cried your eyes out the whole time. And before that, the same thing happened during your senior year of high school, only worse. You crawled into bed for a *week* that time, after whatever stupid boy broke your heart."

My stomach clenches at my father's unwitting reference to Mr. Gates, and the way I imploded after he attacked me. For a solid week after Mr. Gates shoved his tongue down my throat and his fingers into my body, I felt literally dysfunctional. I couldn't sleep or eat or concentrate. I couldn't stop tears from streaming down my cheeks or my stomach from twisting into knots. So, I went to bed and told my father I had the flu. But when he said, "This isn't the flu. Did something happen with a boy?" I took the bait and nodded. And said nothing else.

Dad continues, "That time in high school, you'd just gotten the news you were accepted into UCLA! You should have been on Cloud Nine. But, instead, you were in bed, crying your eyes out for a week over some stupid boy."

Bile rises in my throat. My stomach physically twists. "I don't want to talk about that, Dad. Please."

Dad's face softens. "I'm not trying to upset you. I'm saying you can't let boys get you down the way you always do."

"I don't *always* do that. That's a massive exaggeration."

"My point is only that there are plenty of fish in the sea. And if this latest dumb boy isn't smart enough to want you, then you're lucky to be rid of him. *Ciao, stronzo,* right? Time to move on."

Despite my clenching stomach, I can't help smiling at my father's invocation of my mother's favorite expression. Literally translated, *Ciao, stronzo* means, *Bye, asshole.* But Mom always said it in a broader sense, not just in relation to people. It was her way of saying "good riddance" or "I'm done with you" to any person, place, or thing, even something as small as a malfunctioning can opener that might have broken her nail.

I look down at my mother's wedding ring on my hand and hear her feisty voice, telling me to move on from Reed. *Ciao, stronzo*, she says. *He cheated on you, love. He thought he could buy you with that grant.*

But it's no use. My head might be conjuring my mother's voice to help me move on. But my heart still only wants Reed, despite everything. I could have sworn he was falling in love with me the way I was falling for him this past week. My brain knew it was a long shot, given his renowned womanizing and public declarations of eternal bachelorhood. But, still, my heart *felt* so sure he was experiencing my exact feelings.

Dad brushes his fingertips against my cheek. "What about your job?"

"What about it?"

"Nobody expected to see your pretty face in the office today? It's Monday."

"No. Don't worry, Daddy. I'm not screwing up at work. I worked on Saturday night, into the early morning hours of Sunday, so Zasu told me to take Sunday and Monday off. I just now texted the office to let them know I'm coming in tomorrow to look through some documents."

Dad looks relieved.

"Plus, nobody expects to see me at *Rock 'n' Roll's* offices, just to show my face—not unless I've got a specific meeting. They know I'll be working mostly out of the office this summer. Out in the field, or at home, or at a desk set up for me at River Records."

"Speaking of home, where is that these days? You never texted me the name of your hotel. You know I like knowing where you are."

"Oh, yeah. I wound up staying with my co-worker, Zasu, this past week."

"Oh. How fun. Send me that address, would you?"

"Sure. Of course."

Crap. I think I might be a sociopath. Over the years, I've lied to my father, here and there. Simply because he's always been crazy-strict with me and girls just wanna have fun. But I've never lied to my father about *important* stuff. And I've certainly never told this many lies to him in rapid-fire succession.

I squeeze my father's hand. "Don't worry about me, okay? My job is going great. I'm going to be doing a whole bunch of cool interviews of famous artists in the next few weeks. One of them, as early as this Friday in Seattle, if my boss gives me the green light on Wednesday."

Dad's face lights up. "Any artists I might know?"

"Remember that show I used to watch: *It's Aloha!* on Disney?"

"Oh, sure. You loved that one."

"Aloha Carmichael is a pop star now, signed to River Records, and I'll be interviewing her."

Dad flips out.

"Have you heard of Laila Fitzgerald?"

Dad shakes his head.

"Oh. Well, then I guess you won't be excited to learn I'm interviewing her, too. How about the rock group 22 Goats?"

Dad shakes his head again. "They're called '22 *Goats*'? As in, the farm animal?"

"Yep. They're super popular, Dad. If my boss says yes, I'll be flying to Seattle on Thursday to interview them on Friday."

"Are there twenty-two people in the band?"

I chuckle. "No, only three. You know how random band names can be."

"That's true. What the hell is a 'Led Zeppelin'?"

We talk about nonsensical band names for a bit, and, with each passing minute, my mood lifts and brightens.

"Don't worry, Daddy. I know this job is the chance of a

lifetime. I promise I'm not going to blow it. Not for anyone. Least of all, some stupid boy who doesn't love me back."

Dad juts his lower lip, making a classic "sad face." "Aw, I didn't realize you *loved* this boy."

Crap. How did I let that slip? "I thought I did."

"Aw, honey. I'm sorry."

I shrug and say nothing. Because... what is there to say? I was a fool to give my heart to Reed Rivers, any way you slice it.

Dad says, "Well, then, this *stronzo* is obviously more than dumb. He's crazy."

"It's for the best," I say, trying to convince myself, even more than him. "I should be focusing on my career, not trying to make some dumb, crazy boy fall in love with me."

"Amen. Focus all your energy on your internship and getting hired for that magazine you've always wanted to work for."

"That's exactly what I'm going to do." I bolt upright. "In fact, I'm going to get back to work right now." I point to the cardboard box in the corner—the one filled with the three settled lawsuits I got from the courthouse the other day. For some time now, I've been meaning to read the third lawsuit Reed settled—the one filed by Troy Eklund for breach of contract, fraud, and assault—but I haven't had a spare moment to dig into it. "Could you hand me that box? There's something I've been dying to read, and there's no time like the present."

"Nope. You're going to eat something now and read whatever is in that box later."

"No, I'll eat later. I want to capitalize on this burst of energy."

"What have you eaten today, Georgina Marie?"

My middle name, again? "Coffee this morning, when I took Alessandra to the airport. And a banana."

"And that's it?"

I nod, grimacing.

"That's what I thought. Your appetite is always the first thing to go when you're upset. Well, you're in luck, *Amorina*. I've been slow-cooking meatballs all day."

I fist-pump the air, and Dad chuckles. He doesn't always know how to talk through my feelings with me, though he tries. He doesn't always know how best to console me when I'm down. But the man sure as hell knows how to feed me.

"I'll put together meatball sandwiches for us," Dad says. "While you take a shower and get into some fresh jammies."

"It's a date." I hug him. "Thank you, Daddy. You're the sweetest."

Dad kisses my cheek. "I know you wish Mommy were here to talk to you about boy stuff. And I don't blame you. But I'm here. Any time. If you want to talk."

"Thank you."

"Now, shower while I make us dinner."

"I'll shower after dinner. I've got some texts and voicemails to go through, real quick."

"All right." Dad rises from the bed and points at the cardboard box in the corner. "As long as you don't start reading whatever's in there. I know how laser-focused you get when you work. Two hours pass without you even realizing it."

"I'll deal with my texts and voicemails and come right out."

"Good girl."

Dad kisses my forehead and heads out. And the minute the door closes behind him, I grab my phone, steel myself for whatever bullshit explanations and apologies Reed has left me over the past two days, and swipe into his first voicemail.

Chapter 4
Georgina

I must admit, the desperation in Reed's voicemails makes me smile. He's miserable? Desperate? Tormented? Full of remorse and regret? Good.

After listening to his voicemails, all of which say basically the same things he said to me at the party, I swipe into Reed's first text, which tells me only that he's left me a voicemail that "requires my attention." Pfft.

I move on to Reed's next text, sent an hour later, after he hadn't heard from me regarding his voicemails. This time, his text is about Alessandra. But he doesn't apologize. On the contrary, he says he's got "nothing to apologize for" in regard to my stepsister. "If she follows my advice," he writes, "she could be great. If not, she'll be stuck singing demos her whole career, if she's lucky."

"*That's* your idea of an *apology,* you prick?" I say out loud. But, truthfully, I know he's right. I'm still annoyed he said anything at all to Alessandra about her demo, given his promise not to do that very thing. But when I drove Alessandra to the airport this morning, she told me everything Reed said to her. And, by the time she was done talking, I knew in my bones, at least in regard to Alessandra, Reed didn't do anything unforgiveable. He was clearly only trying to help her, just like he said.

But so what? Even if I were to forgive Reed for making Alessandra cry, he's still got two other strikes against him.

The grant and *Isabel*. In Reed's voicemails, he said he "refuses" to explain himself about either topic, via text or voicemail, but, instead, "demands" that I call him to hear him out. But I'm not in the mood to meet his "demand." Nor am I inclined to let him try to sweet-talk me. He already tried to do that as I was leaving the party, and I wasn't impressed.

I move on to Reed's next text, which he sent around noon yesterday (Sunday):

I get that you're upset, and you have every right to be. But I'd appreciate the courtesy of a reply to my voicemails and texts, even if it's just to tell me to fuck off. I'm worried about you and want confirmation that you're safe and sound. Call me.

Obviously, he received no reply to that command. And so, he sent another text, this one about an hour later.

Per our initial agreement, I've booked a hotel room for you for the summer, at the W in Hollywood. I've also decided it would benefit the special issue if you had access to a car, so I've rented a little convertible for you. It's already sitting in the hotel's parking garage. Keys at the front desk. No need to thank me. I've done all of this for business reasons. All I ask is that you call me, the CEO of River Records, to let me know you're safe and sound.

When Reed received no reply from me about the hotel and car, he sent yet another text, four hours later. This one, on Sunday afternoon.

Guess where I am, Georgie Girl? At Hazel Hennessy's 1st birthday party! Drinking like a fish, sitting in a corner, wishing you were here. You were supposed to come with me to this shindig, remember? In fact, you were excited to come. And now, here I am, a lone wolf. Looks like The Man with the Midas Touch has lost his golden touch, huh? Sure would be awesome if you'd answer one of my fucking texts or voicemails.

Reed's next text came an hour later, at 5:26 pm on Sunday.

I swear I've never wished I could rewind the clock and get a 'do-over' more than I wish that right now. I'm sorry, Georgie. Please, call me. XO

Fifteen minutes later, he sent this:

Georgie, I'd walk a million miles, barefoot, over the shards of my Ferrari's shattered windshield, if it would make you forgive me. Please, call me. Scream at me. Tell me you hate me. Just call and let me hear your voice. I'm losing my mind. I'm sure you're happy about that. I'm sure you're smiling at my misery, and I don't blame you. But if you ever cared about me at all, please, just call me and let me explain. I'm physically sick with the need to talk to you. XO

When he *still* didn't receive a reply from me, Reed sent this little gem at 2:13 a.m. today (Monday):

Congratulations. You've now ignored me for a full twenty-four hours. Are you alive? Are you safe? Should I file a missing person report? I think the punishment far outweighs the crime, at this point. I mean, I get that you're pissed at me. But guess what? I'm pissed at you for smashing my Ferrari as punishment for a fucking kiss! So, let's call it even. A kiss for a Ferrari. Call me, even if it's to tell me to fuck off and die. CALL ME.

I can't help smirking. God, he's terrible at this. Doesn't he realize he should be groveling right now? Not lashing out. Not being cocky. Not telling me he's angry with me. Jesus, he's infuriating. But so am I. Because the pathetic truth is that I kind of like Reed's bad attitude. In fact, knowing he's grouchy and angry and cantankerous and lashing out... all of it kind of makes my heart go pitter pat. How screwed up is that?

When Reed didn't hear from me, yet again, he sent me another text. Surprise, surprise. This one, about thirty minutes later.

I lied. I'm not mad about my Ferrari. Never was. I just texted that to piss you off, so you'd call me. Please, Georgie. Have mercy on me. I've never done this before.

I've never felt this before. There was no way I was going to be able to do this, and to feel this, without stumbling. I fucked up. I know that. Give me another chance. Please.

But I didn't call. Not because I have willpower of steel. Not because I'm heartless or the Bobby Fischer of breakups. But because... I had my phone off. Because I was in bed, wallowing in self-pity.

Well, guess what? My non-strategy strategy finally wore Reed down and forced him to do the one thing he *swore* in his voicemails he wouldn't: explain the grant to me over text. In four messages, all of them sent in rapid-fire succession, he unloaded on me, as follows:

I didn't want to explain any of this to you in a text, but you've left me no choice. CeeCee was going to hire you, regardless. When I called the day after the panel, she'd already fallen in love with you and your writing samples. The only problem? She never pays summer interns and didn't want to open a can of worms by doing it for you. On the other hand, she'd heard about your father's situation, and didn't feel right about offering you a standard unpaid internship. I suggested a solution that would benefit all three of us: I'd donate to CeeCee's favorite cancer charity to get you paid, in exchange for RnR doing a special issue about my label. CeeCee countered that the deal had to include an in-depth interview of me. I said okay. She suggested you as the interviewer. I said yes, because, unbeknownst to CeeCee, that would give me a chance to try to seduce you. And that was that. A win-win-win. So sue me.

You once told me you had parallel motivations the first time we met. Well, so did I. Yes, I wanted another shot at seducing you, but I ALSO wanted to help CeeCee, and you, and your dad. I regret the way the grant turned into such a big secret. That wasn't my intention. I didn't say anything about it because I didn't want to steal your thunder or make you think, even for a second, you hadn't earned your job. Also, I didn't want you feeling any kind of pressure to sleep with me. Yes, I wanted it to happen. Hell yes. But only if you genuinely wanted it, too. Not because you felt a financial obligation to me. That's the truth. On my nephew. Now, stop acting like a petulant child and reply to this text so I know you're safe.

PS I sent the Peloton to your dad's place. If you don't have room for it there, let me know. Also, let me know if you want your Pilates machine. It's much bigger than the bike, so I figured it'd be better to ask before sending.

I'm assuming you're coming to today's team meeting, seeing as how you're still obligated to write an article about me. Please allow me to take you to lunch before the meeting. We'll talk and forgive. I'll forgive you for ignoring me for two days. And you'll forgive me for being a stupid idiot. I'll make a reservation at Nobu. You'll love it. Please reply to confirm. I can't wait to see you. XO

I look up from my phone. Damn that man. He's persuasive. I still need to talk to CeeCee, to hear her unbiased account regarding the grant. But I can't deny Reed's texts have made me cautiously optimistic about that. I'm sure Reed spun some of the facts to make himself sound as innocent as possible. But, even so, I'm feeling pretty sure CeeCee wasn't my pimp, but instead leaped at the chance to create a win-win-win with her trusted friend, for my benefit, and theirs. But so what? None of that would absolve Reed of whatever happened in that garage with Isabel. Sighing loudly, I scroll to Reed's next text, which landed in my inbox about an hour and a half ago—at 6:13 pm this evening:

Miss Ricci, I'm sending this text in my professional capacity. I'm deeply disappointed you didn't come to this afternoon's weekly team meeting. Even if you despise me for personal reasons, you've still got a job to do, and I expect you to fucking do it. You're a writer for the world's top music magazine and you need to start behaving like it. Whatever has transpired between us, personally, it's time for you to put your feelings aside and behave like a fucking professional. I'll expect you to attend next Monday's team meeting. I'll also expect you to respond to all business-related texts from me, going forward, including confirmation that you're safe and sound, within the next fifteen minutes.

I look up from my phone, gritting my teeth. Reed wants me to act like a "fucking professional," does he? Well, all righty, then. How about this? I'll write an article about him that kicks so much ass, CeeCee will have no choice but to publish it in *Dig a Little Deeper*!

Determination flooding me, I hop out of bed and plop myself onto the floor next to the cardboard box and begin sifting through its contents like a madwoman. Quickly, I find the documents pertaining to Troy Eklund's lawsuit. It was filed six years ago, against Reed and River Records, and alleges four causes of action: breach of contract, breach of the implied covenant of good faith and fair dealing, fraud, and assault.

But before I've gotten past the second paragraph of Troy's complaint, Dad pops his head into the room. And the minute he sees me on the floor, surrounded by legal documents, I know I must look to him like a chocolate-smeared kid surrounded by a mountain of candy wrappers on Halloween.

"*Georgina Marie*. You promised not to look at whatever's in that box!"

I grimace. "Sorry. I wasn't lying to you. I just... *forgot.*"

Dad points toward the hallway. "Get your butt into the kitchen and eat the meatball sandwich I've made for you. *Dinner is served.*"

"Sorry, Daddy. I need five minutes. There's a text for work I need to send."

"No."

"It's for work. I swear. I need to send it."

Dad exhales. "You swear on Mommy it's for work?"

Damn it. I hate it when he does that. He knows it's the one thing I'll never, ever fib on. But, luckily, the text I want to send is to Margot. Not about a work-related matter, actually. But, hey, since she works for *Rock 'n' Roll,* I still think a text to her should qualify as something "for work." I say, "Yes. I swear. I just need five minutes."

Satisfied, Dad leaves my doorway, and I pick up my phone, intending to send my text to Margot. But before I've started typing, my phone pings with yet another incoming text from Reed:

The hotel informs me you haven't checked into your room or retrieved your car keys. I'm assuming that means you're staying at your father's condo. Please confirm. If I don't hear from you by 8:00 tonight, then I'll have no choice but to call your father to confirm your whereabouts. If you're not at his place, and he hasn't heard from you, then my next call will be to the police. Your choice, Miss Ricci.

"Bastard!" I whisper-shout. The clever man has found my Achilles' heel. He knows I'd never want the CEO of River Records calling my father about me. How would I explain that to my dad, after the loan on his condo got magically paid off? After a fancy stationary bike showed up at his house? And, especially, now that my father knows I've been in bed, crying for two days because a stupid boy didn't love me back? Damn that relentless man! Gnashing my teeth, I bang out an angry reply to Reed's missive:

Hello, Mr. Rivers. Yes, I'm at my father's condo. I'm planning to stay at the hotel starting tomorrow night. Thank you for the room and rental car. Thank you for having the Peloton delivered. Keep the Pilates machine, please. I missed today's team meeting because I've determined I've got enough information from you, directly, for my article and will now begin gathering information from other sources. Going forward, please keep future communications on a professional basis. Thank you for everything you've done for me and my father. We both appreciate it very much. However, as I hope you have discerned by now, my affection and trust do not have a price tag.

I press send on my message, and not ten seconds later, my phone rings with an incoming call from Reed—which I decline—and then breathlessly tap out a text to CeeCee's personal assistant, Margot:

I know CeeCee will be slammed on Wednesday, since it's her first day back, but I'm hoping to grab a few minutes of her time, one-on-one, before her scheduled meeting with Zasu and me at 2:00. I'm sorry to ask for this favor, but it's an urgent personal matter. Thank you.

After pressing send, I toss my phone onto my bed and march into my father's kitchen, my stomach growling and my head held high. Reed wants me to act like a "fucking professional"? Fine. Great. Then that's exactly what I'll do, *stronzo*.

29

Chapter 5
Georgina

Tuesday, 1:04 pm

I lean back in my chair, blown away. Heartsick. Devastated. How am I going to remain angry with Reed after reading all of *this*?

I'm sitting in a conference room at *Rock 'n' Roll*, having just read the documents comprising the twenty-year-old legal malpractice suit filed by Eleanor Rivers against her divorce attorney—which, in turn, set forth the basic facts of the underlying divorce and custody battle between Eleanor and Terrence Rivers. And I'm feeling like I've just been run over by a Mack truck. I can't imagine what Reed had to do—the fortress he had to build around his heart—to overcome the chaos and abandonments of his childhood.

It's taken me half a day to read everything in the three boxes sent from the courthouse, all of which can be summarized as follows:

Two years before Reed came along, Terrence and Eleanor Rivers had a son named Oliver. When little Oliver Rivers was born, Terrence and Eleanor hired a weekday, live-in housekeeper/nanny named Amalia Vaccaro. Two years later, when Reed joined the family, a weekend nanny named Celeste was added to the payroll. Why did Terrence and Eleanor feel they needed so much assistance with their two young children, when Eleanor didn't work outside the home?

Well, according to Eleanor, it was because Terrence wanted his young wife to be able to "dote on their children" while also having plenty of time to "paint and nap, and read poetry," and, basically, not have to worry about pesky things like cleaning toilets or making the family dinner, or anything else that might cause Eleanor a moment of worry or stress.

According to Terrence, however, he insisted on round-the-clock help for his "unstable and emotional" wife because he knew, from the start, she would make an "unfit mother, if she were left to handle the pressures of motherhood without a lot of help."

Not so, Eleanor retorted in a deposition, pointing out that she'd grown up babysitting her younger sisters and her neighbors' children. "I've always adored babies," Eleanor insisted. "And I absolutely adored mine." According to Eleanor, it was Terrence, *not* herself, who was the unfit parent. "Terrence never showed any genuine interest in being a true father to our boys," Eleanor claimed. "He loves having a family for Christmas cards. But that's about it." Moreover, Eleanor claimed, the reason Terrence "insisted" on hiring their weekend nanny, Celeste, wasn't because *Eleanor* needed her. But because Celeste was "young and beautiful, and Terrence wanted to get her into bed."

But no matter what Eleanor argued in the divorce, it fell on deaf ears. At least, that was my impression when reading the documents—and all because of one tragic fact, which Terrence and his army of lawyers relentlessly hammered on: it was Eleanor who was home alone with her two young sons on the fateful Saturday when little Oliver Rivers drowned in his family's backyard swimming pool.

On that day, the weekend nanny, Celeste, had called in sick, and Terrence was off playing golf. At least, according to Terrence. According to Eleanor, Terrence was off screwing Celeste, the "sick" weekend nanny, that fateful day. In the legal malpractice case, one of Eleanor's biggest beefs with her own divorce lawyer was that she hadn't tracked down Terrence's

31

actual whereabouts that day, either through hotel receipts or witnesses. Eleanor claimed Terrence was a liar and a cheater in the divorce—which, of course, isn't a hard thing to believe, in retrospect, considering Terrence's criminal conviction three years later. She argued proof of Terrence's infidelity on that particular Saturday, and his lies about it in the divorce, would have debunked his entire case, all of which centered on Terrence being a devoted and exemplary husband and father—a pillar of the community. To Eleanor's thinking, proving Terrence was an unfaithful husband and a liar under oath would have given her a fighting chance to retain the right to care for her son, Reed.

Personally, I'm not sure if Eleanor was right about any of that. I have to think, even if the judge had ruled Terrence *was* a liar and a cheater in relation to his wife, it wouldn't have made him decide Terrence was an unfit parent. Otherwise, half the divorced people in the world would lose custody of their kids. But, either way, I felt bad for Eleanor while reading the malpractice case. It was undisputed she'd been alone with her two boys the day Oliver died, which was a tragedy, in itself—and one she was desperately trying to grapple with and explain. But, unfortunately, for Eleanor, that horrible tragedy was all the judge in the divorce case needed to know about, seven years later, to grant Terrence full legal and physical custody of Reed. What did Eleanor get? Once-weekly supervised visitations with her son, for two hours at a time.

Honestly, I have no idea if Oliver's death was Eleanor's "fault," as Terrence claimed. Maybe it was. But I can't help thinking children die tragically in swimming pools every day—sometimes, even in the presence of lifeguards. Sometimes, at a party, when a bunch of parents are standing nearby. Are all parents whose children slip silently underwater, never to rise again, *de facto* unfit parents to their surviving children, based on a few seconds of tragic inattention? And if so, are they *still* unfit parents, a full seven years after the tragedy?

I don't pretend to have answers. I'm just saying, from

what I just read, I feel like the judge in the divorce case believed Terrence's version of events, hook, line, and sinker, without giving Eleanor's version of events, and her desperate pleas for him to listen to her, a moment's sincere consideration. And, in light of what we've since learned about Terrence, one of the world's most notorious liars, I feel in my bones Eleanor was probably given a raw deal.

In Eleanor's version of events, she had the stomach flu the day Oliver died and could barely keep her eyes open. Eleanor testified she "begged" and "pleaded" with her husband to stay home and help her with their children, since the weekend nanny, Celeste, had called in sick. "But Terrence told me to 'suck it up, Buttercup,'" Eleanor testified in a deposition, an excerpt of which was attached to a motion in the malpractice case. "So that's what I did. I put the boys down for their regular morning nap, the same as always, set an alarm so I'd wake up before them, the same as always, and then, I crawled into bed and crashed."

Tragically, when Eleanor woke up and went to check on her boys, she found Reed still fast asleep in his crib... and Oliver nowhere to be found. She testified she looked high and low for her missing son, becoming increasingly panicked, and finally found him in an unthinkable spot. The poor woman described her desperate dive into the swimming pool. She testified about how she pulled Oliver from the water and tried frantically to resuscitate him... But it was too late. She testified, "I had no idea Oliver knew how to open the lock we'd put up high on the sliding door. He'd pulled up a chair to reach it. He'd never done that before!"

A week after Oliver's death, Eleanor tried to commit suicide. She was hospitalized thereafter for a week, and, then, sent to a long-term "mental care" facility in Los Angeles for the better part of a year. While she was away, Terrence was Father of the Year, according to him. Although, according to Eleanor, it was Amalia, not Terrence, who cared for Reed during this period. But since nobody called Amalia as a witness in the divorce case—yet another grievance for Eleanor in the later malpractice lawsuit—the divorce judge, once again, sided with Terrence, even going so far as to praise him for being Reed's "rock" during this time.

Poor Eleanor. She testified in the divorce, "I fully admit I wasn't capable of caring for Reed during the first year after Olly's death. But I knew Amalia was there for him, and that I needed to focus on getting better so I could get out and be a good mother to him. So that's what I did. I got the help I needed. And then I came home and took care of my son for the next six years. I'm not a perfect mother, but who is? Judge, I want to be with my son. I want to be his mother. Please, please, let me do that."

It wasn't enough to convince the judge. Not when Terrence, a man regarded as a "pillar of the community" testified that Eleanor was "useless and non-functional" when she returned home from her year away, and then remained that way for the entirety of the six years preceding the divorce.

In the end, Eleanor got bitch-slapped at every turn by Terrence and his team of lawyers. And then by the divorce judge. And then she got bitch-slapped again in the legal malpractice case. The same way, it seems to me, if I'm reading between the lines correctly, she'd gotten bitch-slapped by Terrence during their marriage.

After the judge in the divorce case granted Terrence full legal and physical custody of Reed, Eleanor swallowed a bottle of pills. It was the same thing she'd done after Oliver died seven years prior. And, again, it ultimately led to her institutionalization in a shitty facility in Los Angeles. Against all odds, she bounced back after about a year and came out with her boxing gloves on. She filed a legal malpractice action against her divorce attorney, the one I've just read, as some sort of last-gasp attempt to prove she'd been railroaded in the divorce, and that she did, in fact, have the wherewithal to care for Reed.

But when the judge in the *malpractice* lawsuit ruled

against Eleanor, the same way the divorce judge had, it was game over for Eleanor's mental health. She snapped for the last time. Once again, she tried to end it all. And wound up in that same, shitty Los Angeles institution. This time, for good, until her hard-working, loyal, and generous son moved her to a posh facility in Scarsdale.

Was Eleanor capable of caring for Reed at the time of the divorce, as she insisted vehemently at trial? I have no idea. All I know is it strikes me as awfully unfair that Terrence had Amalia's full-time help with Reed, and yet the judge expressly commented in his ruling against Eleanor, "A woman shouldn't need a paid nanny to help her care for her own children."

Also, I can't help feeling irate that the judge believed *everything* Terrence said, without question, given that, a mere two and a half years later, the FBI raided Terrence Rivers' sprawling mansion at dawn and arrested him in his underwear for staggering, truly evil financial crimes, thereby rendering his thirteen-year-old son, Reed, whom he'd fought so hard to claim for himself in the divorce, an effective orphan. Was Terrence Rivers any less of an "unfit parent" for mercilessly stealing from countless innocent families who'd trusted him, as Eleanor was for taking a nap, along with her two sons, when she had the stomach flu? I mean, assuming Eleanor's version of the story was true. Which, granted, I don't know.

I scrub my face with my palms, overwhelmed and aching for Eleanor. And Amalia. And Oliver. And, of course, for my beautiful liar, Reed. I've always found his hard outer shell immensely attractive, because it's what makes the rare glimpses of softness and vulnerability all the more breathtaking. But now, I'm realizing Reed's patented poker face, the steely mask he wears so well and often, must have been forged early on in his life as a coping mechanism. A way to survive the chaos. The abandonments. The lack of control he must have felt, at all times.

Even though I lost my mother at a young age, I

nonetheless had the good fortune to observe her passionate, happy marriage with my father before she died. But what has Reed observed of marriage that would make him believe it's possible for one to be happy? If I'd experienced everything Reed has, I'd probably have ten layers of cement around my heart, too. Frankly, after reading all this, I'm in awe of how kind and generous Reed is... exactly as Amalia said to me, that time we were cooking together in the kitchen.

I love him so much.

The thought pops into my head and streaks through my heart.

I love Reed. Even though I fervently wish I didn't.

But so what if I do? I simply have to get over it. Because loving Reed isn't enough. For our relationship to work, I need to love *and* trust him. And I don't see how I could ever get there. Not really. If I were to give Reed another chance, I know, deep down, I'd slowly become jealous, paranoid, and possessive. I'd grow to despise the woman I'd become with him. And he'd despise her, too. Which means it really is time for me to move on.

Ciao, stronzo.

It's what my brain keeps telling me to do. The thing I know is for the best. *Move on, Georgie. There are other fish in the sea. You're too young to have met the great love of your life, anyway, no matter what your foolish heart is telling you. Yes, Mom met her Prince Charming at nineteen. But Mom and Dad's fairytale was the exception, not the rule.*

I tell myself all of these things, as I stare at the conference room wall in a daze. I tell myself these things and stuff down the urge to call Reed and tell him I miss him. I love him. I forgive him. But no. I can't wave a magic wand and make everything the way it was before. Even as my heart wants to hug the tragic, neglected, abandoned little boy who grew up to be a wildly successful, sexy, breathtaking man, my brain knows it's time for me to move on.

Chapter 6
Reed

Tuesday 10:12 pm

I'm grunting. Sweating. Shaking as I finish a savage set of clapping pull-ups in my home gym. Henn texted yesterday to say he'd have something on Gates by Friday. So, at least, there's that. But regarding Georgina herself, I still haven't heard from her, other than that one soul-crushing text she sent twenty-four hours ago, after I threatened to call her father.

To entice her to call me, I did something yesterday morning that's surely going to piss her off when she finds out about it. Hopefully, enough to make her call me and chew me out. Obviously, I'd rather Georgina call me to whisper sweet nothings into my ear. But at this point, I'll do whatever I have to do to hear her voice, even if she's screaming at me.

I finish my pull-ups and look down at my phone on the floor, checking to see if I somehow missed a call from Georgina. But, nope. Grunting with annoyance, I grab my phone and head to a workout bench in a corner. But as I'm getting into position with some heavy dumbbells, it finally happens. *My phone rings with an incoming call from Georgina!*

Gasping like a fish on a hook, I scoop up my phone and briefly fumble with it, like some kind of electrocuted circus clown, and, finally, gather enough control of my fingers to connect the call.

37

"Georgina," I blurt, far more enthusiastically than intended. "You're alive!"

"What the hell do you think you're doing?" she shouts.

I close my eyes and take a deep breath. The sound of her voice, even when she's shouting angrily at me, is a balm for my tortured soul. "Whatever do you mean?" I ask, even though I know exactly what she means.

"I don't have a price, Reed!" she shrieks. "Get it through your head. *You cannot buy me.*"

I feel physically dizzy. I'm a junkie getting his first hit of the good stuff after three torturous days of withdrawal. I sink into the workout bench, feeling blissed out. "What crime have I committed to elicit this shrieking reaction from you, Miss Ricci?"

"You know exactly why I'm screaming at you. My father just called. His email address is the one on record for all my student loans. Apparently, two minutes ago, he checked his inbox for the first time today and discovered he'd received a 'paid in full' notification at noon regarding *all* my student loans!"

I smirk. *God, I'm good.*

"You can't pay off my student loans!"

"It appears I can. Quite easily, in fact."

"I won't let you."

"I already did it."

"Then, *undo* it. Tell the banks to return your money and restore the original loans."

I chuckle. "It doesn't work that way. That money belongs to the banks now. It's theirs."

Georgina mutters something expletive-laden under her breath that makes me smile even wider. "All right," she says, her voice brimming with resolve. "As of this moment, I owe that same exact amount of money to *you*. I don't care how long it takes me, I'm going to pay you back every cent, with interest."

Oh, how I've missed this back and forth with my beautiful fireball. I've only been without her for a matter of days, but it feels like years. "You know I won't accept a dime from you."

"I'm not giving you a choice. I'm going to Venmo payment to you every month, on the first."

"Which I'll decline with the push of a button."

"God, you're impossible! Do you have any idea the trouble you've caused me?"

"Trouble?"

"With my father! He saw that email and freaked out. He was like, 'How did you get your hands on a hundred thousand bucks, Georgina Marie?'"

"Did you tell him about me?"

"Of course, not! I told him that same cancer charity from before came to the rescue again. But he didn't believe me this time. He barely believed me last time, regarding the pay-off on his condo. He was like, 'Tell the truth, Georgie. Where is all this money coming from? Did that same jerk who sent you the expensive stationary bike also pay off your student loans?'"

Admittedly, knowing that Georgina's father thinks I'm a jerk isn't optimal. But, hey, at least, Georgina told him about me. And, even better, she's talking to me again. Which means I can now see a path forward to convincing her to take me back. "Ah, so your father knows of my existence?"

"Only because I couldn't avoid telling him where I got the Peloton."

"So, what did you finally tell him about the loans?"

"That I'm secretly working for a drug cartel."

"What?"

"That was a joke. I wish I could have told my father that. Telling him I'm working for a drug cartel would have been preferable to telling him I fell head over heels for the asshole CEO of River Records, and that, unfortunately, that asshole sneaked off and had sex with a movie star, and now thinks he can buy my trust and affection by paying off my student loans."

Okay, I realize a whole lot of what Georgina said wasn't good for me. Particularly, the part where she's *still* convinced I had *sex* with Isabel. Also, it's not ideal she called me an asshole. But I can't focus on negativity when Georgina started her diatribe with the amazing words: *I fell head over heels for the CEO of River Records.* During our magical week together, Georgina and I never said we were "falling" for each other. We said we felt "addicted." And that we were "crazy about" each other. We said we liked each other "so damned much." But we never once said "I'm *falling* for you"—which, of course, is a close cousin of "I'm falling *in love* with you"— which, in turn, is only one tick shy of "I love you."

"So, how'd you explain the loan getting paid off, if you didn't say you were a drug mule?"

"Well, since my father wasn't buying the cancer charity anymore, I told him the head of River Records is an eccentric billionaire who loves doing random acts of kindness. Which is actually kind of true. So, I told him you'd paid off my student loans, along with the student loans of Zasu, the other reporter working on the special issue."

I scoff. "And he bought that?"

"No. He's not a moron. Don't insult my father's intelligence."

I laugh. "You're the one who told him the lie. Not me."

"I'm his *daughter.* I've been insulting my father's intelligence since I was sixteen and putting pillows under my covers to make it look like I was in bed, fast asleep, when I'd actually sneaked out a window to go to a party."

I chuckle heartily. "You were Ferris Bueller. Oh, God. Please tell me you know that reference."

"Of course."

"There's no such thing as 'of course' when it comes to

you and pop culture references. Did you put pillows under your covers a lot, little Miss 'Sneaky' Ricci?"

"Probably, like, ten times. And it always worked like a charm. Until it didn't. Hoo-boy, the day I finally got caught wasn't a good one."

I laugh, and so does Georgie, which then makes every cell in my body electrify with excitement. Hope. *Love.* "I'm not a billionaire, by the way."

"Huh?

"You told your dad an 'eccentric billionaire' paid off your loans. I'm not a billionaire. Give me twenty years and I will be, though."

"You're a *millionaire*, though, right?"

"About five hundred times over."

"Why are you correcting me on this? Isn't it 'on-brand' for the world to think you're a billionaire?"

My stomach tightens. "I'm not 'on-brand' with you, Georgina, and you know it. I'm just me."

She's silent on the other end of the line, tacitly admitting she knows I'm speaking the truth.

"Georgie, I know you don't trust me as far as you can throw me—which I'm sure would be out a third-story window, if you could swing it—but, please, come home. Sleep in the blue room, while we work this out. My house feels so empty without you. My heart feels like it's rubbing against a cheese grater. Come *home*."

"I can't do that. I'm way too hurt. As sad as it is for me, I think we should agree to be friends and business colleagues, and nothing more."

I scoff. I can't be Georgina's friend and business colleague. Not in a million years. I want every inch of this woman. But, hey, at least she's not telling me to fuck off and die. And she did say it would be "sad" for her to be nothing but my friend.

She says, "Thank you for paying off my student loans. I

appreciate it. But don't you get it? It doesn't change anything between us because I was never with you for your money. We could have been staying in a mud hut for a week, or a rundown motel, and I still would have fallen for you. We could have been eating Taco Bell for every meal, taking hikes with peanut butter and jelly sandwiches, or working out at some local gym filled with nothing but soccer moms. *And I still would have fallen for you.* It still would have been the best week of my life. A fairytale." Her voice cracks. "Because I would have been with *you.*"

Oh, God, what have I done? My heart feels like it's physically breaking. "Georgie, I feel the same way. I know you don't believe it was just a kiss with Isabel, but it was. I know you won't forgive me for that kiss, even if you did believe me. But can you at least forgive me about the grant? You got my texts explaining that, right?"

"Have you talked to CeeCee about that?"

"No."

"Good. Don't say a word to CeeCee about the grant, please. I want to hear what she has to say, in her own words, without any undue influence on your part."

Damn. Kat is good. "Of course. I assumed as much. What about the thing with Alessandra? Can you forgive me for talking to her about her demo?"

"Yes. I was actually about to text you about that, right before my dad called me about the student loans. She's back in Boston now, and she called me earlier today with some fantastic news. She got hired for a weekly gig at a popular coffee place near campus. And she said it was all thanks to you."

"To *me*?"

"She said she almost didn't go through with her audition, she was so nervous. But then, she heard *your* voice in her ear—telling her the same stuff you said at the party—and she realized you were right about all of it. So, she marched onto that stage, the way she wished she'd done at the party, and wound up giving the performance of her life."

My heart is soaring. For Alessandra, of course. For Georgie, who's so obviously elated for her stepsister's victory. But, mostly, selfishly, for myself. The way Georgina is talking to me right now, the joy she's expressing to me, without holding back—it's like she's my Georgie again. We might as well be sitting at my kitchen table, talking while eating a delicious meal Amalia left for us. This, right now, we're *us* again. And Georgie's trying to convince me we're going to be nothing more than *friends* and *business colleagues*? I take a deep breath to gather myself. "Tell Alessandra I'm ecstatic for her."

"I will. The Man with the Midas Touch strikes again. Whatever you said to her, it really helped her out. Thank you so much for breaking your promise not to talk to her about her demo. If you hadn't done that, she never would have gotten this gig."

Oh, my heart. It's physically straining to fuse with hers across the phone line. I swallow hard. "Please, Georgina, come home to me. I'm wrecked without you. I swear, I've learned my lesson."

She exhales audibly. "What would be the point? If we got back together, I'd always feel paranoid and mistrustful. I'd never be able to let go completely with you, like I used to do. I'd always be holding back. And what fun would that be, for either of us, when the thing that was so amazing about us was the way neither of us was ever holding back?"

I'm hurtling toward despair. Feeling like my heart is being wrung out like a sponge. Only, it's my crimson blood, my very happiness, that's oozing from its twisted wreckage. "I don't want Isabel. I only want *you*. And that's exactly what I told Isabel in the garage."

"Oh, yeah? Did you tell her that *before* or *after* you had sex with her?"

I close my eyes. I can't believe I had heaven in the palm of my hand and threw it away. "*I didn't have sex with her.* Hate me. Wish me dead. As long as you believe me when I say I only kissed Isabel goodbye, and it meant nothing." I know Kat told me not to say this next thing, but I don't care. It has to be said. "Georgina, I swear, kissing Isabel only made me realize, without a doubt, I only want *you*."

Georgina snorts with disdain. And now I know, for certain, Kat was exactly right. Georgina thinks I'm only saying what every cheater says when he gets caught. And can I blame her, really? If the situation were reversed, and Georgina had gone into that garage with her ex and "kissed him goodbye," how would I be feeling right now? Decimated. Betrayed. Rejected, beyond repair. That's how. And nothing, no words from Georgina, not even swinging a golf club against one of Georgina's prized sports cars, if sports cars were her thing, would have lessened the pain of that dagger to my heart.

As if reading my mind, Georgina sighs and says, "I wish so badly smashing your car could have made us even. Or maybe given me amnesia, or rewound time. But, unfortunately, it turns out it doesn't work that way."

"I know. I'm so sorry."

"I wish swinging that golf club could have solved every problem I have." She pauses. "I wish it could have made my nightmares about Mr. Gates go away." She sniffles. "I wish it could have brought my mother back to me."

My heart pangs. "Oh, sweetheart. I'd let you smash every one of my cars, including my Bugatti, and then I'd buy another fifty Bugattis for you to smash, if it would bring back your mother to you."

She sniffles again.

"I mean that, sincerely."

"I know you do. Thank you." Another sniffle. "You're really not mad at me *at all* for totaling your Ferrari?"

"No. I'm grateful you spared my Bugatti."

I can hear her smile over the phone line. "The punishment has to fit the crime. I'm psycho but not crazy. You didn't *murder* anyone, for crying out loud."

I clutch my heart, feeling physical pain. I love this woman. I do. I know it as well as I know my own name. I love her, and I betrayed her, and, now, I'm rightly suffering for it. Seriously now, what the fuck is wrong with me?

"I have to go," Georgina says softly. "Thanks again for paying off my loans. But I'm warning you: don't spend another dime on my father or me, or I'm going to come over and smash your Bugatti."

"As long as you come over," I whisper.

"Bye, Reed."

"Wait. Georgie, come on. Can't you feel what's happening between us? We're still *us*. I know I've got to prove myself to you, but I will. The most important thing is that our chemistry, our electricity, it's the same as it ever was. Come home and let's talk until sunrise and figure this out."

"I can't come over."

I look at the clock on my phone. *10:56.* "Yeah, okay, that's probably a good call. I don't want you driving late at night. I'll come to your hotel." Without waiting for her reply, I march out of my gym and race toward my bedroom, planning to take a lightning-quick shower and then drive like a bat out of hell to her hotel.

"Don't go to my hotel, Reed. I'm not there."

I freeze in the middle of my bathroom, already half naked. "Where are you?"

She sighs. But doesn't answer me.

The hairs on the back of my neck stand on end. *"Where are you?"*

"I wasn't planning to tell you this, but, since you're asking, I'm sitting in my rental car, outside a bar, about to head inside."

My heart stops. "It's almost eleven."

"Yeah, that's the time of night when bars have people inside them."

I can barely breathe. I feel sick. "Are you meeting someone? A friend from school? One of my artists?"

"No, none of the above. I'm flying solo tonight."

An odd cocktail of relief and panic swirls inside me. I'm thrilled Georgina doesn't have a date... that she's not, for instance, meeting Savage or Endo for a drink. But if she's truly going to walk into a bar alone at eleven at night, then she won't be alone for long. Is she going to a bar, alone, on a Tuesday night, because she's looking for a casual hook-up? Does she intend to have revenge sex tonight, with some random stranger, in retaliation for the sex she *thinks* I had with Isabel?

"To be clear, if I *were* meeting up with someone at the bar tonight, it wouldn't be any of your business," she says. "When you hooked up with Isabel, you released me from my obligation not to hook up with 'anyone on Planet Earth.'"

Jealousy explodes inside my veins like a Molotov cocktail tossed onto a puddle of gasoline. "Tell me where you are," I say, trying, and failing, to keep my voice calm.

She scoffs. "Why would I do that?"

"What's the name of the fucking bar?" I shout.

"*Calm down*," she says, and I can hear the smirk on her sultry lips. "All I'm going to do is have a drink—only *one*, because I'm driving—and listen to some live music to unwind. I *might* chat with a nice-looking stranger, if the opportunity falls into my lap. But when the musician is done, the plan is for me to head back to my hotel and go to bed, all by myself."

I exhale the equivalent of the Pacific Ocean. "Thank you for telling me that. I almost had a heart attack, imagining you—"

"*Although*... you know what they say about plans, right? Make one, only if you want to make God laugh."

"Georgina."

"I suppose it's *possible* I could meet a handsome stranger at the bar tonight who charms my pants off... *literally*. In which case, I *might* find myself at his place later tonight, screwing the hell out of him... *while thinking of you and Isabel*."

My head explodes. I feel like I'm stroking out. I'm literally blinded by my panic. "That's enough! You're going to head back to your hotel right now to wait for me. Do you hear me? I'm leaving my place now. Meet me at your hotel!"

She giggles with glee. "Goodbye, Reed. I'm hanging up now, and then I'm going to turn off my phone until morning. So, don't blow up my phone all night with texts and voicemails, ya freakin' psycho. *Ciao, stronzo*! Sleep tight!"

I'm stumbling. Tripping as I race to my walk-in closet to throw on clothes over my sweaty body. Forget showering. My house is burning down around me, and I need to grab only my most valuable possession. *I need to grab Georgie!*

"Tell me the name of that bar, Georgina Marie! That's a *command* from the head of the label that's making his artists available to you!" I hop on one foot as I try to throw on jeans with one hand while holding my phone to my ear with the other. "Georgie? Georgina Marie Ricci!"

But it's no use. The line has gone dead.

Georgina Marie Ricci, the most diabolical woman alive, a woman who takes scorched-earth tactics to a whole new level, is gone.

Chapter 7
Georgina

Tuesday 10:57 pm

After I hang up with Reed, I get out of my parked rental car and begin walking the three blocks to my destination: a small bar in West Hollywood called Slingers that features live music every night. Hopefully, Troy Eklund is performing tonight, as Slingers' online schedule promises, because I've got a crap-ton of questions for him.

I haven't decided if I'm going to come right out and tell Troy I'm a writer for *Rock 'n' Roll,* researching an article about Reed Rivers—and, oh, by the way, I've got a bunch of questions about a lawsuit you filed against Reed six years ago!—or if, instead, I'll pretend to be some random chick in a bar with a boner for musicians. My gut tells me I'll get a whole lot more information out of Troy if I play Star-Struck Groupie. But I figure I'll play it by ear and decide on the fly.

Everything I know about Troy, I've learned from two admittedly unreliable sources—the internet and the pages of his six-year-old lawsuit—all of which can be summarized, as follows:

Ten years ago, when Troy was eighteen, he started a band called The Distillery in Sacramento. Troy was his band's front man and guitarist, and, even at eighteen, had so much swagger, you'd have thought the kid had arrived in our world via the future, already knowing his rock stardom was in the bag.

For three years in Sacramento, The Distillery played local bars and gigs, until finally catching the eye of one Reed Rivers—a shrewd and brilliant young businessman with an up-and-coming indie label that had recently scored back-to-back smash debut albums from two young bands: Red Card Riot and Danger Doctor Jones, as well as a number one smash debut single from 2Real.

With the ink barely dry on The Distillery's deal with River Records, Troy and his bandmates moved to LA—into Reed's house, as a matter of fact—where they began writing, and then recording, their debut album with Reed's guidance.

Troy's complaint didn't list the address of Reed's house, but, given that Reed purchased his present hilltop castle five years ago, and the events alleged in Troy's lawsuit happened *seven* years ago, Troy and his band must have stayed in Reed's much smaller first house. A place Reed once told me would have fit inside his present garage. Which means Reed and those Distillery boys almost certainly got up close and personal during those several months together.

According to Troy's complaint, Reed and the band had many "detailed" conversations during the band's stay with Reed, about music, in general, and the band's bright future, specifically. According to Troy, Reed always said the "sky was the limit" for the band—and for Troy, in particular. Troy claimed Reed made multiple promises to him during this time period. Promises Reed didn't wind up keeping.

According to my research, Reed wasn't shy about expressing his admiration for The Distillery during those early months. Reed was variously quoted as saying The Distillery was "lightning in a bottle" and "like nobody else." Regarding Troy, in particular, Reed called him a "future star."

For their part, Troy and his bandmates returned Reed's enthusiasm, calling their deal with River Records a "dream come true" and Reed, specifically, "a genius."

After several months of hard work, The Distillery's

album was completed, and Reed teed up everything for the upcoming release, including having the guys shoot a music video for their debut single. By all accounts, the stars were aligned for The Distillery to take the world by storm in the same way Red Card Riot and Danger Doctor Jones had already done.

But, then, out of nowhere, mere weeks before the band's debut album was scheduled to drop, something happened that made Reed abruptly scrap the album, unceremoniously dump the band from his label, and physically beat the shit out of Troy. What was it that made Reed turn so viciously on a band he'd so vocally supported and admired? *Well, a woman, of course.* What else? Specifically, an "unnamed woman" with whom Reed had previously "been involved"... and with whom Troy had apparently had sex within two weeks of the scheduled debut album release.

In other words, according to Troy, Reed dumped Troy and his band, and physically assaulted Troy, thereby forfeiting all the time and money Reed had invested, merely to exact revenge upon Troy for screwing the wrong woman. Now, really. Does all that sound like something Reed would do?

Hell yes, it does! *Duh.* I saw the way Reed looked at C-Bomb that night at the RCR concert. Like he wanted to kill C-Bomb for merely flirting with me. I also saw the way Reed handled that PA who'd walked in on us. He was absolutely ruthless with that poor girl. Like a mob boss. Plus, backstage at the RCR concert, Reed himself told me he'd "trained" his artists not to hit on anyone he'd been involved with. Well, now I know what he was talking about. He was referring to the incident with Troy.

But even without all that direct evidence to make me believe Reed did precisely what Troy accused him of doing, I'd still believe it, if only because Reed settled Troy's lawsuit. Reed himself told me he doesn't settle a case, unless it has merit, or Reed believes a *jury* will think it does. In regard to

Stephanie Moreland's lawsuit, Reed settled because Leonard advised him a jury would hate him. Also, because California law is clear about the consequences of a boss screwing an employee. But, in this instance, my gut tells me Reed settled Troy's lawsuit because it was flat-out *true*.

What happened to The Distillery after they got unceremoniously dumped by River Records? They broke up. Apparently, Troy's bandmates were too pissed at him for fucking the "unnamed woman," whoever she was—*cough, cough*, Isabel Randolph—to want to continue making music with him. They couldn't release their existing debut album, since River Records owned it, according to the ironclad terms of their record deal. And everyone in the band was far too pissed at Troy at that point to sit down and try to write new music. For crying out loud, the band was even prohibited from *performing* any of the songs on that debut album, without the label's written consent—which, of course, it refused to give. And not only that, according to the complaint, Reed went so far as to "blackball" Troy in the music industry, thereby ensuring Troy's present *and* future music career was DOA.

So, that was that. The Distillery was dead, and Troy thereafter became a lone wolf pariah who eked out a meager music career by performing in small bars. I don't know what Troy received in settlement—there were no details on that in the court file. But whatever payment he got, it obviously wasn't enough to keep Troy off the schedule of dive bars like Slingers a full six years later.

Speaking of which, I reach the front door of Slingers and show my ID to the bouncer, who stamps my wrist and allows me to enter the darkened bar. And there he is. Troy Eklund. Playing an acoustic guitar and belting out a song on a small stage in the corner.

I stand, stock still inside the door for a moment, blown away. No wonder Reed signed this guy. He's mesmerizing. Talented and hot as hell. I already knew what he looked like, thanks to YouTube. But, still, in person Troy Eklund is a smoke show. No wonder the "unnamed woman" screwed him. I'd screw him, too. In fact, who knows? Maybe, if Troy plays his cards right, I'll screw him tonight.

I take a seat at the bar and order a beer, and then swivel around to watch Troy's performance. It doesn't take long for him to notice me staring at him like a hungry dog.

When his gaze mingles with mine, I flash him my most brazen "I'm looking for a sexy good time" smolder. And in response, Troy winks at me, not missing a beat in his song.

Well, damn, that was easy.

Looks like I'll be playing Star-Struck Groupie tonight.

Chapter 8
Georgina

Wednesday 12:37 am

"Good night, everyone!" Troy says into his microphone. His blue eyes flicker to me, the same way they've been doing for the past hour and a half. "I'm Troy Eklund, and I'm here every Tuesday and Friday night! See you next time."

There's a smattering of half-hearted applause, the most energetic of it, coming from me. Troy notices my enthusiastic clapping and raises his beer bottle to me from the stage. So, of course, groupie that I am, I raise my beer to him in reply with a bold wink. And that's all it takes. After sliding his guitar into its case, Troy heads straight to me at the bar.

"Is this stool taken?" he asks.

"I was hoping you'd ask me that. Sit, please. I was supposed to meet a blind date tonight, and he never showed up. So I've been saving that stool for you."

Troy settles onto the seat next to me. "That guy made the biggest mistake of his life, and he'll never know it." He raises his near-empty beer bottle toward the front door of the bar. "Thanks, dipshit! Whoever you are."

I giggle and bat my eyelashes shamelessly. "I think we're both feeling grateful to that dipshit for standing me up. Here's to silver linings."

We clink.

"What's your name, beautiful?"

"Georgina. You're Troy?"

He nods. "I've never seen you here before."

"Mr. Blind Date picked the place."

Troy raises his beer bottle toward the front door again. "Thanks again, dipshit! I owe you one!"

"*Ha, ha, ha.*" I laugh flirtatiously.

"You want another one?" he asks, motioning to my beer.

"No, thanks. I'm driving. But let *me* buy *you* another one to thank you for all that incredible music. Seriously, Troy, you're amazing." It's the truth, actually. The guy is indisputably talented.

"Sure. I'll take another one."

I flag down the bartender and order his preferred beer and a club soda for me. And then settle onto my stool as Troy proceeds to talk my ear off. About himself. And how amazing he is. He tells me about his musical inspirations, not that I asked, and why he wrote such and such song he performed earlier, not that I remember it. He talks about how he first realized he's a natural on guitar. Oh, and did I notice he has perfect pitch? He tells me story after story about himself, and his talent, and his musical inspirations and philosophies, almost all of it unsolicited. And never once does he ask me a goddamned thing about myself. Which is why it takes all of ten minutes for me to realize, with certainty, he's an arrogant asshole. And not the good kind. Not like Reed. No, the kind I genuinely want to punch in the face.

When I manage to sneak in any words into Troy's monologue, it's obvious he's only waiting for me to finish talking so he can say whatever he's got cued up on the tip of his tongue. When, against all odds, I'm able to sneak in a little joke or snarky comment, which I've done about four times, Troy's chuckle isn't sincere. It's made of tin. Nothing more than a ploy to get himself into my pants.

All of which makes me think about Reed, even more than usual. I miss him so much, even though I'm bound and determined to hate him for what he did. But, see, when I talk to Reed, he actually listens. Mostly, anyway. Yes, occasionally, he sits there, smiling like a Cheshire cat while I'm talking, and it's obvious he's thinking I'm silly or amusing or fuckable. But, at least, even at those times, he's *listening,* even if his eyes are blazing with amusement or heat. But this guy? His brain is an echo chamber, filled with nothing but self-congratulations.

Also, Reed *always* laughs at my jokes, no matter how stupid they might be. And Reed's laughter is *always* sincere. True, Reed is always thinking about getting into my pants, every bit as much as this guy is. But it always feels with Reed like he's as attracted to my brain and personality as my body. That might not have been the case in the very beginning. When Reed first saw me in the lecture hall, I know he wanted to bone me, based on nothing but animal attraction. But I'd say the same thing about myself. It certainly wasn't Reed's heart I wanted to bone in that lecture hall. But by the end of our amazing week together, there was no doubt Reed wanted to "bone" my soul, along with my body, every bit as much as I wanted to bone his. Or, at least, that's how it felt to me.

Also, who does this Troy dude think he is? Reed has built an empire from scratch. He started with nothing and put *everything* on the line, because he believed in himself and his vision so much. And then, through sheer force of will and talent and drive, Reed came out the other side a king. *That's* why *Reed* is an arrogant prick! Because he's a legit god among men. But what's Troy's excuse? What has he built from scratch? Sure, Troy's got a soulful voice and he plays guitar well. And he's definitely got that "I know you want to fuck me" smolder down pat. But big whoop. Guys like him are a dime a dozen in this town.

For all Troy's bragging, you'd think he'd cured cancer with his songs. But Reed has *literally* been trying to cure cancer by donating huge amounts of money to cancer charities. And yet, Reed *never* brags the way this guy keeps doing. I only learned about most of Reed's biggest accomplishments and awards and milestones from snooping through his memorabilia and reading up on him online.

Frankly, the more I sit here listening to Troy, the happier I am that Reed eviscerated him. Reed plucked Troy, and his band, out of obscurity and helped them write and record a top-quality album. Reed moved them to LA and opened his personal *home* to this little twat for *months*. And this was a small house, too, so it's not like Troy and his bandmates had their own wing of the house. I'm sure they practically lived on top of each other. Not to mention, Reed invested a ton of time and money in Troy's band. Probably, his whole heart, too, assuming those interactions I witnessed between Reed and 2Real in the studio were indicative of Reed's usual contributions to his artists.

And Troy thanked Reed for all that by *betraying* him? By fucking an "unnamed woman" Reed had been involved with? I can't imagine, after living with Reed for months, Troy didn't *know* the "unnamed woman" had been involved with Reed. There's no way Troy didn't know he was stabbing Reed in the back. But, obviously, he didn't care.

I suddenly realize Troy is staring at me, like he's expecting me to say something.

"Wow, you're so amazing," I say, figuring that's a pretty safe thing to reply, no matter what he just finished saying. "Please don't take this the wrong way. But you're so amazing, I can't believe you don't have a deal with a record label. If you ask me, you should be headlining a world tour."

"I had a record deal once, actually. A big one."

Here we go. "That's so cool! What happened?"

"Oh, you know. The music business is crazy."

I wait, but that's all he says. "Actually, no, I don't know anything about the music industry."

Troy shrugs. "The label holds all the power. No matter how talented you might be, the label can decide to shelve your debut album. And that's that. You're done."

"Really? I didn't know that. That's terrible."

"Yep. They have full control."

"So, they shelved your album?"

He nods.

"But why would they do that for someone as talented as you? Don't they want to make money, every bit as much as you do?"

"Not if the owner of the label decides he doesn't like you for personal reasons and wants to fuck with you out of spite. When that happens, when the owner of the label is a fucking dick, then you're done, no matter how good the album is. Because the contract says the label owns and controls the album, and has the absolute right *not* to release it, ever, if that's what they decide to do."

"Holy hell. That sucks. What label was it?"

"River Records."

I look at him blankly.

"It's a good one. You've heard of their bands, I promise you."

"Let's see." I pull out my phone and google it. "Oh, wow! Red Card Riot, 2Real, Laila Fitzgerald, Danger Doctor Jones, 22 Goats! Holy crap, Troy!"

"Yep. They didn't have all those bands when I signed. The guy who owns the label was planning to build his entire label on my band, Red Card Riot, 2Real, and Danger Doctor Jones."

I point to a photo of Reed on my phone, my heart aching at how excruciatingly handsome he is in the shot. "Is this the guy who screwed you over?"

"Yup. That's him. Reed Rivers. Fucking dick."

Despite everything, hearing Reed's name sends butterflies racing into my belly. "Yeah, that guy looks like he'd be a fucking dick."

Troy chuckles. "He's more than a dick, actually. He's a fucking psychopath."

My eyebrows shoot up. "A *psychopath*? In what way?"

Troy pauses. "I'm actually not allowed to talk about this in any detail. I sued that guy's ass after he shelved my album, and we reached a confidential settlement. If I say too much, and it gets back to him, I'll owe him a shit-ton of money."

"Whoa. You *sued* him? You're such a baller."

Troy looks enamored with himself. "Yep. I brought that bastard to his knees."

"Oh my gosh. I'm *dying* to hear this story. Something tells me it's super-hot." I bite my lower lip suggestively. "Hey, aren't lawsuits public record?"

"Yeah...?"

"So, you're allowed to tell me stuff that's already in the public record. You can't get in trouble for doing that, if it's right there for anyone to find it."

Troy considers that logic for a beat. "Good point."

He empties his beer bottle, and I order him another one. We talk some more. I flirt and laugh and nudge him a bit. And, soon, hallelujah, the floodgates open for me. *Blah, blah, blah,* Troy says, telling me everything I already know from reading his lawsuit, except for a few noticeable edits. First off, he refers to the "unnamed woman" as "the record guy's ex-girlfriend." Which, again, makes me think it has to be Isabel. And, second off, seeing as how he's trying to pick me up, Troy gallantly says he "hooked up with" Reed's ex, rather than explicitly saying they had sex. "And the next thing I knew," Troy says, "the bitch went straight to Reed and told him we'd hooked up, and that's when all hell broke loose. The guy went fucking psycho on me!"

My mind is racing. Reed's ex went straight to Reed after fucking Troy, huh? Now, why would she do that? Could it be she'd only screwed Troy to make Reed jealous? "How did the record label guy go psycho? What'd he do?"

"He dropped my band from his label, shelved our album and music video, and totally blackballed me in the industry, so

I couldn't get signed anywhere else, or hired for any tours or festivals."

I gasp like I'm shocked. "What a dick!"

"Yep."

So, is Troy going to mention Reed beating his ass, too? He made a huge thing about that in his lawsuit, after all. Or does he not want me imagining that smoking hot record label guy kicking his emo ass? "Is that everything the label guy did to you? Anything else?"

"I think he did more than enough. Don't you?"

"Oh, yeah. I just mean, *how* did he blackball you? What did he say?"

Troy takes a drink of his beer. "Oh, you know. He just talked a bunch of shit about me to all his powerful friends in the music industry."

I scoff. "None of it true?"

"Nope."

"What a jerk."

Hmm. Troy just lied to me. I believe most of what he's told me about Reed, actually... but something about this thing—the blackballing—doesn't ring true to me. I can't imagine Reed picking up the phone and spreading flat-out lies about Troy. Reed cares too much about his reputation and name to do something like that. But then again, Reed is a scorched-earth kind of guy. And he *did* settle with Troy, so who knows how far Reed might have taken his vendetta.

Troy babbles for a bit longer, about how great his band was and how big they would have been if Reed hadn't been such a wack job asshole psychopath who thought he "owned" his ex-girlfriend's body for eternity. And while Troy talks, I google Reed on my phone, pretending to get up to speed.

When a photo of Reed and Isabel lands on my screen, I gasp. "Wait. This guy dated *Isabel Randolph*? She's my *favorite*!" I look up, wide-eyed and whisper, "Was *Isabel* the one you hooked up with?"

Troy smirks devilishly, telegraphing the answer to my question is a resounding *yes*. But then he leans forward and whispers, "The woman isn't identified in the public record, though. So you guessed that. I didn't tell you anything."

"Gotcha," I say, returning his wink.

I was already almost positive the "unnamed woman" had to be Isabel, of course. The timing was exactly right. Plus, several articles about Reed and Isabel mention they dated off and on for a while before finally entering into their well-documented two-year relationship. So, it makes sense Isabel could have slept with Troy during an "off" period with Reed, which then brought the pair together again. This time, for two years. But, still, even if I was expecting to hear Isabel's name in relation to all of this, it's nonetheless a blow to actually hear it, and realize Reed went *that* ballistic when another man slept with her.

For a moment, I feel like I'm going to burst into tears at the sense of loss I'm feeling. The rejection. The betrayal. Why did Reed pick a stolen moment in a garage with Isabel over a future with me? I would have given him *everything*. All of me.

I take a deep breath, force my emotion down, and plaster a fake smile on my face. "Here's what I don't get, Troy. Why'd that record label guy settle your lawsuit? Seeing as how he went so scorched earth on you for hooking up with his ex-girlfriend, it seems like he's the kind of guy who'd go equally scorched earth on you in the court case, as well."

Troy takes a swig of his beer and empties it. So, I quickly buy him another one, to keep him nice and loose. "Actually, he told me he'd 'never' settle with me—'not in a million years.' He said he'd 'see me in hell' before he'd pay me a dime." Troy smirks. "Little did he know, though, I had an ace in my pocket, which I used to bring him to his knees."

I lean forward, egging him on. "Oooh, this is gonna be good."

Troy pauses. "Shoot. Sorry. As much as I want to tell you, this part isn't in the public record."

"So, help me *guess* it. What sort of thing was this 'ace in your pocket'? Information?"

He nods. "Confidential information he didn't want anyone to know."

My eyebrows ride up. "About *him*?"

Troy smiles deviously. "No. About his ex."

"The one...?" I point to my phone, referencing the photo of Isabel Randolph I showed him earlier, and Troy nods.

"It was something, to this day, she'd never want the world to know about her. So, I thought, 'Hey, if he cares so much about me hooking up with his ex, then he'll probably pay to keep the world from finding out her secret.' And guess what? I was right."

My heart is thumping. I'm on the bitter cusp of blowing this thing wide open—whatever "this thing" is. "Holy crap, Troy. You're a genius." *And a disgusting blackmailer.* "She told you this secret?"

Troy shakes his head. "Not intentionally. She and I were watching TV together one night, just her and me, when a news story came on TV that made her gasp in shock. It was a news story about a particular woman. So, I was like, *Do you know her*? And his ex said, no, she didn't know the woman in the news story. But it was obvious she was lying." He snorts. "So much for her being a talented actress, huh? So I told her, 'Hey, I know you're lying. And I know why you must be lying. But don't worry, your secret is safe with me.' And I swear I was planning to keep my promise to her. But then, when she went straight to her ex to tell him we'd hooked up, and he went fucking crazy on me, I was like, 'Well, fuck my promise.' So, I told the label guy I'd sell her secret to the highest bidding tabloid, if he didn't settle my lawsuit. And that was that. He settled with me the very next day."

Holy shit. Doesn't this idiot realize what he just

described to me was textbook extortion? Reed didn't settle Troy's *lawsuit*, he succumbed to a brazen blackmail scheme... and only to protect Isabel!

Oh, God. I'm reeling. I don't want to swoon over Reed being Isabel's white knight. I don't want to hear that Reed would slay any dragon for that woman—because it only twists the knife already lodged in my heart. But I can't help swooning, just a little bit, despite myself, to realize, yet again, Reed really is a ride or die kind of guy for the people he loves. Like he told me once, if you're on his short list, he'll do *anything* for you. Too bad I never made it onto his short list. I clear my throat. "Good for you, Troy. That label guy screwed you over, so you screwed him over, even harder. That's *so* hot."

Troy licks his lips. "*You're* so hot." With that, he leans forward, obviously intending to kiss me. Abruptly, I jerk back and take a long drink of my club soda, pretending not to realize I just stiff-armed him.

"So, come on. Give me a little hint about that secret."

I jut out my breasts, and Troy's gaze drifts directly to them, right on cue.

But, dammit, he shakes his head. "For all I know, you could sell the secret to the tabloids, or tell someone else who'd do that. One way or another, the information could get out, and then the psycho would know I'd talked, and he'd sue me for breaching the confidential settlement."

Damn. I bet if I slept with Troy, I could get him to sing to me like a canary about this secret. But that's never going to happen. Not in a million years. Even if I found Troy attractive, which I *don't*, it's clear to me now my heart still belongs to Reed, whether I like it or not. And that means my body belongs to him, too—simply because that's the way I'm wired. When I love, I do it with everything I am. My heart, mind, body, and soul.

Troy touches my arm, making me stiffen, and leans into me. "You have really pretty eyes, Georgia."

I feel no need to correct him on my name. In fact, I'm glad he got it wrong. "Thank you, Troy. So do you."

Troy leans forward, *again,* obviously intending to kiss me, so, I jerk back, *again*, and sip my water. But it's obvious my little jerk-back-cluelessly maneuver isn't going to work a third time. Next time, Troy is going to get up and find someone else to hit on. Someone who'll give him the green light. Which means I need to pry this secret out of this bastard's blackmailing mouth right now, before it's too late.

I put my elbow onto the bar and bat my eyelashes. "I don't normally tell people this, Troy, but I'm super close with someone who writes for *Rock 'n' Roll*. You know, the music magazine?" Troy perks up like a Labrador whose owner is holding up a tennis ball. "I bet if I told this writer about you—and how talented and sexy you are, and how this Reed guy screwed you over—she'd be interested in interviewing you for a featured article."

"Oh my God. That would be *huge*."

"The only thing is," I say coyly. "She's not easy to impress. Honestly, she's always saying she's got a line around the block of musicians wanting her to write about them. So, I think I'd need to tell her you're willing to divulge something more than what's in the public record for the article—or at least, to drop a sizeable hint that will allow *her* to figure it out on her own—*wink, wink*—if you want to have any chance of her coming down here to meet you."

Troy looks pained. "I really can't say anything too specific about that secret."

"Oh, yeah, I totally get it. But you figured it out, based on a news story on TV, right?"

He nods.

"Well... What was the news story? That's got to be in the public record. Maybe this *Rock 'n' Roll* reporter could follow the same breadcrumbs you followed, without a word from you, and figure it out for herself. Maybe this writer for *Rock 'n' Roll* was researching an article about Reed Rivers, so she went to the courthouse to look at the lawsuits filed against him, and she noticed *your* lawsuit, and she read it, and then *happened* to see whatever news story *you* saw... And then, *she* put two and two together, *without a word from you.*"

Troy is lit up. *He gets it.* "Yeah, I think that could work!"

"Of course, it'll work." I lean forward conspiratorially and put my fingertips on his forearm. "Who was the woman in the news story? I'll tell this writer her name, and she'll research it, and take it from there."

Troy pauses, his wheels turning. But, finally, it's obvious his ambition has won out over his fear of Reed. "Francesca Laramie."

My heart is racing. "Francesca Laramie?"

He nods. "Tell your friend to look her up. It won't be hard for her to put two and two together, from there."

With that, he licks his lips and goes in for a kiss.

But I'm outta here. "Let's not," I say, popping up from my barstool. "It kills me to do this, Troy, since you're so hot and talented, and I want nothing more than to go home with you right now and screw the living hell out of you. But if this label guy is as big a psycho as you say, then you have to be extra careful. There shouldn't be any connection between you and me and this writer for *Rock 'n' Roll*." I jut my chin at the bartender. "For all we know, he's reporting back to the record label guy. We shouldn't be seen leaving together." I gather up my purse. "I'm going to tell this writer about you *right now*. Bye!"

"Wait! Georgia! Take my number, at least, so your writer friend can call me!"

"No, no, that's way too risky. If this writer is interested in the story, she'll come to Slingers on a night when you're performing. That way, if Reed ever comes down here, after the article comes out—or God forbid, sues you for breaching the confidential settlement agreement—you'll be able to swear truthfully, under oath, that's how you first met her. She showed up at the bar."

Troy looks vaguely convinced by that. "Yeah... Okay."

I tap my temple and wink. "Bye now, hon. So awesome talking to you!"

And off I go, sprinting out the door, as fast as my devious little legs will carry me, and then laugh to myself like a madwoman as I sprint to my nearby car in the cool Los Angeles night.

Chapter 9
Reed

Wednesday 2:35 am

I roll onto my opposite side and look at the clock on my nightstand. This is pointless. I'm not going to be able to fall asleep while my brain is still wracked with images of Georgina having sex with someone else. Oh, God. I roll over again, feeling like I'm going to puke from stress.

After my horrifying phone call with Georgina ended, I drove straight to her hotel, thinking maybe she was lying to me about not being there, simply to keep me from coming. But she wasn't there. So, I chatted up the concierge in the lobby, trying to figure out what nearby clubs or bars had live music. Specifically, what places might have featured a solo musician tonight, since Georgina said, "And when *the* musician is done performing..." But, unfortunately, the concierge didn't have any useful suggestions.

After that, I drove around aimlessly, like a madman, scoping out random hotspots, in search of Georgina's parked car. And when I didn't see Georgina's car anywhere—not surprisingly, considering I was looking for a needle in a haystack in a city of four million people—I simply kept going. Driving. Searching. Freaking out.

When my search of Hollywood came up empty, I drove to Westwood—the neighborhood immediately adjacent to UCLA—figuring Georgina might have gone back to her old stomping grounds. I even went into Bernie's Place, looking for her. But, nope. She wasn't there, either. At every turn, I came up empty-handed. No Georgina.

And that's when I had a batshit crazy, paranoid thought: what if, when Georgina casually referenced "the musician," she meant to do it? What if that wasn't a slip or an incidental bit of information I'd cleverly picked up on? What if that telltale phrase had been the entire point of Georgina's little speech to me? What if Georgina was actually calling me, *specifically* to tell me, in code, she was heading into a bar to watch a performance... by *Troy Eklund*?

The very thought of Georgina being in the same room with Troy nearly sent me into cardiac arrest. My rational brain knew I was being paranoid, and that the chances were slim. But then again, Georgina did know all about Stephanie Moreland. So, why wouldn't she know about Troy, too?

I googled Troy's name and quickly found out he was scheduled to play at some dive bar called Slingers in West Hollywood tonight. So, off I went, all the way back to that side of town. Even though I knew I'd *literally* commit murder, thereby ruining my life, if I walked into that bar and found Troy with his hands or lips on Georgina.

Thankfully, though, when I got to Slingers, I didn't see Troy, or Georgie, anywhere. And when I chatted up the bartender, I found out Troy had played his set earlier, as scheduled, thereafter flirted with several women, per usual, and then left about fifteen minutes before my arrival with a blonde who'd practically swallowed his face in the few minutes before they'd cut out. Also, per usual. It was all excellent news, obviously. Also, proof I'm losing my damned mind.

Finally, when I'd exhausted all my ideas, I drove to Georgina's hotel. Which was where I saw her convertible in the parking lot. I was glad to see she'd returned to the hotel... but sick to my stomach to think she might not be alone in her room. Oh, God, how I toyed with the idea of going to Georgina's room and knocking on her damned door. But, somehow, I refrained. I forced myself to leave and drive home, even though my heart felt like it was bleeding.

And now, here I am. Tossing and turning as I await a return text from Georgina—confirmation she's alone in that fucking hotel room.

Exhaling in resignation, I grab my phone and tap out another text to her, asking her if she's home yet, even though I know she is... Also, even though I've already sent her three similar texts, none of which she's answered.

Are you back at your hotel yet? PLEASE REPLY.

This time, Georgina texts back immediately.

I told you not to text me, Mr. Rivers.

A huge smile spreads across my face. If she's answering me, then she's alone. Has she been alone all night... or did whatever guy from the bar just now leave?

Me: Just want to make sure you're safe and sound.

Georgina: Do I need to sic my lawyers on you? That's four texts tonight. You've long since crossed into stalker territory, dude.

Me: I thought you said you were turning off your phone until morning.

Georgina: I lied. That's this thing where a person says one thing but does another. Oh, wait, I don't need to explain that to you. You know all about lying, don't you?

Again, I smile. Even when Georgina is bitch-slapping me, she turns me on.

Me: Are you back at your hotel?
Georgina: None of your business.
Me: Just want to be sure you're safe.
Georgina: My safety isn't your concern.

Me: Yes, it is. You're my friend, remember? Also, you're working on the special issue. While you're doing that, your safety is my top priority. If you don't tell me where you are, then I'll call your father to ask him if he happens to know how to use the "Find My iPhone" feature. I'm assuming you're on your father's phone plan?

Georgina: Goddammit! You can't keep doing that! Yes, I'm at my hotel, you wack job! I've been here for well over an hour, doing research on my laptop.

Me: Did you get hit on at the bar?

Georgina: What do you think?

My heart rate spikes.

Me: But did you come back to your room alone?

Georgina: None of your business. But because I'm a saint, and we're friends, I will admit the guy who hit on me at the bar was a turd. He was good looking, but within two minutes of talking to him, I hated his guts. And not in a good way. Not the way I hate your guts. Like, for real.

I sigh with the force of a thousand hurricanes. And smile at the backhanded compliment.

Me: Thank you for telling me that. I had a semi-psychotic breakdown tonight, imagining you going home with someone else. The thought damn near gave me a stroke. I actually drove around for hours tonight, aimlessly looking for your parked car outside random bars.

Georgina: You did not.

Me: I did. Bernie says hi, btw.

Georgina: You went to Bernie's Place? Well, that's not crazy or anything.

Me: You drive me crazy.

Georgina: Good.

Me: Georgie, let me come to your hotel now. I need to see you.

Georgina: It's almost 3:00.

Me: I don't care.

Georgina: Well, I do. I've got important meetings at work tomorrow, including one with CeeCee and Zasu. I need to get some sleep, so I can kick ass tomorrow.

I feel oddly encouraged about this entire exchange. She isn't shutting down the concept of seeing me, really. She seems to be saying now isn't a good time.

Me: Okay, let me take you out to dinner tomorrow night.

Georgina: Zasu and I are doing a working dinner tomorrow night, probably until late into the night.

Me: Lunch tomorrow, then.

Georgina: Like I said, I'm going to be in meetings at RnR tomorrow.

Me: Still, you need to eat.

Georgina: I'll grab a sandwich at my desk.

Me: When can I see you?

Three little dots wiggle underneath my text, signaling Georgina is typing. But, suddenly, the dots disappear. And no text from her arrives for a long moment. I stare at the screen for what seems like forever, willing something to appear, until, finally:

Georgina: I'm sure our paths will cross organically, thanks to the special issue. Let's let fate take the wheel.

Me: Fuck fate. I'm taking the wheel.

Georgina: I've got to get some sleep. Goodnight, Reed.

I stare at my phone. Excitement, disappointment, determination, relief coursing through me. Finally, I tap out my reply.

Me: Goodnight, sweetheart. Sweet dreams. XO

Again, those three little wiggling dots appear underneath my text, and I hold my breath, praying for a little "XO" from Georgina in reply to mine. But another text from Georgina never comes. And so, finally, I put my phone on the nightstand, roll over and force myself to sleep.

Chapter 10
Georgina

Wednesday 11:34 am

Welcome back, CeeCee!" After hugging her enthusiastically, I take the chair across from her at her large glass desk. "Thank you so much for agreeing to see me privately, before our meeting with Zasu."

"Margot said it was an 'urgent' personal matter. Are you okay?"

"Yes, I'm fine. How was Bali?"

"It was wonderful. But let's talk about this personal matter." She looks anxious. "Do you have a problem with Zasu?"

"Oh, gosh, no. Zasu is a goddess. I worship her. No, it's... I don't really know how to say this, so I'm just going to spit it out." I take a deep breath. "It's about Reed Rivers."

"Oh?"

"We had a bit of a fling, CeeCee. A highly mutual, consensual, amazing, fun fling for a week at his house. And then he was an asshole. And now it's over."

CeeCee furrows her brow. "I'm sorry to hear that."

"No, it's fine. It couldn't have ended any other way. But my fling with Reed isn't what prompted me to ask for this meeting, specifically. That's merely context so you understand what I'm about to ask you."

Anticipatory dread overtakes CeeCee's elegant face. "Okay..."

I take a deep breath and proceed to unload the entire, embarrassing, enthralling, heartbreaking story. All of it. Including my discovery that Reed donated the money for my grant. "Honestly, knowing Reed funded the grant is making me question if I got this job on the merits of my writing. Forgive me if this is an insulting question, but did you and Reed broker a deal where you both got the special issue, Reed got access to some tits and ass he wanted, and you got that coveted interview of Reed you've been wanting for two years?"

CeeCee looks ashen. "Oh my gosh, Georgina. *No!* I'm heartbroken you've even had to wonder these things! I promise you, the way the grant happened wasn't like that at all—though I totally understand how it looks that way to you. Darling, I would have hired you, regardless. You're a star. I knew it the minute I met you. And then I read your writing samples, and I knew I had to have you, no matter what."

My shoulders soften. My spirit expands. "Oh, I'm so relieved to hear you say that."

CeeCee explains everything to me, all of which is right in line with what Reed told me in his texts.

"Yeah, that's pretty much what Reed told me in some texts," I admit. "I just wanted to hear it from you before I let myself believe it."

"Do you mind letting me read what Reed texted you about all this?"

"Sure. It's everything you just said."

I pull out my phone and she reads all of Reed's lengthy messages about the grant.

When she's done reading, CeeCee hands my phone back to me. "I agree with almost everything Reed wrote. But, in the interest of transparency, I should tell you there are a couple places where my narrative differs from his." She threads her manicured fingers together onto her glass desk. "First of all, Reed doesn't know this, but I was kind of messing with him during our initial discussion about you. I was going to hire you, no matter what, Georgina. *With* pay, by the way, one way or another. I'd already decided that when Reed called and started asking me about you. I acted like I was on the fence when Reed brought you up, simply because he seemed so damned interested in talking about whether I was going to hire you, and then he was so adamant I should pay you. It was so out of character for him, I wanted to test the waters and see what the hell was motivating him. But the truth is, I wasn't going to let you slip through my fingers, whether Reed had called me or not."

"Thank you so much. That means the world to me."

"It's the truth. But then Reed offered to pay your salary! Ha! And I knew my hunch was right. He'd seen you at the panel discussion and had been flirting with you the whole time, just like I'd thought."

I gasp. "You saw us flirting?"

"Darling, Reed wasn't subtle. And neither were you." She chuckles. "But, still, I never would have assigned you to work on the special issue—effectively serving you up on a silver platter to that horny heathen of a man—were it not for a few things. First off, when I told you about the special issue, you let it slip you'd already looked up Reed on Wikipedia. Well, that's when I knew I'd seen things correctly at the panel. You'd been flirting with Reed, every bit as much as he'd been flirting with you. Why else would you already have looked him up at that point? And then, you expressly *asked* if you could sleep with an interview subject. Ha!" She snorts. "I loved that you did that, by the way. But, again, I knew at that point I wasn't sending Little Red Riding Hood straight to the Big Bad Wolf."

I blush.

"But there was something else that sealed the deal for me. Something that made me feel especially confident about assigning you to River Records." She leans forward and places her forearms onto her desk. "Your father's expensive medicine, darling. Paying for that was Reed's idea, not mine. And that told me you'd caught the attention of more than Reed's libido. I knew, somehow, you'd caught the attention of his generous heart."

My heartbeat is thrumming in my ears. I can barely breathe.

"Plus, your father wasn't the only person Reed helped that day. That generous man donated a quarter million dollars to my favorite cancer charity, even though only a fraction of that sum was needed to cover your salary and your father's medication."

I clutch my heart, feeling overwhelmed with love for Reed.

"And *then,* as if all that weren't enough, Reed agreed to let you peel a layer of his onion. And that was the last straw for me. I knew, for certain, even if Reed didn't realize it himself: you'd caught his attention in a way that far exceeded lust. Frankly, I don't know how you did that from across a crowded lecture hall. That's some special kind of magic, darling. You cast a spell on that man in a way I'd never seen anyone else do, in ten years of knowing him. Now, did I *also* get what I wanted out of the deal? Yes, I did. The special issue was a coup for me. And getting him to agree to a more in-depth interview than he'd given before was also a huge coup. But I did *not* serve you up to Reed as a sexual object. And I did *not* hire an intern I didn't already desperately want to hire. And I did *not* pimp you out or otherwise sell you like a piece of meat."

I bite my lower lip. "I have a confession to make. I didn't cast my spell at the panel discussion. Reed and I ran into each other later that night at the bar where I worked. We talked and flirted quite a bit and really hit it off."

CeeCee palms her forehead. "Now everything makes sense! I was wondering how you'd managed to knock him onto his ass from across a crowded room."

"Well, yeah. I'm good, darling. But I'm not *that* good."

We both laugh uproariously.

"I left the bar with him that night, intending to sleep with him. He drove me to his house, but we never made it inside. We got into a heated argument at his front gate, and I took off in an Uber."

CeeCee hoots with gleeful laughter. "No wonder he was willing to move heaven and earth to get another bite at your glorious apple." She smirks. "And if I'm not mistaken, the apple was rather desperate to get herself bitten, too?"

I blush and nod. "After I cooled down, I was pissed at myself for leaving that night."

Again, CeeCee laughs deliriously. "Oh, my sweet Georgina. You're endlessly entertaining." She sighs. "I'm sorry if all of these shenanigans made you doubt yourself, and the fact that you got hired on your merits. I'm also sorry you doubted Reed. He's actually a wonderful man."

"Except for the fact that he messed around with Isabel when he'd promised to be exclusive with me."

CeeCee frowns sharply. "I'm honestly shocked by that. I never would have expected that of Reed. He's a bit of a fibber sometimes. A good salesman who's spectacularly adept at getting what he wants. But I've never once thought of him as an actual liar or cheater. On the contrary, when it comes to important things—the people he cares deeply about—I've always known Reed's word to be golden."

I press my lips together at the painful thought flickering across my mind: *Yeah, well, ipso facto, I guess that proves Reed never really cared deeply about me.*

CeeCee juts her lower lip in sympathy with whatever she's seeing on my face. "Aw, sweetheart, I don't know what happened between Reed and Isabel in that garage. The only two people who will ever know for sure are Reed and Isabel, unfortunately. But whatever he's been telling you about that, I think it's highly likely he's telling you the truth, the same way he told you the truth about the grant. I'd bet anything on it."

I shrug. "Reed says he kissed her goodbye, and that it only made him realize he only wants me. But I've been cheated on before, CeeCee. And that's *exactly* what my ex said. Plus, I know myself. I'm not going to be able to forgive and forget. I'm not the kind of person who trusts easily in the first place. So, no matter what 'epiphanies' Reed might have gained from kissing Isabel—or doing whatever else he might have done with her— I'm not going to be able to trust him completely, again. And that will doom us. So why hop aboard that train again, when I know it will ultimately lead to Misery Town, USA?"

She nods. "I get it."

"If I knew for *certain* Reed only kissed Isabel, and that it truly made him realize he only wanted me... I think I could forgive and forget and move on. Everyone makes mistakes. We were still so new, and he was saying goodbye to someone he'd been linked to for a long time. I think I could process that. But like you said, the only two people who will ever know for sure what happened in that garage are Reed and Isabel. And I don't want to jump back into a relationship where there's not one hundred percent trust."

She looks pained. "Will this affect your ability to complete Reed's interview?"

"No. I've already got everything I need for my article. I just need to write it now. And it's not like I hate Reed. Honestly, I still like him, despite everything. I'm not sure how that's possible, but I do."

"I know how. He's fatally charming."

"Yes, he is. We've agreed to be 'friends.'"

CeeCee and I exchange a look, both of us acknowledging that's a crock.

"So, did I address all your concerns?" CeeCee asks.

"Yes. Thank you. I'm excited to get to work on all my artist interviews."

She looks at her watch. "Speaking of which, shall I buzz Margot to have Zasu come in? It's still a bit early, but I'm sure Zasu is here somewhere, and I can't wait to hear what you two have come up with."

"Actually, can I run a quick idea past you? Something for *Dig a Little Deeper*?"

She withdraws her hand from the intercom. "Of course."

"What do you think about an in-depth interview of Isabel Randolph?"

CeeCee looks at me like I just threw up on her desk. "As in, the woman who walked into Reed's garage and blew your fairytale fling with him to Kingdom Come?"

"Okay, hear me out on this. Isabel doesn't know I had a fling with Reed, and I won't tell her, or anyone else. I met her at Reed's party, before everything between Reed and me blew up, and she said yes to an interview. She promised to go deeper than her usual interview, CeeCee. To give me something she's never given to anyone. So, why should I pass up this golden opportunity, just because a guy I had a fling with did who knows what with her in a garage? I'm a professional. I can separate my personal and professional feelings."

CeeCee narrows her eyes. "Could it be you're dying to get her alone so you can ask her what happened between her and Reed in that garage?"

My face blasts with heat. If I'm being honest, I have, indeed, *fantasized* about myself doing that very thing. But it doesn't take a brain surgeon to quickly realize that little fantasy would backfire spectacularly on me. First off, Isabel would never tell me the truth, anyway. She's engaged to Howard, after all. So, of course, she'd cling with white knuckles to the story she told me outside the garage—that Reed was showing her his car collection.

Also, asking Isabel about what happened would require me to reveal my fling with Reed. Maybe even that I've developed serious feelings for him. Which, in turn, would cause Isabel to feel duped about the interview and storm out, probably. And then what? Who knows what kind of fit Isabel might pitch for having been ambushed like that? Would she blast *Dig a Little Deeper* and CeeCee for my unprofessional behavior? I think it's likely. And so, in the end, I've realized I can't risk torpedoing my fledgling career, or splashing mud on CeeCee or her magazine, to pull a stunt like that.

"CeeCee, I swear on my mother I wouldn't ask Isabel about what happened between her and Reed. It would almost certainly be a pointless exercise, anyway, and might even backfire on me."

CeeCee shakes her head. "It's still not a good idea for you to interview Isabel, even putting Reed aside. Isabel's not even a good interview subject, Georgina. I know she's a huge star. And with that big franchise deal she signed, I'm probably a fool not to jump at the chance to put her on a cover. But she's notoriously wooden and guarded in interviews. A real dud."

"Yeah, I've heard that. But I think she might open up to me about her engagement to Howard. Maybe I could ask her about that?"

CeeCee makes a face like she just bit into a lemon. "I have no desire to put that man's name inside the pages of my beloved magazine."

I knit my eyebrows together. "You mean Howard?"

"Correct."

"I thought you and Howard were friends. Did you have a falling out in the past ten years?"

CeeCee looks surprised. "Howard Devlin and I aren't friends, and never have been. Who told you we're friends?"

"Oh. Nobody. I assumed it because he was one of the guests at your fiftieth birthday party. I read the article in the George Michael issue."

CeeCee rolls her eyes. "A guest of mine brought Howard to my party as their plus-one. And, trust me, I was livid about it. I can't stand that creep. All my friends know that." She points her finger at me. "Stay away from him, Georgie, if your paths ever cross. From what I've heard, he's all hands with pretty young things like you. Stay. Away."

"Oh, don't worry about me. As a bartender, I've handled more than my fair share of dirty old men."

CeeCee's face turns dark and serious. "No, honey. You don't understand. I've heard some very disturbing rumors about Howard, regarding the young actresses who've worked with him over the years. Nothing I can personally confirm. The rumors have all been second and third hand. But, still, I believe what I've heard. In fact, I've been wanting to do an exposé on that bastard for years. But nobody I've talked to will confirm the rumors. And who could blame them? What young actress would want to torpedo her budding career by pointing her finger at one of the most powerful producers in Hollywood—especially regarding something that would pit her word against his, or maybe even confirm she succumbed to his advances, and slept her way to the top? Howard can make and break careers, at his whim. Look at Isabel! She's been his favorite forever and look at her now. She's landed the biggest four-picture deal any lead actress has ever had. Imagine that."

"All the more reason for me to do that interview of Isabel. I could subtly try to get information out of her about those Howard rumors."

CeeCee scoffs. "Isabel is the last person who'd rat out Howard. Obviously, she's firmly hitched her plow to his wagon. Truth be told, that's one of the reasons I've always said no to Isabel's publicist. Because I'm so annoyed with her for being in Howard's pocket. Especially now that she's wearing his ring, I have zero respect for her. She did what she had to do to get ahead, obviously, but that doesn't mean I respect her."

I think back to my conversation with Isabel at the party. To how charming she seemed. How genuinely sweet. Of course, minutes later, my impression of her was shattered by her smeared lipstick and tousled hair, coupled with Reed's guilty-as-sin expression. But, still, there was genuine sweetness about her when we spoke at the party. And a deep sadness about her, too, especially when her eyes fell on Howard across the party... and she turned and walked in the exact opposite direction.

"Maybe she's more sympathetic when it comes to Howard than you think. Maybe he's been a creep to her, too. Maybe she's marrying him because, it's like, if you can't beat 'em, join 'em."

CeeCee's features soften. "You're kind, Georgina. That's a very kind take on the situation, especially given the fact that Isabel played a part in breaking your heart."

I shake my head. "Isabel isn't the one who broke my heart. Reed did that. For all Isabel knew, Reed was single when they went into that garage together. Yeah, Isabel cheated on her beloved fiancé, but that's her business."

CeeCee studies me for a long beat, her wheels visibly turning. "You really think you could interview Isabel, without breaking down and asking her about Reed?"

"I know I could. I swear to you, I wouldn't ask her about that."

CeeCee narrows her eyes. "All right. Go for it, Georgina."

"Woohoo!"

"Fair warning, though. I might scrap the interview, if it's not interesting enough. But feel free to give it the ol' college try. With those superhero movies all over the news, it's actually a coup for us to get this interview."

"Do I have permission to poke around, gently, about Howard, if I see an organic opening?"

"Yes. But do it subtly, Georgina. I know you're brilliant at that. Don't let her know what you're doing."

"Yes, ma'am. Her publicist already texted me some dates. Isabel's not available until much later in the summer, unfortunately. So, in the meantime, how about I snoop around and see if I can make any progress with some of those young actresses you've heard rumors about?"

"No," CeeCee says firmly, wagging her finger at me. She shoots me a little *Tsk.* "I appreciate your enthusiasm. It's exactly what attracted me to you in the first place. But the Howard exposé is too hot for a newbie to handle on her own. Get yourself some experience and we'll revisit the idea another time. Maybe you'll get something from Isabel that might prove helpful and we'll circle back."

I sigh with resignation, and CeeCee chuckles at my dejected reaction.

"Darling, you've got plenty to do, without running around trying to talk to actresses about their experiences with Howard Devlin. You've got artists to interview for the special issue. Plus, a mind-blowing article to write about Reed for *Dig a Little Deeper*. And who knows? Maybe you'll wind up bringing me something fantastic about Isabel Randolph, too."

Chapter 11
Reed

Wednesday 3:17 pm

I'm sitting at my desk at River Records, listening to some demos forwarded to me by my team. But my heart isn't in it. Because... *Georgina*. Right this very minute, she could be meeting with CeeCee. *And talking about me.*

I've got no doubt CeeCee's recollection of our initial conversation about the special issue and the grant will match everything I told Georgina in my texts. The truth is the truth. But, still, I'd be lying if I said I wasn't a little stressed about their conversation. Is Georgie telling CeeCee that she caught me coming out of my garage with Isabel? And if so, is Georgina erroneously saying I *fucked* Isabel? God, I want to crawl into a hole to think CeeCee is hearing either version of the story. But I'd be especially ashamed for CeeCee to think I fucked Isabel after having the best week of my life with Georgie.

An email notification from Leonard with the notation "URGENT" on the subject line flashes across my screen, so I quickly click out of the marketing plan I've been reviewing and into Leonard's email. It's about the copyright infringement lawsuit against Red Card Riot. We filed a motion for summary judgment on Monday, and it seems the plaintiff's attorney has now offered to dismiss the case, even before the motion gets ruled on by the judge. His only

83

request? We have to agree not to pursue reimbursement of our attorneys' fees from his clients, which is something we'd be entitled to do under the applicable copyright infringement statute, if we were to win the motion.

I type out a quick reply, telling Leonard to take the deal, just to put the thing behind us. "But tell that motherfucker he'd better dismiss his lawsuit within twenty-four hours, or I'm riding that summary judgment motion all the way up his ass until it's coming out his mouth."

I've no sooner pressed "send" on my email to Leonard, when my phone rings with an incoming call—and the minute I see Georgina's name on my screen, my heart leaps and bounds, even as my palms begin to sweat with anxiety.

"Hey, baby," I say, trying to make my voice sound casual, even though I'm freaking out. "Did you talk to CeeCee yet?"

"Yes. At length. And, please, don't call me baby."

"What'd she say?"

"She said she loved every idea Zasu and I pitched for the special issue."

"What'd she say about the grant?"

Georgina pauses. "Yeah... about that. That part of our meeting was... disappointing, Reed. To say the least."

My stomach clenches. *Fuck.* "How so?"

There's another long pause, during which I feel like my stomach is turning inside out.

"Ha! I'm just screwing with you, dude. CeeCee said 'ditto' to everything you said in your texts."

I groan loudly with relief. "Oh my God, you evil woman. Are you trying to make me stroke out? So, CeeCee backed up everything I told you?"

"All of it. Although she did make a few clarifying comments."

My stomach somersaults. "*What* clarifying comments?"

"It doesn't matter. All that matters is that I not only

forgive you for paying my salary and for all my father's expensive medication, I thank you profusely for doing both. Thank you, Mr. Rivers. Sincerely. You're an incredibly generous man, and I'm grateful."

My eyes widen in shock. I look around like a cartoon character for a moment, even though nobody is here with me in my office to see the gesture.

"Hello?" she says.

"Yeah... I was waiting for you to say you're kidding again."

"I'm not kidding. Thank you."

"Wow. That's way more than I was expecting. Thank you."

"No, no, no. Thank *you.*" She laughs again. "Look, I know you donated to that cancer charity because you wanted to get laid. But guess what? I wanted to get laid, too. I understand how a person can have *concurrent* motivations, as we've discussed. The bottom line is CeeCee would have hired me, no matter what. And that's the most important thing."

I feel dizzy with relief. "Let's celebrate my complete vindication. Let me take you to dinner tomorrow night."

"I can't. Sorry. I'm flying to Seattle tomorrow, so I can interview 22 Goats on Friday."

Sorry, she said. Was that a figure of speech, or is she really sorry to miss the chance to have dinner with me? "When will you be back from Seattle? We'll do it then." I've managed to keep my tone casual, I think. But, inside, my body is a riot of excitement and hopeful anticipation.

"I'll be back from Seattle on Saturday," she replies, her tone as breezy and casual as mine.

"Great. I'll take you to dinner on Saturday night, and then to New York on Sunday morning."

"Excuse me?"

My heart is racing. But there's no turning back now. I'm taking my shot. "I promised to take you to an RCR concert this summer, remember? Well, RCR is playing at Madison Square Garden on Sunday night. Your birthday is at the end of this coming week, right?"

"Yes."

"Well, then, we'll call the trip a birthday present. I'll get tickets to some Broadway shows, too. How about *Hamilton*? You should see that one, if you haven't." I hold my breath, awaiting Georgie's reply. For the first time since I dropped an atomic bomb onto my own happiness, I feel hopeful. I feel *optimistic*.

But then I hear Georgina's voice, and I know I'm sunk.

"Reed," she whispers on an exhale. "We shouldn't do this."

"Why not? You said yourself, we're friends now. Well, let me take my *friend* to New York City as a birthday present."

"If I go on this trip with you, and let you try to 'seduce' me again, then what? It won't end well. We're doomed. So, what's the point?"

We're not doomed, I think. *We're destiny.* "Please, Georgie. I won't hurt you again. I promise." She's silent. And I'm desperate. "All right, then. This trip isn't a birthday present. It's a work obligation. I've got full discretion as to when and where I make my artists available for interviews. And I'm only making RCR available to you backstage before their concert at Madison Square Garden. Take it or leave it."

She scoffs. "Seriously?"

"Seriously."

"Wow, great plan, Mr. Rivers. Bully me into falling in love with you again."

My heart stops. It's the first time Georgina's used the "L" word. And it only makes me want to come at her that much harder. "Take it or leave it, Miss Ricci," I say sternly. "You can still interview Dean, individually, in Malibu, like we discussed. But this is the only way I'll serve up RCR to you, as a full band."

I can practically hear her eye roll over the phone line. "Fine, ya big dickhead. I'll take it. But I won't have dinner with you on Saturday night. And I won't fly to New York with you. I'll meet you backstage at the concert on Sunday, with my press pass around my neck."

"God, you're even more stubborn than me. I want to take you to my favorite restaurant in Manhattan."

"And I want to punch you in the face. Sometimes, we can't have everything we want in life."

I chuckle, despite my misery. "Georgina, this is stupid. Every time we talk, the chemistry between us is through the roof, and you know it."

"So what? Chemistry is a shortsighted thing to chase. If I can't trust you with my heart, there's no point in moving forward. Honestly, I wish I could trust you with my heart again, because, apparently, it still belongs to you, whether I like it or not. Along with my body. But I have to get over you, Reed. For my own good. You're nobody's Prince Charming. And yet, that's how I started thinking about you when I was following you around like a smitten puppy for a week. Is that really what you want? For some pie-eyed smitten puppy to start imagining you're her Prince Charming?"

Yes. The word pops into my mind, unbidden. *Yes, yes, yes.* That's exactly what I want, as long as the pie-eyed smitten puppy is *you.*

Georgina continues, "Now, stop trying to bully my affection out of me. Stop trying to buy it. And stop trying to wear me down with all this sweet-talk and razzle dazzle. The answer is *no.*"

"Georgina, you've got to know turning a 'no' into 'yes' is my favorite thing to do, when I want something badly enough. *And what I want is you.*"

"No, you don't. You want the *old* version of me. The one who let go for you, completely, the night of the necklace. Well, guess what? I won't be able to let go like that again, because I'll be imagining you screwing Isabel in that garage."

I feel too defeated to speak. Too full of despair and remorse. For the hundredth time since this disaster happened, I think about doing that thing... the thing that would almost certainly exonerate me... but also risk unleashing the kraken on me, and on Isabel, too, in a way I'd live to regret. Yet again, I decide I simply can't risk it.

"I'll see you in New York, Mr. Rivers," she says, breaking the thick silence. "Backstage at the RCR concert on Sunday night."

"I'll book your travel."

"No. It's official business, remember? *Rock 'n' Roll* will cover it."

Emotion threatens. My eyes sting. But I clear my throat and bite back the wave of emotion gripping me. "All right. I'll see you in New York, Miss Ricci. Travel safe."

Chapter 12
Georgina

After quite a bit of driving around, I find a parking spot in downtown LA and then start trekking the few blocks to my destination—a little hole-in-the-wall restaurant called "Dee-Lish." The eatery opened by Francesca Laramie after her release from prison three years ago. What were the crimes that sent Francesca to The Big House? Procurement of prostitution, conspiracy, tax evasion, and money laundering, all stemming from the high-end escort service she ran in Los Angeles for almost twenty years. All of which leads me to the inescapable conclusion, based on what Troy Eklund told me, that Isabel's secret—the one Troy used to blackmail Reed into settling his lawsuit—was that, at one time or another, America's Sweetheart worked for Francesca Laramie as a paid escort.

But so what? Assuming it's true, is it something I'd write about? No. Just because I've discovered a secret about someone, that doesn't give me the right to reveal it to the world. Even if that someone happens to be a world-famous actress. Even if that someone happens to be the woman who fooled around with my man.

No matter how much Reed hurt me, I'm not going to ruin Isabel's life for a kiss. Or whatever happened in that garage. And I'm sure as hell not the kind of woman who'd shame

89

another woman for doing whatever she wanted with her own body. Isn't that what CeeCee taught me, when I asked her if it was okay for me to sleep with an interview subject? Not to shame another woman for doing whatever the hell she wants with her own body? Well, then, I'm paying it forward. You're welcome, Isabel.

I admit I was devastated when Reed kissed Isabel. Or did whatever he did with her. But what I said to CeeCee was the truth: my issue is with *Reed.* Reed is the one who slipped that ruby necklace around my neck and called me his "queen." Reed is the one who told me nobody is allowed to hurt me, ever again, and then turned around and did just that.

Also, and this isn't a small thing, I have to think Reed hired Isabel as his paid escort the night of CeeCee's birthday party. Why else would they *both* lie about how they met? Why else would Reed say he and Isabel went on a blind date that night, and Isabel say she met Reed through Josh Faraday? Really, it makes perfect sense. Reed had a rented tux that night. A rented limo. So, why not a rented woman, too? He had a plan to convince the power players at that party, especially CeeCee, he belonged there. Apparently, he figured a hot blonde on his arm was the ultimate status symbol. And guess what? He was probably right.

Frankly, this realization about Reed doesn't shock me at all. Reed once told me he figured out how to be an "influencer" before the term was coined. He explained he figured out how to use his curated image as a "cool kid" to conquer the world. Well, bravo, Reed Rivers. If hiring Isabel was part of that strategy, then good for you. Look at you now. I know Reed has hurt me. But he's also done amazingly wonderful things for my father and me. Life-changing things. And for that, he'll always have my loyalty and love. Which means Isabel's secret—and Reed's, too, if I'm right about him hiring Isabel—are safe with me.

So, why am I walking to Francesca's restaurant, then?

Curiosity, I guess. Because she's a breadcrumb to follow, which is my favorite thing to do. And also because... who knows? Maybe talking to Francesca will lead me to something of interest to write about for *Dig a Little Deeper*. And if not, then, oh well. I'll have wasted a couple hours getting to meet a famous madam. No big deal.

I reach Francesca's small restaurant and peek in the window. And there she is. The woman I recognize from my online research. She's standing behind a counter, talking to a stout man in a white apron. As I was hoping, the place isn't bustling at this time of day. In fact, Francesca looks downright relaxed behind the counter.

As I grip the door handle, my stomach ripples with nerves. But I've come this far. I'm not turning back now. "Hi there, Ms. Laramie," I say, coming to a stop before her. "My name is Georgina Ricci. I was wondering if—"

"If you're a reporter, don't bother. I don't talk to reporters."

"Oh, no, I..." *Crap*. What now? "Can we go to a quiet spot? I just need five minutes of your time."

"For what purpose?"

It's a great question—one I don't know how to answer.

"The film rights to my story have already been sold," Francesca says, her arms crossed over her chest. "And I'm not interested in doing any more interviews about my life story."

"I'm not here to interview you like that. I'm just here to... get information for... someone. A friend of mine. One of the girls who used to work for you. She was targeted by a blackmailer. She's too famous to have come here herself. Could we speak privately, please? This is sensitive."

Francesca looks me up and down. And just when I think she's going to tell me to piss off, she turns to the stout guy in the white apron. "Mind the counter for me." She looks at me. "You've got five minutes."

I follow her through the restaurant's tiny kitchen to an

even tinier office that's barely big enough for a small desk and chair. She closes the door, refolds her arms over her chest, and glares at me with hard, suspicious eyes. "Which girl?"

"Isabel Randolph."

Francesca nods. It's a subtle movement of her head, but unmistakable. Which is how I know my assumption about Isabel is spot-on: she did, in fact, work for Francesca at some point.

"Someone figured out she used to work for you, and now he's blackmailing her."

I've fudged the truth a bit. Made it sound like Troy is *presently* blackmailing Isabel, which I don't believe is the case. But I had to think of *something* to justify my presence here.

"Sorry to hear that. But it's not my problem."

In a flash, my mind sorts through the various interviewing tactics I learned in school—ways to get an interview subject to open up—and quickly settles on *confrontation.* "Candidly, Francesca, I thought maybe *you* could be the one blackmailing Isabel. Her four-picture deal has been all over the news. She's a big target now." Francesca opens her mouth, clearly ready to curse me out, but I add quickly, "Although Isabel told me, quite vehemently, you'd never do that to her. I just wanted to come here and meet you and get a read on you myself."

Francesca scoffs. "It's well documented I went to prison for eighteen months longer than I needed to, simply because I wouldn't give up a single name. Not of my girls, or my clients. And I never will." She narrows her eyes. "What are you? A paralegal? Some sort of private investigator?"

I shake my head. "I'm just trying to help Isabel. All her dreams are coming true, and now someone is threatening her."

Francesca shakes her head and exhales. "You know what really pisses me off? That anyone even has any leverage to blackmail her at all. There shouldn't be any shame attached to what she did. Same with what *I* did. There was a demand for a particular service, and I filled it. Simple as that. My girls were adults who came to *me*. I never solicited or trafficked anyone. They were all models and actresses who wanted to earn extra cash in between jobs. And I always told them, they had absolute discretion regarding what they would, or wouldn't do. That's what I told the clients, too. 'Treat my girls right, because if you don't, they won't do anything with you, no matter how much money you offer.' And yet, just because money changed hands, these girls, some of whom went on to become highly successful and famous, like Isabel, have to deal with assholes threatening to 'expose' them for their pasts? Where is the justice in that?"

"It's not fair at all."

"Are the men who used my services looking over their shoulders, worried someone might expose them? No, they're not. Because nobody cares about them. And yet, here I am, a *felon*, just because I ran a business in LA that's perfectly legal in New Zealand. It infuriates me that *I'm* the felon here, when I can think of a client who should have been thrown in jail a long time ago for hurting several of my girls. But does the DA want to pursue *him*? Nope. That asshole terrorized my girls, without consequence, and yet I'm the one who had to go to prison and watch him collecting his Academy Awards on TV."

Holy crap. Was that a reference to Howard Devlin? I have a hunch it was. So, I decide to act like I'm in the know, to suss out more information. "Howard," I say matter-of-factly. Like there's no doubt in the world that's who we're talking about. "Yeah, I know all about him. I've actually been warned to stay away from him, for my safety."

Francesca's eyebrows shoot up. "By *Isabel*?"

And there it is. Confirmation my hunch was right. Because she didn't say, "Howard who?" Or, "I don't know what you're talking about." Nope. She immediately linked the name Howard to the name Isabel. Which tells me everything I need to know. "No, Isabel's never mentioned Howard's grabby hands. An older woman warned me. Someone I trust implicitly, who's very well connected in Hollywood. She told me he's rumored to have assaulted several young actresses—and that she fully believes the rumors to be true."

"She's right to believe them. You're an actress, then? A model?"

"No, I work for the older woman who warned me about Howard. My boss knows lots of celebrities."

"A word of advice? Listen to your boss and steer clear of Howard. Certainly, never accept a drink from him, if you know what I mean."

I inhale sharply, and she nods ominously.

"I didn't know what he was up to for a long time, or I never would have let him near my girls. None of them told me anything, at first. Apparently, he was masterful at dangling all sorts of carrots to get my girls—all of whom were aspiring actresses—to do all sorts of things they didn't want to do, off the books." She rolls her eyes. "And when they finally started tiring of his dangling carrots, and started refusing him services, he'd say he understood, and then invite them to his hotel room to 'have a drink' and 'discuss a part' he supposedly had in mind for them. And the next thing they knew, they were waking up in his bed, naked, groggy, with a terrible headache... and scorching pain in every hole."

My stomach physically revolts. "Oh my God. He needs to be stopped, Francesca. Maybe he's still doing it."

"Who would come forward to accuse him? They all know it'd be their word against his—and career suicide. Add to that, plenty of women are worried he'd out them for having worked for me. Or, possibly, saying yes to him to further their careers."

Crap. I know CeeCee told me not to pursue an article about Howard, but I can't imagine she'll stand by that position, once she hears all of this.

"Francesca, if any of the women who used to work for you came forward to—"

"They won't."

"But, if they *did*, would you—"

"They *won't*. Trust me on that."

"Just hear me out. Please. In a fantasy, a fairytale, an alternate reality where they *did* speak up about Howard, would you be willing to back them up and reveal what you know?"

"It's a pointless question. Nobody's going to say a word."

"Could you play along? *If* I could get some of the women who worked for you to speak up, maybe band together, would you come forward to support them with whatever you know?"

A puff of air escapes Francesca's nose. "I'm a felon, remember? My word is shit, according to the world."

I can barely stand still. *This is it.* The big story I've been waiting for! I feel it in my bones.

"I have a confession to make. My boss, the older woman I mentioned, is CeeCee Rafael—the owner of *Rock 'n' Roll* and another magazine called *Dig a Little Deeper*. I'm a summer intern at *Rock 'n' Roll,* assigned to write about music artists, but CeeCee's given me the green light to find interesting stories for *Dig a Little Deeper*, too. And I think this story about Howard is the one I've been searching for."

Francesca looks annoyed. But, thankfully, slightly amused by my exuberance, as well. "I don't talk to reporters. I told you that, right from the start."

"Yes, I know. Sorry. I didn't mean to mislead you. I really do know Isabel. And someone really *did* blackmail her about her connection to you. Which is what brought me here. Also, my boss really did tell me to stay away from Howard Devlin. But the full truth is that I'm trying to get hired onto the writing staff of CeeCee's magazine that's devoted to investigative journalism. I swear I have no desire to write about you, in particular. You're entitled to your privacy. And your story's already been written about quite a bit. I also promise I won't write about any of the girls you employed or the men who hired them. Except for *one* client. Howard Devlin. Who needs to be exposed and taken down by someone." I puff out my chest. "And that someone is *me*."

Francesca looks outright amused now. She can't hide it.

"Francesca, please. I'm a person who follows my gut. And it's telling me this is my purpose. My *calling*. My destiny."

Francesca presses her lips together. "Show me some proof you work for CeeCee Rafael."

I scramble into my purse and breathlessly pull out my ID and press pass. Also, as further proof I am who I say I am, I also hand her my student ID and a "membership card" from my favorite frozen yogurt place on campus. It's got eight stamps on it at the moment. One shy of getting my next yogurt free. Which proves, I think, I really did attend UCLA, just like my student ID would suggest.

Francesca looks over everything and hands it back to me, seemingly satisfied. "So, one minute you're worried about some asshole blackmailing Isabel, and the next you want to take down her fiancé?"

"I'm not entirely sure how Isabel fits into all this. All I know is she's engaged to a monster, and I'm going to take him down. I have no desire to hurt Isabel, but if she happens to get humiliated because she's engaged to a sexual predator, then sorry not sorry. Was Isabel one of the women who told you about Howard?"

"Like I said, I don't talk about my former girls or clients. Everything I've said in this room has been off the record, and totally confidential, and I'll sue your fucking ass, and your boss's, if you print a word of it."

My stomach twists. "I won't print a word of this conversation. I just want to do the right thing. This is highly personal for me. In high school, someone I trusted tried to rape me and I didn't say anything because he was far more powerful than me and I thought nobody would believe me. Looking back, I realize he was counting on me feeling too powerless to report him. And that's what Howard counts on, too. Well, fuck him. *Ciao, stronzo.* That Italian for—"

"Yes, I know. Bye, asshole." For a long moment, Francesca stares at me, her face unreadable. Finally, she says, "As I've said, Georgina, I make it a firm rule to *never* name any of my clients."

My heart falls. Dang it. For a second there, I thought I had her. "I understand. Thank you for your time."

She puts her palm up. "But if you really think it will help your 'destiny' to be able to tell my former girls I'll corroborate their stories, then, yes, I'll do it. I'll make an exception to my firm rule, just this once. Only for Howard."

Chapter 13
Reed

After our waiter leaves our table, CeeCee leans back and says, "All right, my darling." She pushes aside her empty plate with purpose. "Now that I've got you nice and loose on a fabulous bottle of red, and your belly nice and full on a fantastic meal, it's time to talk about my magical unicorn of an intern. Georgina is obviously head over heels in love with you, Reed. And yet, you were stupid enough to do God knows what with Isabel in your garage?"

Damn. I've been waiting for CeeCee to bring up Georgina, ever since we sat down in this restaurant. Up until now, we've talked about Bali and the special issue. And, stupid me, when CeeCee hadn't yet chastised me for being a dipshit by the time our entrees were served, I started thinking maybe Georgina hadn't told her about The Garage Debacle, after all.

"What did Georgina say I did in that garage, exactly?" I ask calmly, even though my pulse is pounding.

"She doesn't know for sure. So, tell me. What did you do?"

My stomach tightens. "I kissed Isabel. It was a goodbye kiss."

"A little peck?"

I flash her a look that says, *What do you think?* And she smirks and flares her nostrils, nonverbally calling me a cad.

"She's marrying Howard, and I gave her a whopper of a

98

kiss goodbye, to prove my point that she shouldn't marry Howard. Not to be with *me*, mind you. But I gave Isabel a kiss to remind her what it feels like to actually *feel* something. But, damn. The moment my lips touched Isabel's, I knew I was in love with Georgina."

CeeCee swoons. "Well, that's actually kind of romantic, in a twisted sort of way."

"It is, right? That's what I thought!"

"Oh, simmer down. I'm not the one you need to convince. And I'm sixty, for goodness sake. I've been around the block enough times to make your head spin, little boy. To me, one drunken goodbye kiss with an ex would merit an eye roll. But to sweet little Georgina, something like that is the Apocalypse. And understandably so. You broke her trust, Reed. Shattered her little newbie heart. Shame on you."

"Please, don't pile on, CeeCee. I'm well aware I've blown it. By the way, you'll be happy to know that little newbie totaled my Ferrari with a golf club that night in retribution for my transgression."

CeeCee's face lights up. "Seriously?"

"Yep."

CeeCee laughs uproariously. "Ha! My kind of woman."

"Mine, too."

"Yes, you made that abundantly clear, from the minute you first saw her—*at the lecture hall*. Yeah, that's right, Mr. Sneaky Pants. I saw the sparks flying between you two at the panel discussion. And then you called me, feigning curiosity about why I left the hall that day without saying goodbye to you. You actually had the audacity to say you'd only seen Georgina from the back? Ha! And *then* you offered to pay for Georgina's father's medical expenses, not just her salary?" She waves at the air. "Forget about it. I knew you were a goner."

"You knew I was full of shit from the moment I called you?"

"Do you think I'm stupid?"

"You played me like a violin."

"I did. If it makes you feel any better, though, you're a Stradivarius, darling."

"Is that why you sent Georgina straight to C-Bomb, as her 'top priority interview'?"

CeeCee bursts out laughing. "Guilty as charged. Did it work? Did you fall all over yourself, promising Georgina the best interview you've ever given, to lure her away from interviewing—and getting seduced by—C-Bomb?"

"You wicked woman."

"Thank you. That's high praise, coming from you."

"The highest."

We clink wine goblets.

"Don't pat yourself on the back too hard," I say. "I didn't give Georgina anything I wasn't already planning to give her." *Other than my heart.*

CeeCee juts her lower lip. "Aw, Reed. You're miserable."

"I am."

"Well, nothing's fatal except death. Win the girl back."

"That's the plan. When I finally see Georgina again, this Sunday at the RCR concert in New York"—I smile broadly—"I'm going to tell her, for the very first time, I love her." I'm rather impressed with myself. But CeeCee, not so much. "Well, shit. If you've got a better idea, let's hear it."

"I do, actually. Georgina told me she'd be able to forgive and forget, if only she knew for sure you gave Isabel a goodbye *kiss,* and nothing more."

My heart lurches. "Georgina said that?"

"She did. So, I know this sounds crazy, but—"

"CeeCee, did she actually *say* it, or *imply* it?"

"She said it. In those exact words. So, my idea is this: why not ask Isabel to call Georgina and tell her exactly what happened, in confidence? She's marrying Howard now, so she knows she can't have you for herself. Maybe she still cares enough about you to want you to be as happy as she is."

I drag my hand through my hair, buzzing with adrenaline. "No. I know exactly what I have to do now. I've been going back and forth for days on this idea. But I kept nixing it, because I know it'll open Pandora's Box. But now that I know Georgie said that..."

I tell CeeCee my idea—the one I first considered, and rejected, at Hazel's birthday party. And CeeCee expresses extreme support for the idea. In fact, she tells me I'm a fool for not having done it sooner.

"The thing is," I say, "even though I'll be vindicating myself, I'll also be throwing Isabel under the bus—telling Georgina a secret she could use to hurt Isabel."

CeeCee waves dismissively. "So what if Isabel kissed you while wearing Howard's ring. She made her bed. Now she has to lie in it. The same way you've had to lie in your bed with Georgina."

I press my lips together. Isabel cheating on Howard isn't the "secret" I was talking about. I was talking about the same secret of Isabel's I've been guarding for ten years. Can I really divulge that information to Georgina, and trust her to keep it confidential, forevermore, in order to save myself? If I'm wrong about Georgina choosing her loyalty to me, over her shot at writing something salacious for *Dig a Little Deeper,* then it's *Isabel's* life and career that will be decimated, not mine. I *think* I can trust Georgina with this bombshell... but I also know how ambitious Georgina is... and also that she probably hates Isabel's guts for that kiss and would almost certainly revel in taking Isabel down.

But since I can't tell CeeCee about any of that, I decide to reply in a way that lets her continue thinking my concern is Georgina possibly outing Isabel to Howard. "I just need to feel certain Georgina won't use confidential information to try to take Isabel down with a hit piece."

"Have you forgotten I'm Georgina's publisher? I'm not going to publish gossip about Isabel's love life. I'll leave that to the tabloids. If you give Georgina this information and she immediately runs to Howard or includes it in an article on Isabel she submits to me, then I hate to say it, but maybe she isn't the woman you think she is. Or the writer *I* think she is. Which is all the more reason for you to do this. Either you trust her completely, including with this sensitive information, or you don't. It's as simple as that, Reed. You want Georgina to trust *you*? Well, you've got to trust her, too. Trust is a two-way street, sweetheart."

My chest tightens. "You're right. If I want Georgina to trust me, then I have to trust her first."

"Of course I'm right. I'm always right." CeeCee raises her wine glass. "To trust. True love is based on it, my dear. Which, I do believe, has been Georgina's point, all along."

***

After sending CeeCee off in her car, I get settled into my Porsche. Before starting my car, I check my phone, just in case I've missed something important during my dinner with CeeCee. I have. A text from Henn:

Call me ASAP. I've got news on the asshole.

My heart rate spiking, I start my car and immediately place the call.

"Hey," Henn says.

"You found kiddie porn, didn't you?"

"Worse."

Henn tells me the situation, and I'm blown away.

"That's why it took me so long to get back to you," he says. "Once I saw what we were dealing with, I knew I had to follow the clues and hack everyone involved. So, it took a little time."

"You've got everything now?"

"Yep. I've got it all."

"Send it to me. I'm driving home now. I'll look at everything when I get home."

Henn pauses. "You realize this is bigger than your personal vendetta now, right? We have a higher duty than just ruining this asshole's life on the down-low to avenge Georgina. You get that, right?"

"Send me the stuff and we'll talk next steps."

"We're going to have to tell Georgina what I found. This isn't as simple as tipping off the FBI about some kiddie porn. She deserves to know."

I exhale. "Yeah. I know. I'll be seeing Georgina in person in New York in a couple days. I'll talk to her about it then."

"Good. Keep me posted."

"Will do. Thanks, Henny. Seriously. You never let me down."

I end the call with Henn and place another one. This time, to my head of security, Barry Atwater. Unfortunately, though, I get Barry's voicemail.

"Hey, Big Barry. It's Reed. I need your help with something personal and confidential. It's urgent and highly important. Call me as soon as you can."

Chapter 14
Georgina

Friday 9:24 pm

"And this was when Dax and I dressed up as the Wonder Twins for Halloween," Kat says, showing me a photo. "I was sixteen. Dax, twelve."

I'm in Seattle. Sitting on Kat's couch in her stunning home. Earlier today, Dax and the Goats gave me a tour of "their" Seattle, while I interviewed them. Tonight, Kat is regaling me with story after story.

"You two look so much alike," I say, grinning at the photo. "You're both spitting images of your mom." I know this because I met Kat and Dax's mom, Louise Morgan, last night, when I went to "Casa Morgan" for a family dinner.

"Oh, I know. Everyone says that. Gracie, too." That's Kat's spitfire of a daughter. "My mom always says the four of us are Russian nesting dolls. Oh! This is a good one. Dax at age two." She shows me a photo of Dax as a toddler on a couch, looking like he's playing air guitar, while little Kat in the photo, a tow-headed blonde, cheers on her little brother enthusiastically. "According to family lore, Dax saw some hot shot guitar player on TV, and he jumped up and started mimicking him. It's how Daxy got his lifelong nickname: Rock Star."

I giggle. "The Morgans sure love their nicknames."

"Oh, Georgie girl, you have no idea." She pulls out another photo. "This is the Goats rehearsing in my parents' garage. A very common occurrence back in the day. They used to come home from high school every day and head straight to the garage to practice for hours."

"How old are they here?"

"Fifteen or sixteen."

"And Dax already had long hair."

"He always loved having long hair, from day one. My mom said at his very first haircut, he started bawling when he saw his long locks floating to the ground. My mother swears he said, 'But now how will you know which one is me?'"

I laugh and laugh. The same way I did yesterday, when I toured Seattle tourist spots with Kat and her kids, and Kat's best friend, Sarah, and her kids. The same way I did last night, during dinner with Kat's family. Also, during today's fun-filled interview with the band, which Kat tagged along on. Seriously, any time I'm in Kat's presence, I can't stop smiling.

"Do you think Dax would mind me using that 'first haircut' anecdote in my article?"

"Go for it. Dax already told me I could tell you anything."

"Thank you so much. When you offered to put me up in Seattle, I had no idea you'd go all out like this. You've made me feel like family."

"That's because you *are* family, Georgie." She returns to her photos, like she didn't just take my breath away. "Oh, this is a good one. It's from my destination wedding in Maui. This is the night Reed watched 22 Goats play a show for our wedding guests." She smiles. "He signed them to River Records that very night."

Reed. Oh, God, he's gorgeous in the shot. Tanned and relaxed. *I love him.* That's all I can think as I stare at his chiseled face. *I. Love. Him.* Immediately followed by *Why did you screw everything up, you stupid man?*

When I look up from the photo, Kat is staring at me. Scrutinizing my face. Probably looking for signs of

105

heartbreak, since yesterday, while touring Seattle with her and Sarah, I spilled my guts, in nauseating detail, about what happened between Reed and me.

"I'm sorry I showed you a photo of Reed," Kat says. "I didn't think."

"It's fine. Reed and I are friends."

Kat flashes me a look that tells me she doesn't buy that.

Blushing, I return to the photos splayed out before us. "May I use any and all of these for my article?"

"Use whatever you want. The Goats said to give you 'full access.'"

"Thank them for me. I feel like I won the lottery. Not just in terms of my article, but also because I've found you. You're so amazing, Kat."

She touches my shoulder. "The feeling is mutual. You're my spirit animal." She winks. "So, do you have everything you need?"

"For my article about 22 Goats, yes. More than I ever dreamed possible." I pause. "Although... there's another article I'm gathering information for... something for *Dig a Little Deeper*. Would you mind giving me Hannah Hennessy's number? This is highly confidential, but I'd like to ask her about her boss."

Kat grabs her phone. "I just sent you Hannah's contact info and texted her that you want to talk to her."

"Thank you."

She looks up from her phone. "So, by 'Hannah's boss,' do you mean that gray-haired guy who's marrying Isabel?"

I nod. "Howard Devlin."

"You're going to interview him?"

"No. I'm investigating some rumors I've heard about him. I want to ask Hannah if she's heard the rumors, too."

Kat arches an eyebrow. "What kind of rumors?"

"I shouldn't say."

"The ones about him being a pervert groper?"

I gasp. "Oh my gosh! You know about that?"

"Hannah told me. When Howard invited her to get a drink with him at the party, she dragged me along. Later, she told me she did that because it's well known at her company women should always use the buddy system around him."

"Holy hell."

"She said she's almost certainly safe around him, since she's only in PR. Not an actress. Plus, he's apparently a fan of big boobs, and, if you didn't notice, Hannah's Flatty Mcgee. But, still, she didn't want to be alone with him. She's actually looking for a new job. She's heard too much bad stuff about him to want to keep working there."

"Why the hell has nobody reported him? He's the worst kept secret in Hollywood!"

Kat shrugs. "He's a powerful old guy. Those guys always get away with murder." Her phone buzzes and she looks down. "Hannah says she's just putting Hazel down for the night, but we can call her in ten minutes."

My stomach clenches. "Oh, wow. I didn't expect to hear from her quite this fast."

Kat looks perplexed. "Is something wrong?"

I grimace. "The truth is my boss told me not to pursue the Howard story yet. I'm kind of 'going rogue' by talking to Hannah about him."

"She told you not to pursue the story, because she's trying to cover up for whatever he's been doing?"

"Oh, gosh no. My boss wants to take him down, with all her heart. She just thinks I'm too green, and the story too explosive, for me to try to tackle it just yet. But she said that *before* I'd landed my ace in the hole—this woman named Francesca Laramie." I google Francesca and show Kat some articles. Of course, I don't mention Isabel's connection to Francesca, or tell Kat how I found Francesca in the first place. But I tell Kat the gist of my conversation with Francesca about Howard, and the amazing news that Francesca has agreed to lend support to my efforts, if I can get anyone to come forward.

"Impressive," Kat says. "Maybe what Francesca knows about Howard will dovetail with what Hannah knows."

"That's my hope. I'm thinking maybe putting their two lists of names together will crack the whole thing wide open."

"Ooh, I'm getting pumped," Kat says. "Can I be on the call with Hannah?"

"I'd love it. I'm sure Hannah will feel more comfortable talking to me, if you're on the call."

Kat claps her hands and hoots. "Wonder Twin powers, activate!" Laughing, she rises from the couch, her adorable baby bump leading the way. "I'm gonna check on my kiddos real quick, before we call Hannah. Gracie sleeps like a ton of bricks, but Jack always wakes up around this time of night, wanting me, so I want to check on him before we make that call. Why don't you pour yourself another glass of wine while I'm checking on my babies, and then we'll call Hannah to see if she's got any information that might be useful for us to take this motherfucker down."

I could cry. *Us.* That's the word Kat just used. Such a tiny word. But so powerful.

"Oh, hey, you know what?" Kat says, stopping in the entryway of her living room. "Why don't I call Sarah to come over, too?" She's talking about her best friend and sister-in-law, Sarah Faraday, who happens to be a lawyer. The one we toured Seattle with yesterday. "Sarah is crazy-smart—a whiz at research and strategizing. She only lives ten minutes away, and I'm sure her babies are down for the night."

"Wow, Kat. I can't tell you how much your support means to me. I've been really stressed out about tackling this story as an army of one, especially since I'm kind of going rogue here, like I said."

Kat laughs. "The fact that you're willing to go rogue to pursue this story is the best indicator that you *should*." She smiles warmly. "And you're not an army of one anymore, sweetie. You're now an army of *four*—you, me, Hannah, and Sarah." She pats her belly. "Actually, make that four and a *half*. Don't tell my family this, because Josh and I are going to surprise them, but this little peanut is a girl. Arabella."

"Aw, I love it. Congratulations."

She pats her belly. "And you know what I'm going to tell my two daughters one day? And Jack, too. My son needs to know this, too. I'm going to tell them that, once, a long time ago, their mommy helped their Auntie Georgie bring down a truly evil man."

Chapter 15
Georgina

Saturday 2:46 pm

When my flight from Seattle touches down in LA, I turn on my phone, the same as everyone seated around me on the plane. And when I see an email from Reed, with a subject line that reads, "Personal and HIGHLY confidential," my heart stops. My breathing shallow, I read the body of the email:

My dearest Georgina, Attached, you will find a confidential video that's for your eyes only. Audio quality is poor, so watch with sound turned all the way up. It's critically important you watch this video when you're alone, in a quiet place, where you won't be interrupted. Please, I beg you not to share this video with anyone, or even describe its contents. At least, not before you've spoken to me and given me a chance to explain what you've seen. Thank you in advance for granting this request. Please call me after you've watched. RR.

I look around me on the crowded airplane, where passengers have just started grabbing their bags, and realize, much to my dismay, I'll have to wait until I reach my parked car to watch this mysterious video. After shuffling off the plane, I make my way through the maze of LAX and onto a parking-lot shuttle. I get off at the appropriate overnight lot, slip inside my rental car, turn the sound on my phone all the way up, and, finally, breathing hard, press play on the video.

Grainy, black and white video of Reed's garage comes up. It's surveillance video, time-stamped in the bottom right-hand corner with a date from exactly one week ago. In other words, the date of Reed's party. I hold my breath with anticipation, and, a few seconds later, Reed and Isabel enter the garage through the same side door they exited through when I stumbled upon them.

As Reed closes the door, Isabel marches into the expansive garage, looking agitated. She comes to a stand, facing the camera, and Reed stops in front of her.

"What's this supposed 'emergency'?" he says, sounding deeply annoyed. "Make it quick. I've got something important to do."

"That reporter you introduced me to. She mentioned CeeCee's birthday party."

"So?"

"Did you tell her I was with you that night?"

"She asked me how I met CeeCee, so I told her the story of how I crashed the party. And, yeah, I mentioned you were my date. So what?"

"Goddammit, Reed!"

"You're being paranoid, Isabel. It's perfectly fine you were my date. Nobody would ever guess how that came to be."

"She's really smart. I can tell."

"Yes, she is. And she wants to write a flattering interview about you. That's all. She's not looking to write a hit piece. You're being paranoid."

Isabel wrings her hands. "Can you blame me? Every day of my life, I'm waiting for the next Troy to come along to blackmail me."

Reed's back is to the camera, but his shoulders soften. "Isabel, I understand why Troy messed with your head. But he was a one-off. If someone was going to threaten to expose

111

your secret again, they would have done it by now. It's been ten years since you worked for Francesca. If I thought there was an army of Troys out there, lying in wait to take you down, I wouldn't have paid him so much to stay quiet. I'm rolling in money, sweetheart, but even I can't afford to pay off the entire world."

Isabel rubs her face. "Yeah, you're right. I'm being paranoid. I am, right?"

"You are."

"Just don't tell this reporter anything else about me."

"I won't. Now, can we please go back to the party? I just made a little girl cry and I need to fix it."

Isabel steps forward and slides her arms around Reed's neck. "What's the rush? Now that we're here, how about we have a little fun, for old time's sake?"

I hold my breath and squint my eyes, convinced I'm about to see something deeply traumatizing to me. But I needn't worry. Reed immediately disentangles himself from Isabel and says, "That's not gonna happen." He grabs her hand, the one with Howard's massive rock on it, and holds it up. "This means nothing to you?"

She yanks her hand away. "You know I don't want him. I want *you*."

Reed throws up his hands. "Goddammit. Not this again. Things are different now than when you fucked Troy to make me jealous. It's not going to work this time."

She puts her hands on her hips. "You're not going crazy to think of me marrying someone else?"

He scoffs. "No. Would I prefer you marry someone you actually love? Yes. Because I care about you and want you to find happiness. But do I wish you were marrying *me*? Fuck no. Isabel, like I keep telling you. *I'm over you.* I've moved on. So, if you're marrying Howard to manipulate me into action the same way you did when you fucked Troy, only bigger and better this time, then don't bother. Don't marry anyone to try to get a rise out of me. The only thing that strategy will get you is a husband you don't love."

"Why are you always so mean to me?"

"I'm not mean to you. I'm *honest*. I don't want you anymore. We'll *never* get back together. *Never.*"

"I don't believe that."

"Believe it. If you must know, I'm with someone else now. I'm in a serious, committed relationship."

Even in the grainy footage, I can tell Isabel is crushed.

"I'll always care about you," Reed says. "I'll always protect you, as best I can. And your secrets are always safe with me. But the truth is you're more like a sister to me now, than anything else."

Isabel slaps Reed across his face, but he doesn't even flinch. "Who is she?" she shrieks, her tears matching mine as I watch the scene unfolding. "Is she here at the party?"

"No, she's not here," Reed lies. "But if she were, I'd expect you to be nice to her. We haven't been together in *years,* Isabel, and you're engaged to another man. Why do you think you still have any claim on me?"

"Because I'm still in love with you!"

He's exasperated. Irritated. "Why the hell are you marrying Howard?" he booms. "I don't get it! You don't need his money, and you certainly don't need his connections anymore. You're a huge star now. The biggest star on the planet. *You don't need him.* You can get cast in anything from blockbusters to indies, without his help or blessing. I get why you flirted with him when you were starting out, but don't you think saying yes to marrying a man you don't love is taking the casting couch a bit far?"

She shakes her head. "You don't understand."

"I think I do. He's made marriage part of the deal for the superhero movies, hasn't he?"

She drops her head, looking defeated. But says nothing.

"Screw the superhero movies! If he drops you from

them, so what? There are ten other producers who'd hire you in a heartbeat."

She shakes her head. Rubs her face. "You cheated on this girlfriend of yours with me in the Hamptons?"

"No. I hadn't met her yet back then."

Isabel is flabbergasted. "How new is this relationship? Were you lying to me last month when you said you were having dinner with your friends? Were you actually seeing *her*?"

"No. I didn't lie to you that night. I was having dinner with my friends. But then we went to a bar, after dinner, and that's where I met her. She was the bartender."

Isabel gasps. "You want a *bartender* over *me*?"

"Fuck you," I whisper to my screen. At the same moment Reed says something I don't catch because I was talking. I rewind the video to hear whatever I missed, and what Reed says makes me smile from ear to ear: "Fuck you, Isabel." Which he follows with, "I'm not going to talk about my girlfriend with you anymore. All you need to know is she makes me feel things I've never felt before." He pauses for dramatic effect. "*Ever.*"

The meaning is clear. *Not even with you.* And, obviously, by the devastated look on Isabel's face, his message has been received, loud and clear. She bows her head and bursts into tears. And, sweet man that he is, Reed wraps his strong arms around her and squeezes her tight. And, suddenly, I find myself quaking with dread about whatever I'm going to witness next.

They remain still for a long time, holding each other. They're whispering to each other, but I can't make out their words. Finally, Reed pulls back from their tender embrace. He takes Isabel's gorgeous, iconic face in his hands and looks deeply into her eyes for a very long moment, causing her body to visibly wrack with sobs.

"If I could have flipped a switch and made myself fall madly in love with you, Isabel Schneider, I would have done it years ago. You're gorgeous and talented. You've got the world on a string. I know what you went through as a kid. I know how bad it was, and I want nothing more than to see you safe and happy and successful, for the rest of your life. You deserve a happily ever after. But I'm truly not your Prince Charming, and I never will be."

Isabel closes her eyes and tilts her face up. "Kiss me goodbye. One last kiss. Just so I can remember what it feels like to kiss you. What it feels like to actually *feel* something with a man. Please, Reed. At least, give me that."

Reed looks into her tear-streaked face for a long moment, and then leans in and presses his lips to hers. And, somehow, the vision doesn't repel me. It doesn't enrage me. No, in this moment I'm actually in awe of Reed's kind heart. I know this isn't a betrayal of me, as much as one final act of generosity toward a woman he's loved for a very long time. Just like he told me, this truly is a goodbye kiss. Yes, he's technically breaking his promise to me in this moment. That fact hasn't escaped me. But seeing the way the kiss unfolded, I know he didn't kiss her because he doesn't want me. He kissed her because he *does*. Because he's closing the book on their tumultuous relationship, forever.

Um...

Okay, Reed, this kiss is far lengthier, and more passionate than required to close that fucking book. Come on, now. *Enough*.

Finally, Reed pulls away, having given Isabel the kiss of her life. She swoons and wobbles, looking dazed, and I can plainly see Isabel is now wearing the same expression she wore when I stumbled upon her and Reed coming out of the garage. She looks like a woman who just got fucked.

Reed puts his fingertip underneath Isabel's chin. "Don't marry anyone who doesn't kiss you like *that*."

I roll my eyes. Okay, Reed. That was wholly unnecessary, sweetheart. It's time to move along now.

"How can you deny our magic?" Isabel chokes out. "You felt it, every bit as much as I did, during that kiss. Admit it."

"No. The only thing I felt while kissing you was complete clarity that I'm head over heels in love with my girlfriend. I felt guilty while kissing you, to be honest. Because the only one I want to be kissing—the only one I *should* be kissing—is her."

Isabel clutches her heart. And so do I.

Even in grainy black and white, it's clear Reed just dealt her a death blow.

And I couldn't be happier about it.

Reed is unmoved by the expression of pure devastation on Isabel's face. She might as well be the blonde at the bar who tried to give him her demo. He looks at his watch, and sighs. "I need to get back to my party now. Come on. I'm sure your beloved fiancé is wondering where you are." With that, he opens the door to the garage, his urgency to get the hell out of there wafting off him. With a heavy sigh, Isabel drags herself out the door, and Reed follows, at which point the surveillance video ends.

I look up from my screen, practically hyperventilating. Reed told me the truth about everything. *Reed loves me. And he figured it out while kissing Isabel.*

And that's a damned good thing. Because, despite everything, I love him, too. With all my heart.

Breathing heavily, I tap out a text to my man, my love, asking him if he's home. And when he replies instantly, telling me he's not home, but can be there in fifteen minutes, my heart gallops with joy.

Me: Go home now. I'm coming home.

Reed: You got my email?

Me: Yes. Just landed at LAX and watched the video in my car. I'm coming straight to you now. See you soon! XO

Reed: I can't wait to see you, my love. XOXOXO

Chapter 16
Reed

Saturday 4:23 pm

I peek down my street again, awaiting the appearance of Georgina's convertible turning the corner. But, still, nothing. For the past ten minutes, I've been standing in front of my iron gate, staring down my street like a Labrador awaiting his owner's return from work while trying not to freak out. I *think* the "XO" Georgina tacked onto the end of her "see you soon!" text message, combined with the exclamation point she used, and the fact that she said she's coming "home," meant she's coming here to forgive me completely and pick up where we left off. But, when it comes to Georgina, and her temper, I never know for sure what she's going to do or how she's going to react. For all I know, after watching that surveillance video—and the whopper of a kiss I laid on Isabel—she's coming here to take a golf club to another one of my cars.

Either way, I'm surely going to have to field a thousand questions from Georgina about the confusing, and highly intriguing, things Isabel and I talked about in that video. Things like "Troy" and "blackmail" and "Francesca" and "secret." All the things that initially kept me from sending that damned surveillance video to Georgina in the first place, even though I knew it would prove I'd been telling Georgina the truth about that kiss, and what it made me realize. Although, yeah, if I'm being honest, I was also highly skittish about Georgina witnessing the actual kiss. It's one thing for me to tell Georgina I "only kissed" Isabel, and to let Georgina *imagine* it, and another thing for her to *see* it, and get confirmation that, to put it mildly, that smooch wasn't a brotherly peck.

I lean against my gatepost, staring down my street. But, still, there's no sign of Georgina. I look at my watch. She must have hit traffic. *Welcome to LA.*

I've never told a woman I love her before. But, today, for the first time in my life, I've told Georgina. Albeit, indirectly, through that video. Plus, I called her "my love" in my text. Which I'm now thinking might have been a bit premature. I *think* Georgina's "XO" meant she feels the same way I do. I *think* Georgina is coming here to say she's mine. But after this torturous week, and a lifetime of shit hitting fans in ways I never expected, I should know by now, better than anyone, not to count my chickens.

Hallelujah! I see Georgina's car turning onto my street! As she draws near, I wave and smile broadly, the sight of her glorious face sending my heart galloping and my skin buzzing. And, in return, Georgina shoots me a wide, beaming smile that tells me everything I need to know.

She's home.

She forgives me.

She loves me.

She's all mine.

I know we're going to need to talk in detail about everything, including the mysterious things Isabel and I talked about on that video. But, after seeing the smile on Georgina's face, I know we'll talk about all of it later. First things first, I'm going to take that woman into my arms and kiss the hell out of her and tell her I love her, to her face, while looking into her gorgeous hazel eyes. And then, I'm going to take her upstairs and show her, with every inch of me, how much she means to me.

Shaking with excitement, I tap out the gate code and

wave Georgina's little car through, and then sprint after her tailgate as she traverses my circular driveway and comes to a stop in front of my house. When Georgina's car door opens, I'm already there, my arms extended. I swoop her into my embrace, and every atom of my body electrifies at the touch of her.

"Welcome home," I murmur into her lips, just before crushing my mouth to hers. As our tongues tangle, a tsunami of love slams into me. Followed immediately by a hurricane of pent-up arousal. My heart thundering in my chest, I disengage from Georgina's hungry lips and take her magnificent, tear-streaked face in my palms. "I love you, Georgina. I love you madly. Completely. And only *you.*"

Her smile is beaming. Radiant. Breathtaking. "I love you, too. Only you."

"I'm so sorry I hurt you. I'll never do it again."

She smiles. "We'll call it a fair trade: a kiss for a Ferrari."

I chuckle. "Deal."

"That's a one-time deal, by the way."

"It'll never happen again."

She arches her eyebrow. "Can we talk about that kiss, though? Holy hell, Reed."

I grimace. "Yeah. Sorry about that."

She smiles. "It's all right. What you said right afterward made it all worth it." She winks. "But just barely."

Sighing with relief, I kiss her again. And, soon, our kiss becomes voracious. I scoop her up like a bride, making her squeal, and stride into my house like a stallion running for the barn. When I get to my staircase, I take the steps two at a time and then barrel down the hallway toward my bedroom, whispering the entire time to Georgina about how much I've missed her, how much I want her, need her, *love* her, can't wait to touch her, lick her, fuck her.

In my bedroom, I lay Georgina down onto my bed and begin energetically ripping off her clothes, and then mine. In short order, we're a naked blur of greedy fingers and lips and tongues. Warm, bare skin against warm, bare skin. In record speed, I make her come with my fingers, which, not surprisingly, makes her beg me to fuck her.

But not yet.

I open the second drawer of my nightstand and retrieve something I've been keeping there for this exact moment. I return to Georgina, holding up her ruby necklace. And the moment she sees it, she gasps in shock.

"You went back to Tiffany's to get it for me?"

I chuckle. "No, baby. I never returned it."

Her jaw drops comically, making me laugh.

"Sit up. I want you to wear it while I fuck you. My Ruby Queen."

"You've already done too much. I can't accept that."

"Sweetheart, look at my boner. I don't have patience for this conversation. Please, let's fast-forward to the part where you let me have what I want."

She sits up, sighing. "Oh, Reed."

After clasping the necklace around her neck, I kiss her neck and shoulder. And then, finally, do the thing I've been fantasizing about for half my life. I pull Georgina on top of me and guide her to ride me, and as she does, as her body gyrates, and her hips snap back and forth, and her tits bounce with her movement, I tell her, over and over again, that I love her. And it's the best sex of my life, even without the ropes and toys and harnesses.

We're fire together, Georgina and me. We're a pyre. I sit up as her body moves on top of mine and devour her pebbled nipples with fervor. I grab her ass and bite her neck. Inhale her scent and lick the hollow at the base of her neck. I'm delirious with desire for her. Overwhelmed to feel white-hot lust intertwining with all-encompassing *love* inside me, for the first time in my life. Oh, God, the sensation of loving to fuck someone, while actually *loving* them, as a person. I mean, totally and completely and unconditionally *loving* everything about them, and knowing they love me back... oh, fuck. I can't get enough of this sublime pleasure.

I run my fingertips over the dripping gems around Georgina's neck. And then caress her tits and pinch her hard nipples, and suck on her breasts and neck and gorgeous bottom lip, again and again. I grip her hair and run my teeth along her jawline, wanting to physically consume her. To ingest her into my body and keep her there, beholden to me, and only me. I want to fuse with her, in every way possible. I want to capture this beautiful butterfly in my net and never, ever let her go. My nerve endings on fire, my body lit up, I gaze up at the mirror above us and tell her, in graphic detail, what she looks like as she fucks me. I tell her about the way her ass is moving as she rides me. I tell her she's my queen.

Finally, Georgie screams my name and comes, hard, and when I feel her muscles clenching and rippling with her orgasm, it's sheer bliss for me. A direct line to a God I've never believed in, until now. I give myself permission to let go. And not just physically. To let go of fear. I'm hers now. Committed to giving her all of me now, no matter what.

When our bodies slacken, Georgina and I flop onto the bed, onto our backs, and stare at our smiles—and our heaving, panting, naked bodies—in the overhead mirror.

Wracked with euphoria, I grab Georgina's hand. "Please tell me you're home now."

She smiles seductively. "Are you inviting me to stay here, for however long?"

"No, I'm *begging* you. No limitations or expiration date. As in, I want you to go down to the DMV, right after we get back from New York, and change the address on your driver's license."

She opens her mouth and eyes as wide as they'll go.

"Yep," I say, chuckling at her shocked expression. "This is DMV-serious, baby."

Lauren Rowe

Georgina bites her lip. "You're serious? Because I'm not willing to go back down to the DMV again any time soon. It's hell down there."

I sit up and look down at her. "Seriously, Georgie. I'm in it for the long haul with you. I'm sure. Please, tell me you're sure, too. It's you and me, from now on."

She nods. "I'm sure."

I lean down and kiss her. But then pull away excitedly and grab my phone off the nightstand with a loud hoot.

"What?"

"I'm telling Owen to get your bike back here ASAP. I want the Ginger Rogers of Spin to start kicking my ass again, as soon as possible."

Georgina sighs like a Disney princess. "I'm so happy."

"I'm also telling Owen to add you to my flight tomorrow."

"Don't do that. I mean, I'd love to travel with you. But I've already got a flight booked. No sense wasting money."

I roll my eyes. "You're coming with me. We're flying first class."

"Oooh, I've never flown first class!" She giggles. "Okay, I'm coming with you."

We both laugh.

As I get settled onto my back again, she turns onto her side and drags a fingertip down the center groove of my abs. "So... I hate to say this and ruin the afterglow... but I think, before we get too swept away on endorphins, we should talk."

My stomach clenches with dread. Shit. Here we go. Isabel's secrets weren't mine to reveal. But what choice did I have but to send that video? If I'm going to love Georgina, all the way, then I've got to trust her to choose me, and our love, over the chance to use the information on that video to try to land her dream job. Or, worse, to try to destroy Isabel out of sheer spite. I know Georgie didn't fully understand anything she heard on that video, but she heard enough to realize Isabel

122

has a secret. And that some guy named Troy blackmailed her because of it. "Yeah, you're right," I say. "We definitely need to talk."

Georgina looks stressed. "I don't want there to be any secrets between us, Reed. Not anymore. No more lies—even if it's only through omission. It's time to come clean about everything."

"Yeah, I agree," I say, my words overlapping with Georgina's, as she says, "I need to talk to you about *Troy*."

Wow. She's jumping right in. Shit. I take a deep breath. "Yeah, I figured you'd ask me about him. In fact, I'm sure you've got a whole bunch of questions about the confusing stuff you heard on that video. But before I explain who 'Troy' is, I need to emphasize that—"

"Oh, no," Georgina says. She lays a palm on my chest, pausing me. "When I said it's time to come clean about Troy, I meant *me*. *I* need to come clean about Troy."

I blink several times, utterly confused. *Did I hear that right?*

Georgina leans onto her elbow and props her head with her fist. "What you and Isabel talked about wasn't confusing to me at all. I already know all about Troy Eklund."

"Uh." I blink again, my synapses exploding. "What, exactly, do you know?"

"Everything. The fact that he slept with Isabel. And figured out Isabel's secret—which I also know about, by the way. I know he blackmailed Isabel. Well, technically, he blackmailed *you*, and you gallantly paid him off in exchange for him signing a confidential settlement of his lawsuit." She shrugs. "I know everything, Reed."

My brain feels like it's melting. "How...?" But I'm too shocked to complete the sentence.

Georgina continues, "Normally, I wouldn't have said anything. I'd have pretended to be clueless, so you wouldn't fully realize the true nature of the demon you've fallen in love with. But if we're truly going to make this relationship work, if I'm really going to brave the DMV for you—then I feel like I should come clean to you about how clever and diabolical and relentless and... *brilliant*... I truly am." She winks. "I know you've *suspected* all along I'm Bobby Fischer. But I feel like, before I put your address onto my driver's license, which is, to me, as serious as a relationship can be, I should come clean and tell you that... no matter how much you've been thinking I'm Bobby Fischer? Oh, honey. You have no freakin' idea."

Chapter 17
Georgina

I tell Reed everything I know about Troy Eklund. How I read his lawsuit and then tracked him down at Slingers and cleverly pumped him for information without him realizing it. I tell him about Troy's unmistakable hints and body language, and finally, those two little words—Francesca Laramie—that sent me straight to Google, which then led me to deducing Isabel's secret, as well as causing me to assume that Reed must have hired Isabel to be his "blind date" on the night of CeeCee's fiftieth birthday party.

And, last but not least, I tell Reed about my visit to Francesca's restaurant downtown, although I don't drop the bomb on Reed, just yet, about my firmly held belief that Howard Devlin is a sexual predator who's been getting a free pass for decades because he happens to be a wildly successful billionaire movie producer. I'm going to tell Reed about Howard during this conversation, of course. But later. I feel like Reed and I have plenty to talk about, before we get to that.

I take Reed's hand. "I want you to know Isabel's secret is safe with me. And so is yours. Assuming I'm right about you hiring Isabel through Francesca."

"Yes, you're right about that."

"I figured. Rented tux, rented limo, rented girl..."

He nods. "CeeCee's party was actually the last time Isabel ever worked for Francesca. We spent the night together after the party. We hit it off. And I got to feeling a bit protective. Not to mention, possessive."

"You? Shocker."

He smiles. "I offered to pay Isabel's rent for the next year, so she could quit her gig with Francesca and afford to live on nothing but modeling and waiting tables, while she went to auditions and tried to get her big break."

My heart melts. Why doesn't it surprise me to learn Reed forked over a year's worth of rent for Isabel? Or, that Isabel took the deal and quit working for Francesca for him. I can only imagine how hard Isabel must have fallen for the dashing, young client she met the night of CeeCee's party. The smoking hot, scrappy dude who looked better in a rented tux than every millionaire or billionaire at that party with ten tuxes in their closets. In fact, I'd bet anything it was love at first sight for Isabel, when Reed got out of that rented limo to pick her up in front of McDonald's. And, judging from that surveillance video, she never fell *out* of love with him, for the next ten years. I can relate. Lying here naked with Reed, I'm certain I'll never fall out of love with him, either. God help me.

"Isabel and I weren't even an exclusive couple when I told her I wanted to pay her rent, so she could quit Francesca. Our serious relationship came a couple years later. But, right from the start, no matter what, or *who*, she was doing, I didn't want her doing it for money. I always knew she was going to be a star. I wanted to free her up from taking shitty jobs just to pay the rent. I wanted her to make smart decisions for her career."

Oh, Reed. Some things never change. He was a star-maker, right from the start. A man who took intense pleasure from helping others achieve their dreams and shoot for the stars. And he doesn't think he was Isabel's Prince Charming? Clearly, he was, right from night one.

Reed says, "It's funny, at one point, I had a feeling you

knew about Troy. But I convinced myself I was being paranoid. Remember that night I drove all over town, looking for your car outside of bars and clubs? I drove to Slingers that night, looking for you, because I found Troy's name on their performance schedule."

I gasp. "We must have just missed each other!"

"When I got there, the bartender said Troy had left with a blonde fifteen minutes before."

"Holy hell. Thank God you didn't run into him. Now that I know what I do, I never would have dropped that hint about what I was doing that night. I'd never want you and Troy to be in the same room. It wouldn't have ended well. And rightly so. He's such a douchebag."

Reed glowers. "If I'd walked into that bar and found that fucker hitting on you, it's fifty-fifty I wouldn't have been able to stop myself from wrapping my hands around his throat and squeezing the life out of him, right then and there." His dark eyes flicker, and I know he's dead serious.

"Is it wrong I get turned on when you look like you're genuinely capable of committing murder?"

"Everyone is capable of murder, under the right circumstances." His eyes flash. "And *you're* my right circumstance."

I bite my lip.

"As it is, I might have to settle this time for suing Troy's punk-ass for breaching his confidentiality agreement. Tell me again everything he said to you that night. This time, word for word."

I tell him everything Troy told me, and, when I'm done, we both conclude Reed probably wouldn't have a legal leg to stand on, thanks to the fact that it was mostly Troy's facial expressions and body language, combined with my clever deductions, that led me to discover the most salacious and sensitive nuggets of information. Plus, would Reed *really* want to reopen that particular wound, in a forum as public as a lawsuit, now that Reed's fame is a hundred times what it was when Troy sued him six years ago? The answer to that question, we both decide, is a resounding no.

"You were enraged Troy slept with Isabel, huh?"

"I was pissed he slept with Isabel. Yeah. Not gonna lie. But, more than that, I was enraged he betrayed me. When Troy slept with Isabel, I'd already broken up with her months before. So, she wasn't cheating on me. I didn't care if she fucked other people. I was doing the same. But *Troy* fucking her? That was a dagger to my heart." He shakes his head. "I'd loved that asshole like a little brother. I'd taken him into my *home* and under my wing. I'd poured obscene amounts of money into his band and guided him every step of the way. I'd *believed* in him and backed him with my name and reputation. And then, Troy had to pick *Isabel*, of all the women in LA, to fuck? And more than that, he had to do it a mere *two weeks* before his debut album was set to drop? I couldn't believe it. She'd come over lots of times while Troy and his band were staying at my house. He knew all about our relationship. I'd even told him about her one night over tequila. Pfft. Talk about a backstabber."

"Her plan worked, though. You got back together with her after that. Exclusively. For two years."

"Yep. It worked like a charm."

"So, as pissed as you were at Troy, I can't imagine you would have gone *that* scorched-earth on him, if it weren't for your love for Isabel."

He looks at me like I've just said two plus two equals five. "That's what you think? That I dropped Troy's band, and tanked his release, and lost all that money, and all that time and effort because he fucked Isabel? Because you think I *loved* Isabel, that much?"

"Well... *yeah*."

He scoffs. "I beat the shit out of Troy because he betrayed me with Isabel. And because I was jealous as fuck.

But the reason I destroyed Troy's career had nothing to do with Isabel. I'm a businessman, Georgie. I ruined that motherfucker because I'd discovered, thanks to Isabel, he'd put my reputation—my entire *label*—everything I'd worked so hard to create—at risk. More than anything, that's the reason I'll always be grateful to Isabel and have her back. Because she had mine regarding Troy, *big-time*."

I furrow my brow. "But she slept with him."

"To make me jealous. Yeah. But it's what she did afterwards that's the true measure of her heart. Her loyalty. Apparently, when Isabel and Troy were spending some 'alone time' together in the sack, he played her his band's upcoming debut album. According to what Isabel told me, Troy started bragging about how he'd come up with each song on the album, what his 'inspirations' were, blah, blah. And during that conversation, that little shit started bragging to her about how he'd basically ripped off some no-name band's lyrics and melodies on three tracks!"

I gasp.

"Thank God, Isabel had my back, despite everything. She came straight to me to tell me what he'd said to her. And I immediately went and listened to the songs that had 'inspired' Troy, and, holy fuck, he'd literally *stolen* them, practically note for note and word for word."

"Oh my God."

"I mean, all music is derivative in some way. All new songs have been influenced by whatever came before. But there was no question this was outright thievery. Textbook copyright infringement. And on *three* fucking songs." Reed scoffs. "That I knew of. God only knows how many more songs he'd ripped off. So, anyway, right then and there, I knew I couldn't release the album. No way. If someone had figured out the link to those stolen songs after release, River Records never would've weathered the shit storm. We were too new. Still building our reputation. It would have been fatal."

I'm blown away. "This whole time I thought you destroyed Troy because of how much you loved Isabel."

Reed scoffs. "No. I would have released that album, despite Troy sleeping with Isabel, if it hadn't been for those stolen songs. Although, admittedly, I still would have beaten the shit out of him for fucking Isabel."

I can't help chuckling. "What happened with that? Did you head out, expressly planning to beat him up? Or was it a spur of the moment thing?"

Reed smiles wickedly. "I went out, specifically to beat his ass. Isabel came to me and told me about Troy's thievery. And, of course, she made sure I understood she'd acquired the information from Troy while naked in his bed. So, I freaked out, for all the reasons I've described, not just about them having sex. All of it. So, I knew C-Bomb was having a party that night. So I headed over there, and beelined to Troy, and beat the hell out of that punk-ass little bitch, just for the sheer pleasure of it."

I bite my lip. "I guess I'm not the only one who knows how to go 'Left Eye Lopes' on someone, eh?"

He winks.

"Troy didn't tell me about the beating he took at your hands. I guess he didn't want to come off as weak to the woman he was trying to pick up. He also didn't tell me about the copyright infringement stuff. He only said you'd 'blackballed' him to your 'powerful friends' in the industry by telling them a pack of unspecified lies."

Reed scoffs. "Oh, I blackballed him, all right. But only with the truth. I warned anyone who'd listen, even my rivals at competing labels, to steer clear of Troy because he was a liar and a thief." He shrugs. "If that's 'blackballing' someone, then so be it. He deserved it."

"And now he plays every Tuesday and Friday night at Slingers."

"Yeah, when I saw that place, and the bartender

confirmed that's his regular gig, I admit I was damned happy about it. I hope that little shit never plays a venue bigger than Slingers, as long as he lives."

"Backstage, at the RCR concert, when you told me you've 'trained' the guys on your roster not to sleep with anyone you've slept with, you were talking about Troy, I presume?"

"Of course. The guys on my roster have all heard the legend of how Reed dumped a guy's band, and beat his ass, solely for sleeping with his ex. Why should I tell anyone the whole story? The legendary version adds to my mythos as a hard-ass prick. It helps keep everyone in line, in all sorts of ways. Plus, it's a disgrace I never realized Troy's songs were stolen in the first place. Believe me, I'm much more careful and knowledgeable about that sort of thing now. But, yeah. For a whole bunch of reasons, I let everyone think I'm just that ruthless."

I laugh. "I love you so much."

"Glad to hear it. Because I love you."

"So..." I say. "There's something else I want to talk about. Two things I need to come clean about, actually." I take a deep breath. "Stephanie Moreland. I already had a copy of her complaint when I asked you about her in your kitchen."

"I know," he says. "After you got drunk and passed out that night, when I put you to bed, I noticed her complaint sitting in a box at the foot of your bed."

"Oh, snap." I wince. "Were you mad?"

"For a split-second. But quickly, I felt nothing but proud of you. I knew you'd been hired to 'peel my onion.' And that's exactly what you were doing."

Butterflies whoosh into my stomach. God, I love this man. "I hope you know I'd never write about Stephanie in my article about you, any more than I'd write about Troy or Isabel. I only got copies of those three lawsuits—that lease dispute, Stephanie, and Troy—because I was following breadcrumbs. It's what I do. I can't help it. But I've never once considered writing any sort of exposé on you."

"I know that. You were smart to follow every breadcrumb, for both professional and personal reasons. The first night I met you, I told you I admire hustlers. And I meant it."

I beam a huge smile at him. "If you'd snooped a little more into that box, you would have found Troy's complaint at the bottom."

Reed shrugs. "I saw Stephanie's lawsuit on top and didn't have the stomach to root around further. So, what's the second thing you feel the need to 'come clean' about?"

"Yeah. Uh." My cheeks blast with heat. "Howard Devlin. I'm investigating him. Hoping to write an article about him for *Dig a Little Deeper.*"

Reed looks confused. "What's the nature of your 'investigation'? You think Howard has committed financial crimes of some sort?"

I shake my head. "No. I'm gunning for Howard Devlin because I'm ninety-nine percent sure he's a serial sexual predator, and that it's the worst kept secret in Hollywood."

Reed looks deeply shocked, and I know, in my bones, he has no idea about Howard's reputation among the women who've interacted with him.

I tell him everything I know thus far, told to me by CeeCee, Hannah, and Francesca, fully admitting all my information is based on hearsay. All of it adding up to the same conclusion: Howard Devlin almost certainly regularly harasses and/or assaults women. Sometimes, as part of a "casting couch" scenario. Other times, when he's not getting what he wants through coercion and manipulation and dangling carrots, he resorts to flat-out roofie-ing his victims.

"CeeCee gave me the green light to pursue my investigation, full steam ahead, this morning. I called her before boarding my flight and told her about my conversations with Francesca and Hannah. So, I'm a full-fledged investigative reporter now, chasing a story. But I want you to know, I'm not doing it to get back at Isabel, or to hurt or humiliate her in any way. She's irrelevant to my reasons for pursuing this article. But I admit she'll probably feel humiliated, and most likely want to break her engagement, if I'm successful. But I'm not going to hold back on writing this, simply because Isabel happens to be Howard's fiancée and your beloved ex-girlfriend."

"As well you shouldn't. And, to be clear, I didn't love her, Georgie. I never fell in love with her. Now that I love you, I know that for sure."

I touch his cheek. "Do you think Isabel knows about any of those rumors?"

Reed screws up his face. "I can't imagine she does. We've had several conversations about Howard over the years. I used to be annoyed about how obsessed he was with her, and told her so, and she never once said a word about any of this kind of stuff."

"Well, if that's the case, then she's going to get blindsided. People are going to wonder how much she knew, and if she looked the other way, simply because Howard was helping her career. That narrative won't be a good look for 'America's Sweetheart.'"

Reed scrubs the stubble on his chin. "Shit. Maybe I should warn Isabel about him. Or at least, that a potential shit storm is coming her way. I don't know when she's planning to marry him, but she can't go through with it."

"No, Reed. Please. I'm trusting you by telling you about this article. CeeCee told me not to tell anyone. And she specifically told me *not* to let Isabel find out about it, because she's worried Isabel might run to Howard and warn him. And then who knows what Howard might do? What hush money payments he might make to the witnesses I'm going to try to interview?"

Reed looks physically nauseated. And my stomach twists in response.

"If you're thinking of asking me *not* to write this article, then don't. Just like you won't compromise your business judgment for anyone, not even someone you love, I won't compromise my journalistic integrity. This is going to be a huge story. I can feel it. So, please, don't ask me to choose between my love and loyalty to you, and your loyalty to Isabel, versus my convictions and ambition and moral code."

Reed's face softens. He smiles and takes my hand. "So feisty. I love it." He sighs. "Sweetheart, I wasn't thinking, even for a second, of asking you not to write this article. If Howard has done any of this stuff, then I want him taken down, every bit as much as you do."

I exhale with relief. "Really?"

"Of course."

"I thought, maybe, since he's Isabel's fiancé, and you obviously still care about her, you wouldn't want her hit by any sort of scandal."

"I'd rather she's embarrassed by a scandal than married to a monster." He touches my cheek. "And let me be clear about something else, my love. I still care about Isabel. I'm still her friend, whether she believes that or not. But at every turn, at every fork in the road, I'll always, *always* choose *you*, and *us*, and our love, over Isabel or anyone else. *Every fucking time*. That's what I was trying to tell you by sending you that surveillance video. I had the idea to send it to you days ago. But I only did it when I was finally ready to trust you, completely, with the information. Besides trying to vindicate myself, I was telling you I pick you—I pick *us*—over protecting Isabel's secret."

I hug him. "I love you."

"I love you. I choose you, Georgie. Above anything and everyone else."

I kiss his cheek. "I choose you too."

"Write this article about Devlin, baby. Take him down. I'll be with you, cheering you on, every step of the way."

I take a deep breath to quell the surge of adrenaline I'm feeling. "I'm so excited. I really think this article is going to be huge. Plus, I think writing it will give me some much-needed closure about Gates, you know? I need that so much."

Anguish flickers across Reed's chiseled face. He lets out a long, controlled breath. "There's something I need to tell you, love. Something about Gates."

My stomach drops into my toes. "About *Gates*?"

He touches my chin. "Come on. We'll talk about it over dinner. Amalia left food in the fridge for the weekend. Let's eat and have a really nice bottle of wine—and I'll tell you everything."

Chapter 18
Reed

Have you ever heard the term 'white-hat hacker'?" I ask.
Georgina and I are dressed in soft clothes now,
sitting at my kitchen table with one of Amalia's meals and a
bottle of red. And I'm nervous. Yes, *I* know Henn is
completely trustworthy. Even more so than a priest or lawyer.
But *Georgie* doesn't know that. What if she finds out I told
Henn about Gates, out of pure necessity, and decides, once
and for all, she can't trust me to keep a promise? If me telling
Henn about Gates is the straw that breaks Georgina's back,
and she leaves me again—for good, this time—*after* I've said
those three little words to her—words I've never said to
another woman—then I'm positive I won't survive it.

Georgina says, "White-hat hackers are the ones who help
companies find vulnerabilities in their online systems, so the
bad guys can't hack them."

My heart is thundering. "That's right. Well, Henn is one
of the best white-hat hackers in the world. Sometimes, he does
favors for good friends, including me. In fact, if he believes in
the cause enough, he'll even don a grey—or maybe even
black—hat, on occasion."

Georgie lights up. "Oooh! You think maybe Henn would
hack into Howard's computer for me?"

Damn. I probably shouldn't have led with that. "Uh...
No. I mean, maybe. But Howard wasn't the reason I
mentioned Henn." I take a deep breath. "Georgie, I had Henn

gather some information for me about Gates. So I could find something to destroy him with."

Georgina's nostrils flare. But she says nothing.

"When you told me what Gates did, I wanted to kill him. Literally. I still do. But since murder is apparently hard to get away with, according to Leonard, and I very much enjoy my freedom—I decided to destroy Gates in a more indirect way. I figured he'd have a stash of child porn, or maybe Henn would find proof he'd embezzled from the school or something. I didn't know what Henn would find. All I knew, in my bones, was a guy like Gates couldn't be living a squeaky-clean life."

Georgina blinks slowly... and exhales.

"I'm sorry I breached your confidence by telling Henn your secret."

"What, exactly, did you tell him?"

"The gist of what you'd told me. Gates was your teacher in high school, someone you trusted, and he tried to rape you, but you got away. I also told him you've been deeply traumatized by the incident."

"He's the only person you've told about this?"

"Yes. And I told him not to tell anyone, not even Hannah. And I know he hasn't. Please, don't be angry. Please, Georgina, don't leave me."

Her features soften with pity. "Oh, Reed." She gets up and slides into my lap. "I'm not going to leave you. This is DMV-serious, remember?" She touches my cheek. "I like that you felt so protective of me, you roped Henn into helping you." She smiles. "It turns me on that you did that, if I'm being honest."

I'm so relieved, I can only exhale loudly.

Georgina chuckles. "You poor thing. You really thought I'd *leave* you for telling Henn?"

"Georgina, when it comes to you, I never know what you're going to do. And I know we're only just beginning to rebuild trust. I don't want there to be any reason for you to doubt me, ever."

She presses her forehead against mine. "Don't cheat on

me. Don't lie to me. Don't you dare smack me. But anything else, we'll work it out. I'm not going anywhere, ever."

Again, I breathe a sigh of relief. "Don't cheat on me. Don't lie to me. Feel free to smack me, any time. Especially in bed. But, please, for the love of all things holy, do not put a scratch on my Bugatti."

"Deal." She kisses my cheek and returns to her chair. "So, did Henn find something useful?"

"He did. And what he found led him to hacking the principal of your high school and another guy—a renowned criminal defense attorney named Steven Price. AKA the father of the Price Brothers: Brody, Brendan, and Benjamin."

"I remember Brody. He was a year behind me. The star quarterback. I don't remember his brothers, though."

"You wouldn't. Brendan was two years behind Brody, and Benjamin a year behind him, so you were long gone by the time the two younger Price brothers got *their* starting quarterback gigs."

"What does the father of the Price brothers have to do with Gates?"

"Steven Price confidentially paid hush money to two female students who'd been assaulted by Gates."

Georgina gasps.

"There might be more victims besides those two other girls and you. Maybe more girls, like you, who told nobody. But, thanks to Henn, we know, for sure, there were at least three total girls, including you. One before you. One after you. The before you was a sixteen-year-old named Katrina Ibarra. Gates raped her a year and a half before he tried to rape you."

"Oh my God."

"It was smack in the middle of football season, when scouts from all the top colleges were actively trying to recruit Brody Price. Hence, the motivation for Steven Price to keep that information from coming out and disrupting his son's football program."

"This is... crazy."

"The second girl, the one after you, was a fifteen-year-old named Penny Kaling. It's not clear exactly the nature of Gates' sexual assault of her. All we know, for sure, from some text messages, is that Gates forced himself on Penny in some way, and she was scared and ashamed and extremely upset about it the next day."

Georgina looks ashen. "You realize what this means, right? If I'd reported Gates, I could have saved Penny from whatever happened to her."

"Not necessarily. Katrina reported him and it got her nowhere. She told a teacher, who told the principal, who then called Katrina and Gates into his office for separate interviews. After those interviews, the principal, in his infinite wisdom, determined Katrina's claim 'wasn't credible.' And that was that. He swept it under the rug and didn't send it up the flagpole to anyone else."

"How is that possible?"

I shrug. "Gates denied all wrongdoing, and the principal believed him. Gates said Katrina was an unstable girl with a crush who'd thrown herself at Gates and gotten rejected—and, now, she was getting back at him. Lucky for Gates, Katrina wasn't a star pupil. She'd been suspended the prior year for plagiarism. Plus, she was known for being a 'drama queen' after a couple breakups. So, the principal decided it was a 'he said, she said' situation, where the accuser wasn't credible, and the accused was a 'well-respected and admired pillar of our community.' Oh, and by the way, the football team was having an undefeated season at this point."

Georgina hangs her head. "I should have known he'd do it to someone else."

"Look at me, Georgina. You were seventeen and in survival mode. If you'd said something, I doubt it would have made a difference. There were no witnesses to your assault, any more than there were to Katrina's. If you'd accused Gates of trying to rape you, maybe those mean girls from the newspaper class would have come forward to say you'd always had a 'thing' for Mr. Gates. Maybe you would have been labeled a 'drama queen,' the same as Katrina. Has there ever been a time in high school when you lost your temper, or maybe got highly emotional, or displayed some sort of behavior Gates or the principal could have pointed to in order to paint you as an 'overly emotional' and 'unstable' drama queen, too?"

"Well, of course. I was a teenage girl who wound up breaking down every year on the anniversary of her mother's death."

"Well, there you go."

Georgina sighs. "So, how did Steven Price get involved?"

"Gates contacted him and told him some 'crazy' girl was making accusations against him. At the time, Brody was being courted by the best colleges in the country. So, Steven Price told Gates not to worry about it. He'd take care of it. And he did. He paid Katrina off. Well, Katrina and her mother, since Katrina was a minor."

"I can't believe her mother took that money."

"Don't judge her too harshly. Katrina's father wasn't in the picture. Her mother, an immigrant, worked three jobs. So, a hundred grand was life-changing money to that family. All Katrina had to do was transfer schools and shut the fuck up about Gates forevermore. I can't really blame them for taking the deal, especially after the principal had basically called her a liar. I'm sure Katrina figured a hundred grand in her and her mother's pockets would help her a whole lot more than going to the police and being called a liar again."

Georgina looks down at her wine glass on the table, shaking her head. "What about the other girl? Did she get paid off, too?"

"She did. Penny was fifteen when Gates did whatever he did to her. A sophomore on the newspaper staff. Unlike

Katrina, she didn't report him to anyone. But we have text messages between Penny and Gates, where she tells him she feels 'sick' about what she 'let' him do to her and that she'd been crying nonstop about it all day. She says she'd never done anything like that before and she feels like throwing up every time she thinks about it. Next thing you know, Steven Price was wiring Penny and her mother two hundred grand as part of a confidential settlement."

"No father in the picture?"

"No father. Not sure if that was a coincidence or a sign of Gates' MO. Maybe he figured girls with one parent at home, like you, had less of a support system. Or maybe he thought one parent would be easier to convince, later on, that nothing happened. Either way, by the time Gates assaulted Penny, he was Steven Price's man. Brody had gone on to play football at Purdue. His first pick. And the next Price brother, Brendon, was having a golden season and getting courted by top colleges."

"And the principal?"

"It's not clear what he knew about Penny. We found nothing to indicate he knew anything. But who knows?"

Georgina picks up her wine glass and takes a long gulp. When she replaces her glass, she puts her elbows onto the table and sinks her face into her hands. "This is... horrible."

I get up and pull her to me. Take her into my arms. Hold her tight and kiss her cheek. "Don't beat yourself up about not telling anyone. You did the best you could under the circumstances."

"But I'm not seventeen anymore."

"No, you're not."

"But what good would it do to speak up now? It's been almost five years since he tried to rape me—and it'd still be my word against his because those other two girls signed confidentiality agreements. I'd be on my own, the same as always. He said, she said. Only, now, five years later."

"The truth is the truth, whether anyone believes you or not. Maybe, if you speak up, you'll save the next girl. And if you don't, at least you tried."

She makes a tortured sound. "I need some time to think. Can you send me everything Henn sent you?"

"Of course. How about you read it *after* we get back from New York, though? Like you said, it's been almost five years. Surely, it can wait another five days. In the meantime, let's have fun and celebrate your birthday and forget about this shit."

She looks grateful for the suggestion. "Yes. I'd like that."

"In fact, let's kick off that game plan, starting now." Without hesitation, I scoop my beloved butterfly into my arms like a bride, making her swoon audibly. "Come on, beautiful. One giant dose of pleasure-induced amnesia, coming right up."

Chapter 19
Georgina

I'm deliciously tipsy as I stare at Reed's gyrating, muscular ass in the mirrored ceiling. My wrists are bound. So are my ankles. I'm spread eagle as Reed fucks me. Staring at that mouthwatering ass. The way his hard muscles clench and unclench magnificently with each beastly thrust is sublime. And the best part? As Reed claims me, he keeps whispering to me in a husky growl. He tells me he loves me. That he worships me. He says I own him. And in reply, I'm groaning out words like "I love you" and "so good" and "that ass!" And, of course, the words Mr. Hottie told me to say the first time he laid eyes on me at the panel discussion: "Yes... yes... *yes*."

When I reach climax this time, I feel like I'm having a seizure. Which, in fact, I think I am. And, of course, my release sends Reed over the edge, too.

With a soft kiss to my lips, Reed unties me and pulls me to him, and I cleave my naked body to his, leaving not even the slightest space between us, literally or figuratively.

We talk about tomorrow's trip to New York. About how excited Reed is to show me the City for my first time.

"And then you know what we're going to do?" he says excitedly. "On your birthday itself, we'll swing by Boston to see Alessandra."

I shriek with joy and pepper his face with kisses and then, just because I know it's his favorite thing, leap up and do a particularly jiggly happy dance that makes Reed hoot and guffaw and applaud. And, finally, I dive back into bed and assault my man with enthusiastic kisses.

"If it turns out Alessandra isn't comfortable around me," Reed says, "then no worries. I'll give you two money to have a nice lunch or dinner without me."

"Oh, honey, Alessandra will be thrilled to see you. You're the reason she got that gig at the coffee house. I know she's dying to thank you."

Reed looks genuinely thrilled. "Well, in that case, why don't you ask Alessandra if she can get onto the schedule to perform at the coffee house the night we'll be in Boston. We'll do lunch that day, and watch Alessandra that night."

My heart lurches. Oh, man, this could be a *huge* opportunity for Alessandra! If she hits it out of the park, who knows what Reed might do? I take a deep breath and try not to sound like I'm totally freaking out. "Yeah, good idea. I'll tell her. But only if you promise me one thing."

"Anything."

"Don't give me any more gifts, okay? You've already given me too much, and I've given you nothing. This trip to New York and Boston—that's my only birthday present, okay? Nothing else."

"Okay, first off. You haven't given me *nothing*. Every time you give me a happy dance, especially a naked one, it's the best gift *ever.*"

I giggle.

"And, second off, nobody—not even you—is going to tell me what I can and can't give the woman I love. So fuck off with that shit."

I feign shock and flip him off. And he feigns outrage and lurches at me like a bear and then proceeds to eat my extended middle finger, and then my arm, making comical "nom, nom, nom!" noises, as he does.

Finally, when Reed is done devouring my arms and neck and breasts and ears, he pulls back from our silliness and looks down at me with twinkling brown eyes. "This is going to be so much fun," he says. And I know he's not talking about our trip to New York.

Chapter 20
Reed

G eorgina!" Owen says warmly, embracing her. "It's great to see you!"

"It's great to see you! You look dapper."

Georgina and Owen are having this conversation in front of me in a backstage hallway at Madison Square Garden. Owen has been in New York the past few days, working as the point of contact for a documentary film crew shooting tonight's RCR concert for a Netflix special. And, of course, the Intrepid Reporter is here to do a quick interview of RCR.

"And you're perfection!" Owen coos to Georgina. "The lady in red. That ruby necklace is a show-stopper."

Georgina touches the gems around her neck and looks at me. "It was a gift from my generous boyfriend."

Owen already knows that, of course. He's the point of contact for both my accountant and bookkeeper, so he's well aware of any large purchase I might make. But Owen, smart man that he is, plays along. "That was quite a gift. Sounds like someone is smitten. And I can see why."

"Sorry to interrupt this lovefest,'" I say dryly. "Is everything all set for filming? Did Andrew get my notes on those shots I want him to get?"

Owen nods. "Andrew's got a skeleton crew in the guys' dressing room now, capturing that behind-the-scenes idea you had." He looks at Georgina. "The band is expecting you. I told them to allot forty-five minutes. Is that enough time?"

"Double what I need, probably. The special issue will be focusing a lot more on Dean, individually, than the full band, so we only need a quickie with all four."

We head off toward the dressing room, at which point Owen leans into me and whispers, "Wow, boss, this is quite a 'purely professional relationship' you're having."

Inside the dressing room, we find all four guys of Red Card Riot, as expected, plus their usual entourage, plus, a skeleton crew for the documentary. And, last but not least, there are several PAs flitting around the room... including, to my delight, the little waif who walked in on Georgina and me backstage at the Rose Bowl, when I was camped between Georgina's naked thighs.

"You remember Georgina?" I say to RCR. And all four of them—Dean, Clay, Emmitt, and C-Bomb—immediately come over to greet her. But nobody more enthusiastically than C-Bomb—Caleb Baumgarten—who strides over, hugs Georgina with fervor, like she's his long-lost lover.

As small talk ensues, I steal a glance at the little PA from the Rose Bowl to find her looking at me like she's a mutt at the pound who just took a crap in her food bowl. I smile at her reassuringly, but it's no use. She's terrified of me. Not at all happy to see me, to put it mildly.

When I return my attention to the band and Georgina, they've already moved to a nearby sitting area, so I follow them and take a chair behind Georgina, where I've got a direct line to C-Bomb. *Keep your friends close and your enemies closer.*

C-Bomb asks Georgina—but not me—if she'd like a drink. Georgina declines, explaining, "I drank too much champagne on the flight here. It's my first time in New York, plus my birthday week, so I went a little crazy with the bubbly."

C-Bomb looks like a shark smelling blood. "Your first time in New York *and* your birthday week? This calls for celebration. Come to our party after the show tonight, and we'll make you our guest of honor."

Motherfucker.

"Oh, that's sweet of you!" Georgie says. "But I've already got plans tonight."

C-Bomb is undeterred. "How about tomorrow, then? We're not leaving New York until Wednesday. I'll show you all the tourist spots by day. And take you for the best pizza you've ever had by night."

I'm a hair's breadth away from launching out of my chair, grabbing C-Bomb by his mohawk, and dragging his tattooed ass out of the dressing room. But, quickly, it's clear there's no need for me to intervene. My baby's got this.

"Thanks for the offer," Georgina says sweetly. "But I'm here with my boyfriend. He knows New York really well. I'm sure he'll be taking me to a great pizza place."

Oh, how I love this brilliant, gorgeous woman. And, oooooh, how I love seeing Caleb look like he just got punched in the balls.

"Cool," Caleb says. And that's it. He sinks into his chair, looking defeated.

"What are you and your *boyfriend* planning to do while you're in town?" Clay, the bassist, asks, and it's clear his question is only designed to razz his drummer.

"Oh, the usual tourist things," Georgina says. She rattles off everything we've talked about doing during our stay, and then adds, "Plus, we're going to visit family." I'm assuming her comment refers to our planned detour to Boston, until she says, "My boyfriend's mother lives in Scarsdale and he always visits her when he comes to the East Coast."

My heart stops.

No.

How did I not see that one coming?

Georgie has made it clear she wants us to "come clean" with each other—to trust each other "completely," as she keeps saying. And, of course, I'm fully on board with that plan. But only in regard to stuff that *directly* affects Georgina.

Not *everything* about me. And certainly not about my mother. I've spent my entire life lying to people about my mother! Literally, my *entire* life. And I can't suddenly stop doing it, just because I've fallen head over heels in love.

When I was in grade school, I remember telling classmates my mother was a firefighter who worked crazy hours down at the station, which was why my nanny, Amalia, and not my mother, was the one who showed up for school functions. Also, why I had to be so quiet during the day—so my mother could sleep at odd hours. Looking back, it was an interesting choice of profession for her, but my undeveloped brain thought it was a stroke of brilliance at the time.

By middle school, I'd grown savvy enough to realize my mother's slight frame made the firefighting story wholly unbelievable. So, *voila,* she became the US Ambassador to France.

After that, during my first year of high school, once I'd started living at that horrid group home, I remember telling the other kids both my parents had died in a plane crash. Which, in my mind, was a whole lot better than admitting I was in foster care because my mother was in a mental facility and my father in prison for bilking innocent people out of their life savings, and all my relatives had decided I was too big a pain in the ass—my anger issues way too difficult to manage—to deal with me. Not to mention, they'd all figured out there was no pot of gold at the end of the rainbow for anyone who took me in.

Granted, lying about my father's death in high school came back to bite me in the ass a few times, whenever I happened to be talking to a kid who followed current events, and therefore knew all about my notorious father. But, mostly, my lie that I was an orphan worked out just fine, especially in relation to my dead mother. Which was good. The fewer questions about her, the better.

After my father killed himself during my first year of

college, I abruptly stopped telling people Mom was dead. Instead, she became the mother of my current lies. The one living her best life. The one who does yoga and paints and plays Scrabble like a boss. And that's the mother she's going to remain, even with Georgina. Especially with Georgina. Because, now that I'm truly happy and in love for the first time in my life, the only thing I want to do, more than ever, is look *forward*, not back. Why would I want my relationship with Georgina to get dragged down by the shit that's always dragged me down my entire fucking life?

I take a deep, calming breath. It's fine. I'll simply tell Georgina my mother isn't available for a visit this time. I'll say she's got a friend staying with her. Or that she's out of town, visiting a friend in Paris. Or Toronto. And on our next visit to New York, I'll make excuses that time, too. And then, again and again. And if Georgina starts asking me why she *still* hasn't met my mother, down the line, I'll deal with it then. Who knows? Maybe I'll feel ready at some point to tell Georgina the truth. Maybe one day I'll tell her about all the tragedies that have left my mother irrevocably broken. The tragedies sitting like an elephant on my chest every day of my life. But today isn't that day.

Everyone around me chuckles, drawing me out of my thoughts—and I realize Georgina is in the midst of a raucous interview of RCR. I watch her for a moment, marveling at her confidence and charisma. At how obviously she's charmed each and every one of them. Not just C-Bomb.

After a moment, my eyes drift to that PA, the one who walked in on Georgina and me. She's sitting in a far corner, watching the interview. And when her eyes happen to land on mine, she flashes me a pitiful look that practically screams, *I swear I didn't tell anyone what I saw!* before quickly looking away, her face flushed.

I resist the urge to smile at her misery—because, man, it's highly amusing to me—and, instead, shift my eyes to

Dean. My golden goose. The face and voice and brilliant mind that launched my empire. He's a fucking genius, that man. And a great guy, too. Can't say the same thing about his best friend. Speaking of which... my eyes snap back to C-Bomb to find him glaring at me.

Fuck you, I shoot him nonverbally, with a little lift of my chin.

He returns the glare and the gesture. And then does something that makes my blood simmer. He looks at Georgina lasciviously, and then back at me, and flashes me a look that plainly says, *Looks like we both missed out on that one, eh?* He winks, like he's taking great pleasure in knowing I won't get to tap that ass, any more than he will.

And that's it. My blood flash-boils. I look away, forcing myself not to shoot him a smug look that will telegraph I've already tapped that ass, motherfucker... and it was the best ass I've ever had.

Goddammit. Clearly, my scare tactics with that little PA worked *too* well, because there's no doubt in my mind she didn't tell C-Bomb, or anyone else, what she saw going down in that dressing room. Or, rather, *who* she saw going down. When C-Bomb heard I'd nixed Georgina's plans to attend his party and tag along on tour, he must have figured I did that because I wanted Georgina for myself... but *not* because I'd *already* successfully gotten her. And that pisses me off to no end. Sitting here now, I *want* Caleb to know I've fucked Georgina. I want him to know I'm fucking her every night of my life. In fact, I want every fuckboy on my label to know it. Even the nice guys, too. I want the whole *world* to know Georgina is mine. In fact, I want to take out a full-page ad in *Rock 'n' Roll* to broadcast the truth: *I love Georgina Ricci... and, miraculously, she loves me, too, motherfuckers*!

There's more laughter that draws my attention. I look at Georgina. She's having a great old time with the band. And, suddenly, I feel like a man possessed. Obsessed with the idea of C-Bomb, and the other band members, knowing *I'm* the "boyfriend" Georgina just mentioned.

"Awesome, guys," Georgina says. She rises from her seat. "That's all I need."

The guys thank Georgina. Dean wishes her a great time in New York and a happy birthday. The other guys follow suit, with Clay specifically telling her to have fun with her "boyfriend." Georgina wishes the band a great show. And in the middle of all that, Owen arrives with a small group of VIPs who've come to meet the band.

I shake hands with the VIPs and introduce them to the guys, and then to Georgina—but only as a reporter for *Rock 'n' Roll*. Not as my girlfriend. Because that's what Georgina has specifically said she wants, whenever we're interacting with my artists. But this time, unlike all times before, not getting to call Georgina my *girlfriend* is driving me batshit crazy. I want—no, I *need*—the world to know she's mine.

As the VIPs take their selfies with the band, I pull Georgina aside. "I need to talk to you about something."

She looks concerned. "Are you okay?"

I glance at C-Bomb, and force myself, through sheer force of will, not to kiss Georgie, right here and now, so he can see me do it. "No, actually, I'm not. Come on, Miss Ricci. Follow me."

Chapter 21
Georgina

R eed leads me down a hallway into an empty dressing room, where he closes the door and guides me to a couch. "I can't do it anymore," he blurts. "I can't hide that you're mine and I'm yours. I want everyone, especially my artists, to know it."

I exhale with relief. "Oh, God. I thought it was something serious."

He pulls on me roughly, animalistically, sending arousal whooshing between my legs, and guides me to straddle him on the couch. "I want to shout from the highest rooftops, 'She's mine!' I know you don't want my artists to know, but I—"

"Go for it," I say, and Reed's face ignites. "I don't want to hide our relationship, either. If someone thinks I'm too young for you, or they don't take me seriously as a writer because they think you pulled strings—screw 'em. *Ciao, stronzo.*"

Reed crushes his mouth to mine, and we kiss passionately. Until, soon, predictably, we're both on fire. Making out energetically. Groping. Grinding. Devouring. You know. Being us.

Reed pulls my shirt up and deftly unlatches my bra. With a growl of arousal, he buries his face in my breasts and sucks on my nipple, making me moan—

"Oh, no!" a female voice blurts in the doorway, making

me leap off Reed onto the couch and scramble to cover myself.

"Don't leave, little PA," Reed says calmly. "I want to speak to you about this."

And that's when I see her. The *same* PA from the Rose Bowl. Standing in the doorway, her ashen face turned away.

"I didn't see anything, Mr. Rivers!" she shouts. "Not a thing!"

"You can go," I say. "I'm sorry you had to see this again."

"No, you may *not* go," Reed corrects firmly. "Come here. Miss Ricci's got her shirt on now. I want to speak to you."

"*Reed*," I chastise. "Let her go."

"Not a chance. Come here, little PA. Right now."

With a loud sigh, the poor PA drags herself across the room like a shackled prisoner and stands before us, her brow furrowed with anxiety. "I didn't see anything except two people having a conversation."

Oh, man, Reed is smiling like a possum with a sweet potato. Obviously, he's *loving* this. "What's your name, again?" he asks, his dark eyes glinting with the purest form of glee.

"Amy O'Brien. Mr. Rivers, I don't know how this happened again. There must have been a mix-up. Owen told me to come in here, right away, to talk to you. He said you texted him that you needed to see me *urgently*. In *this* dressing room."

Full understanding of Reed's wickedness slams me upside the head. I swat Reed's broad shoulder. "Reed Rivers! You're evil!"

He bites back a smile and calmly addresses Amy. "Remember that time at the Rose Bowl, when you *thought* you saw Miss Ricci and me doing something in a dressing room, but you were mistaken, because we were only talking?"

"Yes, sir. I didn't say a word to C-Bomb or anyone else about—"

"Yes, I know. I believe you. I want to remind you that you're still bound by your NDA with respect to that incident."

"Yes, sir. Same as now."

"No, not the same as now," he says, shocking me. "I mean, you *are* bound by your NDA, of course. But I'm giving you special permission to talk about what you just saw. In fact, I *want* you to talk about what you saw, just now, to anyone and everyone on this tour. *Especially C-Bomb.*"

I inhale sharply, floored by Reed's diabolical machinations. But I must admit, I'm holding back a smile. He's evil, yes. But he's damned sexy, too.

Reed says, "In fact, if you blab to C-Bomb about what you just witnessed, before he takes the stage tonight, I'll personally make sure you get a thousand-dollar bonus added to your next paycheck."

Amy's eyebrows shoot up. Obviously, that's a lot of money to her. "What, exactly, do you want me to say to C-Bomb, sir?"

"The truth. What you saw when you poked your head into the room. For real. Now, to be clear, last time is still off limits, Amy. But *this* time, fire away. In fact, let me give you a little something else to gossip about." He turns and smiles devilishly at me. "Georgina Ricci, I love you, baby."

I can't help smiling broadly. "I love you, too, Reed Rivers."

"And I don't mean that platonically," he adds. "I very much enjoy having sex with you, every single day."

I giggle. "I'm glad. Because I very much enjoy having sex with you."

Reed kisses me briefly, but sensuously—definitely *not* platonically—before returning to Amy with a smirk. "Did you catch all that, Amy O'Brien?"

She makes a face that plainly conveys her mistrust. Like she's wondering, *Is this a trap?* "Uhh," she says. "I think so?"

"We can do it for you again, if you're not clear."

"No, I am. And, congratulations. You two are an incredibly attractive couple. But... I just want to make sure I understand, out of an abundance of caution. You want me to be *honest* about what I've seen and heard tonight... with *Caleb*?"

"Correct," Reed says. "Tell everyone and anyone, as you like. But if you want to earn that bonus, you'll tell Caleb *tonight*."

She looks at me. "Are you okay with me doing this, Miss Ricci?"

"I'm thrilled about it, Amy. But thanks for asking."

"Okay, then. Sure. I'll head straight to C-Bomb now."

"Actually, hold on." Reed grabs his wallet, counts out ten bills, and hands them to Amy. "I trust you to earn it. There's no need for us to deal with payroll on this."

Amy takes the cash with a shy smile and disappears out the door, presumably to babble to C-Bomb about the shocking thing she's just witnessed.

"You're a sadist," I say. "That poor girl was nearly crapping her pants *again*. And you clearly enjoyed it."

"She's a PA on tour with a rock band. If she can't handle walking in on a make-out session a few times, she needs a new profession." He smirks. "Now, where were we, sexy girl?"

"Not so fast. When you texted Owen and arranged for that poor girl to walk in on us again, you didn't know I was going to say yes about you telling the world about us."

He shrugs, not understanding my meaning.

"*What if I'd said no?*"

"Then I would have put the fear of God into Amy O'Brien about her NDA, *again*. But, either way, I would have had the pleasure of getting walked-in on again. One of my all-time biggest turn-ons."

My jaw drops to the floor.

"Oh, please. You love getting walked-in on as much as I do."

"I do *not*."

"Liar. You love it."

"No, I don't."

"Yep. And you can't convince me otherwise."

I twist my mouth. "Okay, I admit it's a turn-on for me to see how much it turns *you* on. But that's as far as I'll go." Laughing, I slide onto his lap again, and we begin making out enthusiastically... until I remember the door to the dressing room is unlocked. "Hold on. Who knows who else you've arranged to 'accidentally' walk in on us." With a little bite to Reed's earlobe, I get up and lock the door—a move that elicits a booming and fervent "Boooo!" from Reed. And when I return to my hot boyfriend, his face, and the bulge behind his pants, tell me he's as aroused as I am.

Standing over him, I reach inside my skirt, pull off my cotton undies, and fling them onto the floor with gusto. And then, licking my lips, I slowly kneel before him, unzip his fly, pull out his hard shaft, lick him from his balls to his mushroom tip, and get to work. I lick and suck and deep-throat him with everything I've got, enjoying every groan and shudder and yank of my hair, until Reed is growling and quaking so fervently, I know he's on the bitter edge.

My heart pounding along with my clit, I get up, straddle him, and slide myself down onto his hardness. And the moment I'm positioned, Reed grabs my hips and roughly leads my movement, until we're both losing our minds. Release comes for Reed first—which isn't a surprise, considering the epic blowjob I just gave him. But after he comes, he kisses and touches me to a rolling, rocking orgasm that curls my toes and makes me wish he already had another erection I could suck.

I collapse onto him, feeling utterly euphoric. Swept away. Closer to him than ever. We're not going to hide our love anymore. From *anyone*. It's a dream come true.

I kiss his cheek. "So, I'm assuming you're planning to visit your mother during this trip, like always, right?"

Reed stiffens against me. "Uh. No, actually. Not this time. My mother is out of town. She's visiting a friend."

I bite my lip, trying not to smile in reaction to his lie. Oh, Reed. My beautiful, beloved liar. . . I was hoping he'd tell me the truth without coaxing. But I suppose old habits die hard. "Oh, yeah? How nice for her. Where does this friend of your mother's live?"

Reed pauses. His chest heaves. "In... I don't know, actually. I didn't ask. She's out of town. Somewhere."

I press my forehead against Reed's and exhale. "My love. I know all about your mother."

His breathing hitches. "What do you mean?"

"I know your mother isn't visiting a friend. I know she lives in a mental facility in Scarsdale. And I know and understand why you don't like to talk about that."

Reed has turned into a trapped animal, looking for a way out. With a soft whisper of reassurance, I caress his chiseled face. Kiss his cheek. Skim his lips with mine. "You don't have to spill your guts to me about her. Or about anything else that's been hard for you in your life. You're a private person, and I get that. I respect it. But you can't flat-out lie to me anymore, okay? Those days are over. We don't lie to each other about *anything*. You don't want to talk about something? You say so. *But you will not lie.* And neither will I. Which is why I'm confessing to you: I know all about your mother. And your childhood. I know about Oliver. And the divorce. I know *why* your mother lives in that mental facility, and why she's lived in one, almost continuously, since you were nine."

Somewhere in the arena, Red Card Riot launches into their first song. But I don't react. Because I don't care if we miss this entire concert *again*. All I care about is making my beloved Reed understand that I love him unconditionally. For real. The good, the bad, and the ugly.

I put my palms on his cheeks. "I'm not trying to force you

to talk about this stuff with me. I just want you to know I love you. The *real* you. And, also, that I *admire* and *respect* you for overcoming so much to become the glorious man you are."

Reed looks flabbergasted. "How the hell do you know all this?"

I tell him about the legal malpractice lawsuit—which, to my surprise, he knows nothing about. He asks me some questions about it, which I answer. He asks me how long I've known about his mother being in a facility, and I tell him I've known since almost day one, thanks to a conversation with Amalia, during which I coaxed her into revealing certain things without her realizing I didn't already know them. "But I didn't read the malpractice lawsuit until a few days ago," I say. "That's where I got a far more thorough understanding of your childhood and everything your poor mother's been through."

Red Card Riot begins playing their debut hit, "Shaynee," in a distant part of the arena. My favorite RCR song. But, again, we don't react.

"I'd like to read those documents from the legal malpractice case," Reed says.

"Of course. You were so young during the divorce. I think reading them now will help you understand your mother, so much better. The deck has always been stacked against her, one way or another. I feel so bad for her." Reed looks like he's fighting his emotions, so I take his hand and bring his knuckles to my lips. "I think *not* talking about, or thinking about, things that are painful for you, has been your coping mechanism for a long time. I can relate. But, speaking for myself, I don't want to do that anymore. Not with *you*. I want to tell you everything. I want to show you every part of me. And I'd love for you to do the same with me. Reed, when we say, 'I love you' to each other, I want us to know the word 'you' means '*all* of you.' Not only the good parts we show everyone else."

Reed's Adam's apple bobs.

I feel overwhelmed with love for him. "Do we have a deal? No more secrets?"

Reed opens his mouth like he's going to say *yes*. But then he closes it and scowls. "No more secrets *at all*... about *anything*?"

I can't help chuckling at his facial expression. It's as if I've asked him to bring me a slice of the moon to put onto a cracker. "Correct. *Zero* secrets. No gray area."

Reed looks dubious. "I don't know, baby. Don't you think that's unrealistic? A guy's got to have *some* secrets. At least, small ones."

"Why? If they're little ones, all the more reason not to have them. Let's be open books."

Reed scrubs his face and exhales.

"What is it?" I say. "Spit it out, already."

He sinks into the couch in surrender. "Your necklace."

"Those aren't real rubies?"

He rolls his eyes. "Don't insult me. Of course, they're real. It's just that..." He exhales. "The necklace is worth quite a bit more than I told you. I wanted to pay off your father's mortgage, and I figured if the price tag for the necklace happened to be the same amount as what he owed, you'd think it was fate and let me 'return it,' so you could use the proceeds to pay off the loan."

I'm slack-jawed. "Our *entire* conversation about the necklace was—"

"A set-up. Yes. I knew what you'd say and do, so I arranged a situation that would lead to you saying and doing all of it, so you'd let me pay off the loan, without you being stubborn and contrary."

"And you think *I'm* the Bobby Fischer in this relationship?"

"Takes one to know one, baby. Don't bother asking me the actual value of the necklace. I think the monetary value of

160

gifts should be exempt from our new 'open book' policy, don't you? But if we're truly going to tell each other the truth about 'everything,' other than the value of gifts, then I guess I should come clean about the necklace being part of my clever strategy to save your dad's condo from foreclosure."

I kiss him enthusiastically. "*Thank you.* You're the sweetest, most generous, most adorable man in the world."

"Only for you. Honestly, I was initially planning to buy something worth exactly eighty grand, so I could return it, and use the proceeds, just like I said. But then, I saw the ruby necklace on display on the other side of the store, and, the minute I saw it, I knew it had to be yours, no matter the price."

I gasp. "You didn't walk past Tiffany's and see the necklace in the store window?"

He snorts. "No. My meeting was in Century City. Not Beverly Hills."

I laugh uproariously, and so does he.

"I'm so relieved," I admit. "When you said you didn't think complete honesty was realistic, I thought you were going to drop a bombshell on me."

"Nah. I've got no more bombshells to drop, sweetheart. I'm done with those."

"So am I." I kiss him again, feeling like my soul is soaring around the small dressing room. "So, it's a deal. No more lies, from either of us. Ever again. Unless it's about the price tag of a gift or, you know, like about a surprise party or something like that. *But that's it.*"

Reed pauses underneath me, and I know he's thinking, *Shit.*

"What now?" I say. I pull out of our embrace and look at him sternly. "Whatever it is, spit it out, dude. Let's get it all out in the open."

Reed flaps his lips together. "It pertains to a gift, so I feel like it could very well be exempt."

"Except you know that's not true, or else you wouldn't look guilty as sin right now."

He grunts.

"Tell me." I pinch his face between my finger and thumb, making his lips part. "The truth shall set you free. *Speak.*"

Reed exhales and I release his face.

"The 'rental car' I got you for the summer?"

I gasp. "No. *Reed.*"

He winks. "Happy birthday, baby. It's all yours."

Chapter 22
Reed

Feel free to go to a diner or something," I say to my usual New York driver, Tony, as he parks the sedan in front of my mother's facility. "I'll text you when we're about fifteen minutes out."

"You got it, Mr. Rivers."

I look at Georgina sitting next to me in the back seat. Never in a million years did I think I'd bring a girlfriend to meet my mother. How did Georgina convince me to do this?

"This is going to be great," she says, reading my mind. "You've briefed me for three days, love. I know what to expect."

She's right. Over the past three days, as Georgina and I have painted Manhattan red, visiting all the usual tourist spots, watching Broadway shows, and eating at fabulous restaurants, she's slowly, but surely, peeled every layer of my onion, all the way down to the nub. Down to my deepest core. To my darkest secrets and sources of shame and embarrassment and pain and insecurity. And to my surprise, with each new layer uncovered, I've found myself feeling *more* comfortable and in love with Georgina. Not less. And, slowly, I've felt that lifelong elephant, who lives on my chest, getting up and wandering off into parts unknown.

"Did you tell your mother I was coming today?" Georgina asks.

"No. I didn't want to answer any questions in advance.

So, don't take it personally when she stares at you, mouth agape, like you're an alien from Mars." I look at the front door of the facility, without moving.

"It's going to be great," she says, patting me reassuringly.

I exhale and open the car door. "Well, here goes nothing."

Inside the lobby, the orderly behind the front desk, Oscar, looks shocked as we approach. And I'm not surprised. In all my years of coming here, I've never once shown up with a plus-one.

I introduce Georgina, calling her my girlfriend, which feels amazing, and then set about leafing through the logbook, as usual, to confirm my mother's paid "best friend" has been doing her job. When I'm satisfied she has, I slide the logbook to Georgina for her signature, and ask Oscar where I might find my mother.

Oscar glances at the wall clock. "With such nice weather, I'd try the garden first."

And off we go.

Once inside the garden, Georgina and I immediately spot my mother from afar, sitting before an easel in a far corner, looking engrossed and attentive.

"She's so beautiful," Georgina whispers. "She looks every bit as lovely as in that framed photo on your desk."

I shrug. "Mom always looks the most beautiful when she paints. It's like a time machine for her. It's when she's not painting that she's lost."

We begin crossing the lawn, and when we're close enough for Mom to notice our approaching movement, she does a classic double-take—followed by her face lighting up in a way I've never seen before. Squealing, Mom puts down her paint brush and rushes toward us. But, to my surprise, she doesn't hug me. She hugs *Georgina*, like she's known her forever.

"You're finally here!" she says. "I'm so glad you came!"

Oh, Jesus. Well, this is new. My mother has a lot of issues, including some cognitive dysfunction, but she's never before mistaken a stranger for someone she knows. Does she think Georgina is one of her long-deceased sisters, come back from the dead?

"Mom, no. This is my *girlfriend*, Georgina Ricci. You've never met her. She came with me from LA."

"Hi, Mrs. Rivers," Georgina says, putting out her hand. "I'm so happy I'm 'finally' here, too."

"*Eleanor.*"

"Eleanor."

"You're beautiful, Georgina."

"Thank you. So are you, Eleanor."

Mom hugs me. "Hello, dear. Yes, I know I've never met Georgina before. You think I don't know that?" She pulls back from our embrace and flashes me a chastising look. "I said I'm glad she's *finally* here because you've *finally* found a woman you like enough to bring her to meet me." Chuckling at my stunned expression, she addresses Georgina. "Please, tell me you like my son, as much as he likes you, or I'll never forgive him for bringing you here, only to tease me."

"I do like your son. I also love him very much. With all my heart."

Mom claps. "*Finally*! And you?"

"I like Georgina, and love her, too. With all my heart. To the moon and back again."

Mom squeals and grabs Georgina's hand. "Come. Sit and talk to me while I continue painting the ocean." She tosses over her shoulder, "Grab a couple chairs, Reed."

"Yes, Mother."

I carry two chairs over and get Georgina settled next to my mother, and myself settled next to Georgina, and then take a good, long look at this week's opus. Not surprisingly, it's more of the same. A Happy Family Portrait, featuring Mom's lost loved ones. This time, set at the seashore.

As usual, a younger version of Mom sits on a red blanket with her two young sons—Oliver and me—and both of us are happily licking ice cream cones. One of Mom's sisters wades in the ocean up to her knees. Another sister turns cartwheels in the sand. A third sister throws a colorful beach ball with her ill-fated mother.

Mom's father is in this happy scene, too, as usual. Although, per protocol, he's set apart from his other family members, just in case the pesky rumor about him setting the house fire that claimed his wife and three daughters was true.

Mom picks up her brush and begins filling in the gray-blue of the ocean. And as she paints, she peppers Georgina with questions. How did Georgina and I meet? How long have we dated? When did she know she was in love with me?

At first, I pipe in, here and there, to supplement Georgina's replies. But, quickly, it's clear I'm a third wheel. *Persona non grata.* So, I sit back and listen, feeling relieved and amused and, surprisingly, relaxed. After a bit, Mom starts asking Georgina personal questions that have nothing to do with me. Does Georgina have siblings? What do her parents do for a living? Which, of course, ultimately leads to Georgina revealing her mother's death.

"Oh, dear. I'm so sorry," Mom says. "My mother died, too." She points to her mother's happy avatar on her canvas. "When I was sixteen."

I brace myself. This is a topic I've avoided talking about with Mom my whole life. Like the plague. Same with Oliver's death. Because, obviously, I don't want to upset Mom or trigger a meltdown.

But Georgina jumps right in. "Oh, no," she says. "How did your mother die?"

I brace myself again. But to my surprise, Mom answers Georgina, in detail, without crying, and then proceeds to regale Georgina with stories about everyone in her painting. When Georgina asks follow-up questions, Mom not only answers them, she tells Georgina lovely, lighthearted stories about her family members, most of which I've never heard. And, suddenly, I realize something huge: Mom has been *dying* to talk about these people!

My eyes drift to Mom's painting again. To her family members, enjoying the sun and surf. To her younger self, sitting on that red blanket with Oliver and me. And I feel deep compassion for my mother washing over me, not disdain or shame or embarrassment. Not only that, I feel pissed at myself for never doing exactly what Georgina is doing right now. *Asking questions.*

"Tell me some happy stories about Oliver," Georgina says. And to my surprise, Mom leaps right in, treating us to three adorable stories about him, which then leads to her telling one about *me* I've never heard before—a story in which I played a concert with pots and pans on our kitchen floor for an enraptured audience of teddy bears.

A bell rings in the distance, signaling lunch is ready in the dining hall, and Mom stands like a Pavlovian dog, saying she's so hungry she could eat a hippo. But for some reason, for the first time, ever, seeing Mom's avatar sitting happily on a blanket with her two young sons has given me an idea.

"Why don't we have a picnic? Right over there, on the grass?"

Mom loses her mind at the idea.

"You two continue chatting and enjoying the sunshine. I'll head inside and get everything we need."

Mom claps with glee, while Georgina flashes me a smolder that somehow simultaneously lights my very soul and sends rockets of desire into my dick. And I know, without a doubt, I just hit a grand slam homerun in the bottom of the ninth.

Feeling light as a feather, I practically skip into the dining hall, where Gerta, the woman in charge of the kitchen, hooks me up with the good stuff, all of it packed expertly into a beautiful basket.

But when I return to my mother and Georgina outside, holding the basket in one hand and a red blanket in the other, Mom bursts into tears at the sight of me.

My stomach drops. Shit. "It's okay, Mom. We don't have to do this if—"

She launches herself at me. "This is the best day of my life!" She pulls back from our hug, smiling broadly. And I'm relieved to realize her tears are happy ones. She asks if I got a sandwich for Lee, her boyfriend.

"Of course. And don't worry, I remembered you telling me once that he hates mustard with a fiery passion, so I specifically made sure Gerta didn't put a drop on his sandwich."

Mom touches her heart, looking like the name "Eleanor Rivers" was just announced after the phrase "And the Oscar goes to..." And, again, Georgina flashes me a look that makes me feel like I could jump, from standing, straight to the moon.

Biting back a wide smile, I say, "Come on, Mom. I know we can't have a picnic without *Lee*. That dude's the life of the party."

Mom looks like she's about to cry again, so I tell her to go find Lee while Georgina and I set up our feast.

Wiping her eyes, Mom heads off, leaving me alone with Georgina... who's now staring at me like I'm Superman who's just saved the world from a hurtling meteor.

"It's just a picnic," I say, my cheeks burning.

"It's not just a picnic."

I'm blushing too much to reply, so I hold up the blanket. "Help me spread this out, will you?"

"My pleasure."

We spread the blanket and lay out the food, and by the time Mom appears with Lee, the blanket looks ready for a photo shoot with *Better Homes & Gardens*. Brief introductions are made between Lee and Georgina, and a conversation about yoga ensues. At first, Georgina tries to include Lee in the discussion, but when she realizes that's a fool's errand, she leaves the silent man alone to quietly eat his mustard-free sandwich and stare at my mother like she walks on water.

And what am I doing in this Happy Family Portrait? A whole lot of nothing, really. Smiling. Looking around at the trees and flowers and birds and bees. Enjoying a damned good sandwich while listening to my mother and Georgina chatter away. *And it's amazing.* I tilt my face up toward the sun and enjoy the sensation. The peace infusing me. The certainty I feel that I've found The One. I can't believe Georgina is here. And that she knows *everything* about me, and loves me, anyway. No, actually, as she's told me repeatedly, she loves me even *more* because of what she's learned about me.

All of a sudden, I feel like I've been hit by a lightning bolt of pure joy and peace and certainty, and I realize this, right here, is the happiest moment of my life. Which is a crazy thought, considering it's such a big, fat *nothing* of a moment. A simple picnic in a garden with my mom and the woman I love. Plus the man my mother loves. But it's enough. It's not the way the storybooks show families. Or love. But this is what I have. And it's mine.

Moisture threatens my eyes, but, as usual, I push it away. I look at Georgina. She's laughing with my mother—who, in this moment, looks ten years younger than she did when I visited her by myself last month. How did Georgina do this? Nobody in my "real life" has *ever* entered this secret vault, this place where I visit my mother and wish in vain she could be different.

But, contrary to my fears, the sky isn't falling to have Georgina here. I feel nothing but good. Happy. *Free.* My eyes drift to a little brown bird hopping across a nearby tree branch. And then to a rosebush that's bursting with colorful blooms. I look at my mother's smiling face as she chats with Georgina. And I know, as surely as I know my name, I truly do love Georgina Marie Ricci with all of me.

Chapter 23
Reed

A re you flying out of LaGuardia or JFK this time, Mr. Rivers?" Tony, my driver, says, as Georgina and I settle into his backseat.

"Teterboro, actually. We're flying private today."

"Yes, sir." Tony pulls away from the curb. "Did you have a good visit with your mother today?"

I look at Georgina and smile. "We had a wonderful visit. My mother wouldn't let Georgina leave until she promised to come back with me next time. Or without me. Either way."

Tony's eyes crinkle in the rearview mirror with his smile. "You're heading back to LA now?"

"No, we're stopping in Boston first. LA, after that."

"Oh, I love Boston. Make sure you walk the Freedom Trail, if you've never done that. Do you need a restaurant suggestion? My cousin lives in Boston."

"No, I've got it covered. It's Georgina's birthday tomorrow, so I'm taking her and her stepsister out to an extra special lunch."

"Ooh. Nice." Tony's dark eyes shift to Georgina in the rearview mirror. "Happy birthday, Miss Ricci."

"Thank you. I'm excited I get to see my stepsister." She tugs on my sleeve and mouths, *Thank you.*

"Your stepsister lives in Boston?"

"She's a student at Berklee. The music college?"

"Oh, yeah. That's a good one. She must be talented."

"Oh, she is." Georgina flashes me a salty look that makes me chuckle, before adding, "My stepsister is a singer-songwriter, and she just got hired to play at a popular coffee house near campus. She beat out lots of other talented people for the job."

"Good for her."

"Tomorrow evening, Reed and I are going to watch her perform there."

"Sounds like a great birthday to me."

"Doesn't it? It's been a great birthday *week*. The best, ever. Tomorrow will be the icing on the cake."

"So, you met Reed's mother today and he's meeting your stepsister tomorrow? This sounds serious, Mr. Rivers."

"That, it is, Tony. That, it is."

"Reed has already met my stepsister," Georgina says. "But he's never seen her perform, so that will be particularly exciting."

"What about your parents, Miss Ricci? Has Reed met them? If so, I'm assuming your father grilled Reed about his intentions, and then threatened to break his legs if he breaks your heart."

Georgina chuckles. "Reed hasn't met my dad yet, no. But that's *exactly* what he'd do. How'd you know that?"

Tony shrugs. "You're *Ricci*. I'm *Borelli*. I've got three daughters of my own, so I know how Italian fathers think. My daughters are still young, but if they brought home a suave guy like Mr. Rivers, I'd let the guy have it. No offense, Mr. Rivers."

"None taken. I've been called far worse things in my life than 'suave.'"

Georgina says, "I've brought home exactly *one* boyfriend in my life. And my father went so freaking Italian on that guy, I've never had the stomach to bring anyone home again."

Tony chuckles. "Sounds like your father is a good egg."

"The best. He was right to dislike that guy I brought home, by the way. He turned out to be a first-class jerk."

"Daddy always knows best."

Tony's eyes in his rearview mirror shift to me, and I flash him a look that says, "Wrap it up."

"Well, I'll leave you two alone now," Tony says. "Would you like some air? Music?"

"Music," I reply. "Something mellow, not too loud."

"You got it, Mr. Rivers."

Soft, soothing music begins playing and Georgina sinks back into the leather seat. "Whew. I was more nervous about meeting your mom than I let on. I'm so glad it went well."

"Let's do it, Georgie."

She glances at Tony and mouths, "*Here?*"

I chuckle, realizing she thinks I want to have sex. "No, sweetheart. Take me to meet your father."

Georgina makes the exact face I'd expect her to make if I'd just now asked her to shave my balls.

"Why is that such a ridiculous request?" I say, laughing at her expression. "We said we're not going to hide our relationship anymore. And you said yourself you don't care what anyone thinks."

"My father isn't 'anyone.' I care very much what he thinks."

"Aw, come on. I brought you to meet my mother, and I was scared to death to do that. And look how fantastically that turned out."

"That's different."

"Why?"

"Because your mother would never think I'm your boss. Because *I* haven't paid off *your* student loans, and your mother's condo, or paid for your mother's expensive medicine."

"Well, I'm not your boss. So, that's not an issue."

"My father won't understand that."

"And I can't fathom your father will have a problem with me taking care of you, and someone you love dearly, to the best of my abilities. Plus, you really shouldn't care what he thinks, Georgina. In the end, all that matters is what *we* think. What *we* feel."

"Yes. That's true, in relation to everyone in the world, except my father."

"Are you planning to see him for your birthday when we get back?"

"On Saturday. I'm going to his house for dinner and cake."

"Then I'm coming with you."

She winces.

"Stop being a coward. We're doing this. We're both open books now, remember? We've got nothing to hide."

"*From each other.*"

I laugh. "Come on, Ricci. Put your big girl panties on. Stop being a wimp."

"He's going to grill you, exactly like Tony said. He won't be happy with anything except you saying I'm the great love of your life."

"Great. Then, we've got nothing to worry about."

Georgina makes that face I love. The one where she opens her mouth all the way, like she can't believe what she's heard.

"Is that a yes?" I say.

She flashes me a million-dollar smile. "Okay, let's do it. But don't you dare tell him I've moved in with you. He still thinks I'm living at the hotel. Let's not give the poor man a stroke."

Tony's eyes crinkle in the rearview mirror at that.

"Don't worry." I touch Georgina's thigh. "I thought today would be a disaster, and it was the best day of my life."

Georgina bites her lip. "It was?"

"Yup. Thank you for pushing me to do it. You were right. It was beautiful. *Freeing.*"

She takes my hand. "What'd I tell you? *The truth shall set you free.*"

173

We rhapsodize about today's visit for a bit. But after a while, Georgina says she's tired, and I open my arm to her and let her crumple against me for a nap. After a few minutes, when I'm sure she's out like a light, I pull out my phone and tap out a text to Josh and Henn.

Me: Georgie and I just finished visiting my mother. It went fantastically well. Tomorrow, we're visiting her stepsister in Boston. Saturday, I'm going to dinner at her father's condo in LA.

Henn: HOLY SHIT!

Josh: Whoa. Mutual meeting of the parents? This is a first for you, right?

Me: Yep.

Josh: Damn, dude. This is as serious as you've ever been with someone, isn't it?

Me: I just told her she's the great love of my life. And saying it felt good, not scary.

Henn: I have no words.

Me: Josh, send me your brother's phone number, por favor. I want to ask him a question.

Josh: You can't ask me?

Henn: Or me? I'm the smart one, remember?

Me: You're not the right guys to answer this particular question.

Josh: Well, now I'm intrigued.

Henn: Ditto.

Me: Don't read too much into this, but I want to ask Jonas what made him decide to propose to Sarah, as opposed to continuing to shack up with her.

Henn: HOLY FUCK! You're thinking of proposing to Georgina?

Josh: Henn, no. Don't be stupid. He's obviously thinking of proposing to Sarah.

Henn: I knew it! When we talked and you said she's

breakfast-worthy, I said you sounded like I did after meeting Hannah. I'm a genius.

Me: Calm down, Peter. I'm simply gathering information, out of curiosity.

Josh: Last time I checked, Henn and I are every bit as married as my brother. We can tell you why we proposed.

Me: But Jonas' situation is the closest to mine. Henn's always known he'd get married and have kids one day. And you, Josh, only proposed after knocking Kat up. Yes, it turned out great for you, but you didn't put a ring on it out of the blue, like Jonas did. I want to talk to a dude who wasn't always planning to get married, same as me, and also didn't knock his girlfriend up.

Josh: I didn't ask Kat to marry me because she was preggers. I was perfectly fine with having a baby momma. I only proposed when I realized I wanted Kat to be my wife.

Henn: And I didn't ask Hannah to marry me because I had some thumping need to marry just anyone. I only asked Hannah because I knew, for sure, she was The One.

Me: I'm not questioning your undying love for your wives, fellas. I just want to know what makes a guy who's never been interested in marriage, like me, suddenly do an about-face and pop the question.

Henn: I'm answering it, whether you like it or not. I knew it was time to pop the question when "girlfriend" wasn't nearly enough.

Josh: Perfect way to explain it. That's how I felt, too. Girlfriend/baby momma wasn't enough. Even fiancée kind of bummed me out after the novelty wore off. I couldn't wait to call her my wife. Mrs. Faraday.

Henn: Same. Mrs. Hennessy. Couldn't wait.

I look down at Georgina, at the top of her dark head. She's the best thing that's ever happened to me. The great love of my life, like I implied a moment ago. But, at least for now, I've got no problem calling her my girlfriend. In fact, when I introduced Georgina as my girlfriend to Tony, and then Oscar, the orderly, and then to my mother, I felt nothing but buzzed and excited each time. But before I've answered my friend's latest texts, my phone buzzes with one from Henn.

Henn: I wanted to propose to Hannah after knowing her for a week. I only waited out of fear of rejection. But, really, the minute I saw her, I thought, Hello, Wife.

Again, I look down at Georgina against my shoulder. I didn't think, "Hello, Wife," when I saw her in that lecture hall. I thought, *Oooh, I want to fuck that one.*

Me: See? That's exactly why you're not helpful to me, Peter. What sane man sees a woman and thinks, "Hello, wife"? Back me up, Faraday. What did you think when you first saw Kat?
Josh: I thought, "OH, GOD, I WANT TO FUCK HER!"

I chuckle. Josh and I have always shared a brain.

Me: So, Josh, how'd you get from that to "I want to call her Mrs. Faraday?"
Josh: It's too much to explain in a text. Can you talk?

I gently lift Georgina's chin to make sure she's fast asleep, and when it's clear her head is dead weight in my hand, I tap out a text, telling my friends I'll call them both, on a three-way call. The call connects. My friends express shock and excitement that I've opened this line of discussion. And, again, I tell them to pipe the fuck down.

"There's no need for you to call Jonas," Josh says, referencing his fraternal twin. "I know exactly what he'd tell you, because he's already said it to me. It was back when Jonas had just proposed to Sarah, after a month or two of dating, and he was hell-bent on having the wedding right away. So, I was like, 'Dude, what's your rush? And why do you need the piece of paper at all? Do you think it makes your love official?' And Jonas looked at me, all intense—you know how he is when he flashes those serial killer eyes—and he goes, 'Josh, I'm not marrying Sarah because I think I need a piece of paper to make our love *official*. I'm marrying her because I want to be there for her, for better or worse, for richer or poorer, in sickness and in health—and I want to let her know that's my eternal promise to her, in the most irrevocable and sacred way known to mankind.' Or something crazy like that."

I chuckle. "And *that* made you want to propose to Kat?"

"No. At first, I was like, 'Well, okay, dude, you do you. That's not how I feel about Kat, so I guess that's further proof I'm *not* the marrying kind.' And then, I saw Kat standing there at Jonas and Sarah's wedding, looking so damned beautiful, and I just... I don't know. Out of nowhere, it hit me like a ton of bricks. I suddenly felt exactly the way Jonas had described it to me. Plus, the thought of Kat marrying someone else made me fucking homicidal."

"I feel like that didn't improve at all on my succinct, but powerful, answer from before," Henn says. "Deep thoughts, by Peter Hennessy: 'You know it's time to pop the question when the word "girlfriend" simply isn't enough.'"

"Yeah, I admit that's pretty damned good," Josh says. "So, do you still want Jonas' number?"

"No, I think I've got what I need."

"What does that mean?" Henn says. "Is the word 'girlfriend' not nearly enough?"

I look down at Georgina sleeping next to me. "No, it's

enough. At least, for now. Like I said, I was just curious. Gathering information. Don't read too much into it, boys."

My eyes meet Tony's in the rearview mirror. He looks away quickly, but not before broadcasting his sincerely held belief that I'm full of shit.

"Of course, we won't read into it," Henn says sarcastically. "Why would we think there's any correlation between you introducing Georgina to your mother, and her introducing you to her father, and you wondering how you'll know if it's time to put a ring on it?"

"I gotta go, guys," I say, my cheeks flashing with heat. "I'll talk to you later."

"Let us know the *minute* 'girlfriend' isn't enough!" Henn says.

But I don't reply. In fact, I disconnect the call, without saying goodbye. And when I see Tony's eyes in the rearview mirror again, I quickly look out the window at a car in the adjacent lane of the expressway.

What the hell am I doing? Georgina is way too young to want the fairytale. I'm sure she wouldn't even want an engagement ring, if I offered her one. Not at her age. I kiss the top of Georgina's head and pull her into me. For fuck's sake, I admitted this woman is the "great love of my life" today. If that's not *enough*, then I don't know what is.

Chapter 24
Georgina

When Reed and I enter the packed coffee house, Alessandra is getting herself situated on a tiny stage. When she sees us, she waves enthusiastically, and Reed and I return the gesture, before joining the back of the line for the counter. Normally, upon seeing my stepsister, I'd rush to her and hug her. But since the three of us spent hours together today, enjoying my magnificent birthday lunch and walking The Freedom Trail, an enthusiastic wave from afar seems natural and appropriate.

After several minutes of waiting, Reed and I finally reach the counter, and when our cashier lays eyes on Reed, her face ignites. "You're Reed Rivers!"

"Last time I checked. Hello"—he looks at her nametag—"Reena. How are you? We'll have a mocha and a cappuccino, please."

But the girl is too frazzled to take Reed's order. "I'm such a huge fan of all your artists. Your label is amazing. *You're* amazing."

"You attend Berklee?"

She nods profusely. "I'm a singer-songwriter. Oh my God. Can I send you my demo? Or will you check out my Instagram?"

She scrambles for her phone, but Reed puts up his palm, making me brace myself for whatever harsh and/or rude thing he's about to say to her. Surely, it will be something along the lines of what he said to the blonde at Bernie's Place.

179

"Sorry, Reena," Reed says. "If I check out your Instagram, I'm going to be bombarded with similar requests all night. And that would make me cranky for two reasons. One, I'm here to scout tonight's performer, Alessandra, and I want to give her my undivided attention."

The cashier and I exchange a look of excitement for Alessandra.

"And, two..." Reed continues. He puts his arm around me. "I'm on a date, with my girlfriend, Georgina, here—the great love of my life—and I'd like to relax with her tonight without being interrupted."

Predictably, the cashier looks disappointed she won't be able to capitalize on this potentially life-changing chance meeting. But she manages to say, "I understand. Enjoy your night, Mr. Rivers."

"Thanks."

I'm thinking that's that. Which, I must admit, is a bummer, simply because this girl is so darling and charismatic.

But when Reed's gaze meets mine, whatever he sees on my face makes him exhale and return to the cashier. He leans over the counter. "Okay, kid, it's your lucky day. Georgina here likes you and wants me to give you a shot, so..." He pulls out his phone. "Tell me your Instagram handle, and I'll send it along to my music scout to take a look. If she likes you, and tells me to take a look at you, then I promise I will."

"Oh, wow. Thank you, Reed! That's amazing."

The girl tells Reed her Instagram handle and he taps out a text onto his phone. And two seconds later, my phone vibrates in my hand with a text from Reed.

Look at this girl's IG for me, Music Scout. Thanks.

"Okay, I just sent a text to my music scout," Reed says to the girl, shoving his phone into his pocket.

"Thank you!"

"As a return favor, would you make an announcement that I don't want to be bothered tonight?"

"Sure thing."

"Aw, Reed," I say. "I'm sure your music scout wouldn't mind checking out a bunch of Instagram profiles for you. In fact, I'm sure she'd be happy to do it."

"Whatever floats her boat."

I address the cashier. "Why don't you make an announcement you'll be collecting Instagram handles and YouTube links for Reed's music scout, to ensure Reed himself won't be bombarded tonight." I turn to Reed. "And in exchange for Reena being a doll and gathering all those links for your scout, maybe you could do something you hardly ever do and check out her Instagram account, *personally*, without using your scout as a middlewoman?"

"I can do that."

"Oh my gosh! Thank you!"

"Maybe you'll even give Reena some brief feedback and guidance about her music, one way or the other?" I look at Reena. "Would that be helpful to you?"

"That would be a dream come true. Good or bad. Please. Just give me brutal honesty."

"That happens to be my specialty, Reena. I'll look it over in the next few days and be in touch."

"Thank you so much! Oh my gosh."

"Reed, as long as you're feeling benevolent tonight, why don't you grab the mic and talk to everyone for a couple minutes about the music industry, before Alessandra starts her performance? When Reena introduces you, that's when she can make the announcement about her collecting handles and links for your music scout."

Reed says no. "It's Alessandra's night to shine," he insists. Blah, blah. But I know he's only being cranky, so I insist he'd be doing a huge kindness for every person in the coffee house. And Reena backs me up.

"Fine. Just a few words, though. This is Alessandra's night."

As I pop over to Alessandra to tell her the plan, Reena heads to the small stage. She introduces Reed and tells everyone they should give any demos and Instagram handles to her, to be forwarded to Reed's music scout. "So, without further ado," Reena says. "I give you... Reed Rivers!"

Enthusiastic applause erupts, during which Reed traipses onstage. He takes a stool and grabs the mic, and begins talking to the crowd about what he believes they all need to focus on as aspiring musicians, if they hope to make an actual career in music. And, just like at the panel discussion, every person in the room is riveted to him. Mesmerized. In awe. After about ten minutes of speaking, Reed opens it up for questions, and, instantly, he's deluged with a roomful of raised hands.

As Reed answers questions, Alessandra leans into me at our small table. "He's so nice to do this."

"I know. He's such a sweetheart."

"He's so much nicer than I thought. I can't believe I thought he was such a jerk."

"I know the feeling."

"I can't wait to show him just how much I've grown since my demo, thanks to everything he said to me at the party."

My stomach twists. "Whatever happens, don't take his word as gospel, okay? A lot goes into Reed's decision-making that has nothing to do with talent."

Alessandra winks. "You don't have to protect me, Momma Bear. I'm scared to death to perform in front of him, but I'm also excited. Whatever happens, I'll be okay."

"Okay, guys," Reed says onstage. "Let's let Alessandra do her thing now. Be sure to tip her, okay? I'll get things started." He pulls out his wallet and stuffs a wad of bills into Alessandra's tip jar, and everyone laughs and applauds and marvels at his smoothness. And I can't help giggling to myself to see my Reed, the man I know and love, morph into Panel Discussion Reed before my eyes. It's not an act, actually, when Reed turns into this dazzling version of himself. The suave, charming, debonair guy who says all the right things, and elicits chuckles and applause at all the right times. That guy is sincerely him. But what I've come to learn is it's only one facet of him. A facet I love... although, I must admit, I've come to love the parts of him that aren't quite as perfect even more.

"Now, if you'll excuse me," Reed says, "I'm going to take a seat with my beautiful girlfriend and enjoy the show."

Alessandra gapes when Reed calls me his "beautiful girlfriend," and I blush.

"He's been calling me his girlfriend every chance he gets during this trip," I whisper.

"Swoon!" Alessandra whispers back.

A moment later, Reed appears at our table, which prompts Alessandra to head to the stage. With rosy cheeks and a heaving chest, she pulls her acoustic guitar into her lap.

"Hi, I'm Alessandra. Happy birthday, Georgie." She takes a deep breath. "This is called 'Blindsided.'" With that, she takes another deep breath, clears her throat, glances at Reed—which only makes her look like she's going to barf, so she quickly looks at me, instead—and then, begins to play.

It's a new song. One I've never heard before. And, holy crap, it's the best damn song Alessandra's ever written. *By far*. Not only that, she's singing it in a way I've never heard her sing before. With less vocal acrobatics and more soul. In fact, as I listen to her, goosebumps form on my skin. Tears well in my eyes. She's magic up there. And anyone who doesn't see that, including Reed, is just plain dumb.

Speaking of which, I steal a look at Reed. And what I find isn't his usual poker face. He's not Business Reed right now. He's not Discussion Panel Reed. He's *my* Reed. My lover. My man. The generous, kind, sweetheart I've come to know and adore. And, much to my thrill, that man, *my* Reed, is smiling from ear to ear.

Chapter 25
Reed

So far, so good. Although I can't help feeling like I'm waiting for the other shoe to drop. Or, perhaps, a hammer. Onto my head.

I'm at Georgina's father's condo, sitting at a small table with Mr. Ricci and Georgina, eating homemade spaghetti Bolognese for Georgina's birthday dinner. It's one of the man's specialties, apparently. Also, one of Georgie's favorites. Which is why I've been shoveling my meal down enthusiastically, even though I rarely eat red meat or simple carbs. But, hey, whatever it takes to get onto this man's good side. Because, frankly, he hasn't welcomed me with open arms thus far. Not that I blame him.

When Georgina and I first arrived this evening, and Georgina introduced me as her "boyfriend," her dad took one look at me and made a face I'd caption as, *You've got to be fucking kidding me.* Which, right away, told me this was going to be an uphill battle. Although, in the man's defense, I wasn't particularly thrilled to hear Georgina call me that word, either. The minute Georgina uttered it in her father's presence, I couldn't help feeling exactly the way Henn and Josh described it to me the other day, only in reverse. *It's not nearly enough.*

I was shocked to think that way. By all rights, I should be thrilled to be introduced as Georgina's boyfriend, seeing as how, mere days ago at the RCR concert, that's the word I coveted. But the thrill is gone now. I've realized "boyfriend" is actually a stupid, juvenile, overly vague word. For crying out loud, it's the same fucking word Georgie used when introducing that bastard, Shawn, to her father.

Also, thanks to the bombshell Georgina dropped on her father fifteen minutes ago—namely, that I'm the guy behind all their recent financial windfalls—he seems suspicious as hell of me. Although, he did thank me profusely for my generosity. But, still, it was abundantly clear he was feeling deeply worried and conflicted. He's already said "I don't know how I'll ever be able to repay you" at least ten times. To which I've replied, every time, "The payments were gifts. No strings attached."

The last time he made the comment, I told him I donated a whole bunch of money to that cancer charity, not just to him and Georgina, in an effort to make him feel less singled out. But, immediately, I could tell the comment had backfired on me. Rather than reassuring him, it only served to make me sound like I was bragging about my wealth. And so, realizing I was only digging a hole for myself, I shut up and let Georgina change the topic. Which she did. To Alessandra. Specifically, to Alessandra's performance at that coffee house in Boston the other day. And that's what she's still talking about, a solid ten minutes later.

"You should have seen Ally's face when Reed told her he wanted to sign her to his label!" Georgina gushes. "She was so excited, I thought she was going to pass out!"

Georgina's father looks at me, his face impassive. "Add that to the list of generous things you've done for my family."

"Oh, it wasn't charity, Mr. Ricci," I say. I pause, hoping he'll correct me regarding his name this time. But yet again, he doesn't. Which annoys me to no end. I mean, I get it. This is his home, and Georgina's his beloved daughter, so, he's clearly exerting his alpha status in this pack. But, come on, this man is only seventeen years older than me, and he's been letting me call him "Mr. Ricci" all fucking night? I continue,

"I was genuinely blown away by Alessandra. Specifically, by a song she performed called 'Blindsided.' To be clear, I've only offered to produce and release that one song, as a single. I told Alessandra, if the single goes well, we'll talk about what comes next, if anything."

"Daddy, trust me, this is such a *huge* deal. Every student at Berklee—every aspiring artist in the *world!*—would sell their soul to have a single released by River Records!"

"Very kind of you, Reed."

Did the dude not hear a word I just said? Forcing myself not to scowl, I say, "It wasn't charity. Alessandra earned her spot. I listened to a demo of hers a while back, and the improvement and growth between then and now was staggering. With the right mentoring and guidance, I think Alessandra will do great things. If I didn't wholeheartedly believe that, I wouldn't have signed her. Not even for one song."

"It's true," Georgina says. "Reed's name and reputation are too valuable to him, not to mention his investment of time and money, to throw it away on anyone he doesn't believe in wholeheartedly. He says that all the time."

"It's the truth."

"A while back, Reed told me he makes it a rule never to take on young artists who need to be coaxed out of their shell. 'Ponies who need to be led out of the barn,' is what he called them. And look at him now, talking about mentoring Alessandra, and breaking his rule, because she's just that good."

Georgina's father shoots me a look like he can see right through me, and I can't help flashing him a look that concedes, *Okay, okay, maybe Georgina is being a bit naïve here.* In truth, Alessandra's performance at the coffee house was amazing. Honestly, I was blown away by her growth, and thrilled with how brilliantly she'd implemented every one of my suggestions. But does Georgina *truly* think I would have given Alessandra this shot, and committed to investing my valuable time and money and mentorship, if it weren't for my all-encompassing love for her? *Really*?

Mr. Ricci smiles at me, ever so subtly, letting me know he saw the white flag I offered, the concession I made, and he appreciated it. Maybe even respected it. He peels his gaze off me and smiles warmly at his clueless daughter, who's still babbling about Alessandra's amazing performance.

Finally, when Georgina stops rambling, Mr. Ricci says, "That's wonderful, honey. I'm so proud of Alessandra. But, as great as she performed, I'm sure part of Reed's motivation to sign her was knowing how much it would mean to you."

"No, Daddy. *Stop.* Reed doesn't compromise his business judgment. *Ever.* Not for anyone. Not even me." She looks at me with little hearts in her eyes. "Not even for someone he *loves.*"

Mr. Ricci's eyebrows ride up. "Oh, you two are in love, are you?"

"We are," Georgina says.

"We are," I confirm. I feel myself blush, but I press on. "In fact, as I've told Georgina, she's the great love of my life."

Mr. Ricci looks shocked.

"And I feel the same way about Reed," Georgina says, her chest heaving. "I met his mom in New York, and she welcomed me into the Rivers family with open arms. And now, Reed is meeting you, and I want you to welcome him into the Ricci family, the same way."

Mr. Ricci gathers himself. He puts his elbows on the table. "How old are you, Reed?"

And there it is. The elephant in the room. He thinks I'm a dirty old man.

"I'm thirty-four."

"Have you been married before?"

"No, sir."

"Any children?"

"No. I've been in some committed relationships. I'd say

I've cared deeply. But now that I'm in love with Georgina, I know I've never actually been in love. Never like this."

Georgina swoons, but her father looks unconvinced.

There's silence in the room for a long beat before Mr. Ricci exhales and says, "Georgie, will you excuse Reed and me? I'd like to chat with him, man to man."

Georgina looks at me, and when I nod, she rises, flashes a warning look at her father, and then an apologetic one at me, and heads out of the room.

"Don't eavesdrop, Georgina Marie," her father calls after her. "I'm well aware the walls are thin."

"I won't eavesdrop," Georgie tosses over her shoulder. But even I can tell she's lying through her teeth.

"Swear on Mommy."

Georgie stops in the doorway and whirls around, looking annoyed. "You can't constantly pull that out for things that aren't critically important."

"This is critically important," he says. And it's clear to me he's dead serious about that.

Georgina seems surprised by that retort. She softens. "Okay, I swear on Mommy. But be nice to him, Dad. *Please*. I didn't bring him here to meet you because I need your permission to love him. That ship has sailed. I brought him here because I want him to be part of our family. Because I love him."

"I understand, *Amorina*. Please, give us a minute— *without* you pressing your ear to the kitchen door."

Georgina rolls her eyes. "I'll be in my room."

"With headphones on and music blaring."

"Fine!"

When Georgina is gone, Marco Ricci leans back in his chair. "These grand gestures of yours, Reed... Aside from the fact that I don't know how I'll ever be able to thank you or repay you—"

"Like I said before—"

"Yes, I know what you said. And I don't want to appear

ungrateful to you. I can't deny you've saved my life. *Literally.* I'll never be able to thank you enough for that. But that's totally separate from my job, as Georgina's father, to protect her to the best of my abilities. I'm sure you can appreciate that."

"Of course."

"So, let's talk about what these grand gestures are communicating to my impressionable daughter. She's obviously enthralled with you. Totally under your spell."

"It's not a spell. This isn't smoke and mirrors. We've gotten to know each other, in a deep and meaningful way, without any bullshit, and we're now as close, and in love, as two people can be."

He sighs. "Georgina doesn't give her heart away easily, but when she does, she falls hard. Which means she gets utterly destroyed on the back end, when she gets rejected. She'd kill me if she knew I was saying this to you, but Georgina isn't always the firecracker you think she is. On occasion, she gets knocked on her ass like you wouldn't believe. Her senior year in high school, some stupid boy rejected her, and whatever happened, she crawled into bed and cried for a full *week*. And then, at UCLA, when..."

He continues talking, but I'm too devastated to continue listening. This man thinks his fierce daughter was nothing but a silly high school girl with a flair for dramatics for a week, when, in actuality, she was trying to deal, all by herself, with a sexual assault?

"My point is this," Mr. Ricci says. "How bad will Georgie get knocked on her ass *this* time, with you—a glamorous man who took her to New York, and signed her stepsister to his label, and paid off all her and her father's expenses? It's one thing for a twenty-year-old to say his girlfriend is the 'great love of his life.' But when *you* say it, under the circumstances, you're creating a much higher expectation. Painting yourself as her knight in shining armor on a white horse. Don't you see, you're implicitly promising my daughter 'forever.'"

Forever.

It's the first time that word has been in play in relation to my love for Georgina. A mighty big word that should, by all rights, terrify me. And yet, it doesn't. It only feels right.

"If Georgina thinks I'm promising her forever, then she's right. I am."

He arches an eyebrow, clearly surprised by that reply. "Answer me this, Reed. What did you do, mere days ago, that made Georgina crawl into bed and cry for two days?"

Shit. My stomach drops into my toes. "I made a couple mistakes. But we worked through them and came out the other side, stronger for it. Whatever crying Georgie did here, with you, you should know, when dealing with me, she was nothing but strong and forceful about the level of respect and honesty she required from me, going forward. Despite what you obviously think, Georgina is an equal in this relationship. In fact, I think it would be fair to say she has the upper hand in some ways. Although, please, don't tell her that, or God knows what she'll do to me."

He doesn't return my smile.

"Look, you don't have to worry about my intentions. All I want to do is to love and protect Georgina, for as long as she'll have me. You asked Georgina to swear on her mother. Well, for me, my most sacred promise is on my nephew. I swear on him, Mr. Ricci, that I love Georgina and my intentions are honorable."

Mr. Ricci remains quiet for a moment, until, finally, he smiles and says, "Marco. Call me Marco."

My heart leaps. "Thank you. But if it's okay with you, I'd prefer to call you 'Dad.'"

Marco can't help himself. He chuckles. So, I chuckle, too. And, just like that, we're both laughing, and all tension between us is gone.

"Do you have any questions of me, Marco? Ask me anything. I'm an open book."

Marco shakes his head. "Nothing else. Just don't hurt my daughter."

"I won't."

He rises from the table. "Why don't you get our little force of nature from her bedroom, while I put some candles on her birthday cake and open a bottle of champagne? It sounds like we've got a lot to celebrate."

Chapter 26
Reed

I knock on the door to Georgina's bedroom, and say her name, but when she doesn't reply, I poke my head inside the room. She's lying on her bed, earbuds in, her eyes trained on an e-reader.

"Georgina?"

Nothing.

I cross the small room, detecting the faintest sound of 22 Goats blasting from Georgina's ears. When I reach the edge of the bed, I stand over her for a beat, waiting for her to look up, but she's too engrossed in whatever she's reading to notice me. Out of curiosity, I peek at the book title in the upper corner of the page she's reading and discover it's a biography of a New York City mobster. The sight makes me smile broadly. How is it possible for someone so gorgeous to also be so damned smart, adorable, and curious?

I could stand here all night, watching Georgina's various facial expressions as she reads. But since her father is waiting on us, I gently tap the top of her head to announce myself.

At my touch, Georgina jolts, tosses down her e-reader, and pulls out her earbuds.

"What'd he say?" she gasps out, her cheeks flushed with anticipation.

"Remember what Tony said a good Italian father would say to a 'suave' dude like me? That's basically what he said."

Georgina winces. "Was it super weird and cringey for you?"

"Not at all. It was awesome, actually. The conversation ended well. And it helped me further clarify my thoughts and feelings about you. About *us*."

Her eyebrows ride up. "What does that mean?"

I sit on the edge of the bed. "Your father told me all these grand gestures I've been doing for you, and him, would imply I'm promising 'forever' to you. And I said, good. That's precisely my intention."

Georgina makes that wide-mouthed, astonished face I love so much. "You actually used the word 'forever' when talking to my *father*—about *me*?"

I nod. "And I meant it." I take her hands. "If I haven't made this clear to you, Georgina, let me do it now. I'm not going anywhere. You're my last stop on the train."

Her chest heaves. "You're mine, too."

"Glad to hear it. But, listen, love. There's something else your dad said... something we should talk about."

I'd noticed Georgina reading everything Henn sent to me about Gates during our flight home from New York, and it was clear to me the information was deeply distressing to her. But she said she didn't want to talk about it yet, so I didn't press. Instead, I simply put my arm around my baby and invited her to sleep on my shoulder for the rest of the flight.

But now, after hearing that thing Marco said to me a moment ago—that thing about Georgina supposedly melting down for a solid week in high school, due solely to some dumb boy—my gut tells me it's time for her to speak up about Gates. At least, with her father.

"While your father was warning me not to break your heart," I say, "he told me a cautionary tale about some unknown boy in high school who broke your heart so badly you crawled into bed and cried for a week."

Georgina scowls. "Ugh. My dad made a similar comment the other day. You realize he's talking about the week after Gates attacked me, right?"

193

"Yeah, that's my point. I understand why you didn't tell your father about Gates at the time. And I'm not trying to push you to do something you're not ready to do. But do you really want your father thinking his daughter spent a week in bed because some stupid high school boy dumped her? No wonder he thinks you're more fragile and naïve than you are. He has no way of knowing what a badass you are, Georgina. A grown man attacked you, at seventeen—a man in a position of power—and you fought him off. Don't you want your father to know *that's* the badass daughter he raised, all on his own?"

"But if I tell my father what Gates did, he'll want me to go to the police. And what good would that do? Like I said before, it's my word against his—only now, a full five *years* later."

I hold her anxious gaze. "Here's what I think, love. Go out there and tell your dad what happened, simply because he loves you and doesn't fully understand you as an adult. From there, I admit, I don't have the expertise to guide you. But you know who does? Leonard. Let's set up a meeting. We'll show him everything Henn found and ask his recommendation on next steps. Should you file a police report? A civil complaint? I have no idea. But I trust Leonard. I know he'll be able to help us figure out what to do next."

Tears moisten Georgina's eyes. "Thank you. Yes. I'd love to talk to Leonard. I trust him, too." Her face contorts, like she's holding back the weight of the world. But only barely.

"Aw, baby. Come here." I hug her to me, and, when I hear sniffling, my heart physically palpitates with love for her.

"Thank you," she ekes out.

"You don't have to thank me. Don't you get it? *I love you.* Your pain is mine. Your happiness mine." I pull back and meet her teary eyes. "The only thing I want is for my beautiful, colorful butterfly to be set free, and to get to see her flying loop-de-loops against a brilliant blue sky, the way she was meant to do."

"*Loop-de-loops*?" She chuckles through tears. "Whatever

happened to you wanting to capture your beautiful butterfly and pin her to paper and enclose her in an airtight frame?"

I brush the tear streaking down her cheek with my thumb. "Well, I guess that right there is the difference between lust... and *love*."

Chapter 27
Reed

Music is blaring. Bright lights flashing. And I'm a little bit drunk. Not because I'm having fun at this stupid birthday party at my Las Vegas nightclub. But because I'm *not*. Because after the past six weeks of bliss with Georgina, I can't stand being away from her. Because I'd rather be shitfaced than have to stand here, completely sober, wishing I were home with my baby. Because, as this five-day business trip has taught me, I'm now hopelessly incapable of being away from Georgina for even one night—let alone, *five*.

The Old Reed traipsed around the world for weeks at a time, without a care in the world. Not missing anyone. Fucking whoever. Never truly letting anyone get to know the man behind The Man with the Midas Touch. But now, it's abundantly clear: The Old Reed is dead. And The New Reed is totally, madly, irrevocably in love with the siren, the bombshell, the fireball known as Georgina Ricci.

It's been a productive trip, from a business standpoint. In San Francisco, Seattle, Phoenix, and Boise, I've scouted bands, checked out potential real estate investments, and attended meetings. All stuff I really needed to do, after six weeks of ignoring far too much work to hunker down in my house with Georgina. I've survived it all, but just barely, knowing it was all stuff I legitimately had to do for work. But, tonight, I'm losing my mind, since this party isn't work related and I'd much rather be home with Georgina. I'm hosting a birthday party for an old fraternity brother named Alonso in my nightclub tonight, and, I swear, if it weren't for an important meeting tomorrow with some business partners here in Vegas, I'd already have hopped a plane back to Georgina.

I tried to get her to come with me on this trip, but she said she had too much work to do. Her final artist interviews to polish. Her Gates article to finalize. Also, the one about me to edit. Plus, on top of all that, Georgina said she's *still* trying her mighty best to get *someone* to talk to her, on the record, about Howard Devlin. It's looking pretty unlikely she's going to be able to pull that particular rabbit out of her hat, despite how hard she's tried over the past six weeks. But, still, she's not ready to give up. Which doesn't surprise me. Georgina Ricci is nothing if not persistent.

Someone jostles my shoulder on their way to the dance floor, and I'm jolted back to my present surroundings. I'm standing near the dance floor with three of my old fraternity brothers—Henn, Luke, and the birthday boy, Alonso—plus, Ethan, an old friend from UCLA who wasn't in my fraternity, but is friendly with that whole group, thanks to regular poker parties at my house the past several years.

I tune into the conversation happening around me and discover Ethan, a successful producer of indie flicks, is telling the group a "behind the scenes" story from one of the films he's produced. Luke and Alonso are listening intently and laughing. But not Henn. He's glued to his phone, looking anxious.

As I watch Henn furiously tapping out a text, my drunken eyes fixate on the gleam of his metal wedding ring. And, much to my shock, I find myself *envying* him for that ring. For being a marked man. For getting to broadcast to the world, he's got a wife somewhere in the world. A woman who pledged her eternal love to him in a legally binding ceremony.

I look down at my bare ring finger and think it must be cool to have a ring like Henn's. I mean, assuming the woman wearing my ring, in return, was Georgina.

"Reed?"

I look up. It's Alonso talking to me. The birthday boy. He's pointing at my empty glass, asking me if I want a refill.

"Yeah. Sure."

"Henn?" Alonso asks.

Henn barely looks up from his phone. "No. Thanks."

Alonso takes my empty and heads to the bar, at which point I lean into Henn.

"Everything all right, buddy?"

Henn sighs and looks up from his phone. "Hazel's running a high fever. Hannah's at Urgent Care with her now. I'm totally freaking out." He rubs his forehead and, again, my drunken eyes notice the gleam of his wedding band. "Hazel's never had a high fever. Only low-grade ones when she's teething."

"Reed!" a female voice says, drawing my attention away from Henn.

It's Corinne. An ex-girlfriend of mine. An actress I dated exclusively for about three months a couple years ago, until boredom set in—at least, for me.

I hug Corinne hello. She kisses my cheek and links her arm in mine as I quickly introduce her to my friends. After introductions have been made, she pulls me aside and tells me she's elated she ran into me tonight because she's been thinking about me *a lot* lately—a *ton,* actually. In fact, she had a dream about me, just the other night! A really sexy one! Ha, ha! Which made her wonder if maybe we should—

I cut her off. Tell her I've got a girlfriend. And that's when it hits me, like a Mack truck. *Girlfriend isn't enough.* Even as I say the paltry word, I can plainly see Corinne's lack of respect for it. And why not? It's what *Corinne* was to me, once, not that long ago. And she wasn't anything special to me, though I liked her well enough. She was nothing but a brief distraction. Not even in the same universe as Georgina.

Suddenly, I can't stand the hideous word. *Girlfriend.* How can I use that word to describe Georgina, when I've already used it on someone like Corinne? And so many others before her? Georgina is the sun. And every woman who came before her, an LED lightbulb. And yet, here I am, slapping Georgina with the same label used for Corinne and everyone else? Shame on me.

In a flash, I'm desperate to get away from Corinne. So, I tell her there's someone she has to meet. I tell her it's "serendipity" she ran into me tonight, so she could meet this particular friend of mine. Without waiting for her reply, I lead her to Ethan at the bar. I tell Ethan Corinne is an actress. "A talented one." Which is true. I tell Corinne Ethan is a "hot-shot producer" of some of the "best independent films I've ever seen. Some of which have made me a shit-ton of money." Also, true. And then I bid them adieu. And why not? Besides the obvious business connection, Ethan is rich and powerful and young and good-looking. And Corinne is talented and magnetic and gorgeous. I hope they fall madly in love and make a minivan full of babies together. *Peace out.*

I turn to go, but before I do, Ethan catches my eye and flashes me a look that plainly asks if she's fair game.

I nod and flash him a resounding, *Godspeed,* in reply. And then I'm gone, heading back to Henn to find out the latest on Hazel.

But Alonso finds me before I've reached Henn and hands me my refilled drink.

"Thanks."

"No need to thank me," Alonso says. "You're the one who bought it." He motions to Ethan and Corinne at the bar. "What the hell, man? I'm the birthday boy. If you didn't want her, why not introduce her to *me* as a birthday present?"

"Because she's an actress, and you sell life insurance."

"All the more reason to help a brother out."

"She's out of your league, Alonso. Actresses don't date insurance salesmen, any more than squirrels date bumblebees."

As I gulp my drink, Alonso babbles a bunch of shit I

don't care about. So, when my drink is done, I ditch Alonso and stride over to Henn. Not surprisingly, he's still tapping furiously on his phone, looking worried and frazzled.

"Any update?"

"Yeah. Thankfully, the doctor isn't too worried. She told Hannah exactly what to do. So, she's heading home with Hazel now."

"Keep me posted."

Henn runs a hand over his face, looking distraught. "I've got to go, man. I'll say a quick goodbye to Alonso. Do me a favor and say my goodbyes to everyone else."

"You bet."

We head over to Alonso. Henn says, "Hey, man, I'm sorry, but my baby has a fever and I need to go home."

"The last flight to LA has already left," Alonso says. "Why don't you go back first thing in the morning?"

Without hesitation, as Henn and Alonso continue talking, I grab my phone and start making arrangements.

"I'm gonna rent a car and drive," Henn says. "This time of night should be smooth sailing. I'll make it home in four and a half hours. Perfect timing for my wife to crash and for me to take over for her with Hazel."

Henn turns to me, clearly intending to hug me goodbye. But I put up an index finger, asking him to hold on for a second. Quickly, I finalize what I'm doing on my phone, and then look up.

"No rental car required," I say. "I just booked you a car and driver, so you can sleep on the way home. It'll be at the front of the club in exactly fifteen minutes."

"Oh my God, Reed. It didn't even occur to me to do that! I'll pay you back."

"Don't be stupid. Go get your suitcase from upstairs and meet me out front. I'll wait outside for the car, in case it gets here before you're out front."

"You're the best. Thanks, brother."

With that, Henn heads toward the front exit of the club, looking like a man on a mission.

Alonso shakes his head as he watches Henn's departing frame. "What the fuck has happened to all of us? Faraday couldn't come to Vegas because his wife is in her third trimester and he won't leave her, even for one night. Henn is running off to hold his sick baby, even though his wife is already there. Cory stayed home because his wife's *sister* is about to have twins. Jake is standing over there, showing everyone a video of his baby's first fucking steps. And you just now turned down a smoking hot actress with the most perfect tits I've ever seen because you have a *girlfriend* waiting for you at home? Seriously now, am I the only one whose balls are still attached to his body?"

"Fuck you," I mutter. "You were always trash in college, and now you've grown up to be a *Peter Pan* asshole motherfucker. I never liked you, Alonso. Not even in college. Not even when I was high on blow. So, why am I here? Why am I *hosting* this birthday party for you?"

Alonso laughs heartily, apparently thinking I'm joking. But I'm not. Why am I wasting my precious time on this planet doing *anything* I don't want to do? More to the point, why am I doing *anything* that takes me away from *Georgina*?

"I'm going outside to wait for Henn's limo," I toss out, and then stride toward the front door without waiting for Alonso's reply.

Outside in the warm Las Vegas night, I bum a cigarette off the security guy out front, even though I don't smoke. Just as I'm stubbing the cigarette out, Henn's limo comes. Two minutes after that, Henn appears with his suitcase, looking frayed. I give my sweet best friend a bear hug and tell him to keep me posted. And then, I send Henn off into the night, on his white horse.

Deciding I'd rather have FaceTime sex with Georgina in my room than return to the excruciating birthday party, I begin crossing the street toward my hotel. But just as I'm heading into the lobby, my phone buzzes with a text from CeeCee that stops me dead in my tracks.

CeeCee: I saw on Instagram you're in Vegas. Francois and I are here, too, for his friend's birthday dinner tomorrow night. Let me know if you have time for a drink.

Me: I have time right now, as a matter of fact.

CeeCee: Perfect timing! We just got back to our room. Bellagio. Penthouse 8. See you soon, darling!

Chapter 28
Reed

Not surprisingly, given that CeeCee's husband is a multi-billionaire, CeeCee's penthouse at the Bellagio is the biggest, most luxurious hotel suite I've ever beheld. Which is saying a lot, considering how much I like to treat myself to the finer things in life.

At first, CeeCee, Francois, and I chat as a threesome while gazing at the neon view of The Strip below. But, after a while, Francois heads downstairs to meet some friends in the casino, leaving CeeCee and me to booze it up as a dynamic duo.

"Okay, darling," CeeCee says when her husband is gone. "Tell me what's going on with you. You're not yourself tonight."

"Yeah, I've got some blood in my boozestream."

She laughs. "No, I've seen you drunk, plenty of times. There's something bothering you. What's wrong?"

I sigh. "I can't stand being away from Georgina. She's my disease and there's no cure. I'm lovesick."

CeeCee pats my arm. "What a glorious reason to be miserable."

"How the hell do you and Francois live on different continents? Are you not in love with him? I won't tell, if you're not. Just tell me the truth."

She bats my shoulder. "Don't insult me. Of course, I'm in love with my darling Francois! I hate being away from him, every bit as much as you hate being away from Georgina. But I've got no choice, at least for now. I'm not ready to retire yet. Not even close. So, we make it work."

I shove my empty glass at her. "Another one, bartendress. Help me numb the pain of my acute lovesickness."

Chuckling, CeeCee gets up to refill my glass. "I don't blame you for falling head over feet for Georgie. So have I. I knew she was going to knock my socks off this summer, the minute I met her. But she's blown away even my highest expectations with everything she's submitted to me. Especially that piece she wrote on Gates! Have you read it, Reed? It's incredible."

My chest swells with pride. "Yeah, I read every draft along the way. It's amazing, isn't it? I'm so proud of her."

She hands me a drink and resumes her seat. "I made it a double."

"Bless you, Saint CeeCee."

"Did Georgina tell you? If she's able to incorporate my final edits and turn in her final draft by tomorrow, we'll be able to sneak it into the next issue of *Dig a Little Deeper,* just under the wire."

"She told me. She's beyond elated about it. Georgie's been dreaming of getting published in *Dig a Little Deeper* for a long time."

"Well, cheers to dreams coming true."

We clink and drink.

"Does this mean you're going to hire Georgina full-time at *Dig a Little Deeper*?"

"Of course, I am. But don't you dare steal my thunder and tell her. When her internship is officially over in two weeks, I'm going to throw her a little surprise party at the office to tell her. I already told Margot to order a cake."

I feel euphoric, like this victory for Georgie is my own. "She'll love a party. She doesn't have a mom, CeeCee. Little things like a party with a cake... the way you've taken her under your wing. That stuff means the world to her. More than you could possibly realize."

"Aw, Reed. You look so smitten right now. Like you're bursting with pride."

"I am. This Gates article... It's been so inspiring to watch her journey. When Georgina told her dad about Gates six weeks ago, she was so nervous and timid. And look at her now. She's unstoppable. That article doesn't pull any punches. It's incredible."

"That, it is." She raises her glass. "Everyone drink to Georginaaaa!"

"Heeeey!"

Again, we clink and drink.

"Can I ask you a kind of weird question?" I ask. "Why did you marry Francois?"

CeeCee looks highly offended. "Because I love him more than life itself. And he asked."

"Yes, I know all *that*. Don't get your designer panties in a twist."

She giggles.

"What I mean is, you've both been married twice before. His main residence is in France. Yours is in LA. And you're both at an age where you're not going to have any babies."

"Francois and I aren't going to have babies? Oh, crap. Don't tell Francois! He only married me for my fertile womb!"

We laugh and laugh.

"But, seriously," I say. "I don't get it. Okay, you both fell head over heels. Woohoo. Congratulations. But why not be 'jet-setting lovers'? Wouldn't that be far more romantic than trying to make a trans-continental marriage work?"

CeeCee looks at me like I'm trying to glue false eyelashes onto a pig. "You think being 'jet-setting lovers' is *more* romantic than exchanging vows of *forever* with the person you're head over heels in love with? And doing it in front of family and friends, in a ceremony that dates back hundreds of years and is *legally binding*? *And,* in my case, getting to exchange those vows of forever, and thereafter partying with said family and friends, in a seven-hundred-year-old castle in the South of France? Pfuff. I mean, to each their own. But I, *personally,* think there's nothing more romantic than any of *that.* Especially considering Francois's wealth. He owns half the world, and yet, he told me his life wouldn't be complete if he didn't spend the rest of it with *me.*"

"But, see, that's my point. Spend the rest of your lives together. Great. Wonderful. *Why get married*? You and Francois both know, for a fact, marriage isn't necessarily forever, no matter what you say in your vows. CeeCee, Francois is your *third* husband."

"He is? Oh, shit! Please, don't tell him that! He thought I was a virgin when he married me." She flashes me a snarky look. "Yes, I'm fully aware marriage might not last *forever,* but the thrill is that it *could.* Did you not hear a word I just said? Marriage isn't about *logic.* It's a leap of faith, you fool."

I bring my drink to my lips as my drunken brain feverishly tries to ignore the crazy shit my lovesick heart is saying to me.

CeeCee arches an eyebrow. "You're planning to propose to Georgina?"

My heart shouts, *Yes*! But I ignore it, as best I can. Because, obviously, that would be a ridiculous thing to do. Georgina is too young for that. And I don't even believe in the institution of marriage, as a matter of principle. "No," I manage to say in a calm voice. "I don't believe in marriage. But even if I did, Georgina is *twelve years* younger than me. She's got a lot of life to live before she'd be ready to commit to 'forever' with me."

"I'm fifteen years younger than Francois, and I was ready to commit to him forever."

"Yes, but you're twenty-*five*, darling. Not twenty-*two*. That's a big difference."

We both laugh at my silly, drunken joke.

"I was twenty-two the first time I got married," CeeCee says wistfully. "And it was so much fun."

"CeeCee, you got *divorced*!"

"Yes, but it was fun while it lasted. And the wedding was a damned good party."

I can't help laughing.

"Have you asked Georgina what she thinks about all this 'forever' business? She's been through a lot at such a young age, you know. Losing her mother. Taking care of her father through his cancer battle. And let's not forget what she went through with Gates. I think maturity has more to do with what's happened to a person in their years of life, rather than how many years of life a person has had."

I swirl my drink. "I'm not going to ask Georgina's permission to *ask* her to marry me. That'd take all the fun out of it."

CeeCee chuckles. "Oh, so you *are* a romantic, underneath it all."

I shrug. "Maybe I am. I decided tonight I hate the word 'girlfriend.' It isn't even close to enough to describe what Georgina means to me. In fact, the word feels like an insult, at this point. A hideous slur."

CeeCee laughs. "Well, I think that's a tad bit dramatic. But okay."

I look out at the neon-lit view, gathering my thoughts. There's something on my mind... something I didn't realize I thought about, until this very moment. But now, suddenly, it's crystal clear. "I think my parents' marriage, and bitter divorce, has messed me up in the romance department. My father was thirty-two when he knocked up my nineteen-year-old mother and married her. I was too young during my parents' marriage to understand the dynamics of their age gap, but looking back, as an adult, I can plainly see my father steamrolled my mother at every turn. He lorded over her, controlled her, squeezed the life out of her. In fact, I'd even venture to say he gaslighted her. Finally, my mother discovered his mistresses—one of whom was nineteen, by the way. Oh, and then *he* divorced *her* when she found him out, as if *she'd* done something wrong because *he* had mistresses. I was only nine when they divorced, so I didn't fully grasp everything, but Georgina recently showed me some legal documents that shed some light on my parents' divorce and custody battle, and I got to see how nasty it was. How scorched earth my father was. And I guess, if I'm being honest, I'm terrified of history repeating itself with me and Georgina. Either with me as the controlling older husband who squeezes the life out of his young wife. Or with me as my mother, who falls apart, completely, when the fairytale doesn't work out."

"Oh, Reed. Who says the fairytale wouldn't work out?" She grabs my hand, her face awash in sympathy and love. "Not every love story ends the way your parents' did. You're not your father, and you're not your mother. You're *you*. A beautiful, brilliant man with a huge heart and a whole lot of love to give. You've kept the best of your love bottled up for thirty-four years, like the finest wine. It's time for you to finally pour that delicious wine into someone's goblet, without holding back. Whether that will translate to marriage for you, I have no idea. Just, please, don't let your parents, and your childhood, keep you from doing whatever is truly in your heart. Whatever that might be."

My eyes feel as though they're on the cusp of tearing up. So, I take a deep breath, and then another, to ward off my threatening emotion.

"Forever is a beautiful thing to promise to someone you love," CeeCee says. "If you're feeling the urge to propose to Georgina, then get yourself a prenup and roll the dice."

Yes! my heart screams at me. But, again, my brain tells

me, *No, it's a non-starter. She's too young. And marriage only ends in pain.*

I wipe my eyes. "I've actually got a better idea than making Georgina sign a fucking prenup."

"Marriage *without* a prenup?" CeeCee gasps. "Reed, being romantic is one thing. Being *stupid* is another."

"Cool your jets, woman. I'm not proposing to her. Why give her a ring to symbolize forever when she could take it *off*?" I drain my glass and put it on a side table. "Come on, Ceece. I'm a man on a mission. I'm going to get something for Georgina that symbolizes forever—that she can't take off. Something far better than a stupid ring."

Chapter 29
Georgina

I'm sitting on the couch in the living room of Reed's house—or, rather, "our" house, as Reed keeps calling it—reading the final version of my article about Gates and his two enablers—the principal of my high school and Steven Price—before submitting it to CeeCee. And I love it. When I met with Leonard the day after telling my father about Gates, Leonard recommended I write this article as my best course of action—and reading it now, six weeks later, I never dreamed I'd write something this powerful.

"What's your goal here?" Leonard asked me six weeks ago.

I replied, without hesitation. "I want to expose Gates and the men who covered up for him, so there will never be another Katrina, Penny, or Georgina at my high school."

"Well, then," he said, "if that's your goal, then I don't think walking into a police station and reporting you were the victim of an attempted rape almost five years ago would be nearly as effective as writing an in-depth, airtight account of what happened. Most people in your shoes don't have a national platform like you do. Use it. I predict all appropriate dominoes will fall after that."

So, that's exactly what I decided to do: write my story, without holding back.

After our meeting with Leonard, Reed and I went straight to CeeCee's office, where I told her about Gates, in detail.

After that, after hugging me and saying some truly beautiful things to me, CeeCee immediately gave me the green light to write the article... *provided* I could get Katrina and/or Penny to contribute, *on* the record.

"Consider it done," I assured CeeCee, brimming with confidence... and then quickly discovered my confidence was a bit premature. In actuality, when I tracked down Katrina and Penny, neither girl wanted to talk to me about Gates. Thankfully, though, after I told each girl about the other, and also about my own harrowing experience at the hands of Gates, both girls ultimately poured their hearts out to me... but only *off* the record. They said they *wanted* to take him down. They truly did. But they were scared to death they might have to pay Steven Price's money back.

And that's when Reed, my knight in shining armor, stepped in to save the day. He told both girls he'd cover any and all legal expenses arising from them speaking up and breaching their "hush money" agreements with Steven Price, and promised they'd never have to come up with that money. And that did it. Both girls agreed to take a leap of faith with me and let me include their courageous, heartbreaking, stomach-churning, no-holds-barred stories in my article.

And now, after six weeks of blood, sweat, and tears, not to mention daily pep talks to myself to be brave, I've finally finished writing my article. It's a five-pager entitled, "Football at All Costs: How a Winning High School Coach Got Away with Sexual Assault with a Little Help from His Friends." And I couldn't be prouder of it. I read the article one last time, attach it to an email, and send it to CeeCee. And the moment I press send, a torrent of pride and relief surges inside me. Also, a touch of fear. But the good kind of fear. The kind that tells me I'm alive. It's a one-of-a-kind moment for me. So, of course, I want to share it with Reed.

My heart bursting, I pick up my phone and tap out a text:

I just submitted my Gates article. I'm terrified, but

mostly excited. I can't wait to celebrate with you. Let me know the minute you've landed. XO

As I await Reed's reply, I send the article to my father and Alessandra, and then wind up chatting with Alessandra on FaceTime. Alessandra gushes about the article. She tells me she loves me and is proud of me. And then, at my request, she sends me the latest mix of "Blindsided," which, she says excitedly, Reed is planning to release in about three weeks. Finally, though, after about twenty minutes of chatting with Alessandra, my phone pings with a reply from Reed and I tell Alessandra I've got to go.

Reed: Landed. Coming straight home to celebrate. SO proud of you!

Me: Woohoo! Can't wait to see you. I've been dying without you here.

Reed: I've been miserable without you, sweetheart. Can't wait to touch you. I'm not going to make it two steps past the front door before I rip your clothes off.

Me: Promise? XO

Reed: Hell yes. XO

My body is vibrating with excitement. I knew I'd miss Reed during his business trip. But I didn't think I'd miss him *this* much—like missing a limb. I thought I was "adulting" when I said I should stay home to finish my mountain of work. In retrospect, though, I wish I would have done the irresponsible thing and joined him on his trip. Because these past five days have been pure torture.

To pass time until Reed gets home, I open my laptop and edit an article I've been writing, off and on, for the past several weeks—a secret article I haven't told anyone about, not even CeeCee or Reed. I'm hoping to ultimately get this piece into *Dig a Little Deeper*. But if not, I'll still be awfully proud of it, and happy I took the time to investigate and write it.

As I'm engrossed in the words on my screen, I hear the best sound in the world: the front door opening behind me.

Squealing, I close my laptop with gusto, sprint across the living room, and hurl myself like a missile into Reed's waiting arms. In a flash, we're kissing and ripping off our clothes, right inside the front door, exactly as Reed promised.

Reed unties his tie and unbuttons his shirt with frenzied fingers. He peels off his shirt, breathing hard... and that's when I see it: a new tattoo to join Reed's collection. This one, on his left pec. *ReRiGeRi.* Instantly, I know what the seemingly random letters mean. They're a tribute to us. To our love. The beginning letters of both our names, inked onto his flesh—over his heart—forever.

"I love it!" I exclaim, bending down to kiss the tattoo. From there, I work my way down Reed's abs, to his treasure trail, and then to his hard penis. But before I take him into my mouth, Reed pulls me up and backs me into the door. His eyes ablaze, he binds my wrists with his necktie and raises them above my head. He opens the front door slightly, throws the long end of his tie over it, and shuts it again, pinning me in place with my back against the closed door and my hands trussed over my head.

With eyes like hot coals and flaring nostrils, Reed sinks to his knees and greedily kisses my belly. And then my thighs. He lays fervent kisses around my clit, never actually touching it, until I'm moaning and begging for more. Finally, he begins lapping at my bull's-eye with confident strokes, until, soon, I'm shuddering and bucking and whimpering with pleasure. I'm wet for him now. Swollen and throbbing and aching. He slides his fingers inside me, and, still devouring me with his mouth, begins stroking my G-spot, over and over again, without reprieve. Without letting up or changing speed. He's a laser beam. An oncoming train. Until, finally, my orgasmic screams echo throughout the expansive living room.

Reed's initial job complete, he rises, grabs me by my naked ass, and fucks me against the door like he's trying to kill me with his cock, growling into my ear with each thrust about his love for me, how good I feel, how hot I am, how much he missed me.

When Reed comes, it's with a primal roar that sends me hurtling into a release of my own, thanks to a little help from Reed's talented fingers. Finally, we're finished and breathing hard. Glowing with sexual satisfaction. Reed frees my wrists from the door and unbinds them, and the minute I'm free, I throw myself into his hard chest and clutch him to me, overwhelmed by the intensity of my feelings. It scares me to know I not only love and want Reed. I physically *need* him. I wish I didn't. It's terrifying to realize someone's got the power to decimate me. To shatter my heart into a billion pieces with one word. *Goodbye.* But it can't be helped. I'm undeniably at his mercy. All-in. Laid bare.

"Never leave me," I whisper, still clutching him.

Reed chuckles. "Don't you worry, little kitty. From now on, you're coming with me on every work trip. I was miserable without you."

"No. I meant... *never leave me.*" I pull back and look him in the eye, my own eyes pricking with moisture. "Never leave *us.* I *need* you, Reed. Like air. It scares me to think how badly I'd drown if I ever lost you."

Reed's features soften. He puts his fingertip underneath my chin. "Georgina Marie, why do you think I got the tattoo? If stamping our combined names onto my flesh for eternity doesn't tell you I'm not going anywhere, then I don't know what would."

Without meaning to do it, I make a face that says, *Well, actually...*

Because, damn, without intention, my mind was just now hijacked by this distinct thought: *Well, actually... I can think of one thing that would say "forever" even more than a tattoo.*

Ugh. Who am I right now? I should be nothing but thrilled and grateful about Reed's tattoo, not thinking, *It's not enough.* The man inked our combined names onto his chest as a surprise gift, as a permanent testament to our love, and I've got the nerve to think, basically, *Thanks, but I'd rather you put a ring on it?* Shame on me. Plus, that's so *not* me. I've never had any thumping desire to get married. I'm not the kind of girl who sits around dreaming of her future wedding. But I can't deny I've had the thought. And, even worse, based on Reed's expression, he knows it.

The air in the room feels thick and still for a moment, like an elephant wearing a sign that reads "Put a ring on it!" just galloped between us.

For a split-second, we're both frozen. Red-faced and stilted.

"I want to get the same tattoo!" I blurt, pointing at his chest. Desperately trying to fill the awkward silence with something that will convince Reed he's misread me. "We're Fred and Ginger. We need to be a matched set. A promise of 'forever' will only work if both of us make it."

Reed exhales with relief. It's subtle. But it's there. "Are you sure? You don't have to do that."

"I'm sure. I want to. In fact, let's go right now."

A wide smile splits Reed's handsome face. "Sounds good. I need a shower, and then we'll go." Chuckling, Reed bends down and begins gathering his scattered clothes, so I follow suit, my heart stampeding. "I'll call my usual tattoo guy now and tell him we're on our way. After the tattoo parlor, how about I take you to a nice dinner to celebrate you submitting the Gates article to CeeCee?"

Our clothes gathered, we head toward the staircase.

"Actually, if it's okay with you, I'd rather do a quiet dinner at home. That's all I've wanted for five days. To be home, alone, with you."

Reed takes my hand and squeezes it as we climb the stairs. "Have I ever mentioned you're perfect?"

I swoon. "I'm so relieved you're home. This house felt so big and lonely without you."

Lauren Rowe

We've reached the top of the staircase. Reed stops walking. He looks down at me, his dark eyes a window into his beautiful soul. He lays a gentle fingertip against my lip. "Now you know how I felt living in this big and lonely house for five years before you walked through the door and finally made it a home."

Chapter 30
Reed

We're back from the tattoo parlor now. Sitting in our comfy clothes at my kitchen table, eating Amalia's delicious meal and drinking Cristal from crystal flutes. And, as Georgina eats and talks and repeatedly brings her fork and champagne flute to her lips, I can't help staring at those tiny letters inked along the inside of her left ring finger... *ReRiGeRi...* and, to my surprise, thinking, over and over again, *It's not nearly enough.*

What's wrong with me? Matching tattoos should be more than enough! Especially considering Georgina got hers on *that* finger. The one reserved for a wedding ring. The one that tells the world she's taken, for life. But, nope. I don't feel the surge of pure elation I thought I would. I don't feel sated. *I still want more.*

Georgina puts down her champagne. "I finished writing my article about you while you were gone."

Shit. My gaze jerks from Georgina's tattooed finger to her eyes, as my spirit thuds into my toes. To be honest, I've been dreading Georgie's article about me for weeks. I've asked to read her early drafts, seeing as how she let me do that with her Gates article, but she's always said no. "I want to surprise you," she's told me. And now, holy shit, the "surprise" is finally upon me.

"I'd like to send it to CeeCee tomorrow," Georgina says, unaware of the intense anxiety brewing inside of me. "I'd love it if you'd read the article tonight and let me know what you think about it."

"Sure thing."

"I had such a hard time writing this one. You know, getting it right. I kept going back and forth on what information to include. What to exclude. It was important to me that the piece has journalistic integrity and a strong voice. I didn't want it to be nothing but a sappy love letter to my boyfriend."

She smiles. But I can't muster one in return. Now that I love Georgina more than life itself, now that her dreams are mine, how could I possibly nix a single word of this damned article—even if she's included information about me I don't want to share with the world? If I'm forced to choose between supporting Georgina's career and ambition, versus guarding my own need for privacy and control, how could I possibly choose anything but what Georgina wants?

She stands, her excitement palpable. "So, can I grab my computer now?"

I take a deep breath. "Of course."

Hooting with glee, Georgina bounds out of the kitchen like a gazelle. And a moment later, she returns and places her opened laptop before me on the table. "Promise you'll read it with an open mind, okay? Fair warning, parts of it are almost certainly going to freak you out, at first. But if you give it a fair chance, and read it with an open mind, I'm sure—"

"Enough," I say, more harshly than intended. "We'll let the article speak for itself."

As Georgina resumes her chair, wringing her hands, I exhale a long, slow breath, place my elbows onto the table, on either side of the laptop, and let my eyes settle on the title of the article that's surely going to hurtle me into a massive existential crisis. It reads, "Reed Rivers: The Man with the Midas Touch Unexpectedly Has a Heart of Gold."

I look up, frowning sharply. "What the hell is this?"

"The article I wrote about you."

"I thought you said you want your article to have journalistic integrity, and not be a sappy love letter to your boyfriend."

She winks. "How about we let the article speak for itself? Read to the end before providing commentary, please. Thank you."

Exhaling with annoyance, I return to the screen, and, after reading only a few paragraphs, easily surmise this article is a fucking travesty. A fluff piece. Shameless propaganda. Georgina describes how "brilliant" and "hands-on" I am, in every aspect of running my "empire." She says I'm "gifted," not only at holistic marketing, scouting, and negotiations, but also, at assisting my artists with "honing, maximizing, and developing their unique talents."

She writes, "But Reed's greatest talent lies in something that's hard to encapsulate in words. Something that's awfully hard to perceive about him, unless you've spent days observing him in his natural habitat. As crazy as it might sound to a casual observer, Reed Rivers is genuinely inspirational. Through more than his words—though his *example*, his persistence, his drive—he inspires the people around him to reach for their best selves and conquer the world."

Georgina goes on to admit I'm not perfect. I can be "shockingly harsh" and "grouchy." "At the office, annoyance and impatience are Reed's default modes. But all of that's okay with his team," Georgina writes, "because Reed's artists, and everyone who works for him, understand and respect his mission." Which, she goes on to explain, is fundamentally built on an "uncompromising commitment to greatness." Georgina further writes, "Everyone who works with Reed is well aware he only commands from others what he commands of himself. Excellence. And that makes them respect the hell out of him, both personally and professionally."

I look up from the computer, scowling. "CeeCee will never publish this tripe in *Dig a Little Deeper,* and you know it."

"Which is why I'm submitting this for *Rock 'n' Roll.* For the special issue."

I pull a face like that's the most moronic thing I've ever heard. "CeeCee explicitly assigned you to covertly try to unpeel my onion and bring her something on-brand for *Dig a Little Deeper.* Come on, Georgina. You're still vying for a spot at *Dig a Little Deeper.* Don't dim your light for anyone. Not even me. You know very well an article about me in *Rock 'n' Roll* isn't an A-plus result for you."

Georgina shrugs. "A's are overrated. C's get degrees, dude."

I stare at her blankly, incredulous. I've told this shark of a woman every fucking thing about me, every embarrassing, sensitive, excruciating, torturous thing... and *this* piece of shit is what she decided to write about me? I'm flabbergasted. Shocked. *Annoyed.* "You're sincerely proud of this... *article*? And, yes, I'm using that term loosely."

She laughs. "Yes, I'm very proud of it. Keep reading, please. No further commentary until you're finished. Thank you."

My pulse thumping in my ears, I return to Georgina's screen and continue reading at the point where I left off. It's the turning point of the article, it turns out. The place where Georgina gets to her true thesis: "But Reed isn't merely a wildly successful and brilliant mogul-innovator-influencer-genius, he's also, surprisingly, a truly good, generous, and kind human being, as well." According to Georgina, I'm a "devoted son" who plays Scrabble and does yoga with his "beloved mother." A loyal big brother who put his little sister through school and adores his nephew. "Reed is loyal as the day is long," Georgina writes. "A man who's had the same best friends since college and who grew up to hire his childhood nanny as his housekeeper, as soon as he could scrape together the funds to do so."

To drive her thesis home, Georgina quotes several of my employees, including Owen, all of whom babble about whatever exceedingly nice thing I've done for them, or their family members, over the years, without fanfare or taking credit for it. Owen, in particular, goes on and on about my over-the-top generosity. "He's a dream boss," Owen is quoted as saying. "There's never a dull moment with that guy. I learn something new every day by watching him."

"This is hideous tripe," I spit out. "I feel like I'm reading my own fucking obituary."

Georgina giggles with glee. "Read to the end, *stronzo*. What part of that instruction do you not understand?"

Begrudgingly, I return to Georgina's screen, only to discover I'm not only a "philanthropist" who "generously" supports such and such causes, I'm also a guy who "regularly" helps good friends and family, and *their* friends and family, with whatever they ask of me, while never seeking acknowledgment or praise for any of my covert good deeds.

"Not true," I mutter under my breath. But I know better than to look up from the screen again. I continue reading: "Why does Reed help so many people, without seeking credit or adulation? As far as this writer can tell, he does it simply because he can. Because helping people gives his life purpose. Because he's a genuinely good man who likes watching other people soar. Of all the wonderful things I've discovered about Reed this summer, I think that's the thing I like best about him. The thing that made me fall in love with him the most.

"Yes, you read that right. This writer has fallen hopelessly and totally in love with Reed Rivers. I didn't mean to do it. In fact, I tried very hard *not* to give him my heart. But it couldn't be helped. He's irresistible. Thankfully for me, though, luck was on my side. When I gave Reed my heart, he gave me his in return. And let me unpeel it, down to the nub.

And that's why I'm able to tell you, with certainty, The Man with the Midas Touch truly does have a heart of gold."

And that's it. The article ends that way, without any mention of my father—not even the golf story I explicitly gave her permission to use. She doesn't bother to mention the fact that I play all that Scrabble and do all that yoga with my "beloved mother" in a mental facility. Similarly, there's no mention of my parents' divorce or Troy Eklund or Stephanie Moreland. For crying out loud, Georgina's article is so *opposite* a hit piece, so unabashedly—and *explicitly*—a sappy love letter to her boyfriend—I mean, for fuck's sake, she *literally* declares her love for me!—it's an embarrassment. Not only to *me,* but also to Georgina.

And then it hits me. *She's playing a prank on me.* Ha! I look up, chuckling. "Good one. You *almost* got me. Now, show me the real article."

Georgina smiles. "This is the real article."

"No more joking around, sweetheart. I'll cherish this forever. It's sweet. But, please, show me the one you're actually planning to submit to CeeCee."

"This is it. I swear on my mother."

I pause, utterly floored. Not to mention, disgusted. "Are you insane? You can't submit this!"

She laughs. "Why not?"

"Because it's everything you said you *didn't* want to write. Propaganda. A love letter to your boyfriend. Not to mention, it's full of brazen fabrications and untruths."

"Name one thing that's not true."

"All of it! It's not any one thing. It's the total effect of it, put together. You've made me sound like a saint."

"The article is well-researched and every word is accurate."

I scoff. "I funded your grant because I wanted to fuck you. Did you forget about that?"

Georgina folds her arms over her chest and leans back

from the kitchen table. "Then why'd you pay for my father's medication, on top of my salary? Why'd you donate so much money to the cancer charity, if your only goal was getting me into bed? Surely, you could have paid my measly little salary and nothing else, if you sincerely didn't have *any* altruistic motivations."

Well, shit. She's got me there. I've already told her, repeatedly, I had parallel motivations on that front. So, fuck, I guess I need another tack. "Yes, okay, but you make it sound like I'm *never* selfishly motivated, in anything I do, and you know that's a bald-faced lie. There's *always* something in it for me."

"Is that so? Why'd you help Keane with his career? His agent wouldn't send him on any serious auditions, so you pulled strings, without a moment's hesitation. What'd you get out of *that*?"

"Where'd you hear about that?"

"Kat."

I roll my eyes. Fucking Kat. It's no wonder her family calls her The Blabbermouth. "Did Kat bother to mention *Josh* asked me to do it?"

"You also helped Hannah get a job."

"Because *Henn* asked me to do it. Whoop-de-do, I sometimes do favors for my two best friends. It hardly makes me a saint. Do you know how many favors they've done for *me* over the years? Josh paid for *every* fun thing we ever did in college. He flew a group of us to Thailand for spring break! Did you know that, after graduation, he's the one who gave me a loan to help me get River Records off the ground? I owe *everything* to Josh for that loan. Just as much as I owe CeeCee for putting *Rock 'n' Roll's* reputation behind a nobody-band called Red Card Riot. And don't get me started on Henn. You already know that guy helps me left and right, in a million ways. And not just regarding occasional hacking. He's my conscience. He keeps me sane and on the right track. So, okay, yes, I do nice things for my friends, sometimes. It doesn't mean I have a 'heart of gold.' It only means I'm not a sociopath. But that's hardly something to praise me for in a gushing piece of tripe."

She giggles. "It means you're fiercely loyal. Which is how I've described you in the article. Yet another thing I've said that's totally true."

I scoff. "I'm almost always motivated by selfishness, Georgina. One way or another. I just mask it well."

She flashes me a look of total incredulity. "What about Zander? Were you being selfish when you helped him land a job as Aloha's bodyguard?"

"Actually, yes! Ha! Aloha needed a bodyguard on her upcoming tour, and I knew Zander would be a perfect fit for her in terms of personality. And I *also,* selfishly, didn't want Barry going on tour with Aloha himself—which was exactly what Aloha, little miss diva, was demanding. I *selfishly* wanted Barry to stay in LA and work on *my* shit. So, I pulled strings and arranged a win-win-win-win."

"That doesn't sound selfish. It sounds brilliant. Which, again, is exactly how I've described you in my article."

"Georgie, I get what I want by giving other people what they want, too."

"Exactly." She laughs. "Wow, Reed, you're such a dick."

I run my hand through my hair. "Why didn't you at least tell the golf story?"

"Do you *want* me to tell the golf story?"

"No. Not particularly. But I don't want you to compromise your journalistic integrity by excluding it."

Georgina shrugs. "I decided that story wasn't on-brand for *Rock 'n' Roll.* Which is the publication I decided to write this for."

I lean back in my chair, bewildered. "This is insane. You make me sound so *nice.* And we both know I'm not. I mean, I am. But not *this* nice. I'm short-tempered. Harsh. Vaguely annoyed at all times."

"I've said all that."

"But not enough. Oh! I'm arrogant, too. But you didn't bother to say that."

"Okay, I'll add it. Fair point. Anything else?"

"Just paint an accurate picture of me, for crying out loud. Come on. *Drag me.*"

"Why would I do that? I had a thesis, which is that you have a heart of gold. Anything not supportive of that thesis isn't relevant."

"Not *relevant?*"

"This isn't a biography, Reed. It's a short little piece for *Rock 'n' Roll* about how unexpectedly wonderful you are—which is something the world doesn't already know about you. And *that,* my darling, was my *actual* assignment from CeeCee. To uncover a side of you nobody has seen before."

I shake my head. "I won't approve the article unless you make it a more accurate depiction of me. You need to dick me up a bit."

"No. If I do that, I'll look like an idiot for falling in love with you."

I grunt. "Yeah, about that ending..."

Georgie's face falls in earnest. "You don't like it? You want me to take it out?"

Oh, my heart. Fuck. "Come here, sweetheart." I pat my thigh, and Georgina leaves her chair and slides into it. "It's my favorite part. Thank you. But you can't leave that part in for the version you send to CeeCee."

"Why not? It's the truth."

"CeeCee will never print that."

"Well, I guess there's only one way to find out." She nuzzles her nose into mine. "Please, let me submit this article, as is. If CeeCee doesn't like something, she'll tell me to change it. But this is the article I want to submit. This is my truth." Before I can reply, she begins laying soft kisses up my jawline to my ear, licking and nipping and kissing as she goes, until I'm rock-hard and feeling incapable of saying no to her. "Say yes," she purrs. "Let me submit this, as is."

"It's propaganda of the worst kind," I whisper, but I'm smiling. Paradoxically, turning to steel underneath her while melting into a puddle of pliable goo.

Georgina's lips find mine and skim softly, making me shudder. "I've peeled your onion, down to your very core, my love. And what I found there, is what I wrote about." She places both palms on my cheeks. "Say yes."

I still can't believe *this* is what The Intrepid Reporter came up with, after everything she's discovered about me. Especially given that she thinks her dream job at *Dig a Little Deeper* is still on the line. Yeah, *I* know CeeCee is planning to offer Georgina a full-time slot, but *Georgina* doesn't know that. And, yet, Georgina is nonetheless willing to submit this puff piece for *Rock 'n' Roll,* rather than something that would surely lock down her dream job. "I just don't want you compromising your professional judgment for me."

She smirks. "Says the man who's about to release a single for my stepsister."

My cheeks flush. "But I'm not compromising anything to do that. Alessandra has all the makings of a quirky little indie star. She just needs some guidance and coaching."

"And you're willing to take the time to give Alessandra that 'guidance and coaching,' *personally*, because... *why?*"

I bite back a smile. She's got me there.

Georgina presses her forehead into mine. "I've written this article about you, for *Rock 'n' Roll,* because I love you with all my heart *and* I believe in this article. Which is the same thing as you producing and releasing Alessandra's song because you love me *and* believe in her. That's love, Reed. It's a two-way street."

Oh, my heart. If anyone is a saint here, it's Georgina. I press my lips to hers. And as I do, a dam breaks inside me. *Girlfriend* isn't enough. Matching tattoos aren't enough. I want it all, and I can't deny it a second longer. I want Georgina to take my name and wear my ring. I want us to pledge forever to each other in the most sacred way known to humankind. *I want her to be my wife.*

I've tried my damnedest to avoid reaching this conclusion. I've shucked and jived and thrown shiny objects into my own path to divert myself from reaching it. But the truth is, with each new ploy designed to convince myself I'm perfectly satisfied with shacking up, with each new label I use—whether it's girlfriend, lover, or partner—and each tiny letter we get permanently inscribed onto our bodies, all of it keeps bringing me to the same place. The same inescapable conclusion. *It's not nearly enough.* I want Georgina to be my one and only wife. Forever. And I won't settle for anything less.

"So, can I submit this article, as is? *Please?*"

I look into her hazel eyes, feeling overwhelmed with love and excitement about the decision I just made. "Just be prepared for CeeCee to say it's not what she wanted."

"I'll take that chance."

"Okay, you win, you relentless force of nature. Submit it. But only if you do a happy dance for me."

Squealing, Georgina gets up and gives me what I've demanded, making me laugh and clap. Breathlessly, she slides back into her chair, as I refill our champagne glasses and say a toast to the "godawful" article.

"So... there's actually one more thing I've been wanting to talk to you about," she says, putting down her champagne glass. "I figured I'd wait until you got home to tell you about it in person."

My stomach tightens. *What now?* "Okay..."

Georgina exhales loudly. "It's Isabel."

Chapter 31
Reed

Georgina strokes the stem of her glass. "Remember I told you Isabel's PR person had contacted me a few weeks ago and said she didn't want to do the skydiving thing, after all? That she decided she wanted to do a conventional lunch interview?"

"Yeah. I thought you said you were going to cancel the whole thing. You said you didn't feel right interviewing Isabel, now that we're together."

"Yeah, and I meant that when I said it." She grimaces. "Turns out, though, I never got around to actually cancelling. I started having this fantasy I could show up to the lunch, and tell Isabel we're together, and let her decide if she wanted to proceed with the interview." She makes an adorable face I'd caption, *Sorry, not sorry.* "And now I've dragged my feet so long on cancelling, I'm in a bit of a pickle." She winces. "I'm scheduled to meet Isabel for lunch tomorrow."

"Georgina Marie."

"I know, I know. I'm a bad girl. It's just that texting her PR woman to cancel feels so anti-climactic and unsatisfying compared to getting to tell Isabel, to her face, I'm your girlfriend, and then watching her expression as she puts two and two together and realizes *I'm* the woman you were talking about in that surveillance video. Although, I promise, I'd *never* mention the video itself or what I saw or heard in it."

Ah. I get it. Georgina can't help wanting that delicious

moment of revenge for herself, every bit as much as I wanted the pleasure of making that PA scurry back to C-Bomb to let him know I'm the "boyfriend" Georgina mentioned during her interview of RCR. And you know what? I don't blame her. Frankly, after the shit I pulled in that garage, I think it's only fair Georgina should get to enjoy a triumphant moment like that.

"If I'm being immature and vindictive, tell me so," Georgina says. "But the truth is, I want Isabel to realize, if she's only marrying Howard to try to win you back, she's going to have to go through *me* to do that."

Oh, my gorgeous fireball. She's a blazing pyre before me. Physically glowing with passion. "You know what?" I say. "Go for it."

"Really?"

"Why not? Once your article about me comes out in *Rock 'n' Roll,* Isabel will find out about us, anyway. You might as well experience the pleasure of telling her yourself, in person. But, if you don't mind, I'd like to come along, so she understands we're a team—that I'm as committed to you, as you are to me."

"Oh my gosh! I'd love that."

"Just be prepared for Isabel to get pissed off and feel like we've ambushed her."

Georgina's eyes ignite. "Yes, please."

I laugh.

Georgina's face flashes with mischief. "Actually, now that an actual interview of Isabel isn't going to happen, I can't see the downside of me asking her about Howard. I still haven't been able to get a single actress who's worked with Howard to talk to me on the record, although several of them have told Hannah and me horror stories, *off* the record. CeeCee said she won't publish anything based solely on anonymous sources. So, I might as well go for broke and ask Isabel if she's heard any of the rumors and see what she says."

"Why not? Although I can't imagine she's heard a thing. Isabel is screwed up in a lot of ways, but I don't believe she'd marry Howard if she knew any of that stuff, no matter what superhero franchise he'd offered her."

"She's truly never said *anything* to you about Howard being a creep?"

I shake my head. "Not in the way you mean. Sure, she's always laughed about how obsessed he was with her, right from the minute he met her at her first big audition. She called him a 'stalker,' but she laughed about it."

Georgina furrows her brow. "Isabel met Howard at an audition?"

"Yeah. It was her big break. He happened to be at the audition, by chance. Usually, that's below his paygrade. But he happened to be there, and when he saw her, he immediately demanded the director give her the part."

Georgina squints. "Did that audition happen before or after CeeCee's fiftieth birthday party?"

"About a year after. Why?"

"Oh, nothing. I'd convinced myself Isabel met Howard at CeeCee's birthday party. I had this whole storyline in my head about that. But I guess not."

"No. She met him at an audition. Howard wasn't even at CeeCee's party."

"Yes, he was. I saw him in a group photo from the party. Hang on." Georgina leaves and comes back with a color copy of the article, which she places before me on the kitchen table. "See?" She points to Howard's face. "That's definitely him. Plus, CeeCee confirmed he crashed her party and she was livid about it."

"Well, I'll be damned. I had no idea. I didn't even know who he was that night, so I never would have noticed him. But I can't imagine Isabel didn't know who Howard was at the time. She was always savvy when it came to..."

I trail off, as my brain starts connecting dots. Suddenly, I remember that twenty-minute gap during the party when Isabel disappeared on me, and later told me she'd been in line for the toilet. Was she talking to Howard then? Did she contact him after the party, and stay in touch with him during that entire next year, working him, hustling her ass off, until he finally agreed to give her that first big break? And did she do all of this, while I was paying her fucking rent because I didn't want her working for Francesca anymore?

Georgina sits in my lap and looks at the smiling group photo that includes Howard. "Maybe Isabel was in the same boat as you. Too young and naïve to realize she was in the presence of a hugely successful movie producer." She runs her fingers through my hair. "Or maybe she was just too damned smitten with her gorgeous date for the evening to notice—"

"No, she noticed," I say, my jaw tight. "Trust me, she knew exactly who he was that night. Isabel is, and always has been, the most ambitious person I know. She's always wanted to be a star, come hell or high water." Again, my brain catalogs the countless times I felt like Isabel was lying to me, early on. The times I felt like what she was telling me didn't add up. But since I was regularly lying to her, too—about my father, mother, childhood, lack of funds—I always let it go.

"Are you okay?" Georgina says.

"I'm fine." I stroke her arm and exhale. "I think it's a great idea for you to keep your lunch date with Isabel tomorrow, and for me to tag along. We'll tell her about us, and, after that, I definitely think you should ask her any goddamned thing you want about her beloved fiancé."

Chapter 32
Reed

I wake up and look at Georgina's sleeping face next to me. *Hello, wife.* The thought pops into my head, without me consciously putting it there. Which means the thumping urge I felt last night to make Georgina my wife hasn't abated in the slightest. In fact, it feels even stronger inside my veins this morning. Which means... hot damn. I need a ring.

I grab my phone off the nightstand and send a quick email to Owen, asking him to set up a private showing with a high-end jeweler this week. After a few gifs expressing excitement and shock, he asks me my budget, to which I reply, "Something between a Bugatti Chiron and a Lamborghini Veneno." Owen replies to that bit of news with two gifs from Disney's *Aladdin.* One of the Genie, granting a wish. Another of Aladdin tossing up a pile of gold coins. And I send him a gif of Leonardo DiCaprio from *Titanic,* where he's shouting that he's king of the world.

Next up, I send CeeCee a text, telling her I've decided to pour every proverbial drop of me into Georgina's wine goblet, and asking her to join me ring shopping this week. As I'm reading her enthusiastic reply, a photo of Hazel Hennessy, looking happy in a bathtub, flashes across my screen, along with a message from Henn:

Hazel's fever broke this morning. Thanks for the limo ride. When I got home, I was well rested and ready to take over for Hannah. You're the best.

I tell Henn I'm relieved to hear the news, and then rope Josh into the chat, at which point I tell my two best friends the shocking news that I've decided to propose to Georgina. The three of us exchange texts and gifs for a while, trying to come up with the perfect location and plan for my proposal, until Georgina stirs next to me in bed and I quickly tell my friends I've got to go.

"Hey, good lookin'," Georgina says, her voice husky.

I put down my phone. "Hey, beautiful. How'd you sleep?"

"Like a baby." She rubs my thigh underneath the covers. "Who were you texting with?"

"Henn. He left early from our fraternity brother's birthday party in Vegas the other night because Hazel had a high fever. He was just updating me. Her fever's broken and she's doing great."

"Aw, that's great. I'm so impressed he left Vegas early to be with his sick baby."

"Yeah, all flights had left already for the night, so he booked a limo and hightailed it home." Okay, yes, Georgina and I have decided to be open books. But there's no reason for me to mention I'm the one who booked the damned limo for Henn. For all I know, she'd slip that little nugget into her atrocious "Reed Rivers Can Turn Water Into Wine" fluff piece.

Georgina snuggles up to me and the touch of her warm flesh against mine makes my heart rate increase.

"Henn is such a good daddy."

"Same with Josh. Both of them love being fathers."

She runs her fingertip down the ridges and grooves of my abs for a long moment. "So, what are your thoughts about becoming a father one day? Is that a firm 'never'? Or is it more like, 'Never say never'?"

Wow. I didn't see that coming. I open and close my mouth a few times, sincerely unsure how to answer the question.

She adds quickly, "Everything I've read says you're not interested in having a kid. But, you know, rule number one of journalism is to go straight to the source, whenever you can."

My heart is clanging against my sternum now. "I think I'll answer your question with a question of my own. Would *you* like to have a baby one day? If your answer is yes, then my answer is, 'Yes, I'd be willing to have a baby with you one day. Not in the near future, please. But, yes. One day.' And if your answer is that you don't want a baby, then my answer would be, 'I'm perfectly fine with not having a baby.'"

I'm thinking this is a monumental answer. Shocking. Earth quaking. But Georgina looks wholly unimpressed.

"I'm asking what *you* want, in your heart of hearts. Not what you think *I* want."

"I just told you what I truly want. What I said is my honest answer."

Georgina flushes, the enormity of what I've said hitting her, full force.

I sit up and look down at her. "So, what do you truly want? Do you want to have a baby one day, in your heart of hearts? Don't tell me what you think I want to hear. Tell me the truth."

She bites her full lower lip, and the sparkle in her hazel eyes makes it abundantly clear what she's about to say. "Well, not any time soon... but, yes. I can't imagine not being a mommy one day. Like, maybe when I'm thirty?"

And just like that, I see my future in Georgina's hazel eyes. I see my future family. And, to my extreme shock, the vision doesn't terrify me. It only makes my heart skip a beat to imagine Georgina with a baby on her hip, the way T-Rod had one at Hazel's birthday party.

"Then I guess we're gonna have a baby one day, baby."

She touches my arm. "I'd never want to bring a child into the world with you, though, if that's not truly what you want."

I take her hand. "Am I chomping at the bit to have a kid, in this moment? No. I'm not. But, sweetheart, if you get to the point where you truly want one, and you honestly feel ready, then, *boom*. Decision made. We're having a baby. I mean, come on, I'm sure as shit not letting you have one with someone else."

She pulls me down and snuggles into me with glee. "I love you so much."

"Good. Because I love you. Just, promise me, we're not boarding the baby train any time soon. I want you all to myself for a while. I want to show you the world. Fuck you in forty countries."

She sighs happily. "Sounds great to me. I want you all to myself for a long while, too. Plus, I want to get established in my career."

"Can't wait to see you do it." I kiss the top of her head. "Now, come on. We don't have tons of time for our workout before we have to meet Isabel for lunch. Annihilate me, Ginger."

Georgina flashes me a wide smile that makes my heart burst wide open. "You got it, Freddie Boy." She hops up and heads to her closet, swishing her naked ass as she goes. And the minute she disappears, I grab my phone, eager to see what I've missed in my conversation with Josh and Henn.

Not surprisingly, my two best friends have roped their wives into our conversation, and all four of them have been littering our group chat with gifs—images of people popping champagne and jumping for joy and getting down on bended knee. Finally, I reach the end of the long text chain, and tap out a reply.

Me: Thanks for the enthusiasm, guys. I can't wait to blow her away. CeeCee already said she'll help me pick out a ring.

Kat: I'M SO EXCITED!!!

Me: Really? I couldn't tell.

Hannah: When, when, WHEN are you going to ask her?

Me: I don't know yet. Once I have the ring, I'll take her somewhere with white sand beaches.

Henn: Josh, you owe me $1000.

Josh: No, the bet was RR getting married, not engaged. I don't have to pay until RR actually says, "I do."

Me: Josh, pay Henny on the bet now.

I look up. Georgina's just now re-entered the bedroom in her workout gear, looking like a wet dream. And there it is again. *Hello, wife.* I return to my phone and quickly finish tapping out my text: **Because, I assure you, the deed is as good as done.**

Chapter 33
Reed

I'm in an upscale restaurant with Georgina. We're sitting in a private dining room, awaiting Isabel. When she finally walks into the room, twenty minutes late, and sees me with Georgina at our table, her features contort with surprise.

"Reed?" Isabel says. "What are you doing here?"

"I came to sit in on the interview," I say, rising and giving her a polite hug. "Also, to tell you some news, so you won't hear it first on social media."

Isabel looks anxious. "Okay." She politely hugs Georgina. "Hello again. Nice to see you."

"You, too."

We take our seats at the linen-covered table, just as a server appears to take our drink orders.

"Water for me," Isabel says.

"Why don't we have martinis all around?" I suggest. "I think you might thank me later, when you hear what I have to tell you."

Isabel's face drops. She looks at Georgina. And then again at me. But since she's an actress by trade, she forces a stiff smile and says, "It's five o'clock somewhere. Martinis it is."

When the waiter leaves, Georgina motions to me, giving me the floor. So, I put my elbows on the table and jump right in.

"I thought you should know Georgina and I are in a

237

committed relationship. She's the one I told you about at my party. The one I'm head over heels in love with. Actually, my love for her has only grown exponentially since that night."

Isabel swallows hard, but otherwise remains stoic.

"Georgina lives with me," I continue. "We're as committed and serious as two people in love can possibly be."

Well, that does it. Isabel can't keep her poker face intact any longer. Her chin trembles. Her eyes flash with acute rejection. And I'm not surprised. How many times did Isabel declare her love for me over the years, and I told her I'm not cut out to say those words in return? "It's nothing personal," I'd always say. "I've never been in love. I'm not cut out for it." How many times did Isabel say she wanted to move in with me, and I'd say, "I value my space and privacy too much to share my bed and home with anyone. It's nothing personal." How many times did Isabel say I "broke her heart" because I wasn't capable of loving her the way she so clearly needed to be loved? And now, here I am, breaking her heart one last time—forcing her to hear that I've given everything she's ever wanted from me to another woman. And not just any woman, but someone who's Isabel's physical opposite in every way. Plus, Georgina is ten years Isabel's junior—a fact that's probably hitting Isabel where it counts, considering how much she's been using Photoshop lately to smooth away all signs of her actual humanity.

But it can't be helped. As much as I don't have any impulse to brutalize Isabel, she needs to understand, without a doubt, my heart is now irrevocably taken. Not to mention, I feel like I owe this moment to Georgina as my final act of penance.

"Why are you telling me this in front of *her*?" Isabel spits out. "Did she demand you do this, and let her watch, as some sort of test of your—"

"Here we go," the waiter says, arriving with our martinis, and we lean back from the table to let him put them down.

"Bring me another one," Isabel says, picking up her glass.

"Make that three," I say.

"Of course," the waiter says. "Would we like to order some appetizers?"

"No, we won't be ordering food," Isabel snaps. "Bring the next round of drinks and then leave us alone."

"Yes, Miss Randolph."

As he scurries away, Isabel trains her ice-blue eyes on mine. "Doing this in front of her is cruel."

"Nobody is trying to hurt you," Georgina pipes in. "We thought it would be more respectful to tell you this, in person, before we started posting 'happy couple' photos on Instagram. And, by the way, I don't see how Reed telling you he's in love and happy could possibly be considered 'cruel' to you, when *you're* the one who's engaged to be married, and you and Reed haven't even been together in *years*."

I bite back a smile. *That's my girl.*

"It's not like you and I are besties," Georgina continues. "So, I don't feel like either one of us owes you an apology for falling head over heels in love with each other and then giving you the *courtesy* of an in-person heads-up about it."

I take Georgina's hand underneath the table, letting her know I've got her back. "I understand you're feeling blindsided," I say. "But Georgina is right. You've got no reason to be upset with me or throw shade at Georgina. You've moved on with Howard. I've moved on with Georgina. Congratulations to us both." I raise my martini. "Cheers."

Georgina clinks with me, but Isabel doesn't.

"You told me your girlfriend wasn't at the party," Isabel says, her nostrils flaring.

"I didn't want you heading straight to Georgina to confront her. I also wanted Georgina to have a shot at getting a good interview out of you."

Isabel scoffs. "*Why*? Why did you care about that?"

"Because I thought it would be a win-win."

Isabel looks at Georgina. "I hope you know you can forget about that interview now, sweetie."

"Yes, I've gathered that, sweetie. Although I do have a couple questions for you. Not for an article about *you*. For something I'm writing about your fiancé."

"Ha! Howard's not going to let you interview him! Not after I tell him—"

"No, no," Georgina says calmly. "My article about Howard isn't going to be an *interview*. It's going to be an exposé."

Isabel pauses, clearly taken aback. "About *what*?"

"I'm glad you asked. But first, a little background, so you understand how this idea was born. I was researching an article about Reed, actually. So I went to the courthouse and got copies of some lawsuits he'd settled. One of which, was this one." She reaches into her computer bag, pulls out Troy Eklund's lawsuit, and slides it across the table in front of Isabel. And the moment Isabel sees the name at the top, she gasps and looks at me, hurtling into full panic mode.

"I want to be clear, I found this lawsuit, all by myself. Without Reed or anyone else saying a word about it. And when I read it, I found it so interesting and mysterious, I decided to track down this Troy Eklund dude and hear his side of it. I went to a bar in West Hollywood, where he was playing on a Tuesday night. Troy and I chatted after his set. Man, he's a chatty motherfucker. Also, a douchebag. But, anyway, based on *that* conversation, I then headed downtown to a restaurant owned by a woman I think you know. Francesca Laramie."

Isabel looks ashen. She looks at me and whispers, "*You told her?*"

"Reed didn't say a word to me about any of this," Georgie says. "He didn't even know I was sniffing around about any of this. I figured everything out for myself."

"Oh my God," Isabel says, burying her face in her hands.

"There's no need for you to worry," Georgina says reassuringly. "I swear on my mother, and that's my most sacred promise, that I'll never tell anyone your secret. No matter what. The only reason I'm telling you about all this is because—"

"Here we go," the waiter says, bringing us the second round of drinks. "Are we sure we don't want to order—"

"We're sure!" Isabel shrieks. "Now go, and don't come back unless you've been expressly summoned!"

"Yes, miss." He scurries away.

"This isn't a shakedown," Georgina says. "I wasn't going to mention this next thing, but I suddenly feel like it would be for the best if I do. I already know that you and Reed kissed in his garage at the party, Isabel. And I want you to know this isn't about that. I want to assure you I'm not going to find out about that kiss later, and snap, and then go back on my word not to divulge your secret. My promise is ironclad. I come in peace. I'm not here to hurt you and I'll never tell *anyone* what I figured out. I love Reed. And whether he realizes it or not, he loves you. And that means, no matter what, I'm not going to hurt or humiliate you. Not directly, anyway. Which brings me to Howard and the reason I'm telling you all this." She takes a deep breath. "When I was talking to Francesca at her restaurant, Howard's name came up. Francesca said she never talks about her girls, or her former clients. But she did say there was one client who used to assault her girls. And when I mentioned Howard's name, she confirmed that's who she meant."

Isabel's lips part in surprise.

"You know why I knew Francesca had to be talking about Howard? Because my boss, CeeCee Rafael, had already warned me about him. She told me not to be alone with him. And then, a young woman who works at Howard's company told me every young woman who works for Howard knows not to be alone with him. In fact, all the young women who work at Howard's studio know to use the buddy system when interacting with him."

Isabel looks like she's having a hard time taking air into her lungs.

"Thanks to this insider at Howard's company, I've now interviewed five actresses who told me detailed stories about Howard sexually assaulting them. Everything from unwanted groping and kissing to coerced sex to being roofied and raped."

Isabel groans like she's about to throw up.

"The only problem? They're all too scared to come forward." Georgina leans forward. "He's a predator, Isabel, and my gut tells me you know it."

"No."

"Don't you want to stop him? Because he's not going to stop, unless someone brave, someone the world will believe, leads the charge. Isabel, that someone is *you.*"

Isabel looks frantic. "You think I know about all this? I don't!"

"Yeah, well, you know something. At the very least, you know what he's done to you, personally. But I'm here to tell you, you're not alone. He's done stuff to others. And he won't stop, just because he's marrying you. He'll never stop."

"What do you want from me?"

"I want you to tell the truth, on the record. Either to the police, or in an interview, or in a press conference. I don't know. I want you to stop him. Because once you speak out, everyone else will, too. And that's the only way we're going to take this man down. If we band together."

Isabel is trembling. And there's no doubt in my mind Georgina is right: Howard's done *something* to Isabel. The thought physically pains me.

"For what it's worth, I have a glimmer of understanding about how hard this is for you," Georgie says. She reaches into her computer bag and pulls out a copy of her Gates article. "This is going to be published in a couple days in *Dig a Little Deeper*. It's an article I wrote about the forty-two-year-old man who tried to rape me when I was seventeen. He wasn't a billionaire movie producer, and I wasn't a young actress with big dreams, who felt like she had no other choice. But he was very powerful in my little world. After he assaulted me—and to be clear, he came as close to forcibly raping me as a person can get, before I wiggled free from his clutches and ran away—after that happened, I was too terrified to say a word to anyone. So I kept it bottled up inside me for almost five years. But, recently, I found out he's hurt other girls, too. And that made me realize he's going to do it again and again, unless someone stops him. So, I decided that someone is going to be *me*."

Isabel picks up her martini with a shaky hand and drains it. But she doesn't speak.

Georgina taps the article on the table. "Pretty soon the whole world is going to read this article and know what he did to me, and to those two other girls. And I can't begin to tell you how fucking proud I am, how *freeing* it is, to know I'm not hiding this secret anymore. And not only that, I'm doing everything in my power, however small, to protect other girls from suffering at the hands of that fucking prick." Georgina reaches across the table and takes Isabel's hand. And to my surprise, Isabel doesn't flinch or jerk away. "You're about to play a superhero on screen. But on your deathbed, won't you be far prouder of yourself for playing a superhero in real life?"

Isabel slides her hand away. But not forcefully. Her demeanor is dejected. Scared. "I'm sorry. I can't help you."

"You can do this," Georgina says. "If I can do it, then you can, too. And, by the way, I don't want you to do this to help *me*. I want you to do it to help yourself. To help the other women he's hurt and the ones he hasn't yet but will."

Isabel's features harden. "You don't understand. You're not *me*. I've got too much to lose."

All of a sudden, I get it. "Howard has been blackmailing you, hasn't he? You met him at CeeCee's party, not at an audition a year later. Howard found out you were a working girl at that party, and he's been blackmailing you about your past, ever since."

Isabel's breathing halts, and, just that fast, I know I'm right. Isabel did, indeed, meet Howard the same night she met me. The night we went back to my hovel of an apartment and fucked like rabbits and talked until sunrise about our dreams and ambitions. The night I told her I didn't want her working for that fucking escort service any longer. The night I told her I'd pay her rent, even though I could barely afford to pay mine, so she could stop selling her body and concentrate on her auditions and making her dreams come true. The night I told her I'd always protect her and have her back, no matter what. And she let me say all that. And do all that for her. She let me think I was her knight in shining armor... and all the while, she was fucking Howard on the side. Or, if not fucking him, then flirting with him. Stringing him along. Wrapping him around her finger until he finally gave in and gave her the big break she'd been trying to coax out of him for a fucking year.

"Did you fuck Howard at CeeCee's party?" I choke out.

"No," Isabel says. "Reed, no."

"But you met him that night."

She exhales and nods. "I flirted with him and gave him my number."

"Why did you lie to me?"

"You'd made it clear to Francesca your date that night wasn't allowed to network for herself. You told Francesca that was rule number one—your date had to be there to support you, and only you, and not her own agenda. I knew you'd be furious with me for hunting Howard down and slipping him my number. I thought you might even demand your money back from Francesca."

I take a deep breath. "You told him you worked for Francesca that night?"

"Yes. And he liked it. It turned him on."

I look down at the table. I can't believe Isabel let me pay her rent that entire year, when she knew how hard I was working to keep my own dreams afloat. I can't believe she did that to me, when Howard was probably slipping her gifts and God knows how much money, at the same time.

"I really did quit Francesca's when I told you," Isabel says. She begins to cry, but I don't believe a single tear. "Howard was my only client after that. But he hired me directly. After a while, though, I told him I'd fallen in love with you and wouldn't be doing anything with him, anymore. And that's when he drugged me. The first time. When I woke up, I told him I'd go to the police, and he said, go ahead. He said he'd tell them, and everyone else, I'd worked for Francesca. He said he'd make sure I never got hired for anything but porn. And that's when he finally gave me that first big role. And then another one. And another. Until my career really started taking off... But then I felt trapped. Like I couldn't get away, even if I wanted to... Which I did, Reed. I swear, I did. But I was in a gilded cage." Isabel wipes her eyes. "He said he'll finally let me go if I marry him. He said he'd never let a 'scandalous' secret like mine come out about his *wife*. Not even his ex-wife."

"And when will that be?" I ask flatly. "What does the marriage contract say, Isabel?"

She looks down. "Five years."

I shake my head. I can't believe how stupid I've been. For so long, I thought I was defective, thanks to my childhood. I thought I was literally incapable of falling in love. I knew I'd felt a glimmer of something special with Isabel that first night. Something I'd never felt before. Not quite that thing everyone writes about in love songs. But, still, it was definitely *something* more than I'd ever felt before. But then, as our relationship progressed, I felt myself constantly butting up against an impenetrable wall. And I thought that was because of *me*. Because *I* was too fucked up to let someone get too close to me. Because *I* was too guarded to ever let someone in, all the way. But now, suddenly, I realize it was never going to work for Isabel and me, not because *I'm* too fucked up to love. I mean, yes, I'm fucked up. But not to the degree I've always thought! No, Isabel and I were doomed because our entire relationship was built on lies, from day *one*. Because Isabel was playing me, and using me, and a piece of my heart always sensed it, and held back out of self-preservation.

"I'm sorry, Reed," Isabel chokes out. "I've always loved you. Only you."

"You don't know what love is," I say. I look at Georgina, my eyes plainly telling her: *But you sure do.* I return to Isabel, my jaw muscles pulsing. "If you're hoping I'll save you from Howard, the same way I've always saved you, then stop hoping right now. I'm not here to save you this time. *Georgina* is. *She's* your white knight. She's the one throwing you a lifeline. So, grab it with both hands." With that, I grab Georgina's hand under the table and squeeze. "Nobody can blackmail you about something you're not hiding. Set yourself free. I don't know if you'll find true happiness by doing that. But what have you got to lose? You're obviously miserable now."

As Isabel sits quietly, her chest heaving, Georgina reaches into her computer bag, and pulls out a pad. She scribbles on it, tears off a sheet, and slides it across the table to Isabel. "I don't blame you for not wanting to talk to me about any of this. So, call my boss, CeeCee Rafael. This is her number. CeeCee's been wanting to expose Howard for years. I've also confidentially listed the names of the women I've spoken to about Howard, several of whom were on Francesca's roster, early in their careers. Talk to them. Hear for yourself what Howard did to them. See for yourself if you feel okay with staying silent after you speak to them."

To my relief, Isabel takes the paper. But, again, she says nothing.

I say, "If Howard's got you brainwashed into thinking you're nothing without him, he's dead wrong about that. You're a brilliant actress, Isabel. And everyone knows it. I know for a fact my buddy Ethan Sanderson—you remember him, right? I know for a fact he's got at least four films in the pipeline he'd *kill* to hire you for. Wouldn't you rather do movies you can sink your teeth into, anyway? That's what you always used to dream about when we were young and poor— not doing *superhero* movies. Chase your *real* dreams, Isabel. Fuck Howard."

After stowing the scribbled paper in her purse, Isabel stands, throws back the entirety of her second martini, and says. "I've got to go."

"Take Georgie's article," I say.

Isabel pauses and eyes the pages on the table. But she doesn't move.

"As a favor to me," I say. "If you ever truly loved me, as you claim, then take that article and read it tonight. It's the only thing I've ever asked of you."

Nodding, Isabel picks up the pages and folds them into her purse. She holds my gaze for a long moment, her blue eyes full of longing and regret, and, finally, leaves the room without saying another word.

The moment the door of the private dining room closes, Georgie melts into her chair. "Holy crap, that was intense."

"You were amazing."

"I was?"

"A superhero."

She smiles from ear to ear. "So were you. We're a dynamic duo."

"Let me take you somewhere, Georgie. Some place where we can relax and fuck and eat and think of nothing but each other."

247

"Sounds amazing. When?"

"As soon as possible. Your internship is officially over at the end of the week, right? So, let's pick up and go then."

"Where?"

"St. Barts... Santorini... the Amalfi Coast? You pick. Anywhere, as long as it's got sun and beaches and is easy to get to from the East Coast. We'll stop in New York, on our way, pay a quick visit to my mother, and then head to paradise."

Her face is glowing with excitement. "I've still got one more article to finish up. A secret something I've been working on as an 'audition' piece for *Dig a Little Deeper.* I should be done with it on Friday."

"We'll head out on Saturday, then. That's actually perfect timing. Several of my bands are performing in New York at a big charity concert this coming week. Why don't we add a few days in New York to our itinerary before we fly to paradise?" My wheels are suddenly turning. "Actually, you know what? I'll fly Alessandra to NYC to catch the charity show with us. And the next day, we'll shoot a simple little music video for her upcoming single."

Georgina shrieks. "What? Oh my God!"

"Don't get too excited. The video won't be anything fancy or complicated. Just a simple little 'performance' video we can throw onto YouTube, to show people how cute Alessandra is. I'll ask Maddy Morgan if she's available to fly in and direct the thing for me. I've always wanted to give her a shot. This is a perfect opportunity."

"Oh my gosh! This is so exciting!"

"And after all that, we'll swing by Scarsdale for an afternoon, and then jet off from there to paradise to relax." *And get engaged.*

"Amazing."

"Now come here, my little kitten." I coax Georgina out of her chair and bring her to my lap, where I kiss her passionately. And, soon, it's clear our kiss is barreling toward something a whole lot more than that.

"We can't do it *here*," Georgina whispers playfully, but she's purring as I reach underneath her skirt and massage her clit. "Reed, the waiter might walk in on us."

"*Oh no*," I say with mock horror, my fingers making her swollen and wet. "That would be *terrible*." I skim her lips with mine, as my fingers continue making her eyelids flutter. "Relax," I coax. "Isabel put the fear of God into the waiter. He won't come back, unless called."

"But what if he does?" she groans out, her pleasure apparent.

"*Oh no*," I say softly, my voice low and oozing with arousal. "Whatever would we do?"

Georgina groans and gyrates into my fingers. "You'd love for us to get caught, wouldn't you?"

I suck on her lower lip. "So much."

With that, I guide her belly against the table, pull off her panties, unzip my pants, and enter her from behind. And then, I proceed to fuck her, hard. She's the woman I'm going to ask to be my wife. The woman who's most likely going to have my baby one day—Jesus fucking Christ! The woman I love. I fuck her without mercy, while continuing to massage that hard, swollen bundle of nerves. Until the sounds of her pleasure become so loud, I have to shove a linen napkin into her mouth to muffle them. Finally, Georgina comes. As her body milks mine, I release and growl loudly and then collapse into her back, seeing stars.

Sadly, our waiter never walks in to discover us fucking like animals against the white-linen-covered table. Nor does he enter the room as we're putting ourselves back together. The consolation prize, though? As we pass the guy on our way out of the private room, the look on his face tells me he heard every telltale sound Georgina made in that room, and he's well aware of what I did to get her to make them.

Chapter 34
Georgina

I did it! I finished writing my last article of the summer!" I walk across Reed's home office and stand over his desk, holding up the printed pages—the secret article I've been working on for the past six weeks. "I never told you about this one. I wanted it to be a surprise. I think you're going to love it."

Reed looks up from whatever he's doing on his laptop. "Uh... what? Hold on." He clacks on his keyboard for a moment. And then looks up again. "Sorry? What?"

I hold up the printed pages of my mystery article. "I just finished writing a super-secret surprise article and I'm wondering if you'll read it now."

"Oh. Wow. Congratulations. Of course, I'll read it."

My chest heaving with anticipation, I slide the pages across Reed's desk, and he calmly picks them up. But when he looks down at the page, and sees the title at the top, his mouth hangs open.

"How did you...? Oh my God, Georgie."

"I know. Crazy, right? Read it. Please. I'm dying."

Still looking flabbergasted, Reed leans back in his leather chair and begins to read, and, in short order, it's clear he's thoroughly engrossed. Mesmerized, I'd even say. After a while, he looks up from the last page. "I can't believe you did all this. I'm in shock."

He asks me some questions about the article. How I gathered the information set forth in it. And I answer him.

"Holy shit," he says. "Would you do me a favor and give this to my mother before submitting it to CeeCee?"

"Of course. That's always been my plan. First, you. Then, your mom. And then, CeeCee, but only *if* Eleanor gives me the green light. I'm planning to give it to your mom, in person, during our upcoming visit, if that's okay with you."

"Perfect." Reed's mind is visibly racing. "My mother is going to have a thousand questions for you. Every bit as much as I did."

"And I'll happily answer them. Do you think she'll like it?"

"I think she'll be as blown away as I am."

My heart is thundering. I'm so relieved Reed likes this article and thinks his mother will, too. My biggest fear was Reed would say this topic was none of my business. I say, "Okay, but, if, for some reason, Eleanor doesn't love it, or wants her privacy, I won't submit it to CeeCee." My phone rings and I look down to find CeeCee's name on the screen. "Speaking of CeeCee, her ears must be ringing." I connect the call. "Hi there. Reed and I were just talking—"

"Sorry to cut you off. I've got big news. Are you at Reed's?"

"Yes."

"Stay put. I'm coming now."

I give CeeCee the passcode for the front gate and disconnect the call. And then drag Reed into the living room, where I pace circles around the cavernous space as we await CeeCee's arrival. Finally, CeeCee knocks on the front door. And the minute I fling it open, she barges into the room and blurts, "I sent advance copies of your Gates article to a few friends in the media, and we've caught two huge whales on our line! Both *NPR* and *Good Morning America* want to interview you about the Gates article, Georgina!"

"No!"

"*Yes*! You'll do a radio interview with *NPR* on Monday morning in Philadelphia. Which is perfect timing because the article will be published online that same morning. From Philly, you'll head straight to New York and do a nationally televised live interview on *Good Morning America* the following morning!"

I'm practically hyperventilating. "You'll come with me to all of that, right?"

CeeCee laughs. "I wouldn't miss it for the world."

I look at Reed, feeling like a deer in headlights. "And you, too?"

Reed chuckles. "Of course I'm coming. And don't worry. We'll rearrange our trip itinerary to make everything work."

CeeCee claps. "We have so much to do! I'll set up a prep session with my PR woman, Jane. She and I will go over talking points with you for both interviews, and also get you camera-ready." She looks me up and down. "Which, obviously, won't be hard to do." She slides into an armchair, a wide smile splitting her elegant face. "Now, listen, Georgie girl. I was going to tell you this tomorrow at the office— Margot and I were going to throw you a little party with a cake when I told you. But I've obviously got to tell you now: you're officially a full-time writer for *Dig a Little Deeper*!"

I leap up from the couch, shrieking with joy. I hug CeeCee exuberantly, and then Reed, and then perform the most enthusiastic happy dance of my life, making Reed and CeeCee guffaw.

"Holy shit, guys," Reed says, looking down at his phone. "When it rains, it pours. I just got a text from Isabel. She's read the Gates article and wants me to tell Georgina she found it 'deeply moving and inspiring.'" He reads, "'After some soul-searching, I reached out to the women Georgina listed for me. I've now met with several of them and decided I can't stay quiet any longer. Let the chips fall where they may. I'm ready to tell the truth. And so are they.'"

"Oh my freaking God," I breathe.

Reed continues reading, "'We're going to consult a

lawyer, and then give statements to the police. After that, we've all agreed we're going to do one, exclusive interview, as a group. Please ask CeeCee Rafael if she wants the exclusive. I don't want to text her, or anyone else. This is highly confidential, and I only trust you. Delete this message right after you get it. I'm sending it from a burner phone.'"

"Tell her yes!" CeeCee shrieks. "Tell her I'm sitting here now, and that I say yes!"

Reed begins tapping away on his phone, while CeeCee looks at me, astonished.

"You're a miracle worker!" CeeCee says. "The *Woman* with the Midas Touch!"

"Okay," Reed says. "I told Isabel you're one hundred percent in, CeeCee." He looks at me. "Isabel wanted me to tell you she's proud of you for coming forward about Gates. She says she wouldn't have made this decision if it weren't for that article."

I feel electrified. On the verge of tears. "Tell her I'm proud of her, too. Tell her we're not enemies. We're *sisters*." Tears well in my eyes. "Tell her she's more of a superhero now, than if she played one in *forty* movies."

Reed pats his thigh. "Come here, little kitty."

I go to him, on the bitter cusp of bawling, and he wraps his strong arms around me. "The Intrepid Reporter strikes again," he coos. "I'm so proud of you."

I nuzzle my face into Reed's neck and inhale his musky scent, somehow, still managing to keep it together. But when I look down at my mother's wedding band on my hand, a tsunami of emotion slams into me. Pride. Relief. Longing for my mother to be here to see this. But, mostly, I feel a deep-seated certainty that I'm fulfilling my purpose in life.

Reed touches my mother's ring on my splayed hand. "She'd be so proud of you," he whispers. "She's watching over you right now and cheering you on."

"I can feel her," I squeak out. And that's it. I can't keep

my emotions at bay any longer. I squeeze my beautiful Reed with all my might, nuzzle into his chest, and give myself permission to sob.

Chapter 35
Georgina

When my article about Gates and his enablers went live three days ago, early Monday morning, my phone lit up like crazy, and my father told me the reaction in our hometown community was like an atomic bomb had gone off. But I was already in Philadelphia by then for my radio interview with *NPR* that same day, so I ignored my phone and social media, choosing instead to focus on not sounding like a clown on live national radio.

Luckily, my *NPR* interview went fabulously well. Better than expected. But, right after that, Reed took me, CeeCee, and CeeCee's PR woman, Jane, to lunch to celebrate, followed by whisking us off to Manhattan. So, again, I didn't have a chance to focus too much on whatever the world was saying about Gates and my article and me.

But once Reed and I got settled into our penthouse suite overlooking Central Park, and CeeCee and Jane came over, we finally looked, as a group, at the world's reaction to the story. And that's when we realized the story of Gates, the high school football coach who was secretly a sexual predator, was rapidly becoming high-profile national news.

One major news outlet called the story "a sexual assault scandal" and summarized it this way: "Three female former students at a California high school allege the school's football coach sexually assaulted them, and also that the school's principal, and a wealthy parent, actively covered for him." I thought that summed it up nicely.

Luckily, according to the vast majority of online commentary, it seemed most people believed Katrina, Penny, and me, and wanted swift justice for Gates and anyone who'd covered for him. On social media, people were sharing the story like crazy, as part of several lines of discussion. One of them about the intersection between sexual assault and sports-hero worship. Another one focused on women often being scared to speak truth to power, for fear of being called a liar or slut. I felt heartened to read all of those discussions. Frankly, I felt immensely proud.

But it wasn't all rainbows and unicorns. In one line of general discussion, people lamented the ability, in the age of social media, for any "disgruntled" or "unhinged" woman to say "anything she wants" about any "innocent man," thereby unjustifiably ruining his life, without due process. Fair enough. I think, generally speaking, we can all agree that's a true statement, in concept. But, when people went so far as to *specifically* call Katrina, Penny, and me "fame-seekers," "opportunists," and "liars," that pissed me off.

A former player of Gates', a guy who went on to play in the NFL, posted his support for Gates on Instagram with the hashtags #innocentuntilprovenguilty and #myhero. Again, fair enough. I totally understood his point, in concept. Gates *is* innocent until proven guilty, in terms of the legal system. But to me, he's not a hero. He's the man who shoved his tongue down my throat and his fingers up my vagina, forcibly. The man who literally ripped my shirt as I tore myself away from his terrifying grasp. He's the man who made me hide, trembling, in bathrooms whenever I saw him across campus. The man who, to this day, occasionally visits me in nightmares that always cause me to break out in a cold sweat.

But that whirlwind is what happened on *Monday*. Day *one*. On day two, I opened a can of whoop-ass on not only

Gates, and his two enablers, but also on the online trolls and detractors who said Katrina, Penny, and I are liars. That morning, I did my interview on *Good Morning America*, with one of my all-time idols, by the way, so, that was a personal thrill. And, thankfully, the TV interview went even better than the radio interview. So much so, by the time Reed, CeeCee, Jane, and I walked out of the studio and into the sunshine on 44th Street, the "high school football coach scandal" had indisputably become a viral story.

Within an hour of my TV interview, both my name and Gates' were trending on Twitter. Gates' name, mostly, because people wanted his head. My name, mostly, because people were supporting me for all the right reasons. But, also, because a popular dude on Twitter had posted a screen shot of me, taken during my TV interview, that captured me looking like a goddamned fire-breathing dragon. Apparently, the Twitter guy decided that particular angry shot of me was incredibly hot. His actual hashtag was #hotwhenangry. And, apparently, a massive amount of his followers wholeheartedly agreed with him.

After that first Twitter guy did his thing, a *second* Twitter guy, someone with the handle @AngelinaFan, picked up on the thread and expanded upon it. Even though @AngelinaFan agreed I was, indeed, "hot when angry," he also felt it vitally important to note I looked uncannily like a young Angelina Jolie—which then, bizarrely, inspired him to start tweeting out all sorts of photoshopped images of me soundly kicking Gates' ass, using screen grabs from the movie *Tomb Raiders* as his starting point.

Along with my actual name in his hashtags, and the other guy's hashtag #hotwhenangry, as well as #TombRaiderRebootPlease, @AngelinaFan *also* transformed me into some sort of Georgina action hero with his additional, numerous hashtags. Stuff like #DoNotFuckWithGeorgina and #GeorginaSaysNotTodayGates   and

#BadassHotChickGeorgina. So stupid. Did he not understand the point of my article was to push back against exactly that kind of objectification?

But, whatever. In truth, I liked all those images of me kicking Gates' ass, as well as that first screen shot of me looking like a fire-breathing dragon. Because, truth be told, those two Twitter dudes, every bit as much as the radio and TV interviews, are what pushed my article into The Viral Stratosphere.

By the time Tuesday afternoon rolled around, all hell broke loose, in the best possible way. Leonard called to tell us that a young woman had come forward to accuse Gates of kissing and groping her when she was sixteen. The following morning, another young woman said Gates had forced her to give him a blowjob when she was fifteen, and also that she'd been paid off by none other than Steven Price to keep her mouth shut about it.

Well, that was when shit got real—when the story no longer lived in the world of Twitter or TV or radio—but, instead, started having real-world implications. Leonard called to tell me Gates and the principal had been put on leave by the school district, pending an internal investigation. Two hours after that, he called again to say authorities in Los Angeles had just announced—in a freaking press conference, attended by national media!—that they'd opened a criminal investigation into Gates *and* the principal. And *then,* shortly after that, Leonard called to report that Steven Price, the father of Brody, Brendan, and Benjamin, had lawyered up.

"I'm not sure what the charges against Price will be," Leonard told Reed and me. "My guess is money laundering and/or tax evasion. Maybe obstruction of justice."

"Oh, tax evasion, for sure," Reed said. "No way Price didn't cook his books to hide all those hush-money payments."

"So, listen, Georgie," Leonard said. "Some of Gates' victims are talking about filing civil lawsuits. Do you have any interest in that?"

I looked at Reed in that moment. Into his chocolate brown eyes. And, instantly, I knew my answer was a resounding *no*. Just that fast, I felt certain it was time for me to move forward. To build my career and a happy future with Reed, and not give another drop of my energy or time or soul to Mr. Gates. "No interest," I replied to Leonard. "I'll cooperate with any criminal investigations. But I'm done. *Ciao, stronzo.*"

Oh, the smile Reed flashed me then. If CeeCee and her PR woman hadn't been in our hotel suite at the time, I would have ripped Reed's clothes off and sunk to my knees to pleasure him, right then and there. Which is exactly what I did, only a few hours later, the minute CeeCee and Jane left.

And now, here I am, sitting in the back of a limo with Reed on Wednesday morning, scouring the curbside at JFK for Alessandra's beautiful face. I'm ready to put the past behind me now. For good. And to have a fantastic time, during the rest of this trip, to celebrate. Playing tourist today and going to the concert tonight. Visiting Eleanor in Scarsdale on Friday. And then heading off to Sardinia on Friday night to start a weeklong vacation in paradise with my man.

"There!" I say, pointing excitedly when I spot Alessandra on the curb with her suitcase.

The driver maneuvers and finds a spot, and I pop out of the car and race to my stepsister. When I reach her, we hug and kiss and jump for joy. And a few minutes later, we're heading off in the limo, excited to enjoy a carefree day of sightseeing in Manhattan, along with Reed's sister and nephew, who we're going to pick up now, while Reed heads off, separately, to the venue for tonight's charity concert. It's going to be a huge show, featuring, among others, some of Reed's biggest stars. 22 Goats, Laila Fitzgerald, Danger Doctor Jones, Aloha Carmichael, Watch Party, and Fugitive Summer. I can't think of a better way to celebrate the first day of the rest of my life.

Lauren Rowe

***

Laughter rises up from the other side of the long dinner table. Apparently, Davey from Watch Party has just told a joke to all the other River Records artists seated near him, as Davey often does—although this restaurant is too noisy, and our table too long, for the group at this end of the table to hear whatever joke Davey's told. But that's okay. I'm thoroughly enjoying my conversation with Alessandra and Fish. Who, by the way, have been joined at the hip since the moment Fish spotted Alessandra backstage at the concert earlier tonight.

This place is a chic eatery in Midtown. We're here to enjoy a post-concert dinner party, hosted by Reed. As I've been chatting with Alessandra and Fish to my left, Reed has been engrossed in an intense conversation with Maddy and Keane Morgan, to my right, about tomorrow's video shoot.

Without warning, however, Reed abruptly turns away from his conversation to address Alessandra. "Hey, Ally. Change of plans for your video tomorrow. I didn't know Maddy was bringing Keane to the shoot to help her. But now that I know he'll be there, I think we'd be missing a golden opportunity not to give him a starring role in the video. Keane says he's up for anything, so Maddy and I just now put our heads together and came up with an entire storyline for him."

Alessandra expresses excitement and enthusiastically thanks Keane.

"Happy to do it," Keane replies. "It sounds like a blast."

Alessandra looks at me, as if to say, *Can you believe this is my life?* And I don't blame her. Keane Morgan's show on Netflix is doing extremely well, from what I've gathered. With each passing day, he's becoming a bigger star. Having him star in her debut music video is huge.

"Now, don't feel any stress about tomorrow," Reed says soothingly to Alessandra, his little lamb. Over the past few weeks, as they've worked on Alessandra's song together, and fine-tuned it, exactly according to Reed's specifications, Alessandra has grown to trust him completely, and Reed has often told me he thinks Alessandra is "absolutely adorable." He continues, "From your end of things, Ally, you'll still mostly be doing what we talked about, okay? You'll still mostly be performing onstage at the coffee house."

"*Mostly?*" Alessandra says meekly.

"Yes. Maddy and I have come up with two storylines. A love triangle involving Keane. Also, a cute little love story involving you and Fish." Reed looks at Fish, who looks astonished to hear his name called. "If you're game, that is, Fish Taco."

Fish chuckles. "Sure. Count me in."

Thankfully, there's been no lasting tension between Fish and Reed, deriving from when Fish ripped into Reed at his party. Backstage at the charity concert earlier tonight, Fish pulled Reed aside and apologized for calling him a prick that night. To which Reed replied, in true Reed fashion, "I don't even know what you're talking about, Fish."

"What will Fish and I have to do for this 'cute little love story'?" Alessandra asks, looking on the verge of panic.

"Don't worry, honey," Maddy says reassuringly. "You'll be the performer onstage at the coffee house, as we discussed, and Fish will play the shaggy barista across the room. All you two will have to do is make googly eyes at each other, from afar, like you're totally smitten with each other."

Fish smiles shyly at Alessandra. "Well, speaking for myself, that shouldn't be hard to do."

Alessandra blushes the color of a vine-ripened tomato, and my heart skips a beat for her. "I think I could manage that," she says, through her lashes.

Reed looks at me. "Georgie, you're going to star in this thing, too."

"*Me?*"

"Yes. You and Laila are going to be in a campy love

triangle with Keane. Laila already said yes. But we need *two* smoking hot women to pull this off, and it's too late to hire someone else on such short notice."

"But I'm not an actress."

"Oh, yes, you are," Reed says. "You're a better actress than half the professionals in Hollywood."

"Georgina, I saw you on *Good Morning America*," Maddy says. "The camera *loves* you."

I make a face that plainly telegraphs I'm freaking out.

"Sweetheart. Pull it together. This is happening. You're always saying you want to give me a present. Well, this is your present to me. From the first moment I saw you in that lecture hall, I fantasized about putting you into a music video. Well, this is my chance. Don't you dare deny me this pleasure."

I laugh. "Okay, okay. Count me in."

Reed smiles at Alessandra. "Wait till you hear this next thing." He motions to the array of artists seated at the far end of our long table, none of whom are paying a lick of attention to our conversation. "See all those rock stars down there? They've all agreed to stop by the coffee house tomorrow to shoot quick cameos for the video."

"*Whaaaat?*" Alessandra blurts, making Reed and Maddy laugh with glee.

"You've hit the jackpot, Alessandra Tennison," Reed says gleefully. "Having all these superstars in your debut video—plus, having Laila, Keane, and Fish in starring roles alongside you—is going to give you so much street cred, it's ridiculous. Without a doubt, all this star power is going to make this video go viral. Which, in turn, my dear, is going to rocket your song to the top of the charts."

Alessandra and I flip out, and then begin peppering Reed and Maddy with a thousand questions, asking them to describe their two storylines in detail. In response, Reed calls Laila over, so she can hear what he's about to tell the group. Plus, he calls Owen to come over, too.

"Hey, O," Reed says. "Do me a favor and arrange to buy a really cheap used car for use in Alessandra's music video tomorrow. We'll need it by midmorning or so. Laila and Georgina are going to beat it to smithereens with baseball bats."

Owen says he's on it, boss, no questions asked, and heads off to look online for some possible candidates. And then, finally, Reed leans back in his chair and, with an exuberant assist from Maddy, tells our group about the concept for Alessandra's music video:

The setting is a packed coffeehouse in Brooklyn. Alessandra is the performer on a small stage, her audience filled with famous faces. Fish is the shaggy barista behind the counter—Alessandra's "secret admirer" who covertly writes her love letters on distinctive pink stationery. Although, sadly, Fish never musters the courage to give Alessandra any of his pink love letters, but, instead, throws them, one after another, into a nearby trashcan.

Meanwhile, Keane is a hot douche-canoe customer who's been shamelessly two-timing *both* waitresses at the coffee house, Laila and me... by giving us both the distinctive pink love letters he finds in the trash. Throughout the video, we see Laila and me, pink letters in hand, separately following Keane into his beat-up love mobile, presumably for some hanky-panky.

Midway through the video, the love triangle explodes, and Laila and I confront Keane together, both of us standing shoulder-to-shoulder as we angrily hold up those distinctive pink love letters and let him have it. After soundly chewing him out—and looking hot as we do it—because, you know, angry women are hot—Laila and I drop our notes to the floor, and march outside the coffeehouse with purpose, as Keane trails behind us, pleading his case.

As the love triangle exits, Alessandra's gaze drifts to the pink love notes on the floor... and then to Fish across the room... who, at that very moment, is tossing yet another "secret admirer" love note into the bin. On that same pink, distinctive paper.

Alessandra connects the dots, and realizes *Fish* is the true author of those love notes on the floor. She also realizes, thanks to the many smitten looks Fish has sent her throughout the video, those notes on the floor must have been written to *her*.

Fish sees Alessandra's gaze migrating from the notes to him. He sees her putting two and two together. With a deep breath, he grabs his latest pink love letter from the trash, smooths it out, and marches toward Alessandra on the stage... who, as he's been doing that, has turned to grab something out of her guitar case. And that's when the audience sees a splayed stack of blue papers in Alessandra's case. A whole bunch of love songs she's secretly written about Fish. We see a shot of the handwritten lyrics, with titles like, "I'm Secretly in Love with a Barista" and "He Makes Coffee and Owns My Heart"—and we know Alessandra has always been every bit as in love with Fish, as he's been with her.

With their love notes in hand, Alessandra and Fish meet in the middle of the coffee house. They exchange their colorful declarations of love, smile like smitten kittens at each other, and then march, hand in hand, out of the coffee house... where they walk past Georgina and Laila furiously beating the crap out of Keane's love mobile with baseball bats, much to his chagrin.

"The End," Maddy says. And her enraptured audience instantly explodes with excitement.

"Can I ask a question?" Alessandra says. "I'm not trying to look a gift horse in the mouth here. I can't believe how lucky I am. But why are all these famous artists willing to make cameos in some nobody's video?"

"Every last one of them owes me a favor," Reed says. "But also, and this is the truth, Alessandra, none of them would do this if they didn't genuinely like you and believe in your song."

Alessandra couldn't be more effusive and adorable in this moment. She thanks Reed profusely and says she's going to hop up and thank each artist around the table, individually.

"No, no," Reed says, laughing. "Thank them tomorrow if they actually show up. Also, there's no need to thank me. I wouldn't be doing any of this if I didn't think I'd make my money back, and then some."

I smile at Reed. *Liar.* I love him for it, don't get me wrong. But I've come to realize Reed isn't trying to make Alessandra a star for money. He's doing it for himself. As a game. Just to see if he can. And, of course, he's doing it for me. The same way I wrote a sappy love letter about him for *Rock n' Roll,* rather than a hard-hitting, revealing piece for *Dig a Little Deeper.*

A waiter comes to refill water glasses and Reed gestures to him. "Open a case of your finest champagne. We're celebrating an amazing charity concert and the imminent birth of a superstar." He indicates sweet little Alessandra with his whiskey glass. "Mark my words, this girl here is about to make every person at this table look like a fucking amateur."

The waiter chuckles. "Yes, sir." He looks at Alessandra. "Congratulations."

As the waiter leaves, I lean into Reed's ear. "When we get back to our hotel room, I'm going to give you a blowjob that will make you pass out."

Reed grins. "Gosh, I wonder what prompted that reaction, Miss Ricci." He winks. His face aglow. "And you thought you didn't have a price."

Chapter 36
Reed

W asn't Alessandra *amazing*?" Georgina gushes.
We're cuddled up together in the backseat of Tony's black sedan, heading to my mother's facility in Scarsdale. Throughout the drive, we've been talking enthusiastically about yesterday's music video shoot for Alessandra's single. Reliving it. Laughing about it. Marveling at how well it went.

"She was adorable," I say. And it's the truth. To my surprise, Maddy was able to coax a delightful performance out of shy little Alessandra. Actually, I think it's fair to say Maddy captured lightning in a bottle from everyone. "Props to Maddy for what she accomplished yesterday," I say. "She impressed the hell out of me."

"Me, too." Georgina lays her head on my shoulder. "You swear I didn't embarrass myself?"

I kiss the top of Georgina's head. "Sweetheart, I promise you were magnificent in the video. A bombshell. A siren." And, again, I'm telling the truth. Not surprisingly, Georgina was a star yesterday, just like I knew she'd be. When I watched her being interviewed the other day on *Good Morning America*, her star power was undeniable. Even CeeCee saw it. During the interview, she leaned into me and said, "I'm not going to be able to hang onto my unicorn for long. She's going to get a whole lot of TV offers after this... and, at some point, she's going to take one."

CeeCee didn't sound the least bit upset when she said

that, by the way. Only proud. Because CeeCee knows, as do I, that dreams are inherently meant to grow and expand. Right out of college, Georgina thinks writing for *Dig a Little Deeper* is the highest peak imaginable for her career. But one day, probably soon, I'd guess, Georgina will realize she's standing at the base of a much, *much* higher peak. She'll realize she was born to take that *GMA* interviewer's job one day, or its equivalent. And when Georgina realizes that, and leaves *Dig a Little Deeper* to chase an even bigger dream, CeeCee will be as excited for Georgina as I'll be.

Tony brings the sedan to a stop in front of my mother's facility. "Will this be a long visit today, Mr. Rivers?"

I touch the ring box in my pocket, reassuring myself, yet again, it's still there. I'm not going to give it to Georgina until we're in Sardinia, standing on a beach at sunset with a photographer there to capture the once-in-a-lifetime moment. But when I took the ring box out of the hotel safe this morning, I didn't feel good about packing something so valuable in my suitcase. And so, here it is. Burning a hole in my pocket. Making me feel physically ill with excitement about what's to come every time it bumps against my thigh.

"It'll be a long visit today, Tony," I say. "Feel free to head to a diner or something. I'll text you when we're close to leaving." I look at Georgie. "You've got a print-out of your article?"

She pats her purse. "God, I hope Eleanor likes it."

I reassure her my mother will love it, even though, in truth, nerves are suddenly gripping me. I'm *almost* positive I'm right about that—that my mother will, indeed, love the article Georgina has written for her. But you never know with Eleanor Rivers. There's always the chance the article will send her spiraling into some sort of unexpected meltdown.

I lay my palm on the ring box again, subconsciously reassuring myself it's there. And then, with a kiss to Georgina's cheek, get out of the car, take Georgina's hand, and lead her up the familiar steps toward the facility.

267

Chapter 37
Georgina

There she is. Eleanor. Curled into Child's Pose, alongside her boyfriend, Lee, at the front of her yoga class. When the instructor sees Reed and me in the doorway, she says something to Eleanor that makes her sit up and look, and the moment Eleanor sees us, her face ignites with childlike joy. She leaps up, shrieking happily, and bounds over to us like a gray-haired gazelle. Only this time, unlike last time, Eleanor flings herself into Reed's strong arms, first—but only to chastise him for it being so long between visits.

"It's my fault," I say. "I had a bunch of deadlines for my summer internship, and I had to hunker down. I promise, I'll never let so much time pass between visits again."

"No, no, it's my fault," Reed says. "I should have come weeks ago, by myself. The truth is, I haven't traveled these past six weeks at all, other than one short business trip out West, because I've enjoyed staying home with Georgina so much." He looks at me and flashes a smile that sends my heart fluttering. "Georgina's living with me now, Mom. Permanently. And, suddenly, the only thing I want to do is stay home and hang out with her."

Eleanor looks pleased. "Well, if you're going to ignore me for way too long, I suppose that's a delightful reason." She waggles her finger at her son. "But never stay away this long again, Reed Charlemagne."

"I won't."

Eleanor looks at me, all smiles. "Did you wind up getting offered your 'dream job' at *Dig a Little Deeper*?"

"Oh my gosh. I can't believe you remembered me telling you about that. Yes, actually, I did. When Reed and I get back from Sardinia, I'll start full-time as a permanent staff writer."

Eleanor claps happily. "I knew it! After your last visit, I told all my friends you were going to nab your dream job. I even bought a subscription to *Dig a Little Deeper*, so I could see why you wanted to work there. I've now read every back issue, and, I must say, I'm impressed."

"Oh, wow. Thank you for doing that, Eleanor."

She leans forward. "I read your article in the last issue about that horrible football coach. I'm so sorry he hurt you and those other girls. But good for all of you for telling the world what he did."

I'm astonished. I've always thought of Eleanor as living in a sort of bubble here in Scarsdale, cut off from the outside world. It never occurred to me she would have read my Gates article. "Thank you so much for reading it. That means the world to me."

"Pish. I not only read the article, I also listened to your radio interview on Monday and watched your TV interview on Tuesday. And so did Lee, and all of my friends and nurses. I'm the president of your fan club." Eleanor pats my hand. "Oh, my, we're going to have such a glorious visit today. They're serving chicken pot pies for lunch. Reed's favorite. And after we eat, I'll introduce you around to the other members of your fan club. And then, we'll play *Scrabble* and cards."

Reed says, "Don't forget, Mom, Georgina and I have a flight to catch today. We're going to make this an extra-long visit, I promise, but it sounds like you've got three days' worth of activities on the itinerary for us."

Eleanor waves at the air, dismissing Reed's comment. "Let me tell Lee we're going to the dining hall, so he doesn't worry. He always worries about me when he can't find me, though I don't know where he thinks I'd go." Giggling, she prances off gaily to the front of the yoga class.

"What the hell have you done to my mother?" Reed whispers out the side of his mouth, his eyes trained on his mother.

"What do you mean? She's positively joyful."

"That's what I mean. That's twice in a row now. I figured her preternatural joy last time was a one-off. Never to be repeated. But here she is again, prancing and giggling like a kid at Christmas... *two* times in a row? That's some powerful magic you've got in your bag of tricks, Ricci. Please, always use your superpowers for good, or we're all screwed."

Eleanor returns and happily grabs my arm. "Come on, my beloved darling. We have so much to talk about!"

"I guess I'll come, too," Reed says dryly, trailing behind. But when I glance over my shoulder at him, Reed is smiling from ear to ear.

We reach the dining room and get situated with our food, and then proceed to talk for quite some time about the Gates article and the various ripple effects it's had over the past few days, including the latest bombshell—that Gates was arrested in Los Angeles this morning, after yet *another* accuser came forward. This one, with a surveillance video of some sort to back her up.

"And not only that," I say. "From what Leonard's been hearing, the arrest of Steven Price is imminent, as well."

"Oh, good," Eleanor says. "I hope all those men get everything they deserve in this life, and then go to hell after that. Especially that horrible football coach."

"I have full faith justice will be served," I say. And it's the truth. I tell Eleanor what Leonard told me this morning, thanks to information he obtained from a buddy at the DA's office. Specifically, that the line of women accusing Gates is so long and credible at this point, and the text messages and settlement agreements so damning, Gates is already apparently asking the DA for a deal in exchange for his guilty plea.

"A deal?" Eleanor asks.

"A lighter sentence than the worst-case scenario he could get, if he's convicted on all counts at trial," I explain. "But don't worry. Either way, Leonard said the DA will make sure, no matter what, Gates goes away for a very long time. The whole world sees him for what he is now. Nobody is going to let this man walk away from his crimes."

"When he goes to prison, I bet all the TV shows will want you to come on. Don't you think, Reed?"

"Absolutely."

She returns to me. "I think you should be on TV, all the time, Georgie. Not just about Gates. But as your actual *job*. You're a wonderful writer, and *Dig a Little Deeper* is a fantastic magazine, but you've got a face for TV. When we were watching you on *Good Morning America,* one of my friends said, 'Georgie should be on TV, every morning!' And I told her I agree and would tell you so when you *finally* came to visit me." She shoots Reed a withering look, nonverbally chastising him for staying away so long, and then returns to me, smiling. "Oh! What if you hosted that show where they 'catch a predator'? You'd be so good at that!"

I can't help smiling. She's so cute. "Definitely something to think about."

"Has *Good Morning America* asked you to come work for them yet? If not, I bet they will soon!"

I laugh. "Weirdly enough, not yet. And I've been waiting by the phone all day!" I wink.

"Did you like being on TV? It sure looked like it."

"I did. I loved it. I was super nervous, right before going on. But then, the minute I got out there, and that little red light above the camera turned on, I felt nothing but excitement."

"I could tell. You didn't seem nervous at all." She pats my arm. "It's settled, then. You're going to be a huge star on TV."

I giggle. "Don't rush me, please. I'm elated about my new job. Writing for *Dig a Little Deeper* has been my dream for a long time."

My phone, and Reed's, both ping simultaneously with incoming texts. I don't look down, since I'm engaged in a conversation with Eleanor and don't want to be rude. But Reed looks down. And when he does, he instantly blurts, "Ho! Maddy says she's uploaded a rough cut of Alessandra's video to the Dropbox!"

With excitement, I quickly explain to Eleanor the context—the backstory of the music video Reed is excitedly cuing up. And a moment later, the three of us are huddled around Reed's phone, watching Maddy's masterpiece.

It's *phenomenal.* Better than anything I could have imagined. When it's over, I look at Reed, and it's clear he's every bit as blown away as I am. In fact, I'll be damned, he's morphing into Business Reed before my eyes.

"This video is going to launch Alessandra to the moon," he declares, his dark eyes blazing. "'Blindsided' will hit Top Thirty in its first week. Top Ten by its third. I'm calling it now." Reed's wheels are visibly turning. His excitement is palpable. "Real talk, Georgie. Do you think your stepsister will be able to handle overnight stardom? I'm talking about the kind of whirlwind success that's going to make her drop out of school. Will she crumple under the weight of that kind of success, or rise to the occasion?"

My heart is pounding. I'm euphoric. "She'll rise to the occasion, the same way she did at the video shoot. She's ready for this, Reed. I promise. It's what Alessandra's always wanted."

Reed nods, apparently reaching some sort of decision. "All right, then. I'll get the machine fired up for a full album. The minute we get back from our trip, I'll pull my team together and get everything scheduled. We'll want to capitalize on the success of the first single. Keep momentum going."

Squealing, I pepper Reed's handsome face with kisses, and thank him profusely.

"There's no need to thank me," he says, laughing. "This time I'm telling the truth. Alessandra is going to make me a mint."

Swooning, I check the time on my phone. "We'll need to call her in a couple hours. She's still on her flight back to Boston."

"This is so exciting," Eleanor says. She leaps up and grabs my hand. "Come with me, Georgie! I'm going to introduce you to all my friends and tell them you've agreed with me you belong on TV one day—and, also, that your cute little stepsister is about to become a star!"

***

In a pleasant, sunlit game room, filled with people playing Scrabble and dominoes and cards, Reed and I are making the rounds, making pleasant small talk with Eleanor's friends and nurses, when a newscaster on a TV in the corner reports something startling: "Breaking news. Howard Devlin, the billionaire studio head and movie producer, has just been arrested by LAPD for rape and various other sex crimes." My jaw hanging open, I snap my head toward the TV in the corner, just in time to see Howard Devlin, in handcuffs, being shoved like a common criminal into a cop car that's parked in front of his sprawling mansion.

I turn to Reed to find him looking as shocked as I feel. We quickly excuse ourselves from the game room and barrel into the hallway. First off, Reed immediately calls Isabel, but gets her voicemail. He calls Leonard, who says he's heard the news, but knows nothing more than what's being reported. Finally, Reed calls CeeCee and hits the jackpot. Confidentially, of course, CeeCee tells us Isabel and her posse went to the police station last night, through a back door and in the cover of darkness, and stayed for hours, giving their detailed statements.

"And this morning," CeeCee says exuberantly, "Isabel's lawyer called to schedule two interviews with me! An exclusive, one-on-one with Isabel, which we'll do on network television. I've already made arrangements. And a second, more comprehensive interview, which will be published in a special edition of *Dig a Little Deeper*, along with individual, exclusive interviews of all the other women, too."

"Holy crap, CeeCee. This is going to be the story of the year. A game-changer."

"I know. Now, listen, Georgina. I want you to do some brainstorming while you're in Italy. When you come back, you're going to need to write an opinion piece for the special edition. Something that draws parallels between Gates and Devlin, from your unique perspective."

"I'd love to. *Yes.*"

"I'll handle both Isabel's interviews, personally, but I'm going to want you to handle some of the other women's interviews for me. We're going to have a short turnaround time on this special edition to make it timely."

"You got it. Thank you for trusting me."

"Trusting you? This is all because of *you.*"

"No, it's because *you* had a gut feeling about him. Because *you* warned me about him. And because, most of all, you've shown me what a kickass woman looks like."

Our excited lovefest continues for a short while longer. But, finally, we end the call and I hand Reed's phone back to him.

Reed looks at his watch. "We should think about catching our flight soon. If you're still planning to show my mom that article you wrote for her, I think you should do it now, sweetheart."

"Okay. Yeah, let's do it."

We head back into the game room, where Eleanor is

chatting with her favorite nurse, Tina. After Reed tells her why that Howard Devlin news story sent us sprinting into the hallway, we lead Eleanor to a table in a quiet corner of the game room. And that's where I reach into my purse and tell her I've brought her a special surprise.

"Since I last saw you," I say, my heart thrumming in my chest, "I've been researching and writing an article inspired by something you told me." I hand her the folded pages of my article. "I wrote an article especially for you, Eleanor."

"For *me*?"

I nod. "If, for any reason, you don't want the world to read what's in your hand, then I promise, I won't submit it to my boss. The only reason I wrote it is to give you a tiny drop of some much-deserved peace."

Chapter 38
Georgina

Looking deeply perplexed, Eleanor puts reading glasses on, squints at the first page in her hand, and reads aloud the words printed at the top: "'A War of Fire: How a Battle Between Rival Mobsters Shattered Innocent Lives.'"

She looks at me blankly.

"It's about your family," I say nervously. "About the fire. After you told me about it during our last visit, I decided to poke around to see if I could solve the mystery of how it got started. I wanted to see if I could clear your father's name. And I did it, Eleanor. I figured out, without a doubt, your father *didn't* set that house fire. I'm positive."

Eleanor looks beyond flabbergasted. She looks at her son, and then at me, before throwing her hands over her face and bursting into wracking sobs.

"Aw, Mom." Without missing a beat, Reed gets up and takes his weeping mother into his arms. "Wait until you hear what Georgina figured out. You're gonna be so happy, Mom."

But Eleanor is inconsolable. Crying so hard, so violently, a nurse comes over to make sure she's okay. And, of course, I'm mortified to have provoked this horrifying reaction. All I wanted to do, the only thing, was to give this poor, tormented soul, who's suffered so much in her lifetime, the tiniest measure of peace. But, obviously, my unexpected news has had the exact opposite effect than intended.

Thank goodness for Reed. This ain't his first time at this

particular rodeo, obviously, and he's smooth as silk with his mother. He holds her tenderly. Strokes her back and whispers to her in a calm, controlled voice. He's so simultaneously confident and nurturing, in fact, I can't help thinking as I watch him, "Damn, this man is going to make one hell of a father one day."

Eventually, Eleanor quiets down and becomes a rag doll in her son's muscular arms.

"How about Georgina tells you the gist of what she wrote, so you don't have to read the article itself?" Reed suggests. "She can tell you how she solved the mystery, like she's telling you a detective story."

Eleanor nods, rubbing her slack cheek against Reed's broad shoulder. "I'd like that."

My stomach somersaults. "Maybe you should tell your mother about the article. I'd hate to say something wrong."

Eleanor shakes her head. "No, I want you to tell me. You're the one who solved the mystery. I want to hear it from you."

I look at Reed and he nods encouragingly.

"Okay. Of course. Whatever you want."

But where to begin?

In my article, I start by setting the stage for the reader. I describe the ill-fated Charpentier family, and the tragic house fire that claimed four of six of them in one horrible night. I describe how Charles' insurance company refused to honor his property claim because of "suspected arson and insurance fraud." And how he fought to clear his name, and secure the funds owed to him, for the better part of the next year, because he wanted desperately to build a new house, and a new life, for his sole surviving teenager, Eleanor.

I explain in my article that, in the end, a defeated and beleaguered Charles Charpentier marshalled every last dime in his bank account and used it to send his bereft daughter to an art school in Paris. And that, when he knew she was safe and sound on another continent, painting family portraits while overlooking the Seine, he put a gun in his mouth and ended his life on the one-year anniversary of the fire.

But, obviously, Eleanor doesn't need to hear about any of those tragedies, seeing as how she lived them, plus many more, once she met Terrence Rivers—a strapping, smooth-talking thirty-year-old American—who happened to be vacationing in Paris.

I turn my article facedown on the table, deciding to ditch the format of the article, and, instead, walk Eleanor through my investigation, step by step.

I say, "After you told me about your family and your father during our prior visit, I couldn't help wondering what investigations might have been conducted at the time, either by the police or the insurance company. I called my favorite professor from UCLA, a woman named Gilda Schiff, and she was excited to help me. Right away, we discovered police records regarding the fire were nonexistent. So, we focused on trying to track down the insurance company's investigation. At my professor's recommendation, I hired a local investigator in New York to help identify the insurance company, and, pretty quickly, she was able to find an archive of old property records that provided the answer."

"Mom," Reed says. "What Georgina isn't telling you is that she hired that private investigator with her own money. I didn't even know she was doing any of this research."

"I didn't want to tell Reed, or anyone, in case I came up empty handed," I say. But the full truth is that I didn't want to say anything to Reed, or anyone else, in case I stumbled upon evidence that suggested, or possibly even confirmed, that Charles Charpentier had set that fire. I continue, "To be clear, though, I only paid for the investigator in the beginning. When my little pot of money ran out, she continued working on the case *pro bono* for me, simply because she'd become as obsessed with the case by then as me."

"I didn't realize that," Reed says. "Give me your

investigator's address later. I'll send her a big, fat check to thank her."

I smile at Reed. "Thank you. She'll be grateful for that. She worked really, really hard on this case." I address Eleanor. "I should mention it was only because of Reed's generosity with me that I could afford to pay that investigator, at all. Thanks to him, I didn't have any expenses this summer."

I pause, thinking Eleanor might say something, but when she only stares at me, wide-eyed and visibly overwhelmed, I realize this isn't going to be a back-and-forth conversation. Plainly, Eleanor is too shell-shocked to do anything but sit and listen to an unending monologue. And so, that's what I give her. The full story, in one long, continuous ramble, summarized as follows:

The private investigator I hired, Carla, quickly figured out the Charpentier home had been insured by a long-defunct company called Shamrock Insurance, which went out of business within a year of the fire, when its owner, Henry Flannery, a renowned New York City mobster, was arrested for money laundering, racketeering, and other criminal enterprises.

After finding out the shocking news about Shamrock being owned by a mobster, I called Leonard with some general questions about money laundering and racketeering, and he told me criminals always run their "dirty money" through legitimate businesses, in order to "clean" it. Or, in other words, to make the money look, on the books, like it didn't come from a criminal enterprise. Leonard explained, "It sounds like Shamrock Insurance was one of the legitimate businesses Henry Flannery used to clean his dirty money."

At that point, I devoured every article I could find on Henry Flannery, and noticed that many of them mentioned his bitter feud with another New York mobster named Giuseppe Benvenuto, who'd famously owned a bustling restaurant in Lower Manhattan called "Sofia's"... until it burned to the ground in a raging fire a mere *six days* before the Charpentier fire.

Bam! For some reason, that fact hit me like a ton of bricks. Just that fast, the investigative reporter inside me knew I'd hit on something big. A restaurant in Manhattan, owned by one mobster, burned down in a *fire*, and less than a week later, a home insured by that mobster's rival *also* burned down in a *fire*? Rationally, I knew it was a stretch to link the two fires. But my gut told me there was almost certainly a connection.

Not knowing what else to do, I read a biography about Henry Flannery, written, with the help of a professional co-writer, by a high-ranking member of Henry's crime organization—a "lieutenant" who'd flipped on Henry during Henry's trial, and then disappeared into the witness protection program. And what I discovered while reading that lieutenant's biography broke the entire cold case wide open.

According to this "lieutenant" dude, Henry ordered Giuseppe's restaurant torched to the ground for some unknown offense. And so, in retaliation, Giuseppe decided to "take down" Shamrock by forcing it to pay out on a whole bunch of property claims, all at once. Specifically, claims that would be filed by Shamrock's handful of few "legitimate clients," whom the lieutenant described in his book as "suckers from rich suburbs, who'd bought cheap insurance from Shamrock, not realizing they were doing business with the mob."

Well, that was it for me. After reading that description, I knew in my gut poor Charles Charpentier had been one of those "suckers." I knew, in my gut, he hadn't set the fire that claimed his family. Giuseppe Benvenuto had. But, obviously, a gut feeling wasn't going to be enough. I knew I needed to find unquestionable *facts*.

When I tried to track down the professional co-writer of the Henry Flannery biography, I learned he'd died a decade ago. But, lucky for me, his adult daughter—a professor at Cornell—was more than happy to chat with me on the phone and relay to me all the detailed stories her beloved, and very talkative, father had told her about the legendary mobster, Henry Flannery.

According to the co-writer's daughter, ninety-five percent of Shamrock's clients were dummy profiles with bank accounts controlled by Henry or one of his family members. Only five percent of Shamrock's client roster was comprised of real people—poor saps Henry counted on, without their knowledge, to prove his company's legitimacy, if needed. Over the years, on the rare occasion when one of Shamrock's few real clients filed an actual property claim, the company always denied it on whatever grounds. And then, as necessary, bribed someone at the Insurance Commission to rule in Shamrock's favor on the claim, if the client persisted.

As Giuseppe correctly surmised, however, this strategy didn't work when *every* legitimate client filed a claim, all at once. As the co-writer's daughter explained to me, "There's only so much greasing the skids a mobster can do before people *not* on the take, whether at the Insurance Commission or NYPD, started noticing suspicious irregularities. That's what wound up happening, and ultimately took Henry down. Someone *not* on the take at the Insurance Commission noticed a whole bunch of denied claims, all at once, and picked up the phone to call a detective friend at NYPD. And the rest is history. Law enforcement saw a way to finally get their man."

By the time I hung up the phone with the co-writer's daughter, I knew I was *this* close to hitting the motherlode. But, still, I needed additional facts. I needed *proof.* So, I asked my investigator, Carla, to research any house fires that might have occurred during the same week as the Charpentier fire, in any "rich suburbs" near New York City. And when Carla got back to me on that task, I knew I'd finally hit the motherlode. I'd proved Charles Charpentier was innocent.

As it turned out, there were no less than *eight* other house fires within forty-eight hours of the Charpentier fire, in eight different nearby suburbs outside of New York City. Some in New York state. Others in New Jersey and Connecticut. But all within an hour of New York City.

"And do you know what company insured all *nine* homes that burned down, including your family's?" I ask, looking into Eleanor's dark brown eyes. "*Shamrock Insurance.*"

I wait, expecting a "wow!" reaction from Eleanor. But she's still too shell-shocked to speak.

Reed says, "Do you understand, Mom? Your family's home was burned down as part of Giuseppe Benvenuto's revenge against Henry Flannery. Your family, and eight others, were unwittingly caught in the middle of a war between rival mobsters."

"Yes, I understand," Eleanor says softly. "Thank you for figuring this out, Georgina."

I nod. "I'm so glad I was able to get a definitive answer."

"Was anybody else hurt in the other fires?"

"Yes. One family lost two members. Another lost one."

Eleanor's face contorts. She looks down. And we're all silent for a long moment, paying our respect to the poor souls lost.

Finally, Eleanor lifts her head. "I need to change this week's painting. I need to move my father in the scene. He should be standing next to my mother—in this painting, and every future one." She looks at Reed. "Can you and Georgina come back to see the revised painting in a few days?"

"No, Mom," Reed says gently. "From here, Georgina and I are flying to Italy, remember? If you don't want us to see this week's painting, as is, that's fine. We'll see whatever masterpiece you've painted the next time we visit."

"No, no, you have to see *this* painting. I made it especially because I knew Georgina was coming." She stands and offers her hand to me, which I take, and then begins leading me out of the game room. "Promise me, when you look at this painting, you'll imagine my father standing next to my mother, with a big smile on his handsome face."

Chapter 39
Reed

At the shocking sight of my mother's latest painting, I inhale a sharp breath. *She's painted something different this time.* I mean, not entirely. In some essential ways, this scene is the same as all those that came before: an idyllic setting—this one, a seashore—featuring Mom and me, and Mom's many loved ones lost, who are all busy frolicking and making merry.

Other than those general similarities, however, this particular painting is strikingly different than its countless predecessors. For one thing, my mother has painted herself at her present age. With gray hair. For the first time, ever, not as a young mother enjoying a picnic with her two young sons.

Also, Oliver isn't tethered to Mom's hip, as usual. This time, for the first time, Mom has allowed the poor kid to run off and play. Specifically, Oliver is throwing a beachball with Mom's youngest sister, down by the water's edge.

Shockingly, I'm not sitting on Mom's blanket, either. And I'm not a little kid. For the first time, she's painted me as a grown man. I'm standing on the sand, wearing a tuxedo, and doing something that makes my head explode: exchanging wedding vows with a beautiful brunette who's clad in a simple white gown and bridal veil.

It's a good news, bad news situation, obviously. On one hand, I'm elated and relieved to *finally* see something new in an Eleanor Rivers Original. It's huge progress. A welcome respite from the usual madness. On the other hand, though, I feel like I'm going to stroke out with my rising panic. Of all the days for my mother to have a massive breakthrough, she had to do it by painting me in a wedding scene with Georgina on the very day I'm whisking Georgina off to Sardinia to propose marriage to her? *Way to steal my thunder, Mom!* Now, when I propose to Georgina on that beach at sunset, she's going to think this painting forced my hand! Or, at least, that it gave me the idea. Hell, Georgina might even think I only asked her to marry me to win my mother's long-withheld approval and love.

Mom is presently babbling about where she wants to relocate her father in the scene, but I'm not listening. My mind is racing far too much to focus on her words. *This is a catastrophe.* I look at Georgina and it's clear the elephant in the room is sitting on Georgina's chest, every bit as much as it's sitting on mine.

"And what do you think about yourselves in the painting?" Mom says, looking mischievous.

Georgina looks at me, wide-eyed and rendered mute, so I say, "We look great, Mom. And so do you. I love your gray hair. Have you shown this one to Dr. Pham?"

"Yes. She liked it. She said I should keep painting myself, and you, too, as we are in the present. And she also liked that I included Georgina."

"So do I," I say.

"Thank you for including me," Georgina manages to say brightly. But her gaiety sounds forced to me. "I'm honored."

"You're family now." She looks at me. "Although I'd be very interested to know when—"

"Well, we've gotta head out now," I blurt. "Georgina and I have to get to the airport so we don't miss our flight."

"But I thought you said you're flying private today. You always say the best perk of flying private is that you can never miss your flight, because everyone is paid to sit around and wait for you."

My heart is crashing in my chest. "Yeah, but we've still got time constraints. You should take a nap, Mom. It's been an emotional day for you."

Mom exhales. "Well, that's true. A nap sounds nice, actually."

"Good. I'll help you get into bed."

I grip her frail shoulders gently and pointedly turn her away from her canvas and guide her straight to bed. My breathing labored, I adjust Mom's covers over her and kiss her forehead. I say one last goodbye. So does Georgina. And then, I grab my woman's hand in a death grip and pull her out the door, with more gusto than intended. But rather than turning left in the hallway, toward the front entrance, I turn right and practically drag poor Georgina toward the back door.

The last thing I want is for Georgina to doubt this proposal is *my* idea. My desire. Or for her to think it's some pathetic attempt to win my mother's approval. On the contrary, I need Georgina to know, without a doubt, I already had her ring in my pocket when I saw my mother's shocking painting, and that I didn't scramble upon landing in Italy to get something overnighted to me.

"Hey, Smart Guy," Georgina says. "The front door is that way."

"I need to talk to you about my mother's painting before we get into the car. I want to talk to you about it in a private spot."

"Oh, Reed. There's no reason to freak out. I've read your Wikipedia page, babe. I'm not expecting—"

"Stop talking, Georgina. Please."

"I'm just saying I'm fully aware—"

"*Stop. Talking.* If you love me at all, don't say another word until I've explicitly told you it's your turn to talk."

Georgina flashes me her patented "Well, you don't need to be a dick about it" look. But, thankfully, she clamps her lips together and stops talking as I guide her into a secluded corner of the garden.

When we come to a stop, anxiety rockets through me. Fear of rejection. When I called Georgina's father, Marco, to ask for his blessing two days ago, he gave it to me. Thankfully. But he also gave me a piece of unsolicited advice: "If I were you," he said, "I'd bring up the general topic of marriage with Georgina *before* popping the question. From what she told me at her college graduation party, she's not going to marry anyone before age thirty."

"Yeah, well, that was before she fell in love with *me*," I replied confidently. And from that moment on, I completely disregarded the man's stupid advice and went about my business, buying Georgina's four-million-dollar ring and planning the perfect proposal in Sardinia. I mean, please. Why would I ask Georgina's permission to ask her to marry me, when my favorite thing in the world is blindsiding her with surprises that provoke jiggling happy dances?

But now that I'm here, and the actual moment is upon me, I'm suddenly feeling a whole lot less confident. Was Marco right? Should I have broached this topic with Georgina, the same way she broached the topic of having a baby with me? Is that what normal people do? I don't *think* Georgina will turn me down. But, then again, I never thought, not in a million years, the FBI would raid my house that fateful morning and drag my father away in handcuffs.

"Are you okay?" she says, disregarding my request to remain silent. And when I look into her concerned hazel eyes, what I see there chases away my anxiety. She loves me. Totally and completely. The same way I love her. For crying out loud, she promised me forever, with letters inked permanently onto her ring finger. Which, I have to believe, whether she realized it or not, was her way of subconsciously asking me to put a ring on it.

"Yeah, I'm fine." I take her hands. "I was planning to say this to you in Sardinia in three days. But, now that I've decided to say it here, instead, I realize this is actually the perfect place. Because it's where I finally understood what it means to let down my guard all the way, and let someone in, without holding back." I take a deep breath and exhale a long, controlled breath. "Georgie, you're the great love of my life. My queen. I'll never want anyone but you."

She bites her full lower lip and whispers, "I love you, too."

"I called your father a couple days ago and asked for his blessing to ask you to marry me."

Her eyes widen like saucers as her mouth hangs open.

"And he gave it to me. Which means, I can now do *this*." With another deep breath, I pull the closed ring box out of my pocket and kneel before her. I look up at her, smiling. "Georgina Ricci, I'll marry you tomorrow, if that's what you want. I'll marry you in a year, or ten. Just, please, say yes to me today. Be my fiancée. And whenever you're ready, be my wife. Say yes." I open the ring box, revealing the fifteen-carat, Princess-cut, pink diamond I picked out for her, with CeeCee's help. And Georgina screams like I just poked her with a very large needle in her ass.

Laughing at her reaction, I choke out, "Georgina Marie Ricci, will you *please* marry me?"

Tearfully, she shrieks out her reply. The very thing I told her to say the first time I laid eyes on her at the panel discussion. "Yes, yes, yes!"

A shockwave of euphoria floods me. Quaking, smiling, swallowing down tears, I slip the rock onto Georgina's shaking finger, lurch up, and take my fiancée into my arms. As I kiss her, joy of a kind and magnitude I didn't know exists washes over me. I feel like I'm on top of the world. Or, perhaps, in the Garden of Eden. Because, surely, this moment, this place, and not any white sand beach in Sardinia, is paradise.

Finally, Georgina breaks free of our embrace to gift me with the best happy dance of her happy-dancing career. When she's done, I scoop her up and swing her around, making her squeal and giggle. I put her down and grab her hand and we both stare in awe at the ring on her hand.

"It's so *big*," she whispers. "I swear I would have been happy with something so much smaller."

I scoff. "Did you not understand the question? I asked you to *marry* me. Not go to *prom*. Go big or go home, baby. You know that."

"Honestly, I'm going to be scared to wear it, unless you're with me. I can't go to the gym wearing a ring like this. Or to the grocery store. This is for, like, the Academy Awards!"

I laugh. She's right, actually. It's pretty over the top. "Okay, when we get back from our trip, we'll go shopping and get you another ring—an 'everyday ring' you can wear to the gym or wherever, and you can wear this one whenever you're dressed up."

"What? No! I didn't mean you should buy me a *second* ring! I meant we should return this one and get something less expensive."

"You don't like it?"

"No, I love it! I just can't believe you—"

"Then that's the end of the conversation. What I spend on gifts for you is none of your fucking business, per an exception expressly delineated in our 'open book agreement.'"

She flushes and looks down at her hand again. This time, with unadulterated excitement. "Thank you so much."

"You're very welcome."

"Why did you have it in your pocket, if you weren't planning to propose to me today?"

"Because there was no way I was going to leave a ring worth more than a Bugatti in my luggage."

The color drains from Georgina's face. "No."

"Yes. Not that it's any of your business, of course."

Laughing at her expression, I stroke her cheek. "Georgie, you're going to be the one and only *Mrs. Rivers,* forever. I'm not going to give my future wife a ring worth anything less than the most expensive sports car sitting in my garage." I scoff at the very thought. "Now, come on, fiancée." I put my hand in hers. "Sardinia awaits."

We practically float through the back door, into the facility, the air between us crackling with our mutual elation.

"Your dad put the fear of God into me when I called him, by the way. He gave me his blessing, no problem, but he suggested I should chat with you about marriage, before proposing, because, last he'd heard, you didn't want to get married to anyone before age thirty."

Georgina scoffs. "Well, yeah. I said that before I met *you.*"

"That's what I told him!"

Laughing, Georgina says, "It's easy for a girl to draw imaginary lines in the sand before she knows Reed Rivers exists in the world."

We reach my mother's door in the hallway and poke our heads inside her room, thinking we'll share our happy news before heading out. But Mom is fast asleep, so we decide to let her stay that way.

"We'll call her after we land," I say, as we make our way down the hallway toward the lobby.

"Let's call my dad and Alessandra in the car, though," Georgina says excitedly. "I'm bursting to tell them. I want to tell the whole world!"

"Me, too. We'll call CeeCee in the car, too. She helped me pick out the ring."

"She did? Aw, that means so much to me." Georgina looks at her hand and giggles. "No wonder it's so big. You and CeeCee shopping together must have been like fire and gasoline. I can only imagine how much she goaded you on to 'go big.'"

"Sweetheart, I didn't need anyone to goad me on to do that. Trust me. If anything, CeeCee kept me from buying something that would make your knuckles physically drag on the ground when you put it on."

Georgina laughs uproariously. "What about Amalia? Did she know you were going to ask me?"

"No. Only CeeCee, Josh, Henn, Kat, Hannah, my sister, and Dax."

"Let's call all of them from the car! I can't wait to tell everyone!"

We've reached the lobby now. But instead of heading out the front door, and straight to Tony's waiting sedan, we pause at the front desk.

"Hey, Oscar," I say. "When my mother finishes tweaking her latest masterpiece, will you do me a favor and ship it to me in California?" I scribble my address onto a piece of paper and hand it to him, along with a bunch of bills. "That's for shipping and your trouble."

"Thanks. Sure. No problem. If you don't mind me asking, why don't you want her latest painting tossed onto the heap, with all the others? Is there something special about this one?"

"Yeah, there's something special about this one." I look into Georgina's sparkling eyes. "This one is going to be a memento, forever, of the happiest day of my life."

Chapter 40
Georgina

One year later

"A nd now, it's time for you both to exchange your vows,"
Henn says. "At least, that's what the template says we
should do now."

Everyone seated in rows on our patio chuckles. And I
don't blame them. For his first time officiating a wedding,
Henn is absolutely killing it.

There was never any serious question that Henn would
officiate our wedding, while Josh served as Reed's best man,
any more than there was a question that Alessandra would be
my maid of honor and Kat my bridesmaid. Or that Reed and I
would get married here, on our patio, surrounded only by the
people we love the most. Reed and I both knew long distance
travel would be difficult for my father, thanks to some lasting
side effects from chemo. And also that Reed's mother would
never want to fly internationally, even if Reed were to arrange
a luxurious private flight for her. Plus, Eleanor hates hotels, so
we knew she'd be most comfortable staying here, at our
house, along with her favorite nurse, Tina. And so, in the end,
Reed and I agreed to get hitched *here,* exactly like this, rather
than in some far-flung exotic locale. And we couldn't be
happier about it.

"Georgie?" Henn prompts. "Why don't you say your
vows first. Show Reed how it's done."

Nerves rocket through me. Not because I have any doubt about pledging myself to Reed forever. But because I'm quite certain what I've come up with for vows won't come close to expressing the depth of my love for Reed—the gorgeous, generous, enthralling man who's become my world. My breathing stilted, I pull a piece of paper out of my cleavage. "Sorry," I mumble, indicating the paper. "I didn't want to mess this up."

"You can't mess it up," Reed says soothingly, squeezing my hand. "No matter what you say, it will be perfect."

I glance down at the paper. And then return to Reed's chocolate eyes. I clear my throat. "Reed, loving you feels like the most natural thing in the world—like breathing and blinking and smiling." I smile. "I never have to think about loving you, because I was born to do it. *Designed* to do it. But 'love' isn't a big enough word for how I feel about you. There's really no word for it, actually. No way for language to encapsulate the depth and endlessness of my devotion to you, any more than the word 'infinite' truly encapsulates the vastness of outer space. Please know that I love you as deeply as a human being can love. I adore you, with every drop of me. I admire and respect you. And I *like* you. My vow to you today is to love you fiercely and faithfully, forever. Until we're old and gray. Which, in your case, will be in about three years."

Reed hoots with laughter, along with Henn and Josh. Plus, I can hear Alessandra and Kat guffawing behind my back, as well, along with everyone in our audience.

"Try the veal, I'm here all week," I say, making Reed chuckle again. I crumple my paper and toss it behind me, and then grab both of Reed's hands. "It boils down to this. My beloved Reed, I promise to be yours, in sickness and health. For richer or poorer—"

"Don't jinx me, baby."

Again, everyone laughs, including me.

"Reed Rivers, I can't wait to spend the rest of my life with you, as your wife. I love you so much. I promise to give you, and only you, all of me. Forever."

"Perfect." He leans in and kisses me gently. "I love you so much."

"I love you, too. So, so much."

"That was so beautiful, Georgie," Henn says. He smiles at his best friend. "Okay, buddy. You're up. Make it good."

"I'll do my best." A huge smile overtakes Reed's face. "To start, I feel the need to correct a few things I've said in the past—things that were true when I said them, but aren't anymore. I once told you I'm a believer in 'going big or going home.' But now that I love you the way I do, I've realized that's not an either-or proposition. Going home *is* going big, as long as I'm coming home to you."

I clamp my lips together to keep my chin from trembling.

"Another thing," Reed says. "I once called you the 'Ginger Rogers of Spin.' But I've since realized that's too limiting. You're the Ginger Rogers of *Life*. A badass at everything you do. Far more so than me. From the outside, people might look at us and assume I'm the teacher here—that I'm some sort of Svengali. But the truth is you've taught me far more than I've taught you. You've taught me how to love, Georgie. You've taught me how to be happy."

Well, that does it. Tears spring in my eyes.

"You're my partner," he says, his chest heaving. But then, his mouth quirks up with a little half-smile. "My *sparring* partner, at times, yes. My partner in crime, for sure. But, always, my equal *partner*."

My breathing hitches as I try not to sob.

He cups my cheek in his palm. "I thought I knew it all when I met you, Georgina Ricci. I thought I had the whole world figured out. But you came along and showed me what I was missing. You completed me and brought me pure joy. And for that, I'm so grateful. My vow to you, my beloved

Georgina, is that I'll always love and protect you and take care of you. You've got me, baby. All of me. And I promise, every day of my life, forever, to make sure I'm the Fred Astaire you rightly deserve."

***

Best. Wedding. Reception. *Ever.*

With a loud whoop, I throw my bridal bouquet up and behind my back. And when I spin around to see where my flowers landed, I'm thrilled to discover it's Zasu, the woman who mentored me during my internship at *Rock 'n' Roll,* who's caught them. It's a perfect result, since Zasu is always telling me horror stories from her "hellacious" dating life. Hopefully, those flowers will bring her a prince, the next time she swipes right on Tinder, rather than yet another frog. Although, given that Tinder is Zasu's primary vehicle for meeting men, I wouldn't count on it.

As Zasu raises her flowers into the air, a loud cheer rises up inside the house—a telltale sign that yet another "super-group" has walked onstage to perform another "typical wedding song" for the party. It's the only wedding gift Reed and I requested: for Reed's attending artists to get up onstage, at some point during the reception, in any combinations, and thrill our guests with their interpretations of classic party songs. Tunes like *Dancing Queen* and *Love Shack* and *Uptown Funk.* And that's exactly what these musical geniuses have been doing all night long. And it's been the best thing, ever.

The iconic piano intro to "I Will Survive" sounds from inside the house, followed by the smooth vocals of the one and only Dean Masterson of Red Card Riot singing the instantly recognizable first line.

"I have to dance to this one!" I shriek. I mean, come on. *Dean Masterson* is singing "I Will Survive"... at *my* wedding? My fourteen-year-old self would need smelling salts.

As if on cue, my new husband appears at my side, looking dapper in his perfectly tailored Armani tux, and leads me on his arm into the house.

As we walk toward the French doors on the opposite side of the large patio, I notice C-Bomb and Dax Morgan sitting on a bench together in a far corner, their body language relaxed and friendly. "Reed, look." I gesture to the unlikely duo, and Reed and I share a huge smile.

Before tonight, we already knew the guys of 22 Goats and Red Card Riot had received our wedding invitations and decided to put their differences aside to party under one roof for the first time in years. But *knowing* Dax and C-Bomb had finally decided to bury the hatchet, in our honor, and *actually* seeing them together, looking like old friends, laughing and smiling... well, those are two different things.

"That happened because of *you*," Reed says.

I scoff. "No. They're here because celebrating with *you* was more important to them than hanging onto whatever originally pissed them off."

Reed chuckles. "Silly Mrs. Rivers. What I meant is they're all so shocked I landed a catch like you, they were dying to see for themselves if you actually went through with saying 'I do.'"

I roll my eyes and he laughs.

Inside the house, we find Dean singing his heart out onstage, as expected, backed by some of the most recognizable musicians in the world, all of them looking like they're having the time of their lives up there, making that campy song their own. When we reach the dance floor, we're welcomed enthusiastically by Josh and Kat—who looks svelte and gorgeous in her tight-fitting blue gown—and, also, by Henn and Hannah—who's sporting an adorable baby bump these days.

Not surprisingly, Henn begins performing one of his patented "break dance moves," making everyone around him laugh and egg him on. And, soon, our little dance party in the middle of the floor is *the* place to be. In rapid succession, we're joined by the Fantastic Four: Keane, Maddy, Zander, and Aloha, who, in turn, are accompanied by Kat's adorable parents, Thomas and Louise Morgan. Soon, the next wave shows up: Reed's sister, Dax, Colin and his date, and Alessandra and Fish, all of whom begin dancing like there's no tomorrow.

Still dancing, Alessandra comes over to me and grabs my hands, and we do a joyful little jig that makes me feel like I've got a jetpack on my back. As Reed predicted, Alessandra's single, "Blindsided," eventually rose as high as number eight on the charts and launched her in a big way. So much so, Alessandra's eventual album, which released four months ago, has already churned out three top twenty hits, including an adorable duet she co-wrote and recorded with Fish called "Smitten," which recently hit number one on the Alternative Chart.

When I disengage from Alessandra, I prance over to Owen, who's dancing with Zasu, and then my father, and Leonard and his wife, before returning to my husband to finish out the song. As I dance, my eyes drift around the room, grazing over all the familiar, happy faces. CeeCee and her husband, Francois. Professor Schiff and her date. Bernie, my old boss from the bar, with his sweet wife. Reed's mom is dancing with Amalia and her nurse, Tina, and the orderly, Oscar, who made the trip, at our invitation and on Reed's dime.

And, suddenly, it hits me like a ton of bricks what a truly magical thing a wedding is in a person's life. The one and only time—at least, when they're alive to see it—when a person is surrounded by literally *everyone* who loves them, from every segment and phase of their life, all under one roof—and *everyone* is full of pure joy.

Feeling overcome with love and gratitude, I hurl myself

at Reed, pull his face to mine by his sexy scruff, and kiss him fervently. "Happy wedding day, my gorgeous hunk of a husband!"

Reed laughs. "Oh, shit. I'm a *husband?*" He looks down at the metal band on his finger. "Wait. Is that what all that ring exchanging and 'I do-ing' meant? Someone should have told me!"

I giggle with glee and kiss his ring. "Sorry, Mr. Rivers. The deed is done, and you can't take it back. I'm all yours, according to a legally binding contract. And you're all mine. Don't you know the first rule of negotiations? Careful what you ask for—you just might get it."

Reed nuzzles my nose, a huge smile on his face. "I wouldn't have it any other way. Happy wedding day, Cinderella."

I swoon. "I knew you were my Prince Charming, the minute I met you."

He laughs. "And this is the part of the fairytale where we get to ride off into the sunset and live happily ever after."

I look into Reed's sparkling, chocolate eyes. "There's no need for us to ride off anywhere, my love. We're already here."

Epilogue
Reed

Eight years later

My heart pounding, I park my small suitcase inside our front door and tear through our moonlit living room. I take the stairs, two at a time, and barrel down the hallway toward Leo's nursery. As I approach the doorway, I hear the glorious sound of Georgina singing "Beautiful Boy" by John Lennon—the song I played for my beautiful wife the day she gave me Leonardo Ricci Rivers seven months ago.

As it turns out, I probably could have made Georgina a pop star, if she'd let me. I would have needed to rely heavily on Autotune, but I swear I could have done it, just for the sheer fun of it. As it is, though, Leo and I have been Georgina's sole audience of two, the lucky ones who get to enjoy Georgina's sweet, soulful voice behind closed doors. I swear, that woman singing to our son, especially this song, is in a three-way tie for my all-time favorite sound. The other two being every noise Leo makes, whether he's laughing, crying, babbling, or eating, and every sound Georgina makes when we have sex. Especially the ones she makes when she comes.

My chest heaving from anxiety and exertion, I enter the nursery, and discover Georgina sitting calmly in a glider, holding our sleeping son in her arms. When she senses my movement in the doorframe, she looks up and her features contort with apology.

"Oh, love. You didn't need to drop everything. I shouldn't have freaked you out like that."

I bend down and kiss her in greeting. "You think I'd stay in Vegas when Leo was running a fever and you were worried sick about it? You insult me." I press my lips against Leo's forehead, and to my relief, his skin feels only vaguely warmer than usual, not "on fire," as Georgina described it to me, earlier today, in a panic. "When was the last time you checked his temperature?"

"About thirty minutes ago. The doctor said to check it every hour."

"Check it now."

I pull up a chair, as Georgina presses a thermometer to Leo's temple. When it beeps, she holds up the reading, with a relieved smile on her face. "It's down again. This time, by point-three." She flashes an apologetic face. "I think it's distinctly possible I overreacted here. I'm sorry. I should have left you alone to have fun."

"Would you stop insulting me, please? I'm glad you called. I'd be upset if you hadn't."

"But your artists were up for so many awards. You should be at your after-party right now. Did anyone win?"

I scoff. "Nobody cares if I'm at the after-party. Truthfully, I was grateful to have an excuse to leave. And yes, we had lots of wins. Read about it on Google." I touch Leo's soft brown hair and gaze adoringly at his features. He's got his mommy's lips and nose. His daddy's dark eyes and face shape. And, man, does this kid have a stubborn, fiery spirit, probably inherited from both of us. "When did Amalia leave?"

"She never left. She's downstairs now, asleep in her old bedroom. You should have seen Amalia with Leo today. She was a baby whisperer. And my dad was so sweet to meet me at the doctor's office before I could get ahold of Amalia. I was so grateful to him." She kisses Leo's little hand. "You've got a lot of people who love you, little dude."

"He sure does. Including his daddy." I reach out. "Hand him over. I've been going through withdrawals. I need my fix." I unbutton and open my tuxedo shirt, and when Georgina hands him over, I press his tiny chest flush against mine—right over the ink on my left pec—which nowadays, as of seven months ago, reads, *ReRiGeRiLeRi*. The same as Georgina's tattoo on the inside of her left ring finger.

It wasn't easy to bring Leonardo Ricci Rivers into the world. It took three grueling rounds of IVF and a whole lot of prayers. Which was why, when I finally saw my son for the first time in that delivery room, I wept like a baby, shedding actual tears—and a whole lot of them—for the first time since age fourteen. And with each tear streaking down my face, I felt myself transforming—turning into the man I was always meant to be.

After Leo's birth, I assumed it'd be another twenty-eight years until my next round of tears. But I couldn't have been more wrong about that. Only four months later, I cried again. Just as hard. This time, when my mother's favorite nurse, Tina, called to tell me my mother had passed. She'd been taken in her sleep, unexpectedly, by a massive stroke.

Of course, I was devastated by the news. But I took solace in a few things. I was relieved to know Mom hadn't suffered. And that Georgina had cleared her father's name all those years ago. I loved knowing Mom had gotten to hold her grandson several times. It also made me smile to think she'd taken so much pleasure in watching Georgina on TV every week, for two years before Georgina took her current extended maternity leave. Mom absolutely loved bragging to nurses and friends that Georgina's skyrocketing TV career was all thanks to her. "Years ago, I was the one who told Georgie she's got a face for TV!" Mom always used to say. And Georgina, saint that she is, would always reply something along the lines of "Yep! I never would have thought to get into TV if it hadn't been for Eleanor's suggestion!"

Georgina and I have been sitting quietly for several minutes in Leo's nursery, both of us staring in awe at the little miracle in my arms, when Georgina's soft voice finally cuts the moonlit silence. "I talked to Amalia about that job offer today."

"Yeah?" I say, even though I know exactly what Georgina is going to say. She's going to tell me she's decided to take the job. Which is a no-brainer, by the way. High-profile TV jobs based in LA, like the one recently offered to Georgina, don't come along very often. Turning it down would be unthinkable, if you ask me. But I've kept my mouth shut this past month, letting her process the offer on her own, and providing input only when asked.

"My conversation with Amalia gave me some much-needed clarity," she says.

"Oh yeah? Good." I wait, and when she says nothing, I add, "Care to elaborate?"

Georgina takes a deep breath. "I've decided to take the job. They said I could work part-time the first year, and start when Leo turns one, so that's what I've decided to do."

"That's wonderful, Georgie. Congratulations."

"You think this is a good decision?"

"I think it's a spectacular decision."

She sighs with relief. "Amalia said she'll come out of retirement to take care of Leo when I go back to work."

"Oh my God. That's amazing."

"I know."

"Did she say she'd *think* about doing that, or she's fully on board?"

"She's fully on board. She said she'd never forgive us if we hired another nanny. So, of course, I told her we'd love it. But I made it clear she won't be Leo's *nanny*. I said, 'You'll be his grandma who just so happens to get a paycheck.' And she loved that."

"Good. I'm glad you said that. I'm sure she was touched."

Georgina smiles. "I told her we're going to teach Leo to call her 'Gramalia,' and she laughed with glee."

"That's perfect. I love it." I bite my lip. "Thank you."

"For what?"

"For preserving 'Grandma' for my mom. It means a lot to me."

Her features soften. "Oh, love. Of course. Your mom will always be Grandma. Mine will always be Nonna. CeeCee will always be CeeCee." She smiles. "And, now, Amalia will always be *Gramalia*. Every one of Leo's grandmas will have her own name."

We share a smile.

Georgina bites her lip and touches my thigh. "Do you think it would be okay if we put him down in his crib for a bit?" Her eyes flash with heat. And I know she's missed me as much as I've missed her.

"I think it's a great idea."

Georgie scoops Leo up and gently lays him down. She checks his diaper. Determines he's good. She turns on a white-noise machine. Double-checks the baby monitor. Adjusts the nightlight and thermostat. And, while she does all that, I take Leo's temperature again, just for good measure.

When we leave the nursery, we do it hand in hand. And as we walk the length of the hallway, the air between us becomes charged with three days' worth of pent-up desire.

We reach our moonlit bedroom, where I guide Georgina onto our bed, peel off her pajamas, and my clothes, and proceed to worship every inch of my wife. I kiss and lick and caress and taste, reveling in her curves and newfound softness, my body vibrating with each sultry sound that escapes her throat.

When she comes, I crawl over her writhing torso and plunge myself deep inside her, and then push myself deep, deep, deep, over and over again, as deep as a man can go. As I make love to my wife, I whisper words of adoration. If I were a bottle of wine, I'd be pouring every drop of me into Georgina's goblet. I'm giving her all of me. No holding back.

When we're done, and our bodies are quiet and still, I creep into Leo's room to find him sleeping soundly—butts up coconut—in his crib. I take his temperature again and sigh with relief at the reading. I change his diaper, through which he sleeps like a rock. And, finally, I return to my room, to the bed I share with my wife, and crawl in. "His fever went down again," I whisper, wrapping my arms around Georgina and pulling her body into mine.

"Thank you for coming home."

"There's no place I'd rather be."

The moonlight is wrapping the room in a serene, blue haze. Georgina's skin is warm against mine. My son is safe and sound and fast asleep, and the baby monitor is turned to high. And so, I close my eyes and give myself permission to drift off to sleep.

As my mind begins to float, a feeling of gratitude and serenity—*pure love*—washes over me. Many moons ago, this fireball in my arms saw something inside me I didn't see in myself. She saw something I didn't even know was there. And now, thanks to her, the one and only Georgina Ricci Rivers, I've become the husband and father—the *man*—I was always meant to be.

THE END

Explore the exciting world of River Records, including articles written by Georgina Ricci for the River Records special issue of Rock 'n' Roll, at http://www.laurenrowebooks.com/river-records!

If you want to know more about the beef between Reed and C-Bomb, and between C-Bomb and Dax Morgan, then read the standalone **ROCKSTAR**, about Dax and his lady love, and be sure to check out 22 Goats' original music and music videos from the book under the "MUSIC FROM ROCKSTAR" tab of Lauren's website.

Lauren Rowe

If you want to read about Keane and Maddy, or Aloha and Zander, then you should read the related standalones: **BALL PEEN HAMMER** and **MISTER BODYGUARD**, respectively. Or, you could start with the related standalones about the two eldest Morgan brothers: **HERO**, about firefighter, Colby Morgan, or **CAPTAIN**, about alpha hottie, Ryan Morgan, who's definitely still holding a grudge about the way Reed flirted with his now-wife, Tessa (T-Rod) in that book. All books in the Morgan Brothers series are related standalones.

If you want to read about Josh and Kat, you'll find their explosive and sexy trilogy beginning with **INFATUATION**. Note: Henn and Hannah's love story also begins in INFATUATION, and continues as a side story in several books of The Morgan Brothers series. However, Henn and Hannah do not have their own separate books.

Or maybe you're in the mood to read a love story about another wealthy, hot dude with demons? Then read about Josh's fraternal twin, Jonas Faraday, who becomes obsessed with an anonymous woman he "meets" online. Start THE CLUB TRILOGY with the first book: **THE CLUB: OBSESSION**.

Be sure to sign up to receive news of releases or giveaways, by email or text:

Sign up for Lauren's newsletter at www.LaurenRoweBooks.com
US ONLY: Text the word "ROWE" to 474747
UK ONLY: Text the word "LAURENROWE" to 82228
Find Lauren on social media @laurenrowebooks on
FACEBOOK - INSTAGRAM - TWITTER

A brief list of books by Lauren Rowe is located at the front of this book. Further details below.

Books by Lauren Rowe

The Club Trilogy

Romantic. Scorching hot. Suspenseful. Witty. The Club is your new addiction—a sexy and suspenseful thriller about two wealthy brothers and the sassy women who bring them to their knees... all while the foursome bands together to protect one of their own. *The Club Trilogy* is to be read in order, as follows:

The Club: Obsession
The Club: Reclamation
The Club: Redemption

The Club: Culmination

The fourth book for Jonas and Sarah is a full-length epilogue with incredible heart-stopping twists and turns and feels. Read *The Club: Culmination (A Full-Length Epilogue Novel)* after finishing *The Club Trilogy* or, if you prefer, after reading *The Josh and Kat Trilogy*.

The Josh and Kat Trilogy

It's a war of wills between stubborn and sexy Josh Faraday and Kat Morgan. A fight to the bed. Arrogant, wealthy playboy Josh is used to getting what he wants. *And what he wants is Kat Morgan.* The books are to be read in order:

Infatuation
Revelation
Consummation

The Reed Rivers Trilogy

Reed Rivers has met his match in the most unlikely of women—aspiring journalist and spitfire, Georgina Ricci. She's much younger than the women Reed normally pursues, but he can't resist her fiery personality and drop-dead gorgeous looks. But in this game of cat and mouse, who's chasing whom? With each passing day of this wild ride, Reed's not so sure. The books of this trilogy are to be read in order:

Bad Liar
Beautiful Liar
Beloved Liar

The Morgan Brothers

Read these **standalones** in any order about the brothers of Kat Morgan. Chronological reading order is below, but they are all complete stories. Note: you do *not* need to read any other books or series before jumping straight into reading about the Morgan boys.

Hero. The story of heroic firefighter, **Colby Morgan**. When catastrophe strikes Colby Morgan, will physical therapist Lydia save him... or will he save her?

Captain. The insta-love-to-enemies-to-lovers story of tattooed sex god, **Ryan Morgan**, and the woman he'd move heaven and earth to claim.

Ball Peen Hammer. A steamy, hilarious, friends-to-lovers romantic comedy about cocky-as-hell male stripper, **Keane Morgan**, and the sassy, smart young woman who brings him to his knees during a road trip.

Mister Bodyguard. The Morgans' beloved honorary brother, **Zander Shaw**, meets his match in the feisty pop star he's assigned to protect on tour.

ROCKSTAR. When the youngest Morgan brother, **Dax Morgan,** meets a mysterious woman who rocks his world, he must decide if pursuing her is worth risking it all. Be sure to check out four of Dax's original songs from *ROCKSTAR*, written and produced by Lauren, along with full music videos for the songs, on her website (www.laurenrowebooks.com) under the tab MUSIC FROM ROCKSTAR.

Misadventures

Lauren's *Misadventures* titles are page-turning, steamy, swoony standalones, to be read in any order.

-*Misadventures on the Night Shift*—A hotel night shift clerk encounters her teenage fantasy: rock star Lucas Ford. And combustion ensues.

-*Misadventures of a College Girl*—A spunky, virginal theater major meets a cocky football player at her first college party... and absolutely nothing goes according to plan for either of them.

-*Misadventures on the Rebound*—A spunky woman on the rebound meets a hot, mysterious stranger in a bar on her way to her five-year high school reunion in Las Vegas and what follows is a misadventure neither of them ever imagined.

Standalone Psychological Thriller/Dark Comedy

Countdown to Killing Kurtis—A young woman with big dreams and skeletons in her closet decides her porno-king husband must die in exactly a year. This is *not* a traditional romance, but it *will* most definitely keep you turning the pages and saying "WTF?"

All books by Lauren Rowe are available in ebook, paperback, and audiobook formats. Be sure to sign up for Lauren's newsletter to find out about upcoming releases!

Author Biography

USA Today and internationally bestselling author Lauren Rowe lives in San Diego, California, where, in addition to writing books, she performs with her dance/party band at events all over Southern California, writes songs, takes embarrassing snapshots of her ever- patient Boston terrier, Buster, spends time with her family, and narrates audiobooks. Much to Lauren's thrill, her books have been translated all over the world in multiple languages and hit multiple domestic and international bestseller lists. To find out about Lauren's upcoming releases and giveaways, sign up for Lauren's emails at www.LaurenRoweBooks.com. Lauren loves to hear from readers! Send Lauren an email from her website, say hi on Twitter, Instagram, or Facebook.

CPSIA information can be obtained
at www.ICGtesting.com
Printed in the USA
LVHW041741011020
667692LV00004B/798